IMMORTAL REIGN

IMMORTAL REIGN

BOOK 6 IN THE

FALLING KINGDOMS

SERIES

MORGAN RHODES

RAZORBILL®

RAZORBILL®

An Imprint of Penguin Random House
Penguin.com

RAZORBILL & colophon is a registered trademark of Penguin Random House LLC.

First published in the United States of America by Razorbill,
an imprint of Penguin Random House LLC, 2018

LIBRARY OF CONGRESS CATALOGING-IN-PUBLICATION DATA IS AVAILABLE

ISBN 9781595148247

Printed in the United States of America

10 9 8 7 6 5 4 3 2 1

This is a work of fiction. Names, characters, places, and incidents either are the product of the author's imagination or are used fictitiously, and any resemblance to actual persons, living or dead, businesses, companies, events, or locales is entirely coincidental.

KRAESHIAN
EMPIRE

JEWEL
OF THE
EMPIRE

THE
SILVER
SEA

THE

AMARANTH

SEA

KRAESHIAN EMPIRE

VENEAS

THE NORTHERN SEA

Mytica

THE IRON COAST

LIMEROS

THE GRANITE COAST

Ravencrest

THE REACHES

The Temple
of Valoria

Scalia

Limerian
Palace

THE IMPERIAL ROAD

BLACK HARBOR

PAELSIA

THE TINGUE SEA

Basilia

Basilius's
Compound

FORBIDDEN MOUNTAINS

TRADER'S
HARBOR

THE WILDLANDS

KING'S
HARBOR

The Temple
of Cleiona

AURANOS

Auranian Palace/
City of Gold

Hawk's
Brow

Elder's
Pitch

THE RADIANT COAST

ISLE
OF
LUKAS

TERREA

CAST OF CHARACTERS

Limeros

Magnus Lukas Damora	Prince
Lucia Eva Damora	Princess and sorceress
Gaius Damora	The king of Mytica
Felix Gaebras	Former assassin
Kurtis Cirello	Lord Gareth's son, former kingsliege
Lord Gareth Cirillo	Grand kingsliege
Enzo	Palace guard
Lyssa	Lucia's infant daughter

Paelsia

Jonas Agallon	Rebel leader
Tarus Vasco	Rebel

Auranos

Cleiona (Cleo) Aurora Bellos	Princess of Auranos
Nicolo (Nic) Cassian	Cleo's best friend
Nerissa Florens	Cleo's attendant
Taran Ranus	Rebel
Bruno	Tavern owner
Valia	Witch

Kraeshia

Amara Cortas	Empress
Ashur Cortas	Prince
Carlos	Captain of the guard
Neela	Amara and Ashur's grandmother
Mikah Kasro	Revolutionary

The Sanctuary

Timotheus	Elder Watcher
Mia	Watcher
Olivia	Watcher and earth Kindred
Kyan	Fire Kindred

PROLOGUE

ONE HUNDRED YEARS AGO

It was her favorite dream.

The golden dagger lay before Valia on a velvet cushion. Beautiful. Powerful. Deadly. She picked it up, the golden hilt ice cold against her skin. The thought of the dark blood magic within it, restrained only by the symbols of *elementia* etched into the blade's surface, sent a shiver up her spine.

This weapon held magic that could be wielded to shape the world however she wanted it. No conflict, no strife, no pain. Her decisions, her kingdom—all of it.

With this blade in her grip, everyone would worship and love her.

Yes, this was her favorite dream—a shining gem in a deep, dark cave of nightmares. And she allowed herself to enjoy every moment of it.

At least, until Timotheus decided to interrupt.

The immortal pulled Valia's unconscious mind into a field of green grass and wildflowers—a stark change from her usual view of ice and snow from her tiny, isolated cottage in the mountains of northern Limeros.

In this dream, she could smell the sweet pollen and feel the warmth of the sun on her skin.

She looked into Timotheus's golden eyes. He was millennia old, but still had the face and body of a handsome man in his early twenties. He'd looked the same since he first came into being, made from the elements themselves, one of the six immortals first created to protect the Kindred and watch over the world of mortals.

The sight of him filled her with equal amounts of annoyance and dread.

"The end is coming," Timotheus said.

His words sent a chill through her down to the very marrow of her bones.

"When?" she asked as calmly as she could. He was standing only two paces away from her in the field of colorful flowers.

"I don't know precisely," he said. "Could be tomorrow. Could be decades from now."

Annoyance now took precedence over dread. "Your timeline is rather unreliable. Why are you bothering me with this nonsense? I don't care what happens or when."

He pressed his lips together, studying her carefully for a moment before responding. "Because I know that you care. That you always have."

This immortal knew her far better than she'd like. "You're wrong, Timotheus. As always."

He shook his head. "Lying was never your strongest ability, my old friend."

Valia's jaw tightened. "I was having a wonderful dream before you interrupted. Get to whatever point you came here to make, since I'd really like to get back to it."

His eyes narrowed as he studied her. Always studying, always watching. He was unnerving, this immortal. Even more so than the others.

"Have the deepening lines on your face led you to any epiphanies about life?" he asked.

Valia resented the mention of her lost youth. She'd smashed the last mirror in her cottage only yesterday, hating the aging woman it had reflected. "Your tendency to speak in riddles has never been your most endearing trait, Timotheus."

"And your lack of empathy has never been yours."

She laughed, as cold and brittle as an icicle hitting the frozen ground. "Do you blame me?"

He raised a brow as he walked a slow circle around her. Rather than follow his movements, she focused on a cluster of yellow daisies to her left.

"You go by a different name now," he said. "Valia."

Her shoulders tensed. "I do."

"A new name changes nothing."

"I disagree."

"I should have visited your dreams years ago. I apologize for my neglect." His gaze moved to her left hand. "I imagine *that* troubles you even more than the lines on your face."

Heat flew to her cheeks at this blunt observation, and she slid her freakishly misshapen hand into the deep pocket of her cloak. "A mere whisper of air magic can do wonders to hide this during my waking hours."

"Whom do you hide from anymore? You've chosen a life of solitude."

"That's right," Valia hissed. "My life, my choice. And none of your business. And what does it matter anyway? If the end is near, as you say, be it tomorrow or a century from now, then so be it. Let it end—all of it! Now go away. My dreams are private.

My life is private, and that's how I like it."

When her voice broke at the end, she hoped he hadn't noticed.

"I've brought you a gift," he said after several long moments of silence. "Something I thought you might want."

In his hands, he held a flat, jagged shard of shiny black rock.

Valia stared at it with shock. It was the Obsidian Blade—an ancient, magical weapon of limitless possibilities.

"You know what magic this could allow you to wield," he said. "And how it might help you."

Breathless, all she could do was nod in reply.

Valia reached out, first with her cursed hand and then with her good one. Afraid to touch it, afraid to give in to the fresh hope that it teased after so many years of growing despair.

Then hesitation set in.

"What do you want in return for this gift?" she asked quietly.

"A favor," Timotheus replied. "One that you will grant me without question when the day comes for me to ask it."

She frowned. "If the end is coming, do you have a plan? Have you told the others? What about Melenia? I know she can be horribly vain and selfish, but she's also powerful, smart, and ruthless."

"Indeed, she is. She reminds me daily of someone else. Someone lost to us so many years ago."

Valia focused on the daisies again, unwilling to meet the immortal's searching gaze. "Melenia is more useful to you than I could ever be."

When she forced herself to look up at him again, there were no answers in his dark golden eyes. "A favor," he repeated. "Do you agree or don't you?"

Her need for immediate answers faded as a familiar greed rose up within her, too thick to swallow back down. She needed this gift, needed it to help strengthen her fading magic and recover her youth and beauty. To help her control what she still could in this seemingly uncontrollable existence.

The Obsidian Blade was only a fraction as powerful as the golden dagger she dreamed about, that she desired more than anything. But she knew she needed it. Desperately.

Perhaps the past didn't matter anymore.

Only magic mattered. Only survival mattered.

Only *power* mattered, in whatever form she could possess it.

Finally, Valia took the Obsidian Blade from Timotheus, the weight of it a great comfort after so many years of pain and struggle.

"Yes, Timotheus," she said evenly. "I agree."

He nodded. "My gratitude to you. Always."

Then the immortal and the dream world he'd pulled her into faded away to darkness. When Valia woke, tucked into her small cot with the hearth's fire burned down to glowing embers, the jagged hilt of the blade was still in her grip.

CHAPTER 1

JONAS

PAELSIA

"*You can't escape your destiny.*"

Jonas lurched up from the hard wooden floor so quickly that a wave of dizziness slammed into him. Disoriented, but with dagger in hand, he scanned the small room to locate exactly what had torn him out of a deep sleep.

But there was nothing there except a beautiful princess with long raven-black hair asleep on the small cot. A tiny baby lay at her side, swaddled in a piece of cloth ripped from Jonas's cloak the night before.

The newborn's eyes were open wide and staring directly at Jonas. Violet eyes. Bright . . . like glowing jewels.

His breath caught. What—?

Lucia moaned softly in her sleep, stealing his attention away from the baby for a moment. When his gaze returned, the baby's eyes were sky blue like her mother's, not violet.

Jonas shook his head to clear it.

Lucia let out another cry from her slumber.

"Bad dreams, princess?" Jonas muttered. "Can't say I'm that surprised, given what we survived last night."

Their journey to get to Lucia's father and brother had been interrupted by Lucia giving birth during a massive rainstorm. Jonas swiftly found them a room at a nearby Paelsian inn so Lucia could recover her strength before they continued onward.

She shifted beneath the blankets, her face twisting. "No . . ." she whispered. "Please, no . . . no . . ."

The unexpected vulnerability in her voice tore at him. "Princess . . . wake up," he said, louder this time.

"You . . . you can't . . . No . . . I—I won't let you . . ."

Without thinking, Jonas sat down on the edge of the bed. "Lucia, wake up."

When she didn't respond, he took hold of her shoulders to gently shake her awake.

In an instant, Jonas was no longer in the small bedroom. He was standing in the middle of a village, and the world was on fire.

Flames shot up as tall as the Forbidden Mountains, their heat an immediate, searing brand on Jonas's flesh. The painful flames didn't crackle like those of a campfire; they screeched like a vicious beast from the darkest corner of the Wildlands. Through the wall of destruction, Jonas watched with stunned disbelief as cottages and villas were set ablaze—people screaming for help and mercy before the flames devoured them whole, leaving nothing but black ashes where they had once stood.

Jonas was paralyzed. He could not cry out or run from the burning pain. All he could do was watch in horror as the destructive fire began to form something recognizable—the figure of a gigantic, monstrous man. This creature of fire stared down at another figure—that of a cloaked girl standing defiantly before him.

"Do you finally see the truth, little sorceress?" the creature snarled, each word the lick of a fiery whip. "This world is flawed and unworthy, just as all mortals are. I will burn all this weakness away!"

"No!" The hood of the girl's cloak blew backward, revealing her flowing black hair. It was Lucia. "I won't let you do this. I'll stop you!"

"You'll stop me, will you?" The creature began to laugh and stretched out his burning arms. "Yet you're the one who's made all this possible! Had you not awoken me after all these centuries, none of this would be happening."

"I didn't awaken you," she said, her tone more uncertain now. "The ritual with Alexius . . . yes, I awoke the others. But you— you're different. It's like you awoke yourself."

"You underestimate the reach of your magic—of your very existence. Melenia knew this. That's why she envied you just as she did Eva. Perhaps this is why she wanted you dead after you'd served your purpose. Just like your mother wanted you dead."

Lucia staggered back from him, as if his words were physical blows. "My mother feared my magic." She turned her face away from the monster long enough for Jonas to see the tears streaking down her cheeks. "I should have let her kill me!"

"Your mortal life is the only one I still value, little sorceress. Take your rightful place by my side, and together we will rule the universe."

Lucia stared at the fire Kindred for a moment in silence. "I don't want that."

The fire god chuckled. "You lie, little sorceress, especially to yourself. Ultimate power is all any mortal wants. You would allow your family, your friends, even your own child, to be destroyed if it meant you could achieve it. Embrace this, little sorceress. Little goddess."

Trembling now, Lucia clenched her fists at her sides, and she screamed, "NEVER!"

The ear-piercing sound froze the fire god in place. In the next moment, he exploded into a million crystal-blue shards, each falling away to reveal the room at the inn behind them. And the girl sleeping in the small bed.

Lucia's dark lashes fluttered. She opened her eyes, and her gaze locked on Jonas.

"What . . . what in the hell did I just see?" Jonas asked, his voice raspy. "Was that just a dream? Or was it a vision of the future?"

"You were in my head just now," she whispered. "How is that possible?"

"I . . . I don't know."

Her eyes widened. "How dare you invade my privacy like that!"

"What—?"

Jonas suddenly found himself airborne, as if a large invisible hand had grasped him and thrown him back from the bed. He hit the far wall hard and fell to the floor with a grunt.

The baby began to wail.

Lucia gathered the child in her arms, her glossy eyes filled with outrage. "Stay away from me!"

He rubbed the back of his sore neck as he pushed himself to his feet and scowled at her. "You think that I did that on purpose? I was only trying to wake you from your nightmare. I didn't know that would happen!"

"I'm beginning to wonder just how much magic you hold inside you."

"Yeah, me too." He willed himself to be patient. "I didn't know I could enter your dreams . . . like . . . like . . ."

"Like Timotheus can," she hissed.

A Watcher. An immortal who'd lived for millennia. Timotheus

lived in the Sanctuary, a world apart from theirs, and Jonas didn't trust him any more than he did the fire Kindred in Lucia's dream.

"This is Timotheus's doing," Jonas mused. "It has to be."

"Get out!" Lucia snapped.

"Listen, I understand that you had a rough night. We both did. But you're being completely irrational right now."

She thrust her hand toward the door. At her command, it flew open and slammed against the wall. Her cheeks were red and tear-streaked. "Leave me alone with my daughter!"

The baby's cries hadn't stopped for a single moment.

Was he supposed to simply ignore what he'd seen in Lucia's dream just because she'd woken up in a foul mood? "I was trying to help you!"

"Once you get me to my father and Magnus I won't need any more help from you, rebel." She jabbed her finger in the direction of the door. "Are you suddenly deaf? I said get out!"

Before he knew it, Jonas found himself shoved out into the hallway by a blast of air magic, the door slamming shut in his face.

So this was the thanks he got for defying his own damn prophecy and saving her life last night by very nearly giving his own: a door magically slammed in his face the morning after.

"Doesn't matter," he said aloud through clenched teeth. "This is almost over. Can't be soon enough for me."

As soon as he delivered the Limerian princess to her hateful family, his association with the Damoras would officially and thankfully come to an end.

In a fouler mood than any in recent memory, he descended the inn's stairway. He focused on finding some breakfast to fill his empty stomach. A traditional Paelsian breakfast of runny eggs and stale bread would be perfect, he thought. He didn't expect to find the exotic fruits and vegetables that graced the dining tables of shiny, pampered Auranians or stick-up-their-arses Limerians. This close to the western wastelands, he'd be lucky to get a wilted piece of cabbage or partially rotting tomato to go along with his meal.

And he was just fine with that!

"Jonas."

He froze momentarily at the unexpected greeting as he entered the shadowy, nearly vacant tavern. Instinctively, he reached for the dagger hanging from his belt. But when his gaze fell upon a familiar face, his scowl was replaced by a grin.

"Tarus?" he asked, stunned. "Am I seeing a spirit right now, or is that really you?"

The young boy with messy red hair and a memorable face full of freckles grinned brightly back at him. "It's really me!"

Without hesitation, Jonas embraced his friend tightly. This welcome face from his past worked as an immediate balm for his wounded soul. "It's so good to see you again!"

Tarus Vasco had given his heart and soul to the rebel cause after his kid brother had been killed in King Gaius's battle to take control of Auranos. Later, after a failed uprising in which countless rebels had been slaughtered, both Tarus and Lysandra had been captured and had nearly lost their heads at a public execution.

Lysandra. The loss of a girl who'd begun to mean so much more to him than just a fellow rebel was still fresh and raw. Any reminder of her made Jonas's heart ache with grief and regret that he hadn't been able to save her.

So many memories came along with Tarus's face—both good and bad. All Jonas had wanted when he'd accompanied the boy back to his home village was for Tarus to be safe, but there was no such thing as "safe" in Mytica anymore.

Tarus gripped him tightly by his upper arms. "I did what you told me to do. I've learned to fight as well as any trained soldier. You'd be proud of me."

"I have no doubt about that."

"I'm relieved that you managed to escape."

Jonas frowned. "Escape?"

Tarus lowered his voice. "Is the witch asleep? Is that how you managed to slip free from her control?"

Jonas suddenly became acutely aware that the tavern was completely empty apart from the three men who stood silently behind Tarus like hulking shadows.

"You've been waiting down here for me," Jonas said slowly and carefully.

Tarus nodded. "As soon as the innkeeper sent word last night that you'd arrived with the witch, we got here as fast as we could."

"You're rebels." Jonas spoke softly, but he could see the truth now right in front of him.

"Of course we are. We heard what happened during Empress Amara's speech—that the witch managed to put you under her dark spell. But it won't last. My grandmama said a witch's magic dies when she does."

This almost made Jonas laugh. Tarus had always had tales to share that he'd learned from his grandmother to help explain the unknown. Jonas had once dismissed magical stories as amusing but utterly worthless.

So much had changed since then.

"I promise we will help free you from her evil grasp," Tarus said gravely. "I know you wouldn't be with Lucia Damora of your own free will."

Jonas flicked a wary glance at the other men. They didn't look at him with concern like Tarus did. The nearby wall torch reflected in their cold, dark eyes. They were filled with distrust.

"I know you'll have trouble believing this," Jonas said, "but Princess Lucia is not what you think she is. There's something else out there . . . someone else. The greatest threat that has ever been unleashed in this world. That's what we need to stop."

"What are you talking about?" Tarus asked quietly.

Jonas licked his dry lips. How best to explain the unexplainable? "I know you're well aware of the legend of the Kindred."

Tarus nodded. "A magical treasure many have sought, thinking it might turn them into gods."

"Right. But the thing is, Kindred magic isn't just magic someone can use for themselves. They're actually gods already—air, water, earth . . . fire. Trapped inside the four crystal orbs. And the fire god has been freed." Lucia's horrific dream flashed through his mind, and he cringed at the memory. "He wants to destroy the world. Princess Lucia is the only one who has the magic to stop him."

Chest tight, he waited for a response, but for several long moments there was only silence.

Then one of the hulking men scoffed. "What nonsense."

"He's definitely under the witch's influence," another hissed. "We gave you a chance to speak with him, Tarus. But our time is running out. What should we do now?"

Jonas frowned. Was Tarus their leader? Did these men look to a boy of only fifteen years of age to command them?

Tarus met Jonas's gaze. "I want to believe you."

"You have to believe me," Jonas said simply, but his voice felt strained. He knew it sounded like the most far-fetched story he'd ever told. Had he not witnessed much of it with his own eyes, he'd be the first to deny such insanity. "You always believed in the possibility of magic, Tarus, and you must believe this. The fate of our world depends on it."

"Perhaps," Tarus allowed. "Or perhaps the witch has a tighter hold on you than I thought she did." His brows drew together, his gaze growing distant. "I saw her, you know. Princess Lucia Damora walked with her male friend amongst the carnage in a village they'd just destroyed as if it were only a pleasant bonfire, set ablaze to warm her cold heart. I remember that she smiled as she walked past the charred corpse of my mother." His voice broke. "I watched both of my parents burn to death right before my eyes, and I couldn't do anything to save them. We were visiting my aunt for a few days. And . . . then they were gone."

Jonas couldn't breathe, couldn't form enough words to speak. To argue. To explain that the male friend had been the fire Kindred, Kyan. It didn't excuse Lucia's behavior or choices while aligned with him. How was he supposed to explain something as horrible as this?

"I'm so sorry" was all he managed to say.

"The King of Blood's daughter belongs to the darklands," one of the other rebels snarled. "And we're here today to send her there. Her and her spawn."

Jonas felt his stomach drop. "You know about the child? And you'd wish to harm an innocent?"

The rebel grabbed a torch off the wall. "The innkeeper told us. It's a demon born of a demon, not an innocent child born of a woman."

Jonas watched with dismay as Tarus also grabbed a torch. "You think Lucia's evil. And perhaps she was . . . for a time. Perhaps we've all done unforgivable things in our lives. I know I have. But you can't help them do this."

"You defend her even though she killed Lys." When Jonas winced as if the name were a slap, Tarus's expression hardened. "Yes, word travels fast."

"The fire god killed her, not Lucia. The princess named her baby Lyssa to show her remorse for what happened to Lysandra."

"That witch doesn't deserve to speak that name," Tarus spat. "Had it not been for her, Lys would still be alive. Countless Paelsians would still be alive!"

It was exactly what Kyan had claimed in Lucia's dream, that everything was her fault.

"It's not that simple," Jonas said through clenched teeth.

Pained disappointment flashed across Tarus's face. "You're a Paelsian. You're a rebel. You know that black-hearted witch is everything we've been fighting against! Why do you waste the breath to defend her?"

Tarus was right. Completely right.

Lucia's magic had released the fire god from his crystal cage. She'd stood by him for months as he laid waste to half of Mytica, killing countless innocents. Even before that, she'd been raised by King Gaius, a monster Jonas had wanted dead more than anyone else.

Until . . .

Until what? he thought with disgust. Until you became an ally of the Damoras? Until the King of Blood himself sent you to find his daughter and return her safely to his royal side so he could harness her magic to regain his sadistic power?

Jonas didn't know what to say, his mind in turmoil. Every choice, every decision, every thought he'd had over the last painful year had all led to this moment.

"Your place is with us, Jonas." Tarus's voice grew quieter again. The boy was now so close that Jonas could feel the heat from Tarus's torch against his face. "If this fire god is real, we'll deal with him. Let us free you from the witch's dark spell so you can help us."

His heart felt like a lead weight in his chest as he pulled the jeweled dagger from the leather sheath at his belt. It was the very same dagger that had killed his brother when it had been wielded by a rich and spoiled lord. Jonas could have sold it for a small fortune on many occasions, but he'd kept it as a symbol of what he fought for.

Justice. Good triumphing over evil. A world where everything made sense and lines between friend and foe were clearly drawn in the sand.

Had a world like that ever existed?

"I can't let you kill the princess," Jonas said firmly. "What you're going to do is let me leave this inn, this village, with her and the baby, unharmed."

Tarus glanced at the dagger, his brows raised. "Impossible."

"You'd be dead if I hadn't saved you from the executioner's ax," Jonas said. "You owe me this."

"I owed you only what you asked of me: that I grow up and get strong. I did that. I'm strong now. Strong enough to do the right thing." Tarus then addressed his men, his voice solemn but firm: "Burn the inn to the ground. If Jonas gets in your way . . ." He sighed. "Kill him too. He's made his choice."

The rebels didn't wait. They moved toward the stairs with their torches in hand. Jonas shoved at one, swiping his dagger at another. In mere moments, they managed to both restrain and unarm him.

He was still weak from last night. From allowing Lucia to steal his mysterious inner magic to survive the birth of Lyssa.

One of the men dragged Jonas across the floor of the tavern, the dagger pressed to his throat as the rebels threw the torches to the wooden floor. It took only a moment for the fire to rise, catching on the dry material and coating the walls.

"Lucia!" Jonas yelled.

The rebel arched Jonas's own jeweled dagger toward his chest to silence him forever, but the weapon froze in place just before it made contact. The rebel frowned as the dagger lurched out of his grip and hovered in the air.

Jonas looked to the stairway. The flames were rising higher, but there was a pathway cleared between them now.

Lucia approached with Lyssa in her arms, her expression full of fury.

"Did you think you could kill me with a little bit of fire?" she said, raising her right hand. "How wrong you were."

All three rebels and Tarus flew backward, hitting the wall of the tavern hard. Their eyes were wide with surprise, and they grunted with effort as they tried to free themselves from where they'd been pinned by Lucia's air magic.

The dagger moved through the air until it reached Tarus.

"Do it, witch," Tarus spat. "Show us all what a cold-blooded killer you are."

"If you insist," Lucia replied.

"No!" Jonas pushed himself up from the floor and stepped between Lucia and the rebels. "Nobody dies here today."

She looked at him incredulously. "They wanted to kill me. They wanted to kill you."

"And they failed."

"Do you think they'll stop trying?"

"I don't care what they do," he said. "We're leaving here."

"We?" She frowned. "Even after how cruel I was to you upstairs, you still want to help me?"

"Let these men live, and we walk out of here together. Tarus asked me what side I'm on, so I guess I've chosen. I'm with you, princess. You're not the monster they wanted to kill here today.

You're better than that." Jonas hadn't believed the truth in the words completely until he spoke them aloud, but they were as honest as he'd ever been with her. Or himself.

Lucia searched his gaze for a moment longer before she flicked her wrist. The dagger flew away from Tarus, embedding itself in the opposite wall.

"Fine," she said. "Then let's go."

Jonas nodded, relieved that no blood would be shed. He looked over at the dagger.

Lucia touched his arm. "Leave it. That nasty thing is a part of your past."

He hesitated just a moment longer.

"You're right," he finally said.

Without looking back at Tarus, the rebels, or the dagger that had stolen the life of both his brother and his best friend, Jonas left the inn with Lucia and her baby.

CHAPTER 2

CLEO

PAELSIA

The guard led Cleo down the dark and narrow dungeon hallway to where the empress of Kraeshia, Amara Cortas, waited. Amara smiled at her in greeting.

Cleo didn't smile back. Instead, her gaze flicked to the brace on Amara's freshly broken leg and the cane she leaned upon. She winced as she remembered the gruesome snap of the bone last night, when Amara had been thrown into a deep pit along with the rest of the group, waiting for their deaths, both rebel and royal alike.

Carlos, the empress's captain of the guard, stood like a menacing yet protective shadow next to Amara.

"How are you feeling?" Amara asked tentatively. "I haven't seen you all day."

"I'm well enough." Cleo fisted her left hand that now bore the water symbol—two parallel wavy lines. The last person who'd shared this marking had been a goddess.

But Cleo didn't feel like a goddess. She felt like a seventeen-year-old girl who hadn't slept at all last night after waking abruptly from a vivid dream in which she'd been drowning. Her mouth, her throat, her lungs filling with a sea of water. The more she struggled, the more impossible it was to breathe.

She woke just before she would have drowned.

Cleo nodded at the wooden door to Amara's right. "He's inside?"

"He is," Amara said. "Are you sure you want to do this?"

"I've never been more sure of anything. Open the door."

Amara gestured toward Carlos, and he opened the door that led into a small room no more than eight paces wide and eight paces long.

A prisoner was inside, his hands chained above his head, lit by two torches on the stone walls on either side of him. He was shirtless, his face bearded, his hair shorn short against his scalp.

Cleo's heart began to pound hard against her chest at the sight of this man. She wanted him dead.

But first she needed answers.

"Leave us," Amara said to Carlos. "Wait in the hall."

Carlos's heavy brows drew together. "You want to be left alone with this prisoner?"

"My honored guest wishes to speak with this former guard— one who would choose to do Lord Kurtis's bidding rather than mine." She sneered at the prisoner. "Yes, I want you to leave us alone with him."

Honored guest. What an strange description for Amara to use for someone she had offered up, along with the others, to the fire Kindred as a willing sacrifice only last night.

Of course, the night had not gone nearly as smoothly as the empress had anticipated.

Very well, I'll play the role of your honored guest, Cleo thought darkly. *But only as long as I have to.*

Carlos bowed, and with a gesture toward the guard who'd led Cleo there, they swiftly departed and closed the door behind them.

Cleo's gaze remained fixed on the bearded man in the shadowy room. Once he had worn the same dark green guard's uniform as Carlos and the others, but now his dirty trousers were in tatters.

The room stank of rot and filth.

The symbol on the palm of Cleo's hand burned.

"What is his name?" she asked with distaste.

"Why don't you ask me?" The man raised bloodshot eyes to look directly at Cleo. "But I doubt you even care what my name is, do you?"

"You're right, I don't." She raised her chin, ignoring any momentary shiver of disgust and blind hatred toward this stranger. If she didn't stay calm, she wouldn't get the answers she needed. "Do you know who I am?"

"Of course I do." The prisoner's eyes glittered in the torchlight. "Cleiona Bellos. A former princess whose kingdom was stolen by the King of Blood before she was forced into marriage to his son and heir. Then the king lost his precious kingdom to the Kraeshian Empire, so now you have nothing at all."

If only he knew the truth. She actually had everything she ever thought she wanted. The symbol on the palm of her left hand continued to burn, as if the lines were freshly branded upon her skin.

Water magic, fused with her very being.

But as untouchable as if a wall divided her from the power of a goddess.

"He's already been questioned to no avail," Amara said. "This may be a waste of our time."

"You don't have to stay," Cleo replied.

Amara was silent for a moment. "I want to help."

Cleo actually laughed at that, a low chuckle in her throat that held no amusement. "Oh, yes, you've been so helpful, Amara. Endlessly helpful."

"Don't forget, we've all suffered because of Kyan," Amara said defiantly. "Even me."

Cleo bit back a response—something cold and cruel and accusatory. A game of who had suffered the most between the two of them.

But there was no time for such pettiness.

Amara had offered all but her very soul to help Kyan in order to gain power. Cleo knew how persuasive he could be, since she had experienced it herself when the incorporeal fire Kindred whispered promises in her ear last night.

Kyan wanted his three siblings free from their crystal prisons and in possession of new flesh-and-blood vessels, and Amara had made sure that a selection of sacrifices were ready.

Kyan had only half succeeded.

Nic. Olivia.

Both gone.

No, she thought. *I can't think about Nic now. I need to stay in control.*

Cleo forced herself to focus only on the bruises on the former guard's face and body. Yes, he'd been questioned like Amara said. But he hadn't been broken yet.

She didn't spare a moment of sympathy for this prisoner and his current predicament. "Where is Kurtis Cirillo?"

She said the name like something she'd spat out and squashed into the ground with the heel of her boot.

The man didn't blink. "I don't know."

"You don't?" Cleo cocked her head. "Are you sure? He is the one you'd begun to take orders from, rather than the empress, isn't he?"

He cast a disparaging glance toward Amara. "I don't take orders from any woman, I don't care who she is. Never have and never will. You have a difficult road ahead of you, princess."

"*Empress*," Amara corrected.

"Is that official?" he asked. "Even with your older brother still alive? I believe the title of emperor is rightfully his."

"Ashur murdered my father and brothers," she replied curtly. "He is my prisoner, not my rival."

Amara's ability to lie was second to none, Cleo thought.

"Answer the princess's questions truthfully," Amara said, "and I promise your execution will be swift. Continue to be evasive, and I promise you will suffer greatly."

"Again"—the man had the audacity to smirk at her—"I don't take orders from women. I have many friends here among your guards. Do you think they'll follow your command to torture me without hesitation? Perhaps they'll refuse such a command. A few bruises and cuts are just for show, to make you think you're in control here. Perhaps they'd free me to torture you instead." He snorted. "You're just a little girl who's deluded herself into think-ing she has power."

Amara didn't react to his rant other than shaking her head. "Men. So full of yourselves, no matter what station you hold. So full of your own bloated self-importance. Don't worry. I would be happy to leave you chained up in here, without food, without water. I can easily make this a forgetting room like we have back home."

"What's a forgetting room?" Cleo asked.

"A room in which one is left in darkness, solitude, and silence," Amara replied, "with only enough plain, tasteless food to sustain life."

Yes, Cleo had heard of such a punishment. Prisoners were left alone until they went mad or died.

Some of the amusement had disappeared from the prisoner's eyes at the threat when he glanced at Cleo. Less amusement, but still no fear.

"I don't know where Lord Kurtis is," he said slowly. "So why don't you be on your way now, little girl?"

"I know you were present when Prince Magnus disappeared." Cleo had to speak slowly to keep her voice from trembling with her growing frustration. "Nerissa Florens has confirmed that you were there. That you knocked him unconscious and dragged him away. This isn't up for debate or denial; it's a fact. Tell me where you took him."

Nerissa had told Cleo not to come here—to let others search for Magnus and Kurtis. She wanted Cleo to rest.

It was an impossible request.

Nerissa had wanted to stay with Cleo today, but Cleo had insisted she join the search for Magnus.

Despite the bruises and cuts on the prisoner's face, his hateful smirk had returned. "Very well. You really want to know? Lord Kurtis had us bring the prince to this very room. Right here." He looked up at the thick iron chains. "These exact restraints. But then Lord Kurtis dismissed me, told me to go back to work. So that's exactly what I did. What happened after that, I don't know. But I do know something . . ."

Cleo had started to tremble as she imagined Magnus here, chained right where this prisoner stood. His face bloody, beaten. His body broken.

"What do you know?" Cleo snarled through clenched teeth, drawing closer to the prisoner. So close that his sour stench became nearly unbearable.

"Lord Kurtis is obsessed with the prince—obsessed with *killing* him, that is. So, my guess? That's exactly what he did."

White-hot pain seared into Cleo, and she swallowed back the urge to sob. She'd already imagined a thousand horrible things Kurtis could have done to Magnus.

More reason to stay awake. More reason to fight for answers, because she wasn't ready to give up.

"Magnus is not dead," she bit out. "I won't believe it."

"Perhaps Lord Kurtis cut him up into many bloody pieces, strewn about Mytica."

"Shut your mouth," Cleo growled.

It was suddenly hard to breathe.

Drowning, she thought with rising panic. *I feel like I'm drowning again, yet I'm wide awake.*

From deep inside the walled compound's prison, she heard a loud rumble of thunder.

"Kurtis promised you something for your loyalty," Amara said. "What? Rescue, perhaps? Fortune?"

She had to be right. Kurtis would need all the help he could get after crossing Amara.

"You *must* know where he is," Cleo said, her voice not much more than a painful croak. Each breath was labored, and the burning sensation in her palm was impossible to ignore.

The man regarded her now with bemusement. "Stupid girl, you're better off without that family alive. You should be thanking Lord Kurtis. And me." His glittering gaze moved to Amara. "Smartest thing you did was lock King Gaius up. He would have slit your throat the moment he could."

"Perhaps," Amara allowed.

"Is he as dead as I am?"

"I haven't decided yet."

After Kyan and Olivia had disappeared last night, Amara had King Gaius thrown into a cell, along with Felix and Ashur. They were three men who presented a threat to the empress, in different ways. Three men she preferred to keep in separate locked cages.

"Did you say that I should . . . thank you?" Cleo managed.

"I said it. I meant it." He laughed, but it sounded raw now. "Some called him the Prince of Blood, didn't they? One who followed in the footsteps of his father? His blood was so red as it hit this dirt floor. And the crunch that his bones made as they broke . . . like music to my ears."

"Shut up," Cleo snarled.

Suddenly, the prisoner's eyes widened. His mouth opened, his lips moving as if he sought his next breath but couldn't find it.

"What?" he croaked out. "What . . . is happening?"

Cleo tried to stay calm, but it had grown more difficult with every hateful word this prisoner uttered. Nerissa was right—it had been a horrible mistake to come here.

She needed to find Taran. He now had the air Kindred within him, battling for dominance of his mortal body. She'd all but ignored him since last night, lost in her own grief, her own suffering.

She shouldn't have. She needed him. She needed to know how he was coping.

Her hand burned. She looked down at the water symbol, and her eyes widened. Small, wispy blue lines had begun to spread out from the symbol itself.

"You're a witch!" the prisoner gasped.

Was that what he thought? That she'd drawn an elemental symbol on her palm, hoping to summon a small piece of water magic like a common witch?

I'm not a witch, she wanted to say.

I don't know what I am anymore.

Cleo looked around at the small, dark room. This was the very room where Magnus had suffered.

"Is he dead?" she managed, her words barely understandable. Then she yelled: "Answer me!"

"By now?" the prisoner gritted out. "I have no doubt that he is."

All the breath left Cleo's body as she stared at this monster.

"You've said enough," Amara snarled at the prisoner.

"Yes, he has," Cleo said.

Then she allowed her hate and grief to surge forward. In an instant, the burning sensation in her left hand turned to ice.

The prisoner's eyes bugged, his mouth opening wide as he let out a pained scream that cut off abruptly. He froze in place, his hands restrained in the metal cuffs, the heavy chain attached to the wall.

"What are you doing to him?" Amara gasped.

"I . . . I don't know."

Her pain and rage had triggered something inside her that she couldn't control. But instinctively she knew what was happening. She sensed every trace of water in the man's body as it turned to solid ice.

A chill fell over the cell like a shroud. When Cleo exhaled, her breath formed a frozen cloud just as it did on the coldest days in Limeros.

Then the prisoner's frozen body shattered into countless pieces of ice.

Cleo stared with shock at what was left of the man as her mind cleared. Stunned silence filled the dungeon cell for several moments.

"You killed him," Amara said, her voice hushed.

Cleo slowly turned to face Amara, expecting to be greeted with a look of horror, of fear. Perhaps the empress would fall to the ground and beg for her own life.

Instead, Amara regarded her with what appeared to be . . . envy.

"Incredible," Amara breathed. "You showed us all a little water magic last night, so I knew it had to be possible. But this? Truly incredible. Perhaps Gaius was wrong about what he said. You—you and Taran—can use the Kindred *elementia* within you without it destroying your mortal bodies."

As if every ounce of strength had suddenly left her in a rush, Cleo collapsed to her knees, bracing herself on her hands. The ground was wet, the icy fragments from the prisoner already starting to melt.

She'd wanted this for so long—to possess the magic of the Kindred.

But now the Kindred possessed her.

Cleo touched the pocket of her gown where she'd placed the aquamarine orb, which was the former prison of the water Kindred. She'd tried to touch it last night, to hold it in her bare hand, but it was impossible. The pain had been so immediate and intense that she'd shrieked and dropped the orb.

Taran had experienced the same thing. He didn't want the moonstone orb anywhere near him, had called it a "cursed marble" and thrown it across the room. Today, he'd joined the search for Magnus with a flank of guards appointed by Amara, along with Enzo—a former Limerian guard—and Nerissa, as far away from the compound as he could get.

Taran's moonstone—along with the obsidian orb that had contained the earth Kindred before it possessed Olivia—now sat in a locked cabinet to which Cleo wore the key on a gold chain around her neck.

But Cleo decided to keep the aquamarine orb with her, protected in a velvet drawstring pouch. She chose to go with her gut on this decision, rather than her brain, which told her to throw it into the Silver Sea and let it sink to the very bottom.

Amara extended her hand to Cleo. After a moment of hesitation, Cleo took it and allowed the empress to help her to her feet.

"What you just did . . . if you could do that at will, you would be unstoppable," Amara said slowly. "You need to learn how to control this magic."

Cleo eyed the girl with fresh skepticism. "Be careful with your advice, Amara. You might accidentally help me reclaim my kingdom."

Amara's expression turned thoughtful. "I only wanted Mytica because I wanted the Kindred. Now Kyan is out there somewhere with Olivia, as we speak. We don't know for sure when they'll come back, but we know they will. And when they do, we need to be ready to fight."

An image of Nic came readily to Cleo's mind, his messy red hair and crooked smile never failing to brighten even her darkest of days.

Kyan had taken Nic away from her as surely as if he'd slit his throat.

She hated Kyan. And she hated this magic inside her.

Amara leaned against the wall, grimacing as she ran her hand gingerly down her broken leg. "We've had our problems, I won't deny it. And you certainly have many reasons to hate me. But now we share the same enemy who could destroy everything either of us has ever cared about. Agreed?"

Cleo nodded slowly. "Agreed."

"Both you and Taran must find a way to use this magic within you to defeat Kyan and Olivia." Amara paused to take a breath. "Succeed, and I will give Mytica back to you and you alone."

Cleo couldn't believe her own ears. It was the last thing she ever would have expected to hear from the empress of Kraeshia. "You would agree to that?"

"I would. I swear this upon my mother's soul." Amara nodded firmly. "Think about what I've said. All of it."

She knocked on the door, and Carlos opened it, looming within its frame. He looked into the room and frowned with confusion at the small chunks of ice melting into the dirt floor.

Amara reached for his waiting arm. "Assist me outside, Carlos. We're done here."

Carlos flicked a look at Cleo, his eyes narrowing with suspicion.

Cleo raised her chin, holding his gaze until he looked away. She didn't trust him. Didn't trust any Kraeshian—especially the ones who made great promises to her.

Defeat Kyan, regain her kingdom.

But they were only words.

If she did harness this magic in a way she could use to defeat Kyan that wouldn't destroy her in the process, she wouldn't need Amara to give her back her kingdom. She would simply take it.

Cleo cast a last glance at the dungeon cell before she left it, her heart a heavy weight in her chest.

I will find you, Magnus, she promised silently. *I swear I will.*

She followed Amara and Carlos down the hallway, up a short flight of stairs chiseled out of heavy stone, and they emerged into the compound grounds that had once been the home of Hugo Basilius, the chieftain of Paelsia. The compound itself was like a small, humble duplicate of the Auranian City of Gold—but with far more stone and mud in its construction than jewels and pristine white marble imported from overseas.

The rainstorm had washed away any remaining traces of blood from the dozens of dead bodies—guards that Selia Damora had murdered with her magic to help the fire Kindred—around the large, thirty-foot-deep pit in the exact center of the compound.

The rain had stopped, but the clouds were thick and dark, making midday appear more like dusk.

She couldn't simply go back to the chambers Amara had lent her, doing nothing. The wait for news about Magnus would drive her mad.

If there was so much magic inside her, why did she feel so powerless?

Then she heard a sound. A loud bang.

It was coming from the closed entry gates, which were twenty feet tall and took six guards great effort to open and close.

A guard rushed up to Carlos, out of breath. "We have a situation, captain."

"What is it?" Amara demanded before Carlos had a chance to answer.

"Someone is at the gates, demanding entry." The man cringed as the bang sounded out again. The ground itself shook with the booming sound.

"It's Kyan, isn't it?" the empress said, her voice filled with fear. "He's returned."

Oh goddess, Cleo thought as panic gripped her throat. *Not yet. I'm not ready.*

"It's not him, empress," the guard said.

Amara's fear disappeared in an instant. "Well, what is it, then? A rebel attack? Wouldn't our scouts have forewarned us?"

"It's not rebels." The guard straightened his shoulders, but it didn't mask how nervous he looked. "It's . . . worse than that."

"Worse?"

Two more bangs made the ground beneath Cleo's feet shudder. The air filled with the sound of guards shouting orders. A hundred men, weapons in hand, flanked either side of the gate just as it splintered down the center.

Untouched, the gate swung wide open from some invisible force.

Guards stormed forward, but then each one flew backward, clearing a pathway for the intruders.

Two cloaked figures, one armed with a sword, entered and walked directly toward Cleo, to where she stood, tensely, with Amara and Carlos to her right.

Cleo realized with shock that one of the cloaked intruders cradled a baby. The intruder pushed back the hood of her black cloak to reveal a familiar face.

Lucia Damora.

"Where is my brother?" she demanded.

CHAPTER 3

LUCIA

PAELSIA

Jonas touched Lucia's arm. "Try to stay calm."

She sent a tense look at him over her shoulder. What did he think she would do? Murder Cleo and Amara where they stood?

Likely, that's *exactly* what he thought she would do.

"I need answers," she gritted out.

Being met at the closed gates of this royal compound by a swarm of Amara's soldiers, their weapons drawn, had stolen what little "calm" she had left in her reserve. She wondered if the rebel was more concerned for Lucia's life or the lives of the dozens of armed guards that now surrounded them.

"Lucia," Amara said, drawing the sorceress's attention away from her far warier companion. The Kraeshian princess leaned on a wooden cane. "Welcome. It's been a long time since I last saw you. Much has changed for both of us."

Lucia narrowed her gaze at the deceitful, conquering empress who, by all accounts, was now her stepmother. "My brother and my father. Where are they?"

The flank of guards drew closer, jostling for position, their swords pointed in Lucia's direction.

Jonas finally lowered the hood of his cloak. "Empress Amara, call off your guards. This isn't necessary."

"Jonas!" Cleo gasped. "It's you!"

The Auranian princess had always been so brilliant at observation, Lucia thought drily.

"Good to see you again, princess," Jonas said, a smile tugging at his lips.

"You too," Cleo replied, her voice strained.

Jonas sounded far happier about the reunion than Lucia felt. Seeing Amara and Cleo standing side by side had raised Lucia's ire tenfold. She'd half expected Cleo to be a prisoner here, at the mercy of the new empress whose army occupied the whole of Mytica, but clearly she wasn't.

"Your father stood against me. He tried to murder me," Amara said evenly. "But I assure you he's unharmed. I'm sure you can understand why I have chosen to keep him under lock and key. He's a dangerous man."

That he certainly was, no argument from Lucia.

"I'm sure you're pleased about that," she said to Cleo.

Cleo's glare was sharp enough to cut. "You wouldn't have any idea how I feel about anything that's happened here."

Lucia tried very hard to hold on to her patience. "Where is he?" she asked Amara.

"I will take you to see him myself," Amara replied, her tone as light and casual as if they discussed nothing more urgent than the weather. "My goodness, Lucia, what a beautiful child. Whose is it?"

Lucia looked down at Lyssa in her arms, her sweet face not showing any distress after her mother had blasted through the locked gates with air magic. In fact, the baby was currently sound asleep.

She raised her gaze to lock with Amara's. "Take me to him now."

Amara hesitated, glancing at the large guard standing next to her, and then regarded Lucia again. "With pleasure. Please follow me."

"Wait here," Lucia said to Jonas.

Her command was met with a glare. "Yes, your highness," he said with mock sincerity.

Lucia knew that Jonas was annoyed with her tendency to issue orders at him as if he were a servant. It was a habit more than a conscious decision.

The thought that this morning he'd somehow entered her nightmare still disturbed her. He was a mystery to her in so many ways, but despite this, she'd come to trust and value him.

However, if he expected her to be sweet and polite all the time, he was traveling with the wrong princess.

Their travels together ended here. Jonas would not have to deal with her foul moods another day.

There was no reason to feel regret over this.

So be it.

Lucia sensed something . . . *unusual* about Cleo as she passed the other princess, but she chose to ignore it as she followed Amara to the compound's prison area. The empress leaned against her guard as well as her cane, limping as she walked. Lucia concentrated, sending out a whisper of earth magic that helped her sense Amara's injury.

A broken leg.

Achieving ultimate power over a newly conquered land did not come without injury, it would seem.

As they moved past the dusty villas and cottages that made up the royal compound, Lucia half expected to feel some sort of familiarity with these grounds. Her birth father had ruled from here—a madman who thought himself a god. She knew nothing about her real mother, only that she'd died as well.

Her sister by blood, Laelia, worked as a dancer in a tavern in the city of Basilia on the west cost of Paelsia. Perhaps one day she might go and ask Laelia more questions about her birth family. At the moment, though, her past was insignificant to her.

Lucia focused now on only three goals.

Reuniting with Magnus and her father.

Ensuring Lyssa's future.

And imprisoning Kyan by any means necessary in his amber orb, which she kept with her in the pocket of her cloak.

Anything beyond these goals was an unwanted distraction.

As they entered the prison, Amara led Lucia down narrow hallways that the injured empress navigated very carefully with her guard's help. She didn't complain once, which Lucia grudgingly respected.

They passed many locked iron doors, but Amara finally came to a stop in front of one at the end of the hallway, which she placed her hand upon.

"If you wish to speak with Gaius," Amara said, "I have a few rules that must be obeyed."

Lucia raised her brows. "Do you?" She flicked her finger at the door, which swung open instantly.

Amara's hulking guard immediately reached for his sword.

"Spare me such displays." Lucia used another blast of air magic to send the sword down the hallway, where it embedded itself into the stone wall, but not nearly as deeply as she'd intended.

Amara's expression didn't shift from one of royal composure;

however, her lips now formed a thin line. "Your air magic is incredible."

Not as incredible as Lucia would like it to be. After stealing Jonas's strange but strong reserve of *elementia* last night to survive Lyssa's birth, Lucia had slowly but surely begun to feel it fading from her again.

But Amara didn't have to know that.

"I will speak to my father in private," Lucia said. "You should hope that he is as unharmed as you claim."

"He is." Amara nodded at her guard, who led her away from the door without another word.

Holding her breath, unsure what she would find within, Lucia turned toward the interior of the cell, unable to see anything within but shadows and darkness.

Amara had kept her father in darkness.

Fury rose within her at the thought.

"My beautiful daughter. More powerful and magnificent than ever before."

The sound of the king's strong voice was such a relief that tears sprang to her eyes. She flicked her hand to light the torches on the walls with fire magic.

King Gaius blinked against the sudden blaze of light, shielding his eyes with the back of his hand.

"Father," her voice broke on the word. She entered the cell completely, closing the door behind her to give them privacy from curious ears.

He had a short beard on his chin and dark circles beneath his eyes as if he hadn't slept in days.

"Apologies for my appearance, daughter," he said. "You seem to have found me in a shamefully unfortunate state."

She couldn't remember the last time she'd allowed herself to cry. She didn't allow it this time, but hot tears still streaked down her cheeks. Her throat was so tight it made it difficult to speak, but she forced the words out. "I'm the one who should apologize. I left you—you and Magnus. I was wrong. And because of my selfishness, so much has happened . . . I can't fix it all, but I'm going to try to fix as much as I can. Please forgive me."

"Forgive you? There is nothing to forgive. I'm just thankful you're alive and well." His dark brows drew together, and he moved forward as if to take her into his arms, but he froze when his gaze moved toward the small bundle in her arms. "Whose child is this, Lucia?"

Again, a shameful swell of emotion made her words difficult. "My—my daughter. Her name is Lyssa."

She expected his kind expression to turn harsh, for his lips to thin, for words of strong reprimand for being so careless.

He pushed the soft cloth away from Lyssa's face and looked down into the face of his granddaughter. "She's as beautiful as her mother."

Lucia stared at him. "You're not angry?"

"Why would I be?" Still, there was a gravity to his words. "She's Alexius's child?"

She nodded.

"The daughter of a sorceress and an exiled Watcher," he mused. "You will need to protect her."

"With your help, I will," she replied.

"This was a swift birth. I haven't seen you in what feels like forever, but it's only been a matter of months."

"I visited the Sanctuary," she said. "Something about being there . . . I'm sure that's what quickened the process."

"She's a newborn."

She nodded. "Last night."

He looked at her, shocked. "You seem so well, considering you just gave birth."

"It wasn't a normal birth," Lucia confessed, needing to share this with someone she trusted. And this man—this King of Blood who'd had her stolen from her cradle, who'd raised her as his daughter because of her prophecy—despite his choices, his reputation, his treatment of others, Lucia could not say he had ever been cruel to her. Only kind. Only forgiving.

Gaius Damora was her father. And she loved him.

"What do you mean?" he prompted.

And she explained it to him as best she could—about Timotheus's prophecy that she would die in childbirth. About finding the magic within herself to survive.

She felt it best not to mention Jonas's mysterious connections to the Watchers and the magic he'd allowed her to take from him.

Lucia told her father that after a wave of agony in which she'd been certain she would lose consciousness, Lyssa was simply . . . there. Lying on the rain-soaked ground, her eyes glowing bright violet in the darkness.

The same violet as Lucia's ring.

Her father listened carefully, not interrupting her once.

"Only more proof that Lyssa is very special," he said. "As special as you are."

"I agree, she is special." Something heavy in her chest that she'd been carrying for months finally eased. "Where's Magnus?" she asked. "Is he in another cell?"

When the king met Lucia's gaze, she saw pain in his dark eyes.

She drew in a sharp breath. "What happened? Tell me."

And he did tell her. About finding her grandmother—a woman she'd thought had died a dozen years ago. About her father and brother's capture by Amara's soldiers. About Amara's association with the fire Kindred and the sacrifices she'd placed at the bottom of a nearby pit. About Kyan's possession of Nicolo Cassian's body and how the ritual was brought to a sudden halt by her grand-mother's death, but not before the other three Kindred had cho-sen flesh-and-blood vessels: that of a Watcher Lucia didn't know, a friend of Jonas's she didn't know, and Cleo.

"And Magnus?" she prompted when she could find her breath again.

"Lord Kurtis Cirillo took him away . . . somewhere. There's a search, I know this. I don't know anything else because I've been locked in this bloody prison. Useless." There was fury in the king's gaze now, tempered with regret. "He hates me for all I've done, and I don't blame him. I tried to help him the only way I could . . ." His breath hitched, and he paused, as if trying to find his composure again. "But I fear it wasn't enough."

It was on the tip of her tongue to ask him how he thought he could help, but her thoughts were stolen away by the name of a boy from her past. Someone hateful and cruel and without remorse.

Kurtis Cirillo.

Lucia had a sudden memory of coming upon a twitching, dying kitten in the corridors of the Limerian palace. Lord Kurtis had been nearby, snickering at her horrified reaction. She'd had nightmares about that poor kitten for weeks afterward.

Magnus had hated Kurtis, but tolerated him only because he was the son of Lord Gareth, a friend and advisor to the king.

"Where is Kurtis now?" she hissed.

"I don't know. He hasn't been located, to my knowledge. All I know is that he had reason to want revenge upon Magnus."

Everything else she'd heard from the king fell to the back-ground. All of it could wait.

"We need to find him together," she said.

"I'm Amara's prisoner."

"Not anymore."

She sent air magic at the door, and it blew right off its hinges. Amara had been standing just outside the room with her guard. Her expression filled with alarm as Lucia left the cell with her father beside her.

"The search for my brother?" Lucia asked. "What news is there?"

Amara's face paled. "Nothing yet, I'm afraid. There is a search party out—thirty, forty men. They may yet find him."

The empress feared her. They all feared her. The reputation she'd built of not only being a prophesied sorceress but one who had no difficulties slaughtering villages might serve her well for a time.

Lucia could not wait for a search party.

Her magic was still strong enough to blast through gates and doors. Perhaps she could channel it another way.

"I need a private room," she said. "And something that belonged to Magnus—something I can get a sense of him from."

With Alexius's guidance, she had performed a very special location spell to find and awaken the Kindred. She'd heard of common witches who could find people or lost things with their magic, enhanced by blood.

She hadn't tried this before, but she was a sorceress, not a common witch. Even with her fading and unreliable magic it had to be possible.

Amara didn't try to stop her or demand that Gaius be put back into his locked cell. She became the perfect hostess, accommodating Lucia's request in an instant.

"Follow me," she said.

Lucia handed Lyssa to her father when they reached the room Amara led them to.

"I want to help if I can," Amara said.

"You can't help," Lucia growled. "Get out."

Amara's eyes narrowed slightly, then she cast a dark look at Gaius but didn't say another word. She nodded at her guard, and they left the room.

Lucia had been given something that belonged to her brother. His black cloak had been found, discarded, in a hallway. The king recognized it, said it belonged to Magnus.

It was torn and bloody.

The sight of it brought fresh panic to Lucia's chest. Her brother had suffered at Kurtis's hand.

I'm so sorry, she thought, clenching the rough material in her hand. *I blamed you, I hated you, I doubted you. I left you when you were the one of the best parts of my entire life. Forgive me, please.*

She would find him.

With her father standing close to her with her baby, Lucia took a seat on a section of the floor clear of any furniture, closed her eyes, and concentrated.

Earth magic seemed to be the right element to call upon. She felt the weight of the cloak in her hand. She pictured Magnus—his tall stature, his dark hair that constantly fell into his eyes since he hated having it trimmed. His square jaw, his dark brown eyes that had gazed at her either seriously or mischievously, depending on the situation and the day. The scar on his right cheek from an injury he said he could not clearly remember.

The image of him shifted to something else then.

Blood on his face, dripping from a fresh cut under his eye. Fury in his gaze.

He strained against the chains that held his arms over his head.

"I can see him," Lucia whispered.

"Where? Where is he?" Gaius asked.

"I think I'm seeing what's already happened . . ." She tightened her grip on the cloak.

Kurtis's weasel-like face came into view, a cruel smile twisting his lips.

Lucia drew in a sharp breath. "I feel Magnus's hatred for Kurtis. He wasn't afraid, even though the coward had to chain him up."

"I will kill him," the king growled.

Lucia tried to ignore him, tried to concentrate only on this vision in her mind. She'd once had another vision of the past—one of the original sorceress Eva's death at the hands of Melenia. The moment the Kindred had made Cleiona and Valoria into goddesses a millennium ago.

She sank deeper into her earth magic and pressed it outward. Even now she could sense its growing limitations, and it frustrated her so much she wanted to scream.

Timotheus told her that Eva's magic had also faded when she'd become pregnant. And this loss of strength and power had allowed her immortal sister the chance to end her life.

Lucia squeezed her eyes shut and focused on Magnus. Only Magnus. She hugged his cloak to her chest and followed the trail of earth *elementia* . . . the trace of his life, his blood, his pain . . .

Earth.

Deep earth.

Shovelfuls of dirt, one after another, hitting a closed wooden box.

"No . . ." she whispered.

"What do you see?" her father asked.

"It's not what I see, it's what I feel. It's what Kurtis did to Magnus after torturing him." Her voice broke. "He—he buried Magnus alive."

"What?" Gaius roared. "Where? Where is my son now?"

Lucia tried to hold on to the horrific feelings and thoughts and scattered images moving through her mind, but they were as difficult to gather as dry leaves caught in a windstorm.

"It's fading too quickly for me to sense that . . ." She cried out. "No—oh, goddess, no. I sensed Magnus's heart beating in the darkness . . . but now . . ."

"Lucia! What do you sense now?" Gaius demanded.

Lucia let out a shuddering sob and finally opened her eyes. It was gone—the magic was gone, and the location spell she'd attempted was over.

"I sense only death." A tear slipped down her cheek, but she didn't have the strength to push it away. "He's dead . . . Magnus is dead."

CHAPTER 4

MAGNUS

PAELSIA

For those who had chosen the path of evil in their mortal lives, the darklands had to feel exactly like this.

Endless darkness.

A slow, torturous suffocation.

And pain. So much pain.

Magnus's broken bones made him useless, unable to fight, to pound at the wooden barrier only a breath above his face.

The expanse of time had felt eternal, but there was no way of knowing how long he'd been there. Trapped underground in a small, stifling wooden coffin. Struggling only made it worse. His throat was raw from screaming for someone, anyone, to find this freshly dug grave.

Every time he slipped away into the escape of sleep, he was certain he wouldn't ever wake up again.

Yet he did.

Again and again.

Limerians weren't buried in wooden boxes like this. As worshippers of the goddess of earth and water, their bodies were laid to rest directly in contact with dirt in their frozen graves, or cast into the waters of the Silver Sea, depending on the family's decision.

Paelsians burned their dead.

Auranians worshipped the goddess of fire and air, so one would think they would favor the Paelsian burial ritual. But rich Auranians favored coffins chiseled from marble, while those of lower status chose wooden boxes.

"Kurtis had me buried like an Auranian peasant," Magnus muttered.

Surely, this had to be the former kingsliege's final insult.

To take his mind off of the horror of being buried alive and utterly helpless, he imagined how he would kill Lord Kurtis Cirillo. After much consideration, he thought a Kraeshian torture technique he'd heard of involving slowly peeling off all the prisoner's skin sounded quite satisfying.

He'd also heard of burying a victim in the ground up to their neck, then covering them with tree syrup and allowing a nest of hungry beetles to consume them slowly.

That would be nice.

Or perhaps Magnus would remove Kurtis's remaining hand. Saw it off slowly with a dull knife. Or a spoon.

Yes, a spoon.

The imagined sound of Kurtis's screams helped Magnus shift his thoughts from his own situation. But these distractions rarely lasted long.

Magnus thought he heard the distant echo of thunder. The only other sound was his own heartbeat—fast at first, but now much slower. And his breath—labored gasping when he'd struggled in the beginning, but now quiet. Shallow.

I'm going to die.

Kurtis would finally get his vengeance. And such a death he'd chosen for his worst enemy. One in which Magnus had plenty of time to think about his life, his choices, his mistakes, his regrets.

Memories of ice mazes and sculptures carved out of chunks of snow in the shadow of the Limerian palace.

Of a younger sister he'd foolishly pined for, who'd then looked at him with horror and disgust and ran away with immortal pretty boys and fire monsters.

Of a beautiful golden princess who rightfully despised him. Whose blue-green eyes held only hate for so long that he didn't remember precisely when her gaze had softened.

This princess who didn't push him away when he kissed her. Instead, she kissed him back with a passion that very nearly matched his own.

Perhaps I'm only fantasizing all of it, he thought. *I helped my father destroy her life. She should celebrate my death.*

Still, he allowed himself to fantasize about Cleo.

His light. His hope. His wife. His love.

In one fantasy, Magnus married her again, not in a crumbling ruin of a temple and under duress, but in a meadow filled with beautiful flowering trees and lush green grass.

Beautiful flowering trees and lush green grass? he thought. *What irrelevant nonsense fills my mind?*

He much preferred the ice and snow of Limeros.

Didn't he?

Magnus allowed himself to remember the princess's rare smiles, her joyful laugh, and, mostly amusingly, the sharp way she'd look at him when he constantly said something to annoy her.

He thought about her hair—always a distraction to him when she wore it down, long golden waves over her shoulders and down to her waist. He remembered the silky brush of it during their wedding tour when he'd kissed her, which had happened only because of the cheering crowd's demands—a kiss he'd despised only because he'd liked it so much.

Their next kiss in Lady Sophia's Limerian villa had struck like a bolt of lightning. It had frightened him, although he'd never admit such a thing out loud. It was the moment he knew that, if he let her, this girl would destroy him.

And then, when he'd found her in that small cottage in the center of a snowstorm, after he'd thought her dead and gone . . . and he'd realized how much she meant to him.

That kiss hadn't ended nearly as swiftly as the others.

That kiss had marked the end of the life he'd known before and the beginning of another.

When he learned she was cursed like her mother by a vengeful witch, to die in childbirth, his selfish desires for her had ground to an abrupt halt. He would not risk her life for any reason. And together they would find a way to break this hateful curse.

But Lord Kurtis had been yet another curse cast upon them.

Magnus remembered the threats Kurtis had whispered to him while chained up and unable to tear the former kingsliege apart. Threats of what he would do to Cleo when Magnus couldn't protect her.

Dark, nightmarish atrocities that Magnus wouldn't wish upon his worst enemy.

Panic swelled within him as these thoughts brought him back to stark reality. His heart pounded, and he strained to break free of this small, stifling prison deep underground.

"I'm here!" he yelled. "I'm down here!"

He yelled it over and over till his throat felt as if he'd swallowed a dozen knives, but nothing happened. No one came for him.

After cursing the goddess he'd long since stopped believing in, he began to bargain with her.

"Delay my death, Valoria," he growled. "Let me out of here, and let me kill Kurtis before he harms her. Then you can take my life any way you wish to."

But, just like his yells for help, his prayers went unanswered.

"Damn you!" He slammed his fist against the top of the coffin so hard that a splinter of wood wedged into his skin.

He let out a roar, one filled with pain and frustration and fear. He'd never felt so helpless. So useless. So incredibly—

Wait . . .

He frowned as he ripped the splinter out of his skin with his teeth.

"My arm," he whispered in the darkness. "What's wrong with my arm?"

Actually, it wasn't what was *wrong* with it. It was what was *right* with it.

His arm—both of his arms—had been broken at Kurtis's command. He hadn't been able to move more than a little without immediate, crushing pain.

He fisted his right hand, then moved his wrist and arm.

There was no pain.

Impossible.

He tried again to move his left arm with the same result. And his leg—the sound of the crack it made when broken and the mind-numbing pain that followed was still far too fresh in his mind.

He wiggled his toes inside his boot.

No pain.

A drop of mud squeezed between the narrow slats of the coffin and splashed into his eye. He winced and wiped it away.

The thunder rolled high above him. The sound had been a constant since he'd been buried. If he concentrated, he could hear rain pounding down upon his grave and soaking into the earth covering his coffin.

He pressed both of his hands flat against the wooden barrier above him.

"What am I thinking?" he mused. "That my bones somehow magically healed? I don't have earth magic like Lucia does. I'm hallucinating."

Or was he?

After all, there *was* a way to keep one alive and well long after they were supposed to die. He'd learned about it only recently.

Magnus frowned at the thought. "Impossible. He wouldn't have given it to me."

Still, he began to search himself with arms that now worked and hands that were previously useless to him. He slid his palms down his sides, over his chest, feeling the suffocating press of wood on either side of him.

He froze as he felt something small and hard in the pocket of his shirt, something he hadn't noticed until this very moment.

Fingers trembling, he drew out the object.

He couldn't see it in the complete darkness, but he could feel its familiar shape.

A ring. But not just any ring.

The bloodstone.

Magnus slid the ring onto the middle finger of his left hand, gasping as an immediate chill spread through his entire body.

"Father, what have you done?" he whispered.

Another drop of mud oozed onto his face, stunning him further.

Magnus pressed his hands against the wooden slats above him that were damp from the rain that had soaked into the earth. His heart lurched at the thought. Damp wood could give easier than dry wood, if he tried hard enough.

"No one is coming for you," he imagined Kurtis's reedy voice mocking him. *"There's no magic that'll keep you alive forever."*

"That's what you think," Magnus muttered.

Along with the chill he'd felt from the bloodstone's magic against his fingertips, strength also filled him again.

He made a tight fist and punched upward, succeeding only in slicing his hand with more splinters from the wet wood. He grimaced, made another fist, and then punched again.

This would take time.

He imagined that the barrier above him was Kurtis Cirillo's face.

"Beetles," Magnus gritted out as he punched at the wood again. "I think I'll kill you with hungry, flesh-eating beetles."

CHAPTER 5

AMARA

PAELSIA

Amara clutched the message that had arrived from Kraeshia in her fist as she limped into the royal compound's prison for the second time in as many days.

Carlos had remained a strong yet silent presence, and she appreciated her guard more than she'd say aloud. Of all the men that currently surrounded her, she trusted him the most. And trust, given recent events, was in extremely limited supply.

She hated this prison. Hated the dank, musty odor it had, as if the scent from decades of prisoners had permanently soaked into the stone walls.

"Well, well, if it isn't the high and mighty destroyer of kingdoms herself blessing us lowly, pathetic creatures with her presence."

Felix Gaebras's painfully familiar voice made Amara's shoulders stiffen. She glanced to her left to see that he had been put into a cell with a small barred window in the iron door that showed part of his face, including the black eye patch covering his left eye.

She remembered very clearly when he'd had two eyes that had once gazed at her with desire.

"I would reply, but I won't waste my breath," she said.

Felix snorted. "And yet that sounded like a reply. And to one as lowly and pathetic as me. Fortune must smile upon me today."

His sarcastic tone had once, not so very long ago, been one of his most endearing traits. Now it was only a reminder of her past decisions and the former assassin's current hatred for her.

He shouldn't be sarcastic to anyone anymore. Had all gone according to plan, he would have been long dead and not yet another problem for Amara to deal with.

"Show respect to the empress," Carlos snarled, his heavy arms crossed over his chest. "It's only by her grace that you haven't yet been executed."

"*Her grace*, is it?" Felix pressed his forehead against the bars and offered her a cold grin. "Aw, perhaps she thinks we can get together again. But sorry, I don't share my bed with snakes."

"Let's move on," Amara said tightly.

Felix smirked. "Have you heard from your good friend Kyan on when he plans to finish reducing this world to ash with your help? A smoke signal? Anything?"

"Say the word, empress," Carlos said, "and I will end this murderer's life myself."

Felix's gaze flicked to the guard. "For what it's worth, she's the one who poisoned her father and brothers without a single blink of regret from those long eyelashes of hers. But I'm sure you won't believe me. Tell me, princess, is Carlos the one warming your bed these days? Will you send him to the torture chamber as a diversion for your next crime?"

His words were the only weapons he had left, but he was a talented assassin. Each one left a wound.

"Perhaps your swift execution is best," Amara said slowly. "I don't know why I'm prolonging the inevitable."

"Oh, I don't know. Guilt?"

She ignored him and, leaning on her cane, began to limp down the hallway to her destination, wishing to leave Felix Gaebras and his accusations far behind her.

"Do you know what I'm going to do to you when I get out of here?" Felix called after her. "I'd tell you, but I don't want to give you nightmares."

Felix had become like a shard of glass, one that hurt more the deeper it sank into her skin.

Carlos spoke next, breaking the silence. "He has been giving the guards great difficulties. He is violent and unpredictable."

"I agree."

"They want to know how you wish to deal with him."

Amara decided to reserve her nightmares for someone much worthier. "I'll leave that decision up to you, Carlos."

"Yes, your grace."

It was time to remove this shard of glass and cast it away forever.

Amara's mood had descended further into darkness by the time they reached her destination. The compound's prison was occupied mostly by rebels. Unlike many Paelsians who embraced Amara's rule after suffering at the hands of King Gaius, these rebels didn't want to be ruled by anyone at all.

Ungrateful fools.

She was ready to be done with the lot of them. And with the sorceress's arrival and Gaius's release from this very prison, the sooner the better.

Carlos stopped at the end of the hallway and nodded at the nearest guard to unlock the iron door.

"Empress . . ." he began.

"I will speak to my brother alone."

His expression held uncertainty. "I'm not sure that's wise, your grace. Even unarmed, your brother is dangerous—every bit as dangerous as the assassin."

"So am I."

She opened the front of her cloak to reveal the blade she wore in a holder attached to a leather belt. Her grandmother had given it to her the day she'd wed Gaius Damora. The traditional Kraeshian bridal dagger was meant to be passed down to one's daughter on her wedding day, a symbol of female strength in a world ruled by men.

Carlos hesitated. "As you command, your grace."

The guard unlocked the door—this one didn't have a window like Felix's—and she slipped inside. The door closed and locked behind her.

Amara's gaze found her brother's instantly. Ashur didn't rise from where he sat in a chair opposite the door. This was a larger cell than Felix's, at least three times as large, and furnished nearly as beautifully as a room in the royal residence. It had been used, quite obviously, for important prisoners of high status.

"Sister," Ashur said simply.

She took a moment to fully find her voice. "I'm sure you're surprised to see me."

He didn't reply for a moment. "How is your leg?"

Amara grimaced at the reminder of her injury, not that she needed it. "Broken."

"It will heal in time."

"You sound so calm. I would have expected . . ."

"What? Anger? Outrage? Shock that you'd have me imprisoned for a heinous crime of which I had no part?" His voice rose.

"What is this? A last visit from the empress before I'm privately executed?"

She shook her head. "Far from it. I mean to release you."

His gaze held naked disbelief. "Really."

"There have been several developments since Kyan stole your friend's body."

Sudden pain flashed through his blue-gray gaze. "Two days, Amara. I have waited in here for two long days wanting information, but no one's told me a damn thing." He inhaled sharply. "Is Nicolo all right?"

"I have no idea."

Ashur pushed himself up to his feet, and Amara instinctively clutched her dagger tighter. He glanced at it, frowning. "You wish to release me, but clearly you also fear me."

"I don't fear you. But your release requires an agreement from you. A very specific agreement."

"You don't understand—there's no time for negotiations," he said. "I need to be released so I can find the answers I need. There is magic out there, sister, that could possibly help Nicolo. But I can't find it if I'm stuck in here."

Familiar frustration welled within Amara. Her brother—rich and handsome and influential—had developed a crush on a meaningless, red-haired former squire to the king of Auranos.

Amara had been one of the few that knew of and wholly accepted Ashur's romantic preferences over the years, but Nicolo Cassian wasn't worthy of the affections of her brother.

"You think you can save him, do you?" she asked.

Ashur clenched his fists at his sides. "Not from behind a locked door I can't."

"Give it another week, you'll forget all about him." She ignored the darkness that slid behind Ashur's gaze at her claim. "I know you, brother. Something or someone new will draw your interest. In fact, I have something right here that might help."

Amara held out the parchment toward her brother.

He snatched it away from her, his glare intense on her before he read the message.

"A message from Grandmother," he said. "The revolution has been crushed in its infancy, and she says that all is well."

Amara nodded. "You can see that she asks me to return immediately to the Jewel for my Ascension."

"Yes, you've been empress in name only up until now, haven't you? Must have the Ascension ceremony to make everything binding for all eternity." He scrunched the message up and let it fall to the floor. "Why tell me this, Amara? Do you wish for me to congratulate you?"

"No." She took her hand off her dagger and began limping in short, nervous lines, the pain in her bound leg a welcome distraction. "I came here to tell you that I . . . I regret very few decisions I've made these last months, but I deeply regret how I've treated you. I've been horrible to you."

Ashur gaped at her. "Horrible? You stabbed me in the heart."

"You betrayed me!" This came out close to a scream before she managed to clamp down on her unhelpful emotions. "You chose an alliance with Nicolo . . . with Cleo and Magnus . . . over one with your own sister!"

"You leapt to conclusions like you always have," Ashur growled. "You didn't give me a chance to explain. Had I not taken the resurrection potion, the death you gave me would have been permanent." He stopped talking, taking a breath to compose himself. "The moment you learned I lived, you blamed our family's murder on me and had me thrown into a pit to become a meal for a monster. Please, sister, tell me how I can forgive and forget?"

"The future is more important than the past. I am empress of Kraeshia—and that will be a fact forever chiseled into history after my Ascension. I make the rules now."

"So what rules would you like me to follow, your grace?"

Amara flinched at his razor-sharp tone. "I wish to make amends between us. I want to show you that I regret what I've done when it comes to you. I was wrong." The words tasted foul, but that made them no less true. "I need you, Ashur. This has been proven to me time and again these last months. I need you by my side. I want you to come back with me to Kraeshia, where I will officially pardon you for the crimes you've been accused of."

Amara raised her chin and forced herself to meet his gaze. He stared back at her with unbridled shock.

"You're the one who accused me of these crimes," he said.

"I will tell everyone that was a plan set forth by Gaius. I've been forced to set him free, so what do I care if there's a target on his back?"

"Why were you forced to set him free?"

"Lucia Damora arrived," she said. "I thought it best not to cross a sorceress."

Amara hated how frightened she was of Lucia, but her magic was as incredible as rumored. In Auranos, Amara had seen only a glimpse of Lucia's power, but it had strengthened and grown since then.

She knew she could not defeat her.

And the child . . .

Lucia had not given more information about the baby she'd arrived with, but there were rumors spreading like wildfire.

Carlos himself had overheard the young man that Lucia had arrived with speaking with a friend about the baby, saying that she was Lucia's own child by blood. Her child and an immortal's.

If true, this would be incredibly useful information.

Between Lucia, Gaius, and the thought that Kyan was out there somewhere, waiting to return to burn everything down around her, Amara had had enough of this tiny kingdom that had only brought her misery.

"All I care about is getting away from here, away from Mytica," she told Ashur. "I will not put myself, or you, in harm's way a moment longer. I'm going home for the Ascension, as our grandmother requests. Perhaps you won't even believe this, given all I've done, but you are the only member of our family that I've ever valued."

Ashur's expression turned wistful. "Neither of us ever fit in, did we, sister?"

"Not in the ways that Father would have liked." She regarded him, her defenses down, as she remembered how good it was to have someone to believe in wholly, someone to trust without question. "Leave the troubles of the past behind. Come with me, Ashur. I will share my power with you and only you."

He held her gaze for a long moment. "No."

Surely she'd heard him wrong. "What?"

He laughed coldly. "You wonder why I sided with Nicolo after knowing him for a handful of weeks? Because he possesses the purest heart I've ever known. Your heart, sister, is as black as death itself. Grandmother has worked her own particular kind of magic in manipulating you to her will, hasn't she? And you don't even realize it yet."

Amara's cheeks flamed. "You don't know what you're talking about."

"Let me be as blunt as I can with you so there's no room for misunderstanding," Ashur said. "I will never in a million years trust you again, Amara. The choices you've made are unforgivable.

I would rather live a life as a peasant than take any power you wish to share with me, knowing that any minute you would gladly plunge a dagger into my back if it served you better."

Amara fought against the tears that stung her eyes. "Are you so much of a fool that you'd give up the opportunity I've given you today?"

"I want no part of your life anymore. You've chosen your path, sister. And it's one that will lead to your destruction."

"Then you've made your final choice." The words came out as a strangled cry. "Carlos! Let me out of here!"

A moment later, the door swung open.

The words like daggers in her throat, she cast one last look at Ashur. "Farewell, brother."

Outside the prison, the sky was dark with rainclouds. Amara leaned against the stone wall, trying to collect herself.

She wondered how much Cleo's water magic had to do with the unpredictable weather over the last two days. The princess was in mourning for her lost husband.

Magnus Damora was dead.

Someone else you betrayed for your own gain, she thought.

She squeezed her eyes shut, wishing to block out the world.

Amara knew she should celebrate Magnus's death—should thank Lord Kurtis for removing one more enemy from her list if he ever showed his face again.

After a moment, she opened her eyes. Amara's stomach lurched. Nerissa Florens was walking across the grounds toward her.

The former attendant to the empress and secret full-time rebel spy—*secret*, at least, until very recently—came to a stop before the empress.

Yet another person Amara would prefer to avoid.

"You're back from the search?" Amara asked tightly.

Nerissa nodded. "The others will be back at dusk, but I wanted to check on Princess Cleo."

"So kind of you."

"You've been crying."

Amara fought the urge to wipe her eyes. "The compound is dusty, that's all."

"You went to visit your brother, didn't you?"

Amara gave her a cutting smile. "Yes, I did, actually. In the very prison you would be in for treason had Cleo not intervened on your behalf. Don't give me a reason to change my mind."

Nerissa didn't react at all to the harshness in Amara's tone. "I know I hurt you."

"Hurt me?" Amara laughed lightly at this. "That's rather un-likely."

Nerissa absently tucked a piece of her short black hair behind her ear. "I need you to know, your grace, that I sided against you only because you gave me no other choice. My loyalty is and always has been to Princess Cleo."

Amara gripped her cane tighter. "Yes, that's become crystal clear, Nerissa."

The betrayal had cut deeper than Amara would ever admit. Nerissa had swiftly become more than an attendant to her, more even than a friend.

Nerissa blinked. "I saw it, you know."

"Saw what?"

"Your true self. A part of you that isn't hard and cruel and hungry only for power."

The pain in Amara's leg shifted momentarily to her heart. But only for a moment.

She forced a pinched smile to her lips once again. "You were only seeing things. Your mistake entirely."

"Perhaps," Nerissa said softly.

Amara eyed the girl with disdain. "I had heard tales about you, most that I had dismissed as only rumors. It seems that your ability to seduce your way into influential beds is second to none. The perfect little rebel spy, aren't you?"

"I seduce only those who are willing to be seduced." Nerissa held her gaze for another small eternity before she bowed her head. "If you'll excuse me, your grace. I must see to the princess."

Amara watched the girl walk away toward the royal residence, her heart a tight knot in her chest.

Her mind was set. It was time to leave Mytica.

Time to plan her next move.

CHAPTER 6

JONAS

PAELSIA

Jonas had stayed at the royal compound far longer than he'd ever intended.

He stayed for Cleo, for Taran, for Enzo and Nerissa. And for Felix, who'd managed to get himself locked up again.

And, it would seem, he stayed to help in the search for his former enemy.

Lucia believed that Prince Magnus was dead, but the search still continued. When she'd asked Jonas to help, he found that he couldn't say no.

After a long, exhausting, and fruitless day of searching the barren Paelsian landscape beyond the gates of Basilius's former compound, Jonas fell into the deepest sleep he could remember. One that blissfully lacked any nightmares.

But then it happened. As if grasped from one world and yanked into another, he found himself standing in the middle of a grassy field facing a man in long shimmering white robes. A man he recognized all too well.

Timotheus wasn't old—or, at least, he didn't *appear* to be old. His face was no more lined than Jonas's brother Tomas's would have been at twenty-two, had he lived.

His eyes, though, betrayed his true age. They were ancient.

"Welcome, Jonas," Timotheus said.

Jonas glanced around, seeing nothing but the grassy field stretched out in all directions. "I figured you were done with me."

"Not yet."

Jonas turned to meet Timotheus's gaze fully, refusing to be intimidated by this immortal. "I defied your prophecy. Lucia is still alive."

"Yes, she is. And she had a child—a daughter named Lyssa, whose eyes glow with violet light on occasion." Timotheus nodded at Jonas's shocked look. "I have ways of knowing many things, so let's not waste time retreading what has already occurred. The child is of great interest to me, but she's not why I need to speak with you now."

Fresh resentment coursed through Jonas. These otherworldly immortals spent centuries watching mortals through the eyes of hawks but provided little in the way of actual help. He preferred it when Watchers were only myth and legend he could ignore at will, not an annoying reality.

Jonas paced nervously back and forth. This didn't feel like a dream. In a dream, everything seemed hazy, and hard to grasp on to.

Here, he could feel the mossy ground beneath his feet, the warm sunlight on his face. He could smell the flowers that surrounded them as fragrant as those in his sister Felicia's small garden.

Roses, he thought. But sweeter somehow. More like the sugar crisps he'd enjoyed as a rare treat as a young boy, made by a kind woman in his village.

He shook his head to clear it of the distracting sensations all around him.

"Then you know the Kindred are free," he said. "Two of them, anyway. And Cleo and Taran . . . they're in trouble. Great trouble." He paused to rub his forehead hard. "Why did you let that happen?"

Timotheus turned his face away from Jonas's accusatory glare. There was nothing in the distance for him to focus on; the lush green field seemed to go on and on forever in all directions. "Does Lucia have possession of all four crystal orbs?"

"Why should I tell you anything when you seem to know it all?"

"*Tell me*," Timotheus said as harshly as he'd ever said anything before.

Something lurched in Jonas's chest, something strange and unpleasant that reminded him of Lucia's ability to draw the truth out of him whether he wished to speak it or not.

"She has three," he bit out. "Amber, moonstone, and obsidian. The obsidian orb had a crack in it, I'm told. But it doesn't anymore."

"It healed itself," Timotheus said.

"I don't know. I would guess it did."

Timotheus's brows drew together. "What about the aquamarine orb?"

Again, Jonas felt a strange compulsion to reply with the truth. "Cleo has that one."

"She can touch it without great difficulty?"

"No, she . . . carries it with her in a pouch," Jonas replied.

Timotheus nodded, his expression contemplative. "Very well."

The strange, magical grip on Jonas's throat eased. "Do you have any idea how irritating it is to be lied to and manipulated?"

"Yes. Actually, I do." Timotheus, his arms crossed over his chest, began to walk a slow circle around Jonas, peering at the rebel with narrowed eyes.

"If you know everything," Jonas said, "you'll know Lucia's in mourning for her brother. If you want her to help you stop Kyan, you could tell us where Magnus is—and whether there's any chance he's still alive."

"You care about someone you wanted dead not so long ago?"

That was a trickier question than he'd like it to be. "I care that Lucia is in pain. And Magnus . . . for all his faults . . . he could be useful in the coming war."

"The war against the Kindred."

He nodded. "Against the Kindred. Against the empress. Against anything that comes our way in the future."

"I'm not here for that."

Jonas hissed out a breath of frustration. "Then what are you here for?"

Timotheus didn't speak for a moment. Jonas realized that despite the immortal's eternal youth, he looked tired and drawn, as if he hadn't slept in weeks.

Do immortals even need sleep? he wondered.

"This is almost over," Timotheus finally said, and Jonas could have sworn he heard pain edging his words.

"What is almost over?"

"My watch." Timotheus sighed, and with his hands clasped behind his back, he began moving again through the long grass. He looked up at the sunless but bright blue sky. "I was created to watch over the Kindred, watch over mortals, watch over those of my own kind . . . I have failed in all regards. I inherited Eva's visions, and they've been no use to me other than to see a thousand versions of what might be. And now it has come to this."

"To what?" Jonas prompted.

"A small handful of allies that I've enlisted to foolishly fight against fate itself. I saw you in my visions, Jonas, years ago. I saw that you would be useful to me. And I've come to realize that that you are one of the few mortals I can trust."

"Why me?" Jonas asked, stunned. "I . . . I'm nobody. I'm the son of a Paelsian wine seller. I stupidly joined a war against a good king and helped put Mytica into the hands of the King of Blood. I've led friends to their deaths because of my idiotic choices to rebel against that king. I've lost everything I've ever cared about. And now I have this strange magic inside me . . ." He rubbed his chest where the spiral mark had appeared only a month ago. "And it's useless to me. I can't properly channel it at will to help anyone or anything—not even myself!"

"You think too much, Jonas Agallon."

Jonas let out a nervous snort of laughter. "No one's ever accused me of that before."

A small smile touched Timotheus's lips. "You are brave. You are strong. And you are worthy of this."

From the folds of his robe, Timotheus drew out an object. It was a golden dagger, beautiful, unlike anything Jonas had ever seen in his life. The blade was covered in etchings. Symbols—some of which appeared to be the symbols for elemental magic.

Something shimmered from the blade. Jonas couldn't see it exactly, but he could sense it.

Magic. But not just any magic—*ancient magic.*

Timotheus placed the heavy golden hilt in his hand. Jonas inhaled sharply as a cool shiver of that ancient magic traveled up his arm.

"What is this?" he managed to ask.

"A dagger," Timotheus said simply.

"I can see that much. But what kind of dagger? What does it do?"

"It can kill."

Jonas glared at the immortal. "Just speak plainly to me for once, would you?"

Timotheus's smile grew, but his eyes remained deadly serious. "This dagger has been wielded by several immortals over millennia. It contains magic that can enslave and control minds and wills. It can kill an immortal. It can absorb magic. And it can destroy magic."

"Destroy magic?" Jonas frowned, his gaze locked upon the golden blade. The sunlight caught the metal and cast a prism of colors down to the grassy ground. "Lucia said the Kindred couldn't be destroyed. Even if I had the chance to get close enough to shove this into Kyan's chest, all I'd be doing is murdering Nic."

Timotheus's expression grew strained. "I can't tell you exactly what you need to do."

Frustration burned in Jonas's chest. "Why not?"

"That's not how it works. My direct involvement—beyond what I've already done—is not allowed. I am a Watcher. I watch. It's all I'm permitted to do. To say any more is literally impossible for me. But hear me, Jonas Agallon. Lucia is and always will be the key to all of this. Kyan still needs her."

Jonas shook his head. "Lucia won't help him. She's different now. She'll do anything to stop him."

Timotheus's jaw tensed, his gaze fixed upon the dagger. "This weapon can stop her as well, even at her most powerful."

Jonas blinked, understanding all too well what the immortal meant.

"I won't kill Lucia," he growled.

"I've seen her die, Jonas. I've seen a precise moment in the future with this very blade in her chest and you standing over her." His expression shuttered. "I've said too much already. This is over. The remainder of my magic is nearly gone, and I have no more to spare on entering the dreams of mortals. You must go forth alone now."

"Wait, no." Panic rose in Jonas's chest. "You need to tell me more. You can't stop now!"

Timotheus glanced to the right of the colorful meadow, seemingly at nothing at all. "You're needed elsewhere."

Jonas frowned. "What? What are you—?"

The expansive field of green shattered, falling away like shards of glass. Jonas realized someone was shaking him awake. He opened his eyes to see Taran Ranus staring down at him.

"Jonas, wake up," he urged.

"What is it?"

"Felix is going to be executed."

The fogginess of sleep left him in a rush. "When?"

"Now."

Jonas sat up so quickly that a wave of dizziness hit him. He noticed something cold and heavy in his hand, and he looked down with shock to see that he held the very same golden dagger that Timotheus had given him in the dream.

But . . . how?

He let go of it as if it had been covered in spiders. The weapon lay there on the blanket, shimmering in the meager light of the room.

"Hurry," Taran barked as he pulled on a shirt.

For a moment, Jonas's mind went completely blank, as if he couldn't make a decision or move or rationalize what had happened.

But then he realized what Taran had said. His friend was in danger.

Nothing else mattered right now.

Jonas grabbed the strange new dagger, thrust it into the empty holder on his belt, and joined Taran as they left the small room the empress had provided for them during their stay at the compound.

"Thought you hated Felix," Jonas said as they rushed toward the prison.

"Only in the beginning. He's a friend now, just like you."

"How did you hear of this?"

Taran frowned deeply. "I heard voices . . . in the air. Guards discussing doing away with a difficult prisoner. They were loud enough to wake me."

Jonas had no reply to this. He knew the air Kindred was inside Taran now, just as the water Kindred was within Cleo, but Taran had barely spoken of it since Jonas's arrival.

They arrived at a small dusty clearing just outside the compound's prison area just as guards dragged Felix out in chains. A small crowd of guards and servants had gathered to watch as Felix was forced to his knees, his head shoved down onto a chopping block.

Jonas pushed through the crowd just as the executioner raised his ax.

Felix's gaze met his.

The defeat in Felix's single eye said it all.

Amara had won.

They were too late. There was no time to yell or fight or try to stop this. Jonas could only watch in horror as the ax sliced downward—

—and stopped only a whisper above Felix's flesh. The guard's muscles bulged as he tried to push down against an invisible barrier.

Jonas shot a look at Taran to see that perspiration coated his forehead. His eyes glowed with white light. Spidery white lines appeared on his hands, wrapping around his wrists.

"You're doing this," Jonas managed.

"I—I don't know how," Taran replied tightly.

The ax went flying, hitting the side of a building so hard that the blade buried itself fully into the stone surface. Then, the guard flew backward as if shoved by an invisible hand.

"Air magic," a nearby woman gasped. All those around her began to speak, to shout, and every gaze in the clearing turned to stare at Taran.

Taran looked wide-eyed at the glowing spiral mark on his right hand. It was surrounded by white lines, spreading and curling around his skin.

"Don't just gawk at me," Taran said through clenched teeth. "Go get him."

Jonas did as Taran said and ran up to the execution platform, cutting through Felix's ropes quickly with his new blade. He offered Felix his hand to stand, and Felix grasped it without hesitation.

"Twice now," Felix said to Jonas, his voice thick. "You've saved my arse twice."

"You can thank Taran for this one." Jonas embraced his friend, slapping him on the back.

The guards who might have intervened at this point all took a step backward as Taran approached. Jonas noted that Taran's face was pale, his deep tan completely gone. Dark circles, like bruises, had appeared beneath his eyes.

"Don't look at me like that," Taran said, wincing. "I hate this."

"I don't," Felix replied quickly. "It's good to have a god on my side of things."

"I'm no god."

Still, when Taran glanced toward the dozens of onlookers, they all took a step backward—servants and guards alike.

"I can't stay here," Taran muttered.

"You're right," Jonas said. This was no place for any of them.

He had to speak to Cleo, to Lucia. He had to convince them to move on, away from the watch of the empress.

Amara wouldn't stop them. She feared them.

He spotted the captain of the guard, Carlos, approaching them fearlessly, his sword drawn.

"We have no fight with you today," Jonas said, spreading his hands. "But you will not execute my friend. Not now, not ever."

"The empress commanded it," Carlos said.

Felix muttered something very dark under his breath about the commanding empress. Then louder: "If the empress wishes me dead, have her come out here and do it herself."

Jonas glared at him. "Kindly shut up."

Felix glared back at Jonas. "I hate her."

"I know." Jonas regarded Carlos again. "You can see that we have power, we have strength. And we will not stand by and let you imprison our friends any longer. We're leaving this place, and Prince Ashur is coming with us."

Jonas had certainly gathered a strange group of friends over the last few months. Tarus had told him that Prince Ashur hadn't betrayed them after all when he'd left their group in Basilia without a word. He'd gone to his sister's side to convince her to halt her evil ways. Clearly, Amara had ignored him.

Prince Ashur Cortas was every bit a rebel as Jonas was himself.

"I'm certain the empress will have no issues with your departure," Carlos said, his eyes narrow and cruel. "But Prince Ashur will not be joining you."

"Perhaps you didn't hear him," Felix said, his fists tight. "Go get him now, or my friend Taran is going to reduce this compound to a pile of rocks. Right, Taran?"

Jonas glanced at Taran, who also appeared ready to fight.

His eyes still glowed.

"Right," Taran said.

Jonas wondered for just a moment if Taran could actually control this godlike power within him that he'd just used to save Felix or if he was bluffing.

"I will tell you again," Jonas said, his attention fixed on the large armed guard. "Free Prince Ashur Cortas immediately."

Carlos's shook his head. "An impossible request."

"Why?"

"Because the prince," Carlos began, his expression grim, "escaped from his cell late last night."

CHAPTER 7

MAGNUS

PAELSIA

For what felt like an eternity, Magnus scratched at the wood in the inky darkness of his minuscule prison. Blood dripped onto his face from his torn-up fingertips, but he continued until the pain became unbearable. He fought against unconsciousness until it claimed him.

When he woke, his fingers had healed.

Without the bloodstone, he would have been dead and broken and worthless.

With it, he still had a chance.

To save his father's life, Magnus's grandmother had literally cut this ring from the finger of an exiled Watcher. He didn't know the bloodstone's origins. Frankly, he didn't care.

All that mattered was that it existed. And somehow, at some time when he hadn't noticed, his father had slipped this invaluable ring into Magnus's pocket.

But why would the man who'd tormented him his entire life, who'd literally tried to kill Magnus not so very long ago, do such a thing? Why would he give up such an incredible piece of magic?

"What game are you playing with me now, Father?" he muttered.

Tormented by a thousand answers to that question, Magnus clawed at the lid of his coffin, aided by the rain-soaked earth that made the wood more pliable. Weaker.

Weak things are so very easy to break.

It was a harsh lesson from his father. One of many over Magnus's life.

He tried to focus only on his seemingly insurmountable task. And on Lord Kurtis.

Magnus had no idea how many days had passed and whether he still had time to stop Kurtis from his horrific plans. The thought made him shake with anger, frustration, and fear.

Cleo had to be smarter than to trust the former kingsliege. She wouldn't allow herself to be alone with him.

It didn't matter, another voice in his head observed. Kurtis could knock her out and drag her away somewhere no one would ever find her again.

A cry of rage tore from his throat as he yanked a larger shard of wood from its place and mud poured through the hole in the lid, covering his face. He roared and pushed it away. But more came, like a cold, wet, demonic blanket meant to smother him. It filled his mouth, his throat. He choked on it, holding on to one single thought that gave him strength.

Nothing can kill me with this ring on my finger.

He shoved, pushed, and dug at the mud and dirt shoveled on top of his unmarked grave.

Slow, it was so painfully slow.

But he did not give up. Darkness had become his entire world.

Now, he kept his eyes squeezed shut to protect them from the mud.

Inch by inch, he pressed upward. One handful at a time.

Slowly.

Slowly.

Until, finally, after a thrust of his fist, the sensation of cool air took him by surprise. He froze for a moment before stretching out his fingers to feel for any further barriers. But there were none.

Despite the strength that had flowed through him after putting on the ring, he wanted to rest, just for a few moments. He needed time to heal.

But then Cleo's face appeared in his mind's eye.

"Giving up so easily?" she asked, raising an eyebrow. *"How disappointing."*

"Trying my best," he growled in reply, but only in his imagination.

"Try harder."

It sounded just like her—more cruel than kind in a moment of great importance. And it helped.

Kindness had never, in Magnus's experience, brought anyone back from their own death.

Only magic could do that.

Muscles screaming with effort, he pushed further, finally freeing his other arm from the hungry earth. He grabbed hold of the muddy ground and pulled himself upward.

It was as if the earth itself birthed him back into the real world.

He lay there, his arm collapsed over his chest, and forced himself to take deep, choking breaths as his heart slammed against his rib cage.

The stars were out, bright in the black sky.

Stars. He could see stars after an eternity of utter darkness. They were the most beautiful things he'd ever seen in his entire life.

When he laughed out loud at the thought, it sounded slightly hysterical.

Magnus slid his dirt-encrusted fingers over the thick gold ring on his left hand.

"I don't understand this," he whispered. "But thank you, Father."

He wiped at his mud-covered face before he slowly, gingerly pushed himself up to his feet on limbs that had very recently been shattered.

He felt strong.

Stronger than he should have, he knew.

Magically strong.

And ready to find and kill Kurtis Cirillo.

Or . . . perhaps he was still buried, moments from death, and this was only a vivid dream before the darklands finally claimed him.

For once in his life, Magnus Damora decided to be positive.

Where was he? He looked around, seeing only a small clearing with nothing to mark his location or indicate how to get back to Amara's compound. He'd been unconscious when Kurtis and his minions had brought him here.

He could be anywhere.

Without another glance at his former grave, Magnus chose a direction at random and began to walk.

He needed food. Drink.

Vengeance.

But first and most importantly, he needed to know that Cleo was safe.

He stumbled on a tangle of roots from a desiccated tree as he entered a wooded area.

"Bloody Paelsia," he muttered with annoyance. "Utterly hateful during the day, even worse in the dead of night."

The moonlight shone down, lighting his path, now flanked by tall, leafless trees, a short distance from where he'd been buried.

He twisted the ring on his finger, needing to feel its presence again, countless questions arising in his mind about where it came from and how its magic worked. What else could it do?

Something caught his eye then—a campfire. He wasn't alone. He instinctively felt for his weapon, but of course he didn't have one. Even before Kurtis had chained him up, Magnus had been Amara's prisoner.

Barely breathing, he quietly drew closer to see who it was, envious of the warmth of the fire after being cold and damp for so long.

"Greetings, Prince Magnus. Come closer. I've been waiting for you."

He froze.

The voice sounded familiar, but it wasn't Kurtis, like he'd half expected it to be.

Magnus clenched his fists. If this was a threat, he was ready to kill whoever had issued it with his bare hands without a moment's hesitation.

At the sight of bright red hair lit by the firelight, relief surged through him, and he relaxed his fists.

"Nic!" Shame slammed into him as his eyes began to sting with tears. "You're here! You're all right!"

Nic smiled and stood up. "I am."

"I thought Kurtis had killed you."

"It seems we both survived, didn't we?"

Magnus let out a hoarse laugh. "Don't take this too personally, but I'm very happy to see you."

"The feeling is mutual." Nic's gaze swept over him. "You're covered in dirt."

Magnus looked down at himself, grimacing. "I just dug myself out of my own damn grave."

Nic nodded thoughtfully. "Olivia sensed you were underground."

Olivia. The girl who traveled with Jonas. Magnus didn't know her well at all, but knew she was rumored to be a witch. "Where's Cleo?"

"At the compound, last I checked. Here, you look thirsty." Nic offered him a flask. "I know you're partial to Paelsian wine."

Magnus grasped the container and tipped it back. The wine was like life itself on his tongue, the purest pleasure in existence as it slid down his throat. "Thank you. Thank you for this. For . . . for being here. Now, we have to get back to the compound." He sent a look toward the forest surrounding them, but it was all in darkness beyond the firelight. "Kurtis means to hurt Cleo, and I'm going to kill him before he does."

Nic took a seat across the campfire from Magnus, cocking his head. "That's right. You don't know what happened, do you?"

How could he act so nonchalant about a threat to his childhood friend?

Something felt off about Nic. Incredibly off. "What do you mean?" Magnus asked, now more cautious.

"The night you disappeared, your grandmother performed a ritual."

"My grandmother?" Magnus blinked. The last time he'd seen her was just before his father had angrily sent her away. "Where is she now?"

"Your father killed her." Nic's expression darkened. "Broke her neck before she was done, and now everything is going wrong."

Magnus gaped at him. "What? What are you talking about? He killed her?"

Nic grabbed a stick and jabbed at the fire with much more force than necessary. "Only the sorceress could have performed the ritual properly. I see that now. I was too impatient."

The wine had quickly worked to ease some of Magnus's stress, but it blurred his thoughts. Nothing Nic said made sense to him. "What nonsense are you speaking? Be clear. I need to know what happened, Nic!"

Nic threw the stick to the side. "You keep calling me that, yet it's not my name."

Magnus hissed out a breath of frustration. "Oh? And what would you prefer? Nicolo? Lord Nicolo, perhaps? You just told me my grandmother is dead at the hand of my father."

"That shouldn't surprise you. Your father is a reckless murderer, just like you have the tendency to be." Nic regarded him for a moment. "It's time to get to the point, I think."

There was something in his otherwise familiar brown eyes that Magnus didn't recognize.

It was the look of a predator.

"Cleo is in danger," Magnus said, more carefully now. "We need to get back to Amara's compound."

"You're right. She is in danger. And I need you to give her a message for me."

Magnus's heart thudded as he studied Nic, trying to figure out why he was so strange tonight. "You're not coming with me?"

"Not quite yet."

"What the hell is going on?"

"Only this." Nic held his hand out, and a flame appeared in his palm. "Have you guessed yet? Or do you still want to call me Nic?"

Magnus stared at the flame as if hypnotized. Then his gaze shot to Nic's eyes. They weren't brown like before. They were blue. And glowing.

It couldn't be.

"Kyan," he managed.

He nodded. "Much better. Knowledge is power, they say. But I think fire is the only power that matters." He stepped closer to Magnus. "Your little golden princess is the chosen vessel for the water Kindred, but the ritual went awry, thanks to your grandmother's weak magic and your father's stupid choice to end her life. You will tell Cleiona that she needs to come with me and Olivia when we arrive. Without a fight. Without an argument."

Magnus grappled to make sense of all this. That Nic was Kyan. That Cleo was in danger—and not only because of Kurtis.

"Go near her and die," Magnus growled.

"Resistant, aren't you?" The fire god blinked, a smile curling the corner of his stolen mouth. "I will brand you with my fire to help ease this along. Then you won't be able to resist any command I give you."

His entire fist lit with blue flames, the same blue as his eyes. Magnus had seen this blue fire before, at the road camp during the battle with the rebels. Bodies touched by this fire shattered like glass.

Magnus stumbled backward as Kyan reached for him, and he frantically eyed the darkness for a way of escape.

"Why did you choose Nic?" Magnus asked, hoping to distract Kyan somehow. "Wasn't there anyone better?"

Kyan laughed. "Nicolo has a soul of fire."

"Because of his hair? More the color of carrots thrown into a horse's trough than fire, if you ask me."

"Outward appearances mean nothing. All mortals are partial to one element. Nicolo's is fire." Kyan raised a red brow. "Just like you."

"Never knew we had anything in common." Magnus moved

backward as Kyan reached for him. "Touch me and you'll lose that hand."

"Quite an empty threat from someone without a weapon." When Kyan reached out again, Magnus grabbed his wrist, wrenching it backward and away from him.

Kyan's fiery hand extinguished in an instant, and the fire Kindred frowned.

"How did you do that?" he asked.

"Do what?" Magnus growled.

The blue glow in Kyan's eyes brightened. "Unhand me or die," he snapped.

"Happy to." Magnus shoved Kyan as hard as he could. With fury flashing through his gaze, Kyan staggered backward and tripped over the campfire.

Magnus didn't wait. He took the opportunity to turn and run into the forest, plunging into darkness immediately. He was certain that Kyan was on his heels, waiting to grab him, to burn him . . .

He slammed into something solid, something—or *someone*— that grabbed ahold of his shoulders.

"Magnus! It's me, Ashur. I was watching you . . . you and Nic."

"Ashur." Magnus searched the Kraeshian prince's familiar face, barely visible as the clouds parted enough to allow a sliver of moonlight. "We have to get out of here. That's not Nic."

"I know."

"How did you find me?"

Ashur grimaced. "I wasn't searching for you."

Magnus had so many questions, but there was no time for answers. "I have to find Cleo."

Ashur pulled the hood of his cloak up over his head. "I'll take you back to the compound. Follow me."

CHAPTER 8

NIC

PAELSIA

Nic remembered being at the bottom of a pit.

Reunited with Cleo.

Reunited with Ashur.

Trapped and unable to escape, but at least they were together.

But a moment of hope for a future—*any* future—was quickly quashed when the incorporeal fire Kindred had taken over his body, sending Nic's consciousness spiraling downward into a bottomless abyss.

He could still see, he could still hear, but he couldn't think. Couldn't process what had happened to him or make any sense of what it meant. It was like being lost in an eternal dream.

But when Magnus grabbed Kyan's wrist, something very strange had happened.

Nic woke up.

The first thing Nic clearly saw was Magnus, covered in dirt from head to toe, staring at him like he was a monster.

The second thing he thought he saw was Prince Ashur Cortas,

barely visible in the shadows behind the Limerian prince.

"Ashur!" he wanted to call out, but he couldn't form the words. Kyan still had control.

Still, Nic sensed Kyan's confusion over the sudden jolt of cold, unfamiliar magic. So much so that the fire Kindred didn't pursue Magnus or even notice Ashur's presence.

What had happened?

Nic knew this much: Prince Ashur had a great interest in magic. He had explored the world far beyond Kraeshia and Mytica in search of any trace of magic.

On a Kraeshian ship, during the trip from Auranos to Limeros before the confrontation in the Temple of Valoria over the water Kindred, Ashur had told Nic about many treasures he'd sought, wishing to acquire, before he and his sister had set their sights upon the Kindred.

"There's an amulet said to allow one the ability to speak with cats," the prince told him one day during a brief visit, his lightly accented voice like honeyed wine.

Nic, the Cortases' prisoner at the time, hadn't been entirely swayed by the prince's palpable charm, but he could never resist a good story. "What kinds of cats? Housecats? Wildcats?"

"I would imagine both."

"Why only cats? Why not dogs, or ice wolves . . . or warlogs, even?"

Ashur frowned. "What in the world is a warlog?"

"It's like a rabbit . . . rat . . . thing. But not a rabbit or a rat. They're quite tasty with the right sauce, actually."

"A rabbit-rat thing," Ashur repeated slowly.

"Exactly."

"Why would you wish to communicate with it if you're going to eat it?"

"I didn't say I wanted to communicate with it, I was just trying to clarify . . ." He sighed. "Forget it."

"No, no. Please continue explaining this to me. The logic of Nicolo Cassian is fascinating." Ashur regarded him in the shadows of Nic's small locked cabin, where Amara believed him to be unconscious or restrained. "Would you tell this warlog that you meant to eat it? Or would you just ask it how its day has been?"

"Well . . ." Nic considered this carefully. "If I could communicate with it, I wouldn't want to eat it. So, yes, I suppose I would like to know how its day had been." Then he scowled at Ashur, his cheeks growing hot. "Are you laughing at me? I'm amusing to you, am I?"

Ashur's smile only grew. "Endlessly so."

The point was, Ashur knew magic. And it wasn't until he'd been present in the forest beyond the campfire that Nic could think as clearly as this, even if it was only to remember a trivial conversation with the prince.

Ashur had done something to help Nic. Some spell, perhaps.

Nic wasn't sure.

And neither was Kyan. The fire Kindred left the campfire and returned to the cottage where he'd been staying since the failed ritual.

Olivia waited for him there. She sat outside on the ground by the door, her hands entwined in a fresh growth of weeds that would be green and lively in the daylight. Beneath the meager moonlight they looked unpleasantly like the grip of a gigantic black spider.

The earth Kindred had spent the last two days surrounding their temporary home—a meager stone cottage—with lush greenery.

Kyan eyed it with distaste. "You'll draw attention to us with all of this fresh life. Paelsia is a wasteland."

"Not for long. I will restore it all to how it was long ago." She looked up at him, unable to mask the cold look in her gaze before he saw it. "I couldn't restore *them*."

Nic knew she meant the former owners of this cottage—an elderly couple that had resisted giving up their home. Their corpses lay close enough that the scent of burned flesh still lingered in the cool night air.

"You don't have that particular power, dear sister." This came out more harshly than Kyan had intended. "Earth magic requires a spark of life on which to grasp hold."

"Oh, much gratitude for explaining that to me, Kyan. I wouldn't know such a thing, would I?"

The cutting manner in which she said this almost made him wince. "Apologies."

"All these mortals will be gone soon enough, anyway. We'll have a fresh canvas on which to start anew." Olivia stood up and brushed her hands on the front of her dress. "Did you find Prince Magnus?"

"No," Kyan lied. "It would have been convenient to have him enslaved to me, but it doesn't matter."

"Fine." The earth Kindred's face twisted with annoyance, distorting Olivia's immortally beautiful features. "Then you need to set your sights on finding the sorceress and wooing her back to our side. We can't finish this without her."

Kyan summoned patience. "I know."

It wasn't as if Nic could hear the fire Kindred's thoughts, but he could clearly sense them. Lucia was vital to them, more so than Kyan had ever believed.

The fact that he had to go to her, this mere girl who had destroyed his former shell, to beg for her help . . .

Kyan would rather burn the world right now and be done with it all.

But he couldn't.

He desperately needed to be reunited with the others—water and air.

Cleo and Taran.

Panic coursed through Nic at the thought that Cleo was in terrible danger and he couldn't do a damn thing to stop it.

He had to try to gain control. If he could think, he wasn't gone. He wasn't dead.

Focus, he told himself.

He focused on his hand. His right hand. He concentrated on trying to move it, something that had once been an easy and totally unconscious decision.

He tried to move it, to raise it up ever so slightly, but not enough for Kyan to notice.

He failed to move his hand. But he did move his little finger—ever so slightly.

Not much, but it's a start, he thought grimly.

"He's still waiting for you," Olivia said as she went to the door of the cottage and opened it. "And asking so many questions I decided I needed the silence of outside."

Kyan followed her into the cottage, sweeping his gaze across the meager home. He nodded at the hearth, and a fire lit within it. Then he shifted his gaze to the young man cowering in the corner.

They'd found him wandering nearby with two of his friends. Kyan had burned the friends into oblivion immediately but thought this one—Lord Kurtis Cirillo—might be useful to him.

"I don't know w-why you're doing this, Nicolo," Kurtis stuttered. "But my father is a great and powerful man. He will pay you as much gold as you want for you to release me unharmed."

Kyan just stared at him, finally allowing himself to smile.

He loved mortals the most when they begged.

"My name is Kyan." He lit his hand up with flames, enjoying the look of terror that entered Kurtis's wild gaze.

Nic, however, felt an odd jerk of sympathy for Kurtis, even though he thoroughly despised the former kingsliege. A swift death would be so much kinder than what Kyan had in mind.

Kyan cocked his head. "Let's begin, shall we?"

CHAPTER 9

LUCIA

PAELSIA

Magnus would have thought her mad to stay here as Amara's guest a moment longer than necessary.

And so Lucia embraced the thought of leaving this strange, dusty compound. It was her birthplace, but it wasn't her home.

Limeros was her home. She craved her chambers at the palace and knew several trustworthy nursemaids there who could help her with Lyssa.

However, they were not headed for Limeros.

Her father wanted to go to the Auranian palace, where he could speak with Lord Gareth Cirillo. Gareth had remained grand kingsliege during the king's lengthy absence.

Through Lord Gareth the king wanted to find his son, Kurtis.

And Lucia wanted to help him.

The evening before they were set to leave for the Auranian palace, Lucia searched the compound for Jonas, finding him sharpening his sword by his temporary quarters.

"Are you coming with us?" she asked. "Or are you staying in Paelsia?"

He looked up from his work, as if surprised to see her. "Should I come with you?"

Lucia had been forced to spend time with Jonas when he'd been tasked to return her to her father and brother, but now—after all this time together—the thought of parting from the rebel felt oddly painful.

But she certainly wasn't going to admit that out loud.

"Cleo needs you," she'd said instead.

Jonas's brows raised. "She said that?"

"When Kyan returns, she will need all the help she can get. And I know Taran has chosen to stay with her until everything is resolved."

His expression grew thoughtful. "You make it sound like a minor inconvenience with a simple solution."

Hardly. Lucia needed time herself to strengthen her magic, to figure out how best to trap the fire Kindred—and now the earth Kindred as well—in their crystal prisons.

"I know it isn't," she allowed.

Jonas studied her. "For what it's worth, I'd already decided to come with you to Auranos. I feel a great need to keep a close eye on you, princess. Both you and Lyssa."

She searched his face, looking for any sign of deception, but found nothing but sincerity.

Jonas Agallon was, quite possibly, the most honest and forthright person she'd ever known in her life. She'd come to value him.

And the thought that she wouldn't have to bid him farewell eased something unnamable within her.

And so they left the royal compound—Lucia and Lyssa, her father, Cleo, Jonas, Taran, Felix, an attendant named Nerissa, and

a guard by the name of Enzo. They began their five-day journey south, with the empress's full permission, taking a ship from
Trader's Harbor to the Auranian City of Gold.

Lucia didn't speak to Cleo. The other princess had gone into
seclusion since learning of Magnus's death.

She loved him, Lucia realized without anyone confirming it for
her in as many words.

This thought made her hate the princess just a little less.

The waters along the channel from King's Harbor to the palace
city were a blue-green that reminded Lucia of the aquamarine orb
Cleo kept with her in a velvet drawstring pouch. A perfect match
for the princess's eyes.

Lucia would rather have that orb safely in her possession, along
with the other three, but she hadn't yet made any demands.

To think that Cleo had the power of a goddess within her . . .

Part of her felt jealous. The other part felt . . . sympathy.

As Lucia watched the banks of the wide river pass from the
deck of the ship, she twisted her amethyst ring, deep in thought.

The ring protected her from her magic, once erratic and nearly
impossible to control. It had protected her from Kyan when he'd
taken his monstrous form, something she dreamed about most
nights, and not only during the dream that Jonas had witnessed.

Kyan had wanted to kill her, and he would have succeeded had
it not been for the mysterious magic within the ring.

A ring that Cleo had given to her of her own free will.

It was the greatest treasure—apart from Lyssa—that belonged
to Lucia. She prayed that it might help her defeat Kyan when the
time came.

And when the time came, she prayed that her magic would also
be there without fail or doubt.

The City of Gold appeared in the distance, a glittering and

spectacular sight under the sun, surrounded by blue water and seemingly endless rolling hills of greenery. Lucia longed for a different sight, that of an obsidian-black castle in the center of stark white perfection.

Home.

Would she ever see home again? Perhaps it would remind her far too much of Magnus—her brother and her best friend.

He was yet another person she had betrayed, and now it broke her heart to know she would never have the chance to make amends for this.

Lucia, with Lyssa in her arms, disembarked from the ship, and as they walked along the lengthy wooden dock to reach a series of waiting carriages that would take them the remaining short distance to the palace, Lucia shielded her eyes from the sunlight to look up at the shining City of Gold with its glittering wall. The towering spires of the palace were in the direct center of the guarded city.

Then her view of the city was replaced by the face of Cleiona Bellos—her skin was pale and the rims of her eyes red, but she held her chin high.

"Yes?" Lucia prompted when she didn't immediately speak.

"The nursemaid who looked after my sister and me is still at the palace," Cleo said. "She was wonderful—kind and sweet, but not weak in any way. I would highly recommend her to look after your daughter."

Lucia looked down at the face of her baby for a moment. Lyssa blinked, her otherworldly purple eyes shifting in an instant to a more normal blue.

A shiver went down Lucia's spin. She didn't know why that happened or what it meant.

"Much gratitude for the suggestion," she replied.

Cleo nodded and went to join her attendant as they entered the palace.

Once inside, Lucia asked for Cleo's nursemaid and found her willing and able to attend to Lyssa. She held back any threats she was tempted to make about her daughter's well-being.

After kissing Lyssa's forehead in the cradle the nursemaid had swiftly readied, Lucia went to join her father for their audience with Lord Gareth.

The kingsliege wished to meet in the throne room, which had once held golden Auranian decorations and embroidered banners emblazoned with the image of the goddess Cleiona and the Bellos family crest, but which now held only a few small reminders of the time when King Corvin had ruled.

Her gaze lifted to the familiar walls, the stained glass windows. An expansive marble floor and columns lined the hall, leading to the dais and golden throne.

Lord Gareth waited for them in the center of the room. His beard had grown thicker and bushier and more streaked with white than the last time Lucia had seen him.

He held out his hands to the king and Lucia. "Welcome, my dear friends. I hope your trip here was pleasant."

The sound of his reedy voice, reminiscent of his hateful son's, made Lucia's blood boil.

"As pleasant as a trip aboard a Kraeshian ship could be," the king replied.

Lord Gareth laughed. "The empress hasn't kept any Limerian vessels for such an occasion?"

"It seems she's had most of them burned."

"And now we are all Kraeshians, as it were. Let's hope only for brighter days ahead, yes?" His gaze swept over Lucia. "You have grown up to be an incredibly beautiful young woman, my dear."

She did not meet the compliment with a smile or a nod or a blush of her cheeks, as would have been expected of her in the past.

"Where is your son, Lord Gareth?" she said instead.

Lord Gareth's pleasant expression dropped. "Kurtis? I haven't seen him since I left Limeros at your father's command to come here."

"But you've exchanged many messages with him," the king said. "Even after he became one of Amara's most loyal minions."

The lord's expression became more guarded. "Your majesty, the occupation has been difficult for us all, but we're trying as well as we can to adjust to the choices you've made for Mytica's future. If anything my son has done seems disloyal, I can assure you he has only tried to fit in with the new regime as best he can. News reaches me only today that many of the empress's soldiers have been called back to Kraeshia. I wonder if this means that the occupation will slowly and steadily be scaled back to next to nothing."

"That is very possible," the king allowed. "I think Amara has lost her interest in Mytica."

"Good." Lord Gareth nodded. "Which means we can all get back to business as usual."

"Did Kurtis tell you that he recently lost his hand?" the king asked casually, moving toward the stairs leading to the throne. He glanced over his shoulder. "That my son sliced it from his wrist?"

Lord Gareth blinked. "Why, yes. He did mention that. He also mentioned that it was as a result of your orders, your majesty, that he came upon such an unfortunate injury. You asked him to deliver Princess Cleiona to you, and it seems that Prince Magnus . . ."

"Disagreed," the king finished for him when he trailed off. "Rather strongly, yes, he did. My son and I have not seen many issues quite in the same way. Princess Cleiona is most definitely one of them."

Lucia watched on, suddenly fascinated. She hadn't heard any of this before now.

"Magnus chopped off Kurtis's hand . . . to save Cleo," she said aloud, bemused.

"It was an impulsive choice," Lord Gareth replied, a thread of distaste in his tone. "But it cannot be undone, so let's put it behind us, shall we?"

"Have you heard from Kurtis recently?" the king said as he sat down upon the magificent, gilded throne and leaned back, gazing down at Lord Gareth at the bottom of the stairs.

"Not in more than a week."

"So you don't know what he's done now."

Lord Gareth frowned deeply, his quizzical gaze moving to Lucia for a moment. "I do not."

"Not even a rumor?" Lucia asked.

"I have heard many rumors," Lord Gareth replied thinly. "But mostly about you, princess, not my son."

"Oh? Such as?"

"I don't think there's any need to indulge the whispers of peasants."

She hated this man, had always hated the simpering manner he used around the king, pretending to be friendly and helpful when she saw the deviousness behind every word he uttered and every move he made.

"Perhaps they are the same rumors I've heard," the king said. "That Lucia is a powerful sorceress, one who has reduced many villages across Mytica to ash. That she is a demon I summoned from the darklands seventeen years ago to help me strengthen my rule."

"Like I said"—Lord Gareth watched the king as he stood up from the throne and began to descend the stairs again—"the rumors of peasants."

"A demon, am I?" Lucia said under her breath, tasting the word and not finding it as unpleasant as she would have thought.

People feared demons.

She had quickly learned that fear was a very useful tool.

"Your majesty," Lord Gareth said, shaking his head. "I am your humble servant, as always. I sense that you are unhappy with Kurtis and, perhaps, with me as well. Please tell me how we can make amends."

The king's face was a mask, showing no hint of his emotions beneath. "*Your majesty*, you say. As if you haven't pledged your devotion to Amara and only Amara."

"Only words, your highness. Do you think she would have let me stay here without such a promise? But I have no doubt your power will be restored now that she has departed these shores."

"So you admit that you're a liar," Lucia said.

He frowned at her. "I admit no such thing."

"Where is Kurtis?" she bit out, her patience swiftly waning.

"Right now? I don't know."

Lucia glanced at her father, who nodded. She returned her attention to the weasel before her. "Look at me, Lord Gareth."

The man shifted his gaze to hers.

She concentrated, but found it difficult for a moment to summon her magic. Difficult, but not impossible. "Tell me the truth. Have you seen your son?"

"Yes," Lord Gareth said, the word shooting out of his mouth as swiftly and heavily as a cannonball. His forehead furrowed. "What did I . . . ? I didn't mean to say that."

Lucia kept his troubled gaze locked with hers, while grappling to hold on to her own magic, which felt like sand slipping from between her fingers. "When did you see him?"

"Earlier today. He begged for my help. He said he'd been

tortured—that Nicolo Cassian had burned him. And he confessed to what he'd done to Prince Magnus."

Gareth clamped his mouth shut so hard his teeth made a crunching sound. Blood began to trickle from his nose.

The blood helped.

Even a prophesied sorceress could use blood to strengthen her magic.

"Don't try to fight against this," Lucia said. She couldn't focus on the jarring mention of Nic Cassian right now. That could wait for later. "What did Kurtis confess to you?"

"He . . . he . . ." Gareth's face had turned red, nearly purple, as he strained against Lucia's magic. "He . . . murdered . . . Prince Magnus."

The confirmation was a blow, stealing her breath. She fought to hold on to the magic she used to draw the truth from the lord's lying lips. "How?"

"Buried him alive . . . in a nailed wooden box. So he . . . would . . . suffer before he died."

Lucia's throat constricted, and her eyes began to sting. It was just as she'd seen during the location spell. "Where is Kurtis now?"

His eyes glazed over, and the blood from his nose dripped to the white marble floor. "I told the little fool to run. To hide. To protect himself however necessary. That the king's heir wasn't someone to be thrown away like the contents of a chamber pot, that there would be ramifications."

"Yes," Lucia said, her expression one of sheer hatred. "There most definitely will be."

With that, she released her tenuous magical control of the man. He produced a handkerchief from the pocket of his overcoat and wiped at his bloody nose, his gaze frantically moving to Gaius, who had silently listened to his confession.

Trembling with outrage, it took every last ounce of Lucia's control not to kill Lord Gareth where he stood.

"I'm glad you've spoken the truth, even if it had to be under duress," Gaius said, finally, when all had gone silent.

Lord Gareth gasped. "Your highness, he's my son. My boy. I fear for his safety even though I know he's done such horrible and unforgivable things."

The king nodded. "I understand. I feel the same"—a small muscle in his cheek twitched—"*felt* the same way about Magnus. I know my own reputation for being unforgiving when crossed. I'm not ignorant to the fears I raise in others and how strongly they would want to avoid punishment."

"And I have stood by your side as you've doled out those punishments. Approved all . . . all until now. And now I must beg you for lenience."

"I understand why you did it—why you'd wish to help your son. What's done is done."

Lord Gareth straightened his shoulders. "I am so relieved that you understand my position in this unfortunate matter."

"Yes, I do. I would have done exactly the same."

Lord Gareth let out a shuddery sigh as he clamped his hand down on the king's shoulder. "Much gratitude, my friend."

"However, I find I cannot forgive you." In one swift motion, Gaius pulled a knife from within his surcoat and sliced it across the lord's throat.

Lord Gareth's hands flew to stanch the immediate flow of blood.

"When I find Kurtis," the king said, "I promise that he will die very, very slowly. Perhaps he'll even scream for you to save him. I look forward to telling him that you're already dead."

Lucia couldn't say she'd been surprised by her father's actions. In fact, she wholly approved.

Lord Gareth fell to the floor by her feet in a growing pool of his own blood while Lucia and Gaius moved toward the exit.

Gaius wiped the bloody blade of his knife on a handkerchief. "I've wanted to do that since we were only children."

"We will find Kurtis without him," Lucia said calmly.

He eyed her. "You aren't upset by what I just did?"

Did he expect her to feel the same horror of a small girl coming upon a dying cat left for her to find?

"If you hadn't killed him," Lucia said, "I would have."

The look in the King of Blood's gaze then as his daughter admitted her desire for murder wasn't one of approval, she thought.

It held a whisper of regret.

"So the rumors about you are true," he said solemnly.

She swallowed past the lump that had suddenly formed in her throat. "Most of them, I'm afraid."

"Good." He continued to hold her gaze when she wished she could look away. "Then be a demon, my beautiful daughter. Be whatever you need to be to put an end to the Kindred once and for all."

CHAPTER 10

CLEO

AURANOS

Her childhood. Her family. Her hopes and dreams and wishes. All were contained within these golden walls.

"If I pretend hard enough, I can almost believe that it's all been a horrible nightmare."

She said this aloud to Nerissa as her friend brushed the tangles out of her hair before the same mirror where she'd gotten ready for countless parties and banquets in the past.

The silver hilt of the brush only served as a painful reminder of a time when Magnus brushed her hair, uncertain whether such a strange act was befitting of a prince, but willing to try because she'd asked him to.

He'd loved her hair. She knew this because he'd never failed to mention how annoying it was that she wore it down, rather than pulled back from her face.

She'd learned to interpret Magnus's particular way of speaking. He rarely said exactly what was on his mind.

But sometimes he did.

Sometimes, when it counted the most, he said *exactly* what was on his mind.

Nerissa placed the brush down on the vanity. "Do you want to pretend it's all been a nightmare?"

"No," she answered immediately.

"I am here for you, princess. Whatever you need."

Cleo reached for her friend's hand, squeezing it, wanting something to help anchor her here. "Thank you. Thank you . . . for everything you've done for me. But can you do me one huge favor?"

"Of course. What is it?"

"Call me Cleo."

A smile touched Nerissa's lips, and she nodded. "I can do that." She turned Cleo's hand over, studying the mark on her palm. "The lines haven't changed since we left Paelsia."

"I haven't used the water magic again."

Not since freezing the guard, she thought, shuddering at the memory.

"Have you tried?"

Cleo shook her head. "Amara thought I should try to control this magic, but I haven't yet." She was afraid to try, although she didn't admit this aloud. "And the weather . . . I'm not even sure I'm responsible for that. Not consciously, anyway."

Storms had followed them from Paelsia, sudden downpours of rain that seemed to correspond to Cleo's darker moments of grief.

"What about Taran?" Nerissa asked. "The lines spreading from his air magic marking are more extensive than yours. They're all the way up his right arm now."

Cleo's gaze snapped to hers. "Really?"

Nerissa nodded. "His air magic saved Felix's life, but after that . . . I don't know if he's been trying to control it. Enzo is worried about him. He's worried about you too."

Cleo wanted to focus on something else, anything else. "Is Enzo worried about *you*?"

Nerissa gave her a small smile. "Constantly. He's the jealous type, I'm afraid."

"He's in love."

"That would make only one of us, unfortunately." She sighed. "He was fun in the beginning, but now he wants something from me that I don't think I can give him." She visibly grimaced. "Commitment."

"Perish the thought." Cleo very nearly laughed out loud at that. "So you're saying that you're not ready to get married and have a dozen babies with him."

"That would be putting it mildly," Nerissa replied. "No, unfortunately there's someone else on my mind lately. Someone I've come to care about more than I'd like."

Such talk, despite what it meant for poor Enzo, had helped to brighten Cleo's dark mood. It reminded her of a simpler time when she gossiped with her sister about the love lives of their circle of friends.

"Who?" Cleo asked. "Do I know him?"

Nerissa's smile grew. "Why do you assume it's a him?"

"Oh." Cleo's eyes widened. "Well, that's certainly a good question, isn't it? Why would I assume such a thing?"

"I've found in my life that love and attraction can take many forms. And if one is open to unexpected possibilities, there are no boundaries."

That certainly was true, Cleo thought. It had been for her and Magnus. "You're not going to tell me who it is, are you?"

"No. But don't worry—it's not you, princess." Nerissa frowned.

"I mean *Cleo*. Using your name rather than your title might take some getting used to. Now, I will wish you goodnight. You need sleep. And tomorrow, if you want to begin channeling this magic within you, I will be readily available to help you practice."

"Perhaps," Cleo allowed.

After Nerissa left, Cleo pondered Nerissa's seemingly overcomplicated love life as she tried to fall asleep and think about anything other than Magnus.

She failed.

The lines spreading out from the water magic symbol on her palm glowed in the darkness, pulsing with the beat of her heart. She pulled up the sleeve of her nightgown and traced her fingers along the lines, like branches of a tree . . . or veins.

Or scars.

Scars like the one on Magnus's cheek.

Cleo forced the thought of his face away from her. It hurt too much to dwell on everything she'd lost.

She had to focus on what she still had.

This magic—this water goddess residing within her . . . what did it mean?

Could she use it to regain her power?

Magnus would approve of that, she thought.

Unable to sleep, she dressed herself in a light silk cloak in the dead of night and decided to go to the palace library and read until dawn. Certainly, she could find more books about the Kindred. She'd glanced at some in the past but had never paid close enough attention to them.

The palace had a scattering of Kraeshian guards on duty, but not nearly as many as there had been when Amara's occupation had started. Some were stationed in the same places where Auranian guards once stood. They were as still as statues, not seeming to pay her any attention or ask where she was going.

It wasn't nearly the same as it had been when she'd been here last, a prisoner of war forced to marry the conquering king's son, watched closely with every move she made.

I could leave here, she thought. *Run away and start a new life—put this one far behind me.*

Cleo scratched her left palm, knowing such thoughts were full of weakness and fear and utter denial.

She refused to be weak or fearful.

Entering the library, blazing with torchlight even in the wee hours of the night, felt like truly coming home. She'd only recently developed a love of books after ignoring the treasures in this expansive space for most of her life.

Thank the goddess that King Gaius had not burned them.

The library was even larger than the throne room, with shelves carved from mahogany wood that stretched thirty feet high with gold ladders to climb in order to obtain books higher than an arm's reach. The titles and scribes of these thousands upon thousands of volumes of story and history were kept in yet another book, one that she remembered trying and failing to decipher one day when the curator wasn't around.

Cleo couldn't find that thick ledger tonight, so instead she traced her index finger along hundreds of spines until she found one that called out to her.

It was simply titled: *Goddess.*

The brown leather cover had two golden symbols upon it—the symbols for water and earth magic.

She opened the book up and held it toward a torch so she could read it easily. It held the accounts of one who was Valoria's personal scribe when she was in power in Nothern Limeros a thousand years ago, and it held sketches of the goddess Cleo had never seen before.

"The real truth about Valoria?" she mused to herself. "Or just the personal opinions of some lovestruck scribe?"

Despite Valoria's rumored sadistic nature—rivaling only that of King Gaius's—she was said to be as eternally beautiful as any immortal who'd ever existed.

Still, this book seemed like one worth reading.

Cleo tucked the book under her arm, deciding to take it back to her chambers to read more. She and Valoria had one important thing in common, something she couldn't ignore: the water Kindred.

Sleep didn't tug at her yet, so she continued to explore the library. She found an alcove that held a great surprise. On the wall, flanked by two small lanterns, was a portrait of her mother.

Cleo hadn't seen this painting in years. She had assumed it had been burned with the rest of the Bellos royal family.

The fact that it hadn't been destroyed filled her heart with a sudden burst of joy and relief.

Queen Elena Bellos looked so much like Emilia. Cleo wished she'd had a chance to know her.

Beneath the portrait was a glass case, similar to the ones that her father had stuffed with the gifts from royal families from overseas who'd come to visit and brought shining treasures from their kingdoms.

This cabinet held only one piece.

A jeweled dagger.

Cleo moved closer, realizing that there was something on the ground.

A piece of torn parchment.

Unable to stifle her curiosity, she picked up the parchment to find it was a letter written in a feminine hand. Part of it had been ripped away, leaving only a few lines for her to read.

My darling Gaius,

I know you must hate me. It's always seemed to be that way between us—either love or hate. But know as I enter this marriage that I do so out of my obligation to my family. I can't turn my back on my mother's wishes. It would have killed her had I run away with you. But I love you. I love you. I love you. I could repeat it a thousand times and it would never stop being true. If there were any other way, know that I would—

The letter had been torn after that line, and Cleo felt a desperate grief within her at not being able to know more.

Her mother wrote this.

She wrote this to King Gaius.

With a trembling hand, Cleo reached into the case and picked up the dagger.

The hilt was encrusted with precious jewels. A beautiful treasure, one that struck her as oddly familiar.

Aron Lagaris, Cleo's former betrothed, had owned a jeweled dagger, but it was not nearly as grand as this. Jonas had kept Aron's dagger for months after the tragedy at the Paelsian market that day, a reminder of losing his brother, a reminder of the vengeance in the rebel's heart.

Another dagger came to Cleo's mind then—one that Prince Ashur had given to her on her wedding night.

"This is a Kraeshian wedding dagger," she breathed.

"Yes. Yes, it is."

Cleo froze at the sound of King Gaius's voice. She took a deep breath in and straightened her spine. "You're the one who put it here," she said.

"I gifted that to your mother upon her marriage to your father."

It took her a moment to find her voice. "What a strange gift from a Limerian."

"It is, isn't it? I wanted her to kill Corvin with it in his sleep."

Cleo turned to glare at him. The king wore a cloak as black as his hair, as dark as his eyes. For a moment, he looked so much like Magnus that it stole her breath.

"If you gave her such a gift," she managed to say, "I can see why she hated you."

"I dropped that letter earlier this evening." His gaze fell upon it still clutched in Cleo's hand, and in a single motion he snatched it away from her. "If you read it, you know that hate was only one of the emotions she held for me." The king's attention shifted to the portrait above her. "Elena kept the dagger. I saw it again in a treasure cabinet like this when I came to visit your father twelve years ago."

Cleo's gaze went to it again. "Is this the same dagger that Magnus saw during that visit? One so beautiful that he wanted to steal it? And you—"

"Cut him with it," he said bluntly. "Yes. I did. And he bore the scar from that day to remind me of that moment when I lost control of myself, lost in my grief."

"I can't believe my mother would have ever . . ." A pain squeezed her heart, both of grief and outrage. "She loved my father."

Gaius turned his face away so it became shrouded by shadows. "I suppose she did, in her way. Her deeply obedient, devoted to her bloody goddess, myopic family way." His smile turned into a sneer. He studied the portrait now with disdain rather than reverence. "Elena was a treasure that your father wished to add to his growing collection. Your grandparents were thrilled that the Corso family name—certainly noble, but not important enough to earn the right to a villa in the City of Gold—might become truly royal. They accepted the betrothal without even consulting Elena about it first."

Cleo was equal parts thirsty to know more and appalled by any slight against her beloved father. "Your mother made it sound like you had fallen for each other much earlier, on the Isle of Lukas. If this was true, why didn't you marry her? You were a prince."

"How clever. Why didn't I think of that?" Such coldness to his tone, such sarcasm. She flinched from it. "Alas, there were rumors about me even then, rumors that met with her parents' disapproval. I was . . . tainted, you might say. Dark and unpredictable, dangerous and violent. They worried for the safety of their precious daughter."

"Rightfully so."

"I would never have harmed Elena. I worshipped her." His dark eyes glittered as he focused on Cleo. "And she knew it. She nearly ran away with me a month before she married him."

She would have denied this very possibility if she hadn't first read the letter. "But she didn't."

"No. Instead I received this message. I wasn't very happy to read it."

That would explain why it had been torn in half.

Cleo tried to figure it out. "My grandparents intervened . . ."

"My *mother* intervened." He scowled. "I see it all now, far more clearly than ever before. How much she controlled when it came to her plans for me. Her control over me."

"Selia spoke to my grandparents? Warned them?"

"No. After I received this"—his grip on the parchment tightened—"my mother saw how distraught I'd become. How distracted and obsessed. She knew I would never give Elena up. So she had your grandparents murdered."

"What?" Cleo gasped. "I know they died years before I was born, but . . . I was never told how."

"Some feel that painful tales are best kept from innocent ears. They were killed by an assassin sent by Queen Selia Damora herself. Until that moment, I believed there was still a chance that Elena would walk away from the wedding to be with me instead. But in her grief, Elena believed the rumors that I was the one behind this act. She married Corvin and made it clear that she hated me. I didn't take the rejection well, so I did what any fool would do. I became everything she thought I was."

Cleo's mind reeled. "So you weren't always . . ."

"Evil and sadistic?" The small, cold smile returned. "I was never kind, at least not to those who didn't deserve it. And very few did. This, however . . . it worked exactly as my mother wished. I tried not to care when I heard of your sister's birth. I tried not to give a damn again about anything to do with Elena." He snorted softly. "Then one day I received another letter from her. She wanted to see me again, even heavy with her second child. She asked me to visit the following month. But the following month, I learned she was dead."

Cleo's throat felt thick. For a moment, she couldn't even attempt to speak.

The king's gaze locked on the painted eyes of Queen Elena Bellos. "My mother found out about my plans to see her again, and she . . . intervened. And for years I believed her lies about the witch's curse and that you were the one who killed her. I supposed I wanted to believe it." He let out a pained snarl. "My mother destroyed my entire life, and I allowed it."

"She . . . she wanted the fire Kindred to use your body as a host, not Nic's." Cleo had been trying to rationalize this since it had happened. "If she wanted ultimate power for you, had planned it all her life, that doesn't make any sense."

King Gaius nodded. "I agree, what happened was not according to Selia Damora's plan. But I know my mother enough to know that she would have found a way to shift control back to me. Back to *her*."

Cleo's mind was in turmoil over everything the king had shared. She went over what he'd just said. "If you believe that, do you think there's a way to bring Nic back?"

He sneered. "I don't know, nor do I care about that boy's fate."

"*I* care," she said. "My mother is dead. My father and sister are dead. My dear friend Mira is dead. And now Magnus is *dead*." Her voice broke, and a layer of frost suddenly began to spread across the walls in the alcove. "But Nic isn't. Not yet. And if there's something I can do to help him, then I have to try!"

King Gaius eyed the icy walls uneasily. "Are you doing that with water magic?"

Cleo's hands shook, but she held them out in front of her. The glowing, spidery blue lines had begun to spread over her wrists. "I—I can't control it."

"Don't try to control it," he said. "Or it will kill you."

"What do you care?" she spat.

Gaius's eyebrows drew together. He looked pained. "Magnus loved you. He fought for you. He defied me again and again in order to save you, even if it meant his own destruction. He was worthy of you in a way that I was never worthy of Elena. I see that now. And for that alone, you must survive this, Cleiona Bellos." Then he scowled at her. "But know this. I would personally kill you in an instant if it meant that my son could live again."

Cleo didn't have a chance to reply before the king walked away, swallowed by the darkness of the library.

CHAPTER 11

MAGNUS

PAELSIA

When Magnus and Ashur returned to the walled royal compound by way of the Imperial Road, they found it all but deserted.

Amara and half her soldiers had set sail for Kraeshia.

King Gaius and a handful of others—including Cleo—had left for the Auranian palace.

"Do you think we can trust what he says?" Ashur asked.

"Oh, I don't know." Magnus pressed the blade he'd stolen harder against the Kraeshian guard's throat. The guard had been patrolling outside the gates when Magnus and Ashur grabbed him and dragged him behind a thatch of thorny bushes out of sight of other guards. "He seems sincere enough."

The guard's eyes moved wildly between them. "I wouldn't lie, not to you, your highness. I don't believe your sister's accusations about you."

Magnus sent a sidelong look toward his companion. "I don't think he's addressing me."

Ashur stepped closer. "Amara has accused me of horrible crimes against my family and against the empire itself."

"And many refuse to believe her. Your sister doesn't deserve to ascend to empress. You are the rightful emperor of Kraeshia. Say the word, and I will give my life for yours."

"No," Ashur said, a shadow crossing his gray-blue eyes. "I want no one else to sacrifice themselves for me. I don't want the royal scepter my sister desires more than anything else. I never have."

"Tell me more about Princess Cleiona," Magnus growled at the guard. "Did Kurtis Cirillo return here? Is she safe?"

"I only saw her briefly when she left with the king's entourage. Lord Kurtis hasn't been heard from in days."

Magnus already knew what had happened during the ritual. After the shocking realization that the fire Kindred now resided within the body of Nic Cassian, Ashur had filled him in on what had happened to Cleo.

He needed to get to her. To see her for himself if she was suffering in any way from this unexpected affliction.

Magnus always believed her to be a goddess; he just never thought she'd become a literal one.

"There's nothing here for us," Magnus growled, pulling his blade away from the guard's throat. "Let's leave."

"Your highness?" the guard ventured. "Will you stay? Will you lead us against your sister?"

Ashur didn't respond to the guard. Instead he turned his back and kept pace with Magnus as they left the compound.

No one followed them.

"Fool," Magnus muttered.

Ashur glanced at him. "Are you referring to me?"

"You have great power within your grasp, and you consciously choose to ignore it."

The Kraeshian prince clenched his jaw for a moment before replying. "I don't want to be emperor."

"Just because you don't have a craving for an apple doesn't mean you need to upend an entire cart of them out of spite." Why did he even care to comment? Amara and her lust for power didn't register as important for him at the moment.

All he wanted was to get to the Auranian palace.

That was as far into the future as he currently thought.

They'd walked along the Imperial Road for hours in silence. It would lead them through the Wildlands and into Auranos without the risk of being seen at the docks of Trader's Harbor. For every guard who might claim loyalty to Prince Ashur, Magnus knew there were a dozen more who'd been commanded by Amara to kill him on sight.

Magnus washed the remainder of the dirt off himself in the first body of water they came upon. Since it was Paelsia, it was a thin, muddy river.

He hated this place.

Finally, Ashur spoke again. "Are you curious at all about what I *do* want?"

"I hope you're going to say a pair of horses," Magnus replied. "Or, even better, a horse-drawn carriage."

"I want to find a witch."

Magnus eyed him. "A witch."

Ashur nodded. "I've asked around to see whether there is one in this land who has enough power to be of help to us. And there is. She's rumored to be an exiled Watcher who has retained her magic. She lives in solitude, hiding the extent of her magic from the world."

"Rumors and feathers," Magnus muttered.

"What?"

"Both usually hold very little weight." He shook his head. "It's an old Limerian saying."

"I was told by a Paelsian woman I met when we were in Basilia that there is a tavern in Auranos where I can find more answers and learn how to contact Valia. We will pass this tavern on our way to the city."

"Valia," Magnus repeated. "You even have a name."

"I will seek her out by myself, if I must."

"And then what? What exactly do you expect if you do find her and she isn't some common witch who can barely light a candle with her weak *elementia*? Do you think she's going to have any more effect on Kyan than Lucia would?"

"Lucia won't have any effect on Kyan. Your sister is as useful in helping to save Nicolo as Amara would be."

Magnus stopped walking, turning to face Ashur. "I believe in Lucia. I'll never stop believing that she will return to us and do what is right."

Ashur cocked his head. "You choose to live in a dream when it comes to your sister. Lucia has shown us all what she wants to do—and it's to help Kyan."

Fury rose within Magnus in an instant. "You're wrong."

Ashur studied him, frustration in his blue-gray eyes. "Where was your sister last night when Kyan was about to burn you? To make you into his slave? Did she magically appear to save you? She doesn't give a damn about you anymore, Magnus. Perhaps she never did."

Magnus really didn't mean to hit Ashur as hard as he did.

But he hit him anyway.

Ashur covered his nose as it gushed blood with one hand and shoved Magnus back with the other. "I think you broke my nose, you *basanuug*."

"Good. You were too perfect-looking before. It'll give you some character." Magnus started walking again. "I'm going to assume *basanuug* doesn't mean 'good friend.'"

"It's Kraeshian for the arse of a pig."

He nodded. "Fitting."

"Don't dare hit me ever again," Ashur growled.

"Don't speak ill of my sister again and I won't have to," he snapped back. "Lucia will return. She will help us. She won't side with Kyan again, not after she sees what he's done."

When it came to his sister, Magnus needed to believe this more than anything else.

Their progress along the Imperial Road was far too slow and tried Magnus's patience, but they finally entered Auranos.

Ashur's tales of this witch named Valia had piqued his interest, though he'd never admit it.

Not far from the Temple of Cleiona and the end of the Imperial Road, they came upon the village and the tavern that Ashur sought. Magnus didn't care about the name of it, only that it might serve wine and good food along with the answers Ashur wanted.

The pair entered the busy tavern and took a seat at a table in a dark corner. They ordered food and drink from a barmaid.

Ashur drew the girl closer. "I'm looking for someone," he said.

She gave him a flirtatious smile and twisted a piece of dark hair around her finger. "You've found her."

"That's not exactly what I mean, lovely girl." He whispered something in her ear.

She nodded. "I'll see if he's here, handsome."

When she walked away, Magnus regarded Ashur with bemusement. "The world's most sought-after unmarried prince who could have anyone he wants . . . cares only for Nicolo Cassian."

Ashur met Magnus's gaze without flinching. "You wouldn't understand."

"Likely not," he agreed.

Not long after, the girl brought them roast chicken and a bottle of wine from Agallon Vineyards. Magnus glared at the etched marking for a moment before he uncorked it and took a deep drink, squeezing his eyes shut to allow the sweet liquid to move over his tongue and down his throat.

"I didn't think Limerians drank inebriants," Ashur said.

"They don't," Magnus replied. "Except for the ones that do."

He scanned the tavern with impatience and suspicion, waiting for one of its patrons to approach them, ready to fight or kill. But every one of them minded their own business, filing out after their meals, drunk and full.

"Amusing," Magnus said drily.

"What is?" Ashur asked.

"Auranians have survived very nicely, given all that has transpired in Mytica this last year. They're still hedonists to their very core."

"People have different ways of dealing with adversities. It doesn't mean they're happy."

"Ignorance is happiness."

"Then let's toast to ignorance." Ashur raised his goblet. After a moment, Magnus raised his bottle. "And to my sister Amara," he continued, "who can rot in what Myticans call the darklands—if such a place exists—where she has surely earned her spot for leaving us with such a mess to clean up."

Magnus nodded. "I'll drink to that."

A man approached their table from across the busy tavern. He had white hair, a lined face, and an impossibly wide smile.

"You asked to speak with me," the man said.

"You're Bruno?" Ashur asked.

Bruno nodded, his smile growing even wider. "Not just one but two princes in my tavern this evening! How utterly marvelous. I wish my son were here to see this!"

"Quiet, you fool," Magnus snarled, scanning the area to see if anyone overheard.

"Why should I be quiet about such an honor?"

"Kindly lower your voice," Ashur said.

"Oh, your accent is just as delightful as they say it is, your grace. My goodness, yes. Lovely, just lovely!"

Magnus placed the edge of his blade against the man's wrist. "I said *be quiet*."

Bruno looked down, his white eyebrows high. "Of course, your highness."

"I was told that you might have information," Ashur said, "about how to contact a woman named Valia."

"Valia," Bruno said, nodding. "Yes, I know her."

"I need to speak with her."

"Valia doesn't speak with just anyone. She values her privacy."

"She's an exiled Watcher? One who's retained her magic?" Magnus asked in a hushed tone, still resistant to this possibility.

Bruno's pleasant expression grew warier. "What interest do you have in contacting Valia?"

"I need to know if her magic might help to save a friend of mine," Ashur said.

"Save them from what?"

"From the fire Kindred."

Bruno twisted his hands, his face paling. "One shouldn't speak aloud of such legends. The hawks may hear us." He peered out the window next to them, into the midday sunshine. "Valia hates the hawks, you know. They're her favorite meal—roasted with sour panberries. I think it's because of what happened to her hand, you see, although she would never admit such a thing."

Ashur let out a small grunt of frustration. "How do I contact her? Through you?"

"If you seek Valia, she will know." He shrugged. "But she'll also respond to a blood sacrifice along with a recited summoning."

Magnus pushed his empty bottle of wine away from him. "I think we're done here."

"What kind of summoning?" Ashur persisted. "Does she live in this village? Will you let her know I'm seeking her help?"

"I haven't seen Valia in years. Frankly, I have no idea where she is now. But if you do the blood ritual and the summoning properly, and she is curious, she will come forth." Bruno turned to Magnus, his smile returning, especially now that Magnus had sheathed his blade. "I saw you on your wedding tour. You and the princess made quite the pair—a portrait of light and dark, night and day. The Prince of Blood and the beautiful Golden Princess. A stunning couple, truly." He shook his head. "It's a memory I treasure to this day, despite how much I despise your evil father."

"Ashur," Magnus said with an impatient sigh, "I'm going to the palace now. Are you going to join me, or do you wish to call out names while sacrificing random forest creatures?"

"You don't believe," Ashur said.

"What I believe is irrelevant. What I *need* is to get to Cleo."

"I've heard a recent rumor about you, Prince Magnus," Bruno said. "I'm so pleased to see it's not true."

"Oh? And what is it?"

"That you're dead." Bruno cocked his head. "You look very well for a dead man."

Magnus brushed his fingers over the ring on his left hand. "Ashur?"

Ashur stood up, his face etched in doubt. "Yes, I'm coming with you. I can't waste time chasing after useless stories, and that's what this sounds like to me."

Magnus heard the pained disappointment in the prince's voice.

He couldn't help but feel it himself.

There would be no simple solution to this puzzle. It had become a giant, complicated ice maze in which one might freeze to death before they ever found their way out.

But Magnus still believed in Lucia.

And he believed in Cleo.

That would have to be enough.

CHAPTER 12

LUCIA

AURANOS

Ever since drawing the truth from Lord Gareth's lying mouth yesterday, Lucia felt more of her magic slipping away.

She barely slept last night thinking about how to solve this crushing problem.

Other than draining Jonas of more of his strange magic—which would possibly kill him the next time—she came up with no solid answer.

Even Lyssa's nursemaid noticed the strain and worry on Lucia's face and told her to go outside and get some sunshine and fresh air.

Instead of ignoring her, Lucia decided to do as suggested.

She had enjoyed the palace courtyard the last time she'd been there, relished in walking its mosaic pathway through the olive and willow trees and beautiful flower gardens tended daily by a full roster of talented gardeners.

The sound of buzzing bees, the chirp of songbirds, and the warm Auranian sun on her face calmed her.

It wasn't home, but it would have to do for now.

The king said they would stay at the Auranian palace until he found Kurtis, who, perhaps, might return to the palace seeking his father's assistance.

So be it.

From the pocket of her gown, she pulled out the amber orb that had once been Kyan's prison. After he'd taken corporeal form, he had kept this with him until the magic from her ring had destroyed that form.

This orb was of value to the fire Kindred.

And it was a threat to him. But only if Lucia could summon the full strength of her magic to imprison him again.

While seated upon a stone bench in the center of the courtyard, she held the small crystal sphere in the palm of her hand and tried to levitate it with air magic.

Lucia concentrated, gritting her teeth with the effort, but nothing happened.

She failed again and again to shift the object even a fraction.

Oh, goddess, she thought with growing panic. *My magic is completely gone.*

"Lucia."

The sound of Cleo's voice made her jump, and she quickly tucked the amber orb back into her pocket.

"Apologies if I startled you," Cleo said, wringing her hands.

"Not at all," Lucia lied, managing a tight smile. "Good morning."

Cleo didn't reply. She simply stood there, studying Lucia nervously.

She wore a lovely blue gown today with orange and yellow flowers embroidered along the hem of the skirt. Lucia would have envied her for it in the past. Limerians, even royalty, rarely wore bright colors. Lucia's mother had always insisted on looking proper, polished, and well-tailored—provided the colors one wore were gray, black, or olive green.

Yet Lucia had always been drawn to brighter colors. She had hated Lady Sabina Mallius, her father's former mistress, but envied her ability to wear red. While it was the official color of Limeros, such a color rarely found its way onto the clothing of anyone but a palace guard.

Perhaps I should have confiscated Sabina's wardrobe after I murdered her, Lucia mused.

It seemed so long ago—her first burst of uncontrollable magic that had led to a death. How horrible Lucia had felt about it at the time.

But that was then, and this was now.

"That is a beautiful gown," she said.

Cleo looked down at herself as if just realizing what she wore. "This is the work of Lorenzo Tavera. He has a dress shop in Hawk's Brow."

Lucia found she didn't care about such things anymore, not really.

No, now that Cleo was right in front of her, she had much more important subjects on her mind. Her gaze moved to Cleo's left hand, the one that bore the water magic symbol. She'd seen the same symbol a thousand times on statues of the goddess Valoria.

To see it in reality, on the palm on the Auranian princess, felt rather surreal.

There were more markings on Cleo's skin—thin, branching blue lines that extended from the water symbol itself. At first glance, they appeared like veins visible through translucent skin, but they were far more ominous than that.

"I need your help," Cleo said, simply.

Something caught in Lucia's chest, something cold and hard and tight.

"Do you?" she replied.

Cleo bit her bottom lip, her eyes cast downward. "I know you hate me for what I did. I convinced you we were friends, and you allowed me to take part in the awakening ritual. When you confronted me about telling Jonas where to find the crystals, I denied it."

Lucia watched her carefully, surprised by the words coming out of her mouth.

Cleo blinked hard as she crossed her arms tightly over her chest. "I did only what I felt like I had to do to survive. But know this: I had come to value you as a friend, Lucia. If it had been another world, another lifetime, perhaps we could have been just that without any difficulties. But instead, I betrayed your trust for my own gain. And I truly apologize for hurting you."

Lucia found herself momentarily at a loss for words. "You mean this."

Cleo nodded. "With all my heart."

Lucia had been terribly hurt by the betrayal. And she'd reacted the only way she knew how—with anger and violence. She'd nearly killed Cleo that day, just before she'd foolishly run away with Alexius.

Cleo had always seemed so perfect—so effortlessly beautiful, so poised . . . a girl who drew everyone's eye and appreciation. So very different from Lucia.

A part of her had wanted to destroy this small, golden piece of perfection.

Especially when it became clear that Magnus had begun to take interest in her.

Was it jealousy Lucia had felt? Not romantic jealousy, certainly.

Lucia had never loved Magnus as more than a brother. But all her life she'd had his full attention and possessed his whole heart.

Magnus had belonged only to her until Cleo came into their lives.

No wonder I've hated her all this time, Lucia thought with shocked realization.

She reached out a hand to the other princess. "Let me see your mark."

Cleo hesitated a moment before taking a seat next to the sorceress and holding out her left hand. Lucia studied the water magic symbol and the lines branching out from it, her brows drawing together in concentration.

"The magic is unpredictable," Cleo said, her voice hushed now. "And so powerful. It can control the weather. It can create sheets of ice out of nothing at all. It can freeze a man to death . . ."

Lucia quickly looked up at Cleo, searching the other princess's face for the truth.

"You killed someone with this water magic," she said.

Cleo nodded. "A guard who had helped to torture Magnus."

Lucia's grip on Cleo's hand increased. "I hope you made him suffer."

"That's just it . . . I didn't try to do anything at all. It just happened. The magic manifests when I'm angry, or sad, or in pain. I can feel it—cool and bottomless within my skin. But I can't seem to control it."

"When it does manifest, are these lines the only side effect?"

"My nose bled the first time, but not since. These lines appeared, yes. And I also have nightmares, but I'm not sure if they're related. Nightmares that I'm drowning. And not only when I'm asleep . . . sometimes I feel like I'm drowning in the middle of the day."

Lucia pondered this for a moment. In the beginning, her magic was also overpowering, lashing out when her emotions became erratic.

"So you want my help," she began, "to rid yourself of this affliction."

"No," Cleo said without hesitation. "I want your help to learn how to control it."

Lucia shook her head. "Cleo, do you realize what this is? This isn't a simple and accessible thread of water magic that could be contained within a common witch—or even within me." Or, at least, how Lucia had been for a short time before her pregnancy. "You have the *water Kindred* inside you—a thinking, feeling entity that wants to gain full control over your body, like how Kyan now controls Nic. The water Kindred wants to live, to exist, and to experience life . . . and you're the only one now standing in its way."

Cleo's expression turned stubborn. "I've been reading more about Valoria in a book I found in the palace library. She also had the water and earth Kindred within her, but she could control that magic at will."

"Valoria was an immortal, created from magic itself," Lucia explained. "You are mortal, flesh and blood, and vulnerable to pain and injury."

Cleo eyes grew glossy, and her grip on Lucia's hand tightened. "You don't understand." She looked down at the water symbol. "I have to figure out how to use it. I have to save Nic and my kingdom. My sister, my father . . . they told me to be strong, but I"—she drew in a ragged breath—"I don't know if I can be strong much longer. What I've always believed about my family, about my mother and father and the love they shared . . ." Her voice broke. "Everything has fallen away into ruin, and I'm lost. Without this magic, I have nothing left. Without this magic . . . *I am nothing.*"

Lucia had hated Cleo for so long for reasons she'd all but forgotten, but the princess's pain tugged on a heart she'd thought had turned hard and black months ago.

"You're not nothing," she said firmly. "You are Cleiona Aurora Bellos. And you are going to survive this. You're going to survive because I know my brother would have wanted you to."

Tears streaked down Cleo's cheeks, and she stared into Lucia's eyes for a long time before she finally nodded.

"I'll try," she said.

"Do better than try."

Cleo fell silent for a moment, her brows drawn together. "Taran wants the air magic out of him. He must have even less control over his emotions than I do, because the lines have gone far higher on his arm than mine have." She stared down at them, touching the blue lines gingerly with her right hand. "He . . . he says he'd rather die than become nothing but a vessel for the air Kindred."

Lucia didn't blame Taran at all for this. To have one's body and one's life stolen away by a greedy god . . .

Death would be kinder.

"I swear I will figure out how to imprison Kyan again and stop this—all of this. I won't let him win." Lucia stood up from the bench. "I need to check on my daughter now."

"Of course," Cleo whispered.

As she walked down the stone path and into the palace, Lucia's mind spun with a thousand different scenarios of how to stop Kyan and help Cleo. Not so long ago, she wouldn't have cared about the princess's fate.

The nursemaid met her halfway to the room that had been designated as Lyssa's nursery.

"Have you left my daughter unattended?" Lucia asked, alarmed.

"She's fine," the nursemaid assured her. "She's sleeping soundly.

Nicolo stopped by and said he'd watch over her while I took my midday meal."

Lucia froze. "Nicolo Cassian?"

She nodded. "It's so good to see him again. I practically raised him and his sister as I did the princesses. Such a sweet boy."

Lucia didn't listen to another word. She shoved the old woman out of her way and ran to her chambers, flinging open the door.

He stood in front of the cradle with his back to Lucia, his red hair and the distinctive lankiness of his body silhouetted by the light from the balcony.

"Get away from her," Lucia warned, desperately trying to summon magic, any magic, to her hand.

"She's as lovely as her mother," he murmured, turning to show that he cradled Lyssa in his arms. The baby's gaze was fixed on his red hair as if fascinated by the bright color.

Lucia's heart stuttered to a stop at the sight of her daughter in the grip of a monster. "Put her down, *Kyan*."

Kyan turned and raised an eyebrow, his brown eyes finally fixing upon Lucia. For all he looked like Nic, right down to the freckles on his pale face, she could see the ancient fire god that now existed behind his gaze.

"So, you've heard that I've found a new home," he said.

"I swear, I will end you, right here and now." Lucia pulled the amber orb from her pocket, knowing she didn't have the magic to live up to her threats—not today—but she prayed he didn't realize that.

"I only came here to talk," Kyan said. "This doesn't have to be unpleasant."

"Put my daughter down."

"I feel like an uncle to this little one. Lyssa is like family to me." He gazed down at the baby's face. "Aren't you? You can call me

Uncle Kyan. Oh, we'll have great fun together if your mother ever forgives me for my horribly bad behavior."

Lucia gaped at him for a moment before she began to laugh. It sounded more like a hiccup. "You want me to forgive you?"

"This young and healthy body has given me a fresh outlook on life." He kissed Lyssa on her forehead before he gently placed her back into her cradle. "Your pregnancy was impossibly swift, wasn't it? Magically so, I'd say."

When he turned to face Lucia again, she struck him hard across his face.

So hard that her hand stung from the blow.

Kyan's brown eyes flashed with blue light, and he wiped the trickle of blood at the corner of his mouth with his thumb.

"Don't ever do that again," he hissed.

Lucia fisted her hand, appalled at her own lack of control. But she'd needed to strike him, needed to try to hurt him.

And she'd made him bleed.

Kyan didn't bleed. In his former body—that of a fellow immortal Melenia had chosen to be his original shell a small eternity ago—she'd watched as his hand was impaled by a dagger. It had been a bloodless injury that had healed in moments.

If he bled, that meant that he was vulnerable.

His gaze narrowed on the amber orb still in her grip.

"You know what I can do," Lucia said as evenly as she could. "You know I have the magic to imprison you just like Timotheus can."

It was the biggest bluff of her entire life, and she prayed that he couldn't sense her dwindling *elementia*.

"I didn't come here for a confrontation," he said simply.

"Funny how seeing you holding my daughter after sneaking into the palace feels very much like a confrontation to me."

Kyan shook his head. "It's unfortunate that we've come to this, little sorceress. We got along very well for a time. You helped me and I helped you until our unfortunate disagreement."

"You turned into a monster made of fire and tried to kill me."

"Not a monster, little sorceress. A god. And you should know, your grandmother's magic was a pale comparison to yours. She failed in doing what I needed her to do."

Lucia took a breath, tried to remain in control of her erratic emotions. "I heard."

Kyan's gaze flicked to the orb again. "Olivia is close by. If anything happens to me, anything at all, she will summon an earthquake great enough to send this kingdom and everyone in it into the sea, like nothing more than a tiny pebble cast into a deep pond."

She wondered if he too was bluffing. If he was weak and vulnerable, the earth Kindred could be the same, despite being within the shell of an immortal Watcher.

Finally, she pocketed the orb. "Say what you came here to say."

He nodded, then ran a hand through his messy red hair. "I need to apologize for my treatment of you, little sorceress. And then I need to ask for your help."

Lucia almost laughed out loud at this.

First Cleo, and now Kyan.

It had been quite a day so far.

"Go on," she said.

Kyan frowned and turned toward the balcony. "All I wanted was to be reunited with my siblings—flesh and blood, unlike we've ever existed together before. Free from our prisons to experience what it means to truly exist. And yes, I still believe this world is flawed. And yes, I would still burn it to ash and begin again." He spared a glance at her. "But I would be satisfied simply to rule over this imperfect world. And you could be my most trusted advisor."

Ah, so he'd decided to be "charming" Kyan again. The same one who'd lulled her into the belief that she could be friends with a god.

"Is that all?" she replied drily. "You just want to rule the world."

"Yes."

"And for that, you need my magic."

"Even if your grandmother hadn't been killed, the ritual she partially performed still wasn't right." He stared down at his hands. The triangle symbol for fire magic was visible on his palm, but pale like an old scar.

She frowned. "What's not right about it?"

"Nothing has been right since my awakening. Melenia intervened, as she always did. She helped me take form more than a millennium ago, and I suppose she felt herself knowledgeable enough to do it again when the time came. I woke in my former body without your direct intervention. I'm certain she sent one of her slaves to raise me with his or her blood—strengthened by the massacre of the battle I awoke to—far weaker than I should have been. Far weaker than if you'd done it yourself as it was meant to be."

Lucia fell silent, allowing Kyan to speak. She had wanted to know this since the beginning, why she had been able to see his location on the glowing map of Mytica during the location spell with Alexius, but she'd sensed that he was already awake.

Idiotic Melenia, allowing her impatience to be reunited with her lover to taint her decisions.

Perhaps Lucia should thank Melenia for her impatience, though. It had kept the fire god from awakening as powerful as he could have been.

"Tell me, how are Cleiona and Taran?" Kyan asked after falling silent for a moment, seemingly lost in his own thoughts.

"Fine," she lied.

He sent an amused look at her. "I find that hard to believe."

"They seem fine to me. Totally in control of themselves and their bodies . . . unlike Nic and Olivia. It only shows me even more how my grandmother failed you."

"She certainly did," he agreed.

"Perhaps they will learn to channel the magic within them as well as I can."

"You think so, do you?"

"Sure." It was what Cleo said she wanted—to control her magic.

Kyan shook his head. "Cleiona and Taran cannot control what doesn't belong to them. And if they try, they will fail and die." He turned to lock gazes with her. "But I think you know this already."

Lucia tried so hard not to react, but she felt the truth of what Kyan said deep in her gut. "How do I save them?"

"You can't. Their lives are forfeit. Their bodies have already been claimed by my siblings."

"Then find other bodies, if you must." Her heart pounded hard as she resisted what he said. "Is that even possible?"

Impatience flickered in his brown eyes. "You aren't listening to me, little sorceress. I am offering you the chance to salvage what is left of this world, to join with me and my siblings as we become all-powerful."

"With my help," she reminded him. "With my magic."

Magic she didn't currently possess at even a fraction of the strength she needed.

She couldn't help him even if she wanted to.

"Everything was so perfectly aligned that night," he said with annoyance. "The sacrifices, the storm, the location. It should have worked. But nothing worth having comes easily, does it? I need you to perform the ritual again, little sorceress—with your blood, with your magic. Fix what your grandmother began."

Of course this was why he needed her. It was not to apologize and make amends. It was to gain ultimate power.

"When?" she whispered. "Do you want me to perform the ritual now? Will you threaten to kill everyone in this palace if I refuse?"

"You do despise me, don't you?" His jaw clenched. "No, I will not make any further threats today. I don't want it to be that way between us anymore. All I need from you right now is a promise to help us."

"And if I refuse?"

He sent a dark look toward her. "If you refuse, Cleiona and Taran will suffer greatly before they finally lose their fight against my siblings. The air and water Kindred will take control of their new shells. It's only a matter of days. Then—even if it's at a slightly lesser level than I'd planned—the Kindred will be reunited. And we will cause great pain and damage to this world that you value, little sorceress. You've seen what I can do, even at a fraction of my true strength, haven't you?"

Suddenly Lucia could barely breathe, remembering the many villages he'd set ablaze. The screams of his victims.

The screams of *her* victims.

"When?" she asked again, her voice barely audible.

A smile touched his lips, erasing the serious look he'd had a moment before. "Pardon me for being vague, little sorceress, but you'll know when. You are a part of this—your magic, Eva's magic. It's been a part of this from the very beginning."

Lucia squeezed her eyes shut, wanting to block him out by any means necessary.

"You've said what you came here to say," she whispered. "Now please leave."

"Very well. Oh, and please don't blame the nursemaid for leaving the room. She trusts this face. Many do. It's a good face, don't you think? Nicolo is not nearly as tall and conventionally handsome as my prior form, but I'm quite partial to his freckles." He paused, as if waiting for a reply. When none came, he continued. "I will see you soon, little sorceress."

Kyan left the room without another word, and all she could do was watch him go. When he was out of sight, she rushed to the side of the cradle.

Lyssa was fast asleep.

CHAPTER 13

MAGNUS

AURANOS

"I don't think you understand," Magnus said to the green-uniformed Kraeshian guard at the palace gates. "I am Prince Magnus Damora."

The guard pursed his lips, casting an appraising look over the length of him.

"I'll admit, you do bear a striking resemblance to the portraits I've seen of him," he replied. "But the real Prince Magnus is dead."

"Clearly, you're new around here." Magnus glanced at Ashur, who wore the hood of his gray cloak over his head to keep his face from view.

Ashur just shrugged.

No help there.

"I demand an audience with King Gaius," Magnus said with as much royal dignity as he had left. "Who is *my father*. We'll leave the determination of the status of my existence to him, shall we?"

The guard sighed and waved the pair through.

"He likely doesn't care if he just allowed a potential assassin access to the palace grounds," Ashur muttered to Magnus.

Likely not.

Upon entrance into the palace itself, they found themselves in a vast, seemingly endless hallway, every column along its length chiseled with artistic perfection.

Some said the palace had existed in this very place when the goddess Cleiona ruled. Someone had to be blamed for importing this much annoyingly white marble into Mytica.

"Frankly, I'm surprised your sister didn't take my father's life when she had the chance," Magnus said, his voice now echoing against the marble walls.

"I'm surprised too," Ashur replied. "It's very unlike her."

They encountered a guard who wore red as they walked.

"Where is the king?" Magnus asked him.

The guard's eyes widened. "Your highness! I'd heard that you were—"

"Dead?" Magnus finished for him. "Yes, that seems to be the general consensus. Where's my father?"

The guard bowed. "The throne room, your highness."

He felt the guard's surprised gaze on him as he and Ashur continued down the corridor.

"Limerians and Kraeshians working side by side," he said under his breath. "How friendly."

"Amara has no further interest in Mytica," Ashur said. "I'd be surprised if this occupation lasts more than another month before she requires the full strength of her army at the next place she plans to conquer."

"Let's not count it as a victory until it actually happens."

"No, definitely not."

Ashur thought it best that Magnus see his father by himself.

Magnus agreed. The pair parted ways as the hallway forked into two directions.

The tall doors to the throne room appeared before Magnus, and he came to a halt, taking a deep breath into his lungs. Nervously, he twisted the heavy golden ring on his left hand as he summoned the courage he hadn't thought he'd need today.

Finally, he stepped forward and pushed the doors open.

The king sat upon the throne, a position Magnus had seen him in—here and in Limeros—a thousand times before. There were six men at the bottom of the stairs leading up to the royal dais, each holding a piece of parchment.

The business of a kingdom must continue, he thought. *In good times and in bad.*

King Gaius looked up, and his eyes locked with Magnus's. He stood up so quickly that the silver goblet he held clattered to the floor.

Then he looked down at the men. "Leave," he said. "Now."

They didn't argue. Collectively, they filed past Magnus and swiftly exited the room.

"Don't let me interrupt," Magnus said, his heart pounding hard.

"You're here," the king said, his voice hushed. "You're actually here."

"I am."

"So it worked."

Magnus knew exactly what he meant. He touched the ring, then pulled it off of his finger. "It did."

His father drew closer, his face pale as he inspected Magnus, walking an entire circle around him. "I had held hope for so long that the bloodstone's magic might save you, but that hope had faded completely."

"It seems that everyone believes me dead," Magnus said.

"Yes." The king drew in a shaky breath. "We know Kurtis buried you alive. And that he tortured you first. But you're right here in front of me. Not a spirit, not a dream. You're here, and you're alive."

Magnus's throat constricted, and he found himself at a loss for what to say, what to think. He didn't realize it would be this difficult. "I'm surprised you seem to care. It's not as if you haven't attempted to send me to my grave long before Kurtis did."

"I fully deserve that."

Magnus held the ring out to him. "This is yours."

The king didn't reach for the ring. Instead, he embraced his son so tightly that it became difficult for Magnus to breathe.

"Unexpected," Magnus managed. "Quite unexpected."

"I have failed you as a father so many times that I've lost count." Gaius gripped Magnus's face between his hands. "But you're here. You're alive. And now I have the chance to try to make amends to you."

"This certainly helped." Magnus indicated the ring again. "Take it back now. It belongs to you."

King Gaius shook his head. "No. It's yours now."

Magnus frowned. "Don't you need it?"

"Look at me," the king said. "I have recovered from my afflictions. I have no need for the bloodstone's magic anymore. I feel strong—stronger than I have in many years and ready to rule again . . . with your assistance, if you'll give it to me."

Magnus swallowed hard. "I will. Of course I will."

"I'm very glad to hear that."

"I heard what happened with the ritual," Magnus said when he found his voice again. "Is Cleo all right? Is she suffering at all?"

King Gaius pursed his lips, his expression souring. "She seems as fine as possible, given the situation. You've heard about every-thing? About your grandmother?"

He nodded again. "Ashur found me and told me what hap-pened. Where is Cleo now?"

"Likely shoving her unwelcome nose into the private affairs of others," the king muttered.

After worrying about her safety for days, this was an incred-ible relief. "And Kurtis?"

"I have a search in progress for him," the king said. "He hasn't been spotted in days, but I feel he may return to the palace to see his father."

"Lord Gareth is here?"

"He was." The king paused. "Lucia has returned to us. If she hadn't, I doubt that Amara would have allowed us to leave without difficulty."

Magnus's mind went blank for a moment. "Lucia . . . is here?"

"Yes." Gaius's gaze shifted past Magnus. "Actually, she's stand-ing right behind you."

His breath catching in his chest, Magnus turned slowly around.

Lucia stood, framed by the throne room's doors, her eyes as wide as saucers.

"Magnus?" she whispered. "I—I saw you dead. I *felt* it in my very soul. But you're here. You're alive."

The last time he'd seen her, she'd been aligned with the fire Kindred, searching for magical stone wheels on the Limerian pal-ace grounds. She had been cruel, quick to violence, and she had used his love for her as a weapon to manipulate and wound him.

But when Kyan had tried to kill Magnus, Lucia saved his life.

Despite Magnus's claims that his sister would return, that she wasn't continuing to help Kyan, in his heart he had honestly thought he'd never see her again.

But here she was.

Magnus tentatively moved toward Lucia, half of him on guard for something horrible to happen. But nothing did.

Her eyes were filled with tears as she gazed up at him.

"I'm alive," he confirmed.

"I—I'm sorry," she blurted then, the tears spilling to her cheeks. "I'm so, so sorry for everything I've done!"

He almost laughed at such a surprising and uncharacteristic outburst. "No . . . no apologies, please. Not today, my beautiful sister. The fact that you're here with us again after everything that's—" His voice dropped off as he suddenly realized that there was a strange bundle in his sister's arms.

A baby.

"Who is that?" he asked, stunned.

She gazed down at the infant, a smile touching her lips. "This is my daughter," she said as she pulled the blanket away from the baby's face. "Your niece."

His niece.

Lucia had a baby.

A baby girl.

Exactly *how* long had he been trapped in that grave?

"How?" was all he managed to blurt out in reply.

"How?" She grimaced. "I really hope I don't have to explain such things to you."

"Alexius."

She nodded.

Magnus squeezed his eyes shut, fighting against the hot wave of rage that threatened to hit him.

"I'd kill him if he weren't already dead," he growled.

"I know."

Magnus glanced at his father.

"Lyssa is going to be a very special young woman one day," he said.

Clearly, the king had had much more time to come to terms with this world-jarring revelation.

"Lyssa, is it?" Magnus touched the soft blanket and looked into the baby's blue eyes. Blue like Lucia's eyes. "Well, she's gorgeous, but how could she be anything but?"

Lucia touched his hand. "Magnus, how did you survive?"

Before he could answer, he noticed that she was staring down at his ring.

"What magic is this?" she asked breathlessly. "I've never felt anything like it before."

"The bloodstone," the king said.

"This is the bloodstone? It is dark magic—the darkest I've ever felt."

"Yes, I'm sure it is. And it's the only thing that saved both your brother's life and my own. For that, and only that, we can thank your grandmother."

"This must have been what I felt," Lucia whispered. "This dark-ness . . . this feeling of death surrounding this ring. I don't like it."

"Perhaps not, but without this piece of dark magic, your brother and I would both be dead," the king said solemnly. "Magnus, I'm very glad you arrived today. I plan to give a speech at midday tomorrow to show that I am again in power here and that Amara has abandoned her new kingdom. I need the citizens of this city to believe in me."

"First time for everything," Magnus countered.

"I want you by my side. And Lucia as well."

"Of course," Magnus said without hesitation. He turned to Lucia. "We will talk more soon."

"Why not now?" she asked.

"I need to find Cleo. Where is she?"

"Currently? I have no idea. But she can't be far." Lucia appeared as if she wanted to argue against his plans, but she closed her mouth and nodded instead. "Go find her."

Magnus was already halfway out the door.

CHAPTER 14

CLEO

AURANOS

If Lucia couldn't—or wouldn't—help her, then she had to help herself.

Cleo decided to scour the library for more books on Kindred magic and on any record of the goddess Valoria in particular. The goddess had water magic within her. By all accounts, she had been considered the embodiment of this magic.

Cleo had come to learn that Valoria had been a greedy Watcher, one who'd stolen the crystal orbs from the Sanctuary. By touching them with her bare hands, she'd become corrupted by them.

Corrupted, Cleo thought as she studied the squiggling lines on her left palm. What a strange word to use for being possessed by an elemental god.

Valoria and Cleiona were enemies, and in a final fight to gain ultimate power, they had destroyed each other. At least that was how the legend went.

She studied an illustration of the goddess drawn by the scribe of the first book about Valoria she'd taken from the library.

The symbols of earth and water magic were on her palms. She had dark flowing hair, a beautiful heart-shaped face, a glowing crown upon her head. The gown she wore in this picture was low enough in the front that it showed off half of the spiral marking on her chest. It wasn't the same spiral that Taran bore that linked him to the air Kindred; this was different, more complex in shape. Cleo now knew this marked Valoria as a Watcher before she'd become a goddess.

As she flipped through the pages, she glanced down at the goblet of peach cider Nerissa had brought her.

"I froze the guard, I can make it rain, I can coat walls with ice," Cleo whispered to herself. "Surely I can do something with this cider. Simple magic. Something to show me I have a chance to control this."

Her heart now pounding, she held the goblet in her hand and focused on the liquid within. She willed it to freeze within its container.

She concentrated until perspiration broke out on her forehead, but nothing happened.

Finally, she slammed the goblet down on a nearby table and let out a small shriek of frustration as its contents splashed over the side. But her scream was cut short by a sensation she'd become entirely too familiar with.

That of a wave of water flowing over her, covering her eyes, her nose, her mouth.

She was drowning.

"No . . ." She staggered backward until she felt the cool stone wall at her back. She pressed her hands against it as she forced herself to take slow, even breaths.

This wasn't real. She was fine, she wasn't drowning, she wasn't dying.

Cleo looked down at her hand to see that the water magic symbol glowed with blue light, and more vein-like lines branched out from the ones already there. The marking now wrapped around her entire hand and forearm.

A chill of dread went through her at the sight of it, and she had a sudden, painful realization of what it might be.

The water Kindred, slowly working its way to the forefront of Cleo's consciousness.

Fighting Cleo for control of her own body.

Cleo burst from her room, needing to be somewhere, anywhere else. She moved down the hallways of the palace so swiftly she nearly got lost as she tried to find the exit back into the courtyard.

Finally outside, she managed to take in great gulps of fresh, sweet air.

Something moved beyond the trees, and she heard the sound of metal clashing. Alarmed, she drew closer to see what or who it was.

She let out a sigh of relief.

Jonas and Felix were practicing their swordplay under the shade of the arched pavilion in the center of the courtyard.

"You're getting rusty," Felix said. He was bare-chested, his muscles flexing as he thrust his sword forward. "Haven't fought in a while?"

Also shirtless and with his back to Cleo, Jonas managed to block the move with a grunt. "Not with a sword."

"You've been relying on your new girlfriend to save your arse with her fancy magic. It's making you soft."

"Princess Lucia is not my girlfriend," Jonas growled.

Felix smirked at him. "Don't worry, I won't challenge you for her. I'm through with complicated women with too much power to wield. She's all yours."

"I don't want her."

"Whatever you say." Felix snorted. "I think we're done for today. You might want to put on your shirt before anyone gets a glimpse of your little secret."

"Good point." Jonas grabbed a white shirt from the ground nearby, pulling it on over his arms. When he turned, Cleo saw exactly what Felix referred to.

Jonas's little secret was a mark on his chest.

The spiral mark of a Watcher.

For a moment, she couldn't move, couldn't think. But then Cleo forced herself to follow them out of the courtyard and back into the palace, still unseen by either of them.

They parted ways at a branch in the hallway.

Cleo followed Jonas, hurrying to keep up with his long strides. She followed him right out of the palace and into the City of Gold.

Where was he headed?

As she followed him through the winding streets, she wracked her brain, trying to remember if she'd ever seen that marking before—or if she'd ever seen him without his shirt on.

She had—in the Wildlands, when he'd kidnapped her in a rebel plot to coerce King Gaius into stopping construction of his Imperial Road. Instead, the king had sent swarms of his soldiers out to search for the princess he'd betrothed to his son in hopes of ingratiating the Damora family with their new Auranian citizens.

Jonas had been injured—shot with an arrow. He'd needed Cleo's assistance to bandage the wound.

There had been no mark on his chest then.

The rebel left the walled city entirely, a bow and quiver of arrows slung over his shoulder. Cleo pulled up the hood of her cloak, staying far enough behind him so as not to be noticed.

He took a pathway toward an inlet the ship that had brought

him and the others to Auranos had sailed past on their way to the palace docks. He walked as if he knew exactly where he was going. As if he'd been there before.

It was a small, secluded cove that Cleo and her sister had visited regularly in simpler times, one shielded by a steep cliff. From the small sandy beach, they would watch ships pass by on their way to and from the palace docks.

Waves lapped against the shore of the wide canal, so wide that Cleo could barely see the other side of it. Seabirds waded in the shallow shore water, hunting for food.

Carefully navigating the pathway down to the cove itself, she watched as Jonas paused, aimed his bow and arrow, and let it go. Jonas swore under his breath as a fat rabbit scampered away.

He was the guest of King Gaius with a banquet of food ready from dawn to dusk . . . and he was hunting rabbits.

"Watch your step, princess," Jonas said without looking up at her.

She froze in place.

"Yes, I know you've been following me since we left the palace," he said.

Feeling oddly exposed, Cleo joined Jonas on the small sandy beach with her head held high. "Why are you hunting rabbits?"

"Because hunting rabbits makes me feel normal," he replied. "Wouldn't that be nice? To feel normal again?"

"Perhaps." She scratched her left arm that bore the twisting, vine-like blue lines. "Please don't kill anything. Not today. There's no need for it."

Jonas paused, giving her a sidelong look. "Do I have to explain to you where the meat on your dinner plate comes from?"

Cleo took a deep breath and let it out slowly. "Why do you have the mark of a Watcher on your chest?"

He didn't speak for a moment, but he put his bow and arrow down on the sandy ground and looked out onto the calm water.

"You saw that," he said.

She nodded. "I saw you and Felix in the courtyard."

"I see. And now you have questions," he said, turning to face her.

"Only the one, really," she admitted.

Jonas rubbed his chest absently. "I'm not a Watcher, if that's what you're thinking. But it seems like I have this well of magic inside me—one I can't easily access no matter how hard I try."

"I know a little of what that's like."

"Yes, I'm sure you do." Jonas turned to stare out at the crystal-blue water. "An immortal named Phaedra gave her life to save mine a while back, just after she'd healed me a moment from death. I've been told that I . . . absorbed her magic. I don't understand it. I don't know why, only that it happened. And then Olivia healed me too, and . . ." He shook his head. "And that original magic acted like a sponge, soaking up more and more. Soon after that, the mark appeared."

"Oh," Cleo said. "That actually makes sense."

He laughed. "Perhaps to you it does."

"But you say you can't use this magic."

"No." His gaze moved to the markings on her arm. "What is the plan, princess?"

Cleo looked up at him, startled. "The plan?"

"The plan to fix all of this."

"I honestly don't know." She studied him for a moment in silence. "Show me your mark."

He hesitated at first before he slowly unbuttoned the front of his shirt. She moved closer to him, placing her hand on his skin and feeling his heartbeat as she looked up at him.

"My mark glows sometimes," she said.

He looked down at her hand before he met her gaze fully. "Lucky you."

A smile tugged at her lips. Jonas could always make her smile.

"Oh, yes, so lucky."

"I have no illusions about your feelings for me anymore, princess," he said. "I know you loved him, that you mourn him. And I'm sorry for your loss. It will be a very long time before that pain goes away."

Cleo's throat had quickly become so thick that it was impossible to respond with anything except a nod.

Jonas tentatively reached for her hand. When she didn't pull away from him, he took it in his and squeezed it. "I am here for you, princess. Today and always. And you need to find a way to control this magic within you by any means possible."

"I know," she replied. "I asked Lucia to help me."

His gaze flicked to hers again. "And what did she say?"

"She said she'd try."

His brow furrowed. "I should check on her. I haven't seen her yet today."

"How strange to think that the two of you have become friends."

"Very strange," Jonas agreed. His gaze held an intensity then, and for a moment Cleo was certain he was going to say more to her. His hand brushed against the sheath at his waist, and she saw the golden hilt of a dagger.

"Do you still have Aron's horrible dagger?" she asked. "After all this time?"

Jonas pulled his hand away from the weapon. "I need to go back to the palace now. Are you coming?"

Cleo turned to the canal to see that a ship was passing in the distance on its way from the palace to the Silver Sea.

"Not yet. I'll be back shortly. Go, check on Lucia. But promise me something . . ."

"Yes?"

"Don't kill any rabbits."

"I promise you," he said solemnly. "No harm will come to a single Auranian rabbit today."

With one more glance back at her, Jonas left Cleo there in the sandy cove.

Alone on the beach, Cleo walked toward the water, which lapped at her golden sandals. She focused all her attention on the ocean, trying to feel some sort of affinity with it since it matched the magic within her.

But she felt nothing here. No sense of drowning. No desire to walk into the salty water until it covered her from head to toe.

She tentatively looked down at the mark on her hand and its branching blue lines.

She didn't want to be tentative or frightened. She wanted to be strong.

He would want her to be strong.

I miss him so much, she thought as her eyes began to burn. *Please, please let me think of him and let that memory make me stronger.*

Cleo wasn't even sure whom she prayed to anymore, but she still prayed.

"Well, that was quite a romantic sight, wasn't it? The rebel and the princess, together again in their mutual admiration."

"And now I'm imagining his voice," she whispered.

His jealous, angry voice.

"I'll let it be your choice entirely, princess. Shall I kill him slowly or quickly?"

Now Cleo frowned.

He sounded so real—far more real than any fantasy.

Cleo turned around slowly to see the tall, broad-shouldered figment of her imagination standing no more than three paces away from her. Scowling.

"I know I should be concerned about your situation." Magnus gestured toward her. "My wife, the water goddess. And even before I'd learned what had happened, I'd been beside myself in my haste to get back to you, thinking you might be Kurtis's prisoner by now."

She gaped at him. "Magnus?"

"And I am deeply, painfully concerned—don't think I'm not. But to follow you here from the palace only to see you with Jonas Agallon," he growled. "It's not all right with me."

She could barely form thoughts, let alone words. "Nothing happened."

"It didn't look like nothing."

Tears splashed to her cheeks. "You're alive."

The remainder of the fury faded from his brown eyes. "I am."

"And you're here right in front of me."

"Yes." His gaze fell to her left hand and the marks from her ongoing internal battle with the water Kindred. "Oh, Cleo . . ."

With a ragged sob, she threw herself into his arms. He lifted her off the ground to embrace her tightly against his chest.

"I thought you were dead," Cleo sobbed. "Lucia—she saw it. She did a location spell and sensed you were dead, and I . . ." She rested her head against his shoulder. "Oh, Magnus, I love you. And I've missed you so much I thought I might die from it. But you're here."

"I love you too," he whispered. "I love you so much."

"I know."

"Good."

Then he crushed his mouth against hers, kissing her hard, stealing her breath and giving her life at the same time.

"I knew you'd be fine, no matter what," he said to her when their lips parted. "You're the bravest and strongest girl I've ever known in my life."

Cleo ran her hands over his face, his jaw, his throat, wanting to prove to herself that this was real and not just a dream. "I'm sorry, Magnus."

He finally placed her back down on the sandy ground, holding her gaze intensely. "For what?"

"It seems I'm apologizing a lot today, but I have to. I'm sorry that I lied to you, that I hurt you. I'm sorry I blamed you for everything horrible that happened. I'm sorry that I didn't see how much I loved you from the very beginning." She wiped at her tear-filled eyes. "Well . . . not the *very* beginning."

"No," he allowed with a wince. "Certainly not."

"The past is forgotten." She placed her hands against his chest, reveling in the feel of him—solid and alive. And here. "Know only this: I love you with all my heart, all my soul." Her voice broke on the raw truth in her words. "That losing you destroyed me, and I never, never, ever want to feel that way again."

Magnus stared down at her now, as if shocked by the intensity of her words. "Cleo . . ."

Cleo pulled his face down so his lips could meet hers again. And it was as if the thousand-pound weight that had been attached to her ankle for more than a week, pulling her further into the depths of the ocean, drowning her slowly and painfully, had finally released.

His kiss was everything. So deep and true and perfect.

Magnus picked her up again, his strong arms easily holding her weight as he moved away from the edge of the water.

"I've missed you so much," he breathed against her lips as he pressed her up against the side of the cliff so she could feel every line, every edge of his body against hers. "I swear I will make it up to you, all the horrible things I've said and done. My beautiful Cleiona . . . say it again, what you said just now."

She almost smiled. "I think you heard me."

"Don't tease," he growled, his gaze intense. "Say it again."

"I love you, Magnus. Truly and madly. Forever and ever," she whispered, hungry for his kiss again. Starving for it. "And I need you . . . Now. Here."

She'd already begun to loosen the ties of his shirt, desperate to feel his bare skin against hers with no barrier between them.

His mouth was on hers again, desperate and hungry. Magnus groaned deep in his throat as Cleo ran her fingernails up his chest, pulling his shirt over his shoulders. He slid his hands beneath the edge of her embroidered skirt before he froze, his lips parting from hers.

A deep frown creased his brow. "Damn it."

"What's wrong?" she asked.

"We can't do this," he whispered.

A breath caught in her chest. "Why not?"

"The curse."

For a moment, Cleo had no idea what he meant. But then she remembered, and a small smile parted her lips. "There is no curse."

"What?"

"Your grandmother made that story up to deceive your father, to explain why my mother died in childbirth. But it's not true. There's no witch's curse on me. It was all a lie."

Magnus didn't move. He studied her for several moments as he held her, pressed up against the cliff's side, their faces at the same level—eye to eye.

"No curse," he whispered, and his lips curved into a smile.

"None at all."

"And the Kindred magic within you . . ."

"It's a big problem, but not at this exact moment."

"So we can deal with it later."

She nodded. "Yes, later."

"Are you certain?"

"Completely certain."

"Good."

This time when Magnus kissed her, there was no restraint. No stopping or waiting, no doubt or fear. There was only this exquisite moment that Cleo wanted to last forever, finally reunited with her dark prince.

CHAPTER 15

MAGNUS

AURANOS

Magnus knew they should have returned to the palace hours ago.

But they hadn't.

Instead, they watched the sun sink into the horizon in the west, turning the sky shades of purple, pink, and orange.

"I like it here," he said, his fingers threaded into Cleo's long golden hair. "It's officially my favorite place in all of Auranos. And this rock at my back . . . my favorite rock in all of Mytica."

Cleo nodded, nestling closer to his side. "It's a good rock."

He took her left hand in his, tracing the blue lines that spread from the water magic symbol on her palm. "I don't like this."

"Neither do I."

"But you said you're in no distress."

"I said it. I meant it. But . . ."

"But what?"

"But . . ." she began. "It is a problem."

"An understatement, certainly."

"I want to figure out how to use this water magic, but I can't. It doesn't work that way. At least, not that I've discovered yet."

Magnus remembered stumbling through the forest that dark night, coming upon the campfire of the fire Kindred.

"I saw Kyan," he said.

Cleo gasped and pulled away so that she could look into his eyes. "When?"

"After . . . the grave." He'd already told her some of what he'd gone through, not wanting to dwell on the darker moments. She knew his father had given him the bloodstone and that if he hadn't, Magnus would be only a memory now. "He let me believe he was still Nic for a while, like he was toying with me. He wanted me to tell you that when he arrives, you need to join him. I would have torn him apart right then, but he looked so much like Nic . . ."

"He is Nic," Cleo said, her voice pained. "For a moment, right after it happened, I nearly stabbed him in the heart—even knowing it would kill Nic. I wasn't thinking straight. I'm so grateful that Ashur stopped me."

That sounded like something the Kraeshian prince would do. "Of course he did."

"I'll never go with Kyan," she said, shaking her head. "Not for any reason."

Magnus's chest tightened at the thought of losing her. "He was going to brand me, somehow, making me into his slave with magic so I'd do as he said. He reached for me and . . . stopped. Something stopped him, and it gave me the chance to escape."

"What was it?" she asked, breathless.

He tried to remember that dark night full of pain and confusion. "I don't know. I thought it might have been Ashur, that he'd found some magic to fight against the Kindred, but it wasn't him. Still, something helped me get away."

"Could it have been Nic himself? Fighting against Kyan somehow?"

"Possibly," he allowed. But the more he thought about it, the more he wondered if it could have something to do with the bloodstone. Lucia had been repelled by its magic.

Perhaps Kyan felt the same.

Still, Cleo, with the water Kindred within her, seemed fine being close to him with this kind of magic—dark magic, as Lucia called it—on his finger.

Cleo shook her head. "To think, our troubles used to consist of a battle for the throne. It seems so inconsequential now."

"Well, I wouldn't say entirely inconsequential," he said. "It will be nice when every trace of Amara Cortas leaves this kingdom."

"I forgot all about her for a moment."

"So did I." He kissed her forehead, threading his fingers through her sun-warmed, silky hair. "We will find a way to save Nic, I promise we will. You and Nic and Olivia and even Taran." He grimaced. "If we must."

Cleo laughed nervously, burying her face against Magnus's chest. "Taran is trying to be strong, but I know he's terrified about losing control of his life like this."

"I have no doubt that he is." Magnus knew he'd feel exactly the same.

He watched the sun sink further over the water. There was very little daylight left. They had to face reality again, far too soon.

"Best slip your gown on before Agallon strolls back here looking for you and gets far too much of an eyeful of my beautiful wife." Magnus reached to the side and grabbed his shirt. "Wouldn't want to break his heart any further by seeing you like this with me. Although . . . come to think of it, I'd be all right with that. Final nail in the coffin, if you'll excuse the expression."

"Jonas is a good person," Cleo said firmly as she dressed.

He watched her with great appreciation, every move, every gesture. "Stellar. Of course he is."

"He cares a great deal about Lucia."

Magnus made a sour face. "Don't even put that potential pairing into my mind. I have enough foul dreams to deal with as it is."

Magnus stood up and took Cleo's face between his hands so he could kiss her again. He knew he would never tire of the taste of her lips—a near magical mix of strawberries, salt water, and the individual and intoxicating taste of Cleiona Bellos herself.

Far more delicious than even the finest and sweetest vintage of Paelsian wine.

She reached up to stroke the dark hair off his forehead, then traced her fingertips slowly along his scar to his lips. "Marry me, Magnus."

His eyebrows shot up. "We're already married."

"I know."

"You can't possibly forget that day in the temple, can you? The earthquake? The screaming and blood and death? The vows forced upon you under threat of torture and pain?"

Cleo's expression turned haunted, and he regretted reminding her of that horrible day.

"That was no proper wedding," she said, shaking her head.

"I agree." A smile touched his lips. "Actually, that was one of my fantasies while in that hateful coffin: marrying you under the blue sky of Auranos in a field of beautiful flowers."

She let out a small laugh at that. "A field of beautiful flowers? Clearly you must have been hallucinating."

"Clearly." Magnus pulled her to him, gentler now, as if afraid she might break. "We will live through this, my princess. All of this. And then, yes, I will marry you properly."

"Promise?" she asked, a tremor in her voice.

"I promise," he replied firmly. "And until then, I have faith in my sister that she will end Kyan and find a solution to this hateful magic inside of you."

Magnus and Cleo returned to the palace slightly disheveled, but determined to find a solution to the long list of problems that plagued them.

After Magnus had heard the twentieth "I thought you were dead" comment, he chose to retire to his chambers with his beautiful wife.

And there they discussed every moment that had passed for each of them since they last saw each other.

Cleo slid her fingers over the golden ring on Magnus's left hand. "I hate your father. I always will." she said, just before she fell asleep in his arms. "But I will be eternally grateful to him for this."

Yes. The bloodstone definitely complicated his already complicated feelings for the man who had made his life far more painful than it should have been.

Perhaps tomorrow, the king's speech would mark the beginning of a new chapter in their lives as father and son.

Magnus knew he, himself, had changed so much over the last year. Change could happen—if one wanted it to.

Perhaps there was room for hope.

The next morning, they lingered far too long in their sleeping chambers, taking breakfast there instead of joining King Gaius and Lucia.

And Lyssa.

Magnus still could not believe his sister had an infant daughter, but he knew he could accept it. He already loved Lyssa and knew he would do anything to protect his newborn niece.

As Magnus lay in bed, he propped himself up on his elbow

to watch as Cleo pulled on her slip and fiddled with the laces, expecting at any moment for her to ask him for assistance.

But then she froze in place.

Her eyes locked on the wall in front of her, and her mouth twisted in pain.

Magnus jumped up and grasped hold of her shoulders.

"What's happening?" he demanded.

"D-drowning," she managed. "I—I feel like I'm . . . drowning."

His gaze shot to her right hand, to the vine of blue lines spreading from the water magic symbol. Before his very eyes, the lines traveled up higher along her skin, encircling her upper arm.

"No," he said, panic clawing at his chest. "You're not drowning. You're here with me, and everything is fine. Don't let this overwhelm you."

"I—I'm trying."

"And you, water Kindred"—he stared fiercely into her blue-green eyes—"if you can hear me, you need to release your hold on Cleo, if that's what this is. I will destroy you. I will destroy all of you. I swear it."

Cleo collapsed in his arms, gasping for breath like she'd just come up from the depths of the ocean.

"It's passed," she managed a moment later. "I'm fine."

"You're not fine. *This* is not fine," he snarled back at her, the pain of being unable to save her from this nearly unbearable. "This is as far from fine as anything that has ever been!"

She righted herself, pushing away from him and quickly donning the dark blue gown she'd chosen to wear today. "We have to go . . . your father's speech. He needs you there."

"I'll get Nerissa to attend to you. You don't have to be on the balcony with us."

"I want to be there." She met his gaze, and he could see the strength in her eyes, along with the frustration. "By your side. So everyone can see us together."

"But—"

"I insist, Magnus. Please."

He nodded, grudgingly in agreement, and placed a hand on her back, guiding her out of the room to join his father and Lucia in the throne room.

"So nice of you to join us," the king said thinly.

"We were . . . otherwise occupied," Magnus replied.

"Yes, I'm sure you were." His attention moved to Cleo. "You look well."

Cleo met his gaze directly. "I am well."

"Good."

"I wish you the greatest luck with your speech," she said, a steady smile on her face. "I know how much the Auranian people love a good speech from their beloved king. Your recent . . . decisions with Amara will be all but forgotten, I'm sure."

Magnus shared an amused look with Lucia, one that reminded him so much of those they'd shared over the years whenever they witnessed the king say something unkind to a guest. But he always managed to say it in a way that almost sounded like a compliment.

Almost.

"Indeed," the king replied.

It seemed the king and Cleo had far more in common than Magnus ever would have thought.

From the throne room, accompanied by guards, the four took a winding staircase, located behind the dais, to the third floor and the large balcony overlooking the palace square.

The last time Magnus and Cleo had been present for a speech by the king on this very balcony, they had been betrothed, much to their mutual surprise and abject horror.

Lucia's beautiful face held pain, her blue eyes as serious as Magnus had ever seen them.

"Is there something wrong?" Magnus asked his sister as they stepped onto the balcony to the cheers of the thousands gathered below.

"What isn't wrong?" she replied quietly. "Shall I give you a list with Kyan at the very top of it?"

"Not necessary."

"Silence, both of you," the king said under his breath before he grasped hold of the marble railing and turned to the Auranians who milled below in the palace square, gazing up at the king with both interest and skepticism on their faces.

Then Gaius began to speak in a strong and powerful voice that traveled easily across the distance.

"In Limeros, our credo is: *Strength, Faith, and Wisdom*," the king began. "Three values that we believe can see us through any adversity. But today I want to talk about truth. I've come to believe it is the most valuable treasure in the world."

Magnus watched his father, unsure just what to expect from this speech. It would be unusual for the king to speak truthfully in such public appearances. Normally, he projected the illusion of a king who cared more for his people than he did for power. Not everyone knew the real reasons behind his nickname of the King of Blood.

The spell that had been cast upon Gaius Damora by his mother seventeen years ago had helped him to focus on his drive for power and the ruthlessness and deception that were necessary to keep his crown and eventually deceive Chief Basilius and crush King Corvin in a single day.

That was the only father Magnus had ever known.

"Today I also ask you all to look toward the future," the king continued. "For I believe it will be brighter than the past. I believe this because of the young people who stand with me today on this very balcony. They are the future, just as your sons and daughters are. They are our truth."

The king glanced at Magnus.

A bright future, Magnus thought. *Does he really mean this?*

King Gaius turned toward the crowd again. "Perhaps you feel that you cannot trust me. Perhaps you hate me and all I have stood for in the past. I don't blame you, not one of you, for feeling that way. I had reached an unavoidable crossroads when I chose to align with Kraeshia, leading to the occupation of Mytica these last months. Had I not made this difficult decision, there would have been war. Death. And, in the end, tremendous loss."

Magnus agreed, to a point. Still, he believed his father had been unforgivably hasty in his decision to align with the Emperor of Kraeshia and his duplicitous daughter.

Then again, there was a time not so long ago when his father suggested that Magnus marry Amara to help forge an alliance between Mytica and the empire.

To his recollection, Magnus had laughed in the king's face at the thought of it.

"What I would regret is if I allowed it to continue a day longer than necessary," the king said. "Some have come to believe that Amara Cortas represents the future of Mytica. But they are wrong.

"She has chosen to leave Mytica and return to her home, where she can be safe from the fallout from her greedy choices. More than half of her army has departed with her, with no announcement, no promises for the future. Amara Cortas's truth is that she doesn't care at all about the future of Mytica or its people. But I do."

There were murmurings of disbelief coming from the crowd now. Magnus glanced at Cleo, who had kept a pleasant, attentive smile on her lips since the speech began, as if she believed and endorsed every single word spoken by the king.

An enviable talent, indeed.

"Mytica is not only my kingdom," King Gaius said. "It is my home. It is my responsibility. And I have failed to live up to my promises, to my position as your leader, from the moment I first took the throne of Limeros. My choices for more than two decades have been fueled by my own greed and desire for power. But today begins a new era in this kingdom, one of truth."

Cleo reached for Magnus's hand and squeezed it. He realized he'd been holding his breath. His father's words were so unexpected and edged with an honesty he'd never witnessed before.

King Gaius continued: "My daughter Lucia stands with me today. There are rumors that she is a witch, one of the few I have allowed to live during my reign. Some say that makes me a hypocrite, since she is dangerous, far more dangerous than any common witch in recorded history."

Magnus tried to catch Lucia's gaze, but his sister's expression was blank, her attention fixed on something in the distance beyond the golden walls of the city. She did not share Cleo's talent for being present and poised in such a situation.

Lucia had never enjoyed being under close scrutiny. She and Magnus might not share blood, but they shared that much.

"My daughter possesses great magic, and yes, she is most certainly dangerous—dangerous to those who wish to do harm to us."

So it would seem that Lucia's secret was no longer a secret.

Magnus wondered how she felt about this revelation.

"Some won't believe me. Some will think me a bitter man whose new wife has turned her back on him and returned to her homeland. They again are wrong." The king produced a parchment from beneath his surcoat, holding it up so all could see it. "This is my agreement with Emperor Cortas, before his death, to make Mytica a part of the Kraeshian Empire. It is signed in blood. *My* blood. Signed before I married Amara as a part of this deal."

The king tore up the contract and let the pieces of parchment fall off the balcony.

A collective gasp came from the crowd.

Magnus wasn't sure how much weight this gesture held. It was, after all, a simple piece of paper. But the crowd seemed to gobble it up, every word, every gesture.

"Today I shall begin to make right what has gone so terribly wrong during my reign," the king promised. "The empress is not welcome in my kingdom, nor is her army. From this day forward, we will stand together, united against—"

Then the king fell silent.

From the far corner of the balcony, Magnus waited for him to continue, certain that all of this was a dream. A speech filled with unity and hope and grit—and quite a lot of anti-Amara sentiment, of which Magnus certainly approved.

But then Cleo's grip on Magnus's hand suddenly became painfully tight.

A single cry sounded out from the crowd, and then another. Soon, many were screaming, wailing, shouting, and pointing up at the balcony.

"Father!" Lucia gasped.

Magnus dropped Cleo's hand and raced to his father's side.

An arrow protruded from the king's chest. He looked down at it and frowned. Then, with all his strength, he gripped it and yanked it out with a loud, pained grunt.

But then another arrow hit him.

And then another.

And another.

CHAPTER 16

LUCIA

AURANOS

Four arrows. Each precisely finding its mark in her father's heart.

King Gaius collapsed to his knees and fell to his side with a heavy thud.

The life faded from his dark brown eyes.

Lucia found herself frozen with shock, unable to think or move.

Magnus frantically pulled the arrows out of the king's flesh and pressed his hands over the wounds, but it did nothing to help stanch the flow of crimson blood.

"No, you are not going to die. Not today." Magnus's hands were slick with his father's blood as he slid the bloodstone ring onto the king's finger.

Magnus then took several gulping breaths before he cast a pained look at Lucia.

"It's not working. Do something!" he shouted at her. "Heal him!"

Lucia staggered to the king's side and fell to her knees. She could sense the dark magic from the ring, the same magic that had saved both her father's and brother's lives before. The coldness of this magic repelled her. She had to force herself to get closer to it.

"What are you waiting for?" Magnus roared.

Lucia squeezed her eyes shut and tried to will earth magic into her hands—the healing magic that had saved Magnus during the battle to take Auranos when he was moments from death. Since then, she'd mended his broken leg and countless cuts and scrapes. Such magic had become second nature to her.

She sensed a trace of this valuable magic within her, but far less than a prophesied sorceress should possess.

And far less than she'd need to heal an injury as profound as this.

Lucia already knew the horrible truth: Even if she had all the magic in the universe, it wouldn't help.

Her gaze flicked to Cleo, who'd covered her mouth with her hand at the bloody sight before her, eyes wide and filled with horror. The princess came forward and put her shaky hand on Magnus's shoulder, the thin, winding blue lines visible past the lacy sleeve of her violet gown.

Magnus didn't push her away; his attention was far too fixed on Lucia.

"Well?" he demanded.

Hot tears streaked down Lucia's cheeks. "I—I'm sorry."

"What do you mean *you're sorry*?" Magnus stared down at his father's face, at his glazed, unblinking eyes. "Fix him." His voice broke. *"Please."*

"I can't," she whispered.

The king was dead.

Lucia struggled to her feet. Tears streamed down her face as she ran from the balcony to her chambers.

"Get out!" she screamed at the nursemaid.

The nursemaid rushed out the door.

Lucia moved to the cradle and looked down upon Lyssa's face, not with the love of a mother, but with blind fury.

Her eyes glowed with violet light.

"You've stolen my magic, haven't you?" she hissed.

If her *elementia* had been close to the surface, easily accessible at the merest of thoughts, Lucia might have reacted quicker—after the first arrow hit.

But her senses had become dulled, useless.

And now her father was dead because of it.

"You've destroyed everything!" she snarled at the child.

Lyssa's eyes shifted back to blue, and she looked up at her mother for a moment before she began to cry.

The sound pierced Lucia's heart, and guilt washed over her.

"I am evil," she whispered as she sank to the floor, pulling her legs up to hug them against her body. "It's my fault, all my fault. It should have been me who died today, not Father."

She stayed in that position for what felt like a very long time while Lyssa cried only an arm's reach away. After a while, Magnus came to her door.

Lucia's eyes were dry and her heart was empty of all emotion as she looked up at her brother.

"The assassin was captured before he managed to escape," Magnus said. "I've asked to personally interrogate him."

She waited, not speaking.

"I would appreciate your help, if you're willing," he said.

Yes, Lucia most definitely would be willing to interrogate their father's murderer.

She pushed herself up to her feet and accompanied Magnus out of her chambers. The nursemaid waited patiently outside, glancing nervously at Lucia.

"My apologies for my harshness," Lucia said to her.

The nursemaid bowed her head. "Not at all, your grace. My deepest condolences to you for your loss."

Silently, her heart a lead weight deep within her chest, Lucia followed Magnus through the halls of the palace, barely seeing anything to her left or right, only putting one foot in front of the other as they made their way out of the building and down to the dungeon.

The prisoner was a young man, in his early twenties. He had been placed in small room, his wrists and ankles bound in iron chains and shackled to the stone wall.

"What is your name?" Magnus asked, his voice cold. He wore the bloodstone ring again, his hands now clean of the king's blood.

The man didn't reply.

Lucia had had so much to say to her father that would forever remain unsaid.

This assassin had stolen that from her.

Lucia turned a look of sheer hatred upon him.

"You will die for what you did today," she spat.

The man glanced up at her only long enough to sneer. "You're the witch daughter he spoke of," he said. "Are you going to use your magic on me?"

"You don't sound afraid."

"I'm not afraid of any common witch."

"Oh, I'm much more than that." Lucia moved close enough to grab the man by his throat, digging her fingernails into his flesh and forcing him to meet her gaze. "Who are you? A rebel? Or an assassin?"

She tried to pull the truth from his mouth like she'd done with Lord Gareth, but he simply eyed her with defiance.

"I did what I did for Kraeshia," he hissed. "For the empress.

Do your worst to me, I have fulfilled my destiny."

"For the empress," Magnus repeated, his dark eyes narrowed. "Did Amara command you to kill the king, or did you make that decision all on your own?"

"And what if she did? You have no chance for revenge. She is far above all of you in this minuscule kingdom." The killer narrowed his gaze at the prince. "Your father was a coward and a liar—a mere worm in the presence of magnificence—and he squandered his chance at true greatness by acting and speaking against the empress. I was commanded to kill him publicly so that everyone would know he's dead."

"Is that so?" Magnus said, the words so quiet Lucia could barely hear them.

Her fists shook with the overwhelming need to reduce this man to ash.

Her brother drew closer to the man. "I find that I must pay you a compliment in that your marksmanship is second to none. I've never seen anyone as skilled with a crossbow before. The guards tell me you were at the back of the crowd when you took aim at the king. Four arrows, not missing your target once. Amara must value you very much."

The killer snorted. "Such a compliment is meaningless from anyone but the empress her—"

The blade of the dagger glinted in the torchlight just before Magnus thrust it upward into the man's chin and straight into his brain.

Breath tight in her chest, Lucia watched as the man twitched then slumped over, perfectly still.

Magnus glanced at Lucia.

"What is wrong with your *elementia*?" he asked, his tone cold and controlled.

Her first instinct was to lie, but the time for lies was past.

"It's failed me," Lucia admitted, the words like broken glass in her throat. "Lyssa . . . I don't understand it, but she's been stealing my magic since even before she was born."

Magnus nodded slowly. He wiped the sharp edge of his blade with a handkerchief, the red blood appearing black in the shadows of the dungeon cell.

"So you can't help Cleo," he said. "And you can do nothing to defeat Kyan."

A flash of anger ignited within her at this dismissal. "I didn't say that."

"That's what I heard."

"I'm trying to find a solution," she said. "I won't let you down again."

Her brother's expression was unreadable to her, void of emotion. She couldn't tell if he was upset or angry or disappointed.

Likely all three.

"I certainly hope not," he finally replied.

Magnus didn't say another word as she left the dungeon and slowly made her way back to the palace.

The first thing she noticed when she entered her chambers was the scent of burning flesh.

Her gaze fell with horror upon the blackened, smoldering corpse of the nursemaid in the center of the room.

A cry escaped Lucia's throat, a pained screech that barely sounded human.

She ran to the cradle to find it empty.

Lyssa was gone.

CHAPTER 17

JONAS

AURANOS

Jonas didn't attend the king's speech. He already knew far too well what to expect.

False promises. Lies. More lies.

Typical political horse dung.

Instead, he and Felix scoured the City of Gold looking for Ashur. Since his arrival yesterday in the palace city with the very much *not*-dead Prince Magnus, the Kraeshian prince had been visiting local taverns where, he said, the tongues of patrons were loose and ready to reveal secrets their sober selves might not provide.

Secrets about magic.

Secrets about local witches.

Secrets about someone, anyone, who might be able to lend their skills to help end Kyan the moment he showed his stolen face.

Jonas had his own secret means of ending Kyan, safe in the sheath on his belt. From what frustratingly little Timotheus had shared with him about the golden dagger, he thought that it would end the fire god very nicely.

However, it would also end Nic as well. And so they searched for other possibilities.

Jonas walked with Felix down the busy street, lined with shops and bakeries and places where Auranians could buy shiny baubles to wear clipped to their ears and strung around their necks.

Many people were walking in the direction of the palace, ready to stand in the palace square shoulder to shoulder in the blazing heat of midday to listen to King Gaius's most recent set of lies.

A man in a dark blue surcoat embroidered with what looked like sparkling diamonds bumped into Felix. He glared at him and pushed his way past.

"Do you ever want to start killing people at random just because they're a bunch of rich, pompous arses?" Felix muttered to Jonas, watching the man walk away.

"I used to," Jonas admitted. "I hated royals. Hated Auranians just for having the privileges denied to us in Paelsia."

"And now?"

"The urge is there, but I know it would be wrong."

Felix groaned. "Perhaps, but it would feel so good. Right? Let out some pent-up frustration." He nodded at a pair of green-uniformed Kraeshian soldiers watching over the flow of citizens up ahead. "We could start with them."

The sight of Amara's dwindling but continuing occupation was a reminder of more oppression. "Frankly, I wouldn't stop you."

"Did you see Enzo in his guard's uniform this morning?" Felix scrunched his nose as if he smelled something foul. "He finally went back to work at his post . . . said it was his honor to do so."

"He's Limerian down to his red blood. He can't help but be bound to duty and honor, even if it means taking orders from King Gaius himself." Jonas gave his friend a wry look. "Sometimes I forget that you're Limerian too. You don't exactly fit in with the rest of them, do you?"

Felix smirked. "Part of my charm is that I fit in wherever I am. I'm a chameleon."

There was no part of Felix Gaebras, eye patch and glowering, intimidating presence combined, that fit in wherever he was. But Jonas chose not to argue with him.

"You are indeed a chameleon," he said instead, nodding.

"Perhaps that's why Enzo's been in such a bad mood the last couple of days," Felix said as they paused in front of a shop with impressively clear windows that showed a selection of decorated cakes and pastries. "Insufferable, really."

Jonas already knew far too much about Enzo's moods. "He proposed marriage to Nerissa."

"What?" Felix regarded him with shock. "And what did Nerissa say to that?"

"She said no."

Felix nodded, his expression turning thoughtful. "Clearly, that's because she's fallen madly in love with me."

"She hasn't."

"Give her time."

"You believe what you want to believe."

"I will."

Jonas glanced over his shoulder in the direction of the palace, which lay in the direct center of the city. He could see its highest golden tower above the shops surrounding them. "I wonder how long the king is going to talk?"

"Hours, likely. He enjoys the sound of his voice far more than anyone else does." Felix cast a look at the maze of storefronts and buildings around them. "We're never going to find Ashur if he doesn't want to be found. Remember when we were in Basilia, and—poof—he'd just be gone? Just wandered off and didn't even tell anyone? Kraeshians are so sneaky."

"Ashur's just doing what he needs to do."

"So . . . him and Nic, huh?" Felix said, raising a brow above his eye patch. "I knew there was something there, but it didn't completely click until we were in the pit. And then I'm all: 'I knew it!' Because I did know it. You can just tell these things."

Jonas frowned at him. "What are you talking about?"

"Ashur and . . . Nic." Felix spread his hands. "They're—"

The sound of a scream caught their attention. It was followed by more shouts and a commotion coming from the palace area.

Felix gave Jonas a grim look. "Must have been some speech."

"We need to get back," Jonas said.

They hurried back to the palace without another word. Jonas's heart pounded fast and hard as he caught a man's shoulder going past him.

"What's going on?" he asked.

"The king!" the man said, his face pale and his eyes round. "The king is dead!"

Jonas stared after him as the man scurried away.

Once they reached the palace, they found it in chaos. Every guard they passed had his sword drawn, ready for battle.

"It can't be true," Jonas said as the pair rushed through the corridors. "I don't believe it."

They found Nerissa walking swiftly down the hallway that led to their bedchambers.

"Nerissa!" Jonas called out to her. "What's going on? The commotion in the city—some say King Gaius is dead."

"He is," she confirmed, her voice small. "It happened during his speech . . . an archer in the audience. He was captured before he could escape."

It still seemed far too surreal for Jonas to accept. "You saw it?"

She nodded. "I saw everything. It was horrible. Lucia and Magnus and Cleo were with him on the balcony."

"Is Lucia . . . ?" he began. "Is Cleo . . . ?"

"They're fine—or as fine as can be expected, given the circumstances. I can only assume the king's death was instant, or else Princess Lucia should have been able to heal him with her magic."

"A rebel," Jonas said, shaking his head. "Some rebel finally took the king out."

"Yes." Nerissa's expression didn't hold any grief, but her eyes were filled with worry. "I assume the assassin will be publicly executed after he's questioned."

Felix crossed his thick arms over his broad chest. "Is it wrong that I'm slightly envious that I wasn't the one to do it?"

Nerissa glared at him. "Seriously, Felix?"

"He left me behind in Kraeshia to take the blame for the emperor's murder—not exactly something I can forgive and forget. I'm glad he's dead!"

"I would strongly advise you to keep that opinion to yourself," Nerissa said. "Especially around Prince Magnus and Princess Lucia."

Jonas barely registered their conversation. He was deep in thought, remembering the time when he'd shoved a dagger into the king's heart, certain that he'd finally done what no one else had been able to do. But it was an injury the king survived because of some spell cast upon him by his witch mother.

"I can't believe he's dead," Jonas said, shaking his head. "The King of Blood is finally dead."

Jonas had to agree with Felix. This assassination had brought with it more good than bad. Perhaps the rebel had been working with Tarus Vasco.

Perhaps it had been Tarus himself.

He was about to ask Nerissa more about the archer, but his attention moved to someone who'd appeared at the end of the hallway.

Princess Lucia swiftly moved toward them.

Despite his hatred for the king, Lucia was his daughter—and she'd witnessed his death. Certainly, she mourned him and was in pain.

Jonas swore he would not make that pain worse than it already was.

"Princess," he said softly. "I heard what happened."

Her sky-blue eyes met his, her brows drawing together. "I told her this was all her fault . . . and she cried so hard, harder than I've ever heard her cry before. It's *my* fault this happened. Perhaps I should have said yes right away and he wouldn't have done this. I'm such a fool. Such a stupid, stupid fool."

"Lucia," Jonas frowned. "What are you talking about?"

Then his gaze fell with horror on the dagger in her grip. Her other hand dripped blood on the marble floor.

"What did you do?" he demanded. "Did you cut yourself?"

Lucia looked down at the injury: a deep slice over the palm of her right hand. "I'd heal it, but I can't."

"Princess, why did you do this to yourself?" Nerissa asked as she pulled a handkerchief from her pocket and quickly wrapped it around the princess's hand.

Lucia looked blankly down at the bandage. "That night, so long ago, I summoned him with the symbol for fire magic drawn on the snowy ground in my own blood. Alexius told me how to do it before he died. But nothing happened this time. I—I don't know how to find him and get her back."

"Who are you talking about?" Felix's voice was much harsher

than either Jonas's or Nerissa's when addressing the princess. "You're not saying you tried to summon Kyan here, are you?"

Lucia's gaze moved to Felix's single eye. "He took Lyssa."

"What?" Jonas gasped. "No, that's impossible."

"The nursemaid is in ashes. It happened when I was with Magnus and my father's assassin in the dungeon. When I came back to my chambers . . . Lyssa was gone!" Her breath hitched sharply, and she let out a sob. "I need to go."

She tried to move past them, but Jonas grabbed hold of her wrist to stop her.

"Where are you going?" he demanded.

"I need to find Timotheus. I need his answers. And I need his help." Her expression hardened then to one of cold steel. "And if he refuses, I swear on Valoria's heart that I will kill him. Now let go of me."

"No," he said. "You're not making any damn sense. I know your father just died, and that was a true horror for you to witness. Perhaps you're imagining things. What you need is rest."

"What I need"—her tone turned to jagged ice—"is for you to let go of me."

She wrenched her arm away, and Jonas was suddenly airborne, tossed halfway down the hall. When he hit the hard marble floor, it knocked the breath from his lungs.

"Lucia, stop!"

She didn't stop. He saw only the swish of her dark gray skirt as she turned a corner up ahead and disappeared from view.

Felix's hand appeared before his face. He took it and let his friend help him back up to his feet.

"Who in the hell is Timotheus?" Felix asked.

Only an immortal who'd seen a future that included the same golden dagger Jonas now possessed embedded in Lucia's chest.

Before he could answer Felix's question aloud, someone else headed down the hallway toward their trio.

"I need to speak with you, Agallon," Magnus growled.

The Damora siblings were equally forthright and equally unbearable. "About Lucia?" he asked.

"No."

Jonas itched to follow the princess, to try to stop her from whatever carnage she was bound to cause in her grief and confusion.

But the best course of action was to sit down and calmly formulate a plan.

He had changed a lot since his days as a rebel leader, and he wasn't sure if such hesitation was an asset or a liability.

"Then what is it?" Jonas asked impatiently.

"I need you to go to Kraeshia."

His gaze shot to the prince. "Why?"

"Because Amara Cortas needs to die."

"What?"

Magnus absently stroked his scarred right cheek. "She is responsible for my father's murder. I won't allow her to get away with it without penalty. She is a threat to everything and everyone."

Jonas forced himself to take a breath. Both Lucia and Magnus were in mourning, causing them to act irrationally and recklessly.

"Your vengeance is understandable," Jonas said, keeping his voice steady. "But that's an impossible request. Even if I agreed, I couldn't get close to her without discovery, let alone manage to escape after an assassination attempt . . ." He shook his head. "It's impossible."

"I'll go," Felix said simply.

Jonas shot him a look of surprise. "Bad idea, Felix."

"Disagree," he replied. "It's a *great* idea."

"Your highness," Nerissa said. "With utmost respect, I must ask: Is this the right move at this time? I thought your position was that our focus needed to remain on the Kindred and on help-ing Cleo and Taran."

Magnus turned a dark look on the girl. "That is still my focus. But this is also the right move, one that should have been taken months ago. Amara is responsible for countless atrocities commit-ted against innocents."

"So was your father," Nerissa said, not flinching when Mag-nus's glare intensified. "Apologies, but it's the truth."

"I'll leave immediately," Felix said. "Happy to serve. I've been waiting for this chance."

"Chance to do what?" Jonas said, glaring at his friend. "Get yourself killed?"

"It's a chance I'm willing to take." Felix shrugged and spread his hands. "This is what I do, and I'm damn good at it, your highness. Jonas has perhaps a few too many pesky morals in place when it comes to the thought of killing a woman. But me? Right woman, right time, right blade—or, hell, my bare hands—and she won't be anyone's problem anymore."

"Good," Magnus said with a sharp nod. "Leave today, and take whomever you need as backup."

"I'll need no one but myself."

"I'll go with you," Nerissa said.

Felix rolled his eyes. "What, to try to stop me? To remind me that everyone deserves a shiny chance at redemption? Save your breath."

"No. I'll go to make sure you don't get yourself unnecessarily slaughtered. I came to know Amara very well during my short time in her service. And I believe she trusts me, despite my choice to side with Princess Cleo."

Felix eyed her with doubt. "You won't try to stop me."

"No. I'll help you."

"Good," Magnus said. "You will go with Felix. And kindly let Amara know before she draws her last breath that this was on my orders."

Felix bowed his head. "It will be my pleasure, your highness."

Magnus turned as if to leave, but Jonas knew he couldn't let him.

"Lucia's gone," he said.

Magnus's shoulders tensed. He turn around slowly and glared at Jonas—a look so menacing that Jonas nearly winced from it.

"What?" he snapped.

"She believes Kyan was here just now, that he kidnapped Lyssa. She's gone after him."

Magnus swore under his breath. "Is it true? Was Kyan here and no alarms were raised?"

"I don't know for sure. But Lucia most definitely seemed to think so."

"I can't leave. Not with Cleo here . . . not with everything that's happened today." A thread of panic had entered Magnus's deep voice. Then he swore again before he looked at Jonas. "You."

Jonas frowned. "Me?"

"Go after my sister. Bring her back. You're certainly not my first choice, but you did it once, and you can damn well do it again. This is a command."

Jonas glared at him. "A command, is it?"

The fierceness in Magnus's dark eyes fell away, replaced by worry. "Fine. I won't command you. I'll ask you . . . *please*. I trust you to do this more than anyone else. Please find my sister and bring her back. If she's right, if this was Kyan's doing, together we will search for my niece."

Jonas couldn't speak. He nodded once.

He would do as Magnus asked him.

But he wouldn't drag Lucia back here kicking and screaming. He didn't think he could even if he wanted to. Instead, he would follow her. And he would help her.

And, he thought with pained determination, *if Timotheus is right and she ends up using her magic to help Kyan, dooming the rest of the world and everyone in it . . .*

He slid his hand over the golden dagger at his hip.

Then I will kill her.

CHAPTER 18

AMARA

KRAESHIA

Amara knew that because of her, a monster was free—one that would destroy the world unless it was stopped. And she'd left the mess behind her for others to clean up.

She'd hoped that the farther she sailed from the shores of Mytica, the freer she'd feel, but the invisible chains tying her to what she'd done did not break even as the Jewel of the Empire finally loomed into view before her.

Her beautiful home would also be destroyed if Kyan wasn't imprisoned again.

She would have to have faith in Lucia. And in Cleo.

For now, that faith would have to be enough.

Costas, the only member of her guard Amara knew she could trust, remained in Mytica to keep a close watch over the royals. She'd commanded him to send a message of any news, no matter how small or insignificant it seemed.

A celebration awaited her as the ship docked, a crowd of

cheering Kraeshians holding up signs proclaiming their love and devotion to their new empress.

"Welcome home, Empress Amara!" they called out to her.

As she disembarked, children and mothers looked upon her with hope in their eyes, hope that she wouldn't be the same as her father—an emperor who had been focused only on power, conquest, and unlimited fortune.

Amara would be different, these women believed.

Better. Kinder. More benevolent and focused on unity and peace in a way male rulers in the past hadn't been.

Amara smiled at them all, but found that the tight feeling in her chest wouldn't ease.

All these people . . . they would all perish at the hands of the Kindred if Lucia failed.

Lucia couldn't fail.

Amara had confidence in the sorceress's magic, in her prophecy, in the determination she'd seen in Lucia's eyes when she'd first entered the compound searching for her brother and father. For a moment, just a moment before the king's entourage had departed for Auranos, Amara had wanted to ask Lucia if she might heal her broken leg with her earth magic, as a favor.

But she had held her tongue, doubting that the reply would be positive.

"I earned this injury," she whispered to herself as she leaned against her cane. The pain had eased, but walking was awkward and slow. She shrugged off the assistance of the guards who surrounded her, preferring to hobble along without any help.

She took in the sights of the Jewel on the carriage ride to the Emerald Spear—the royal residence she'd lived in since birth. Sometimes she forgot how beautiful the Jewel was. It hadn't received its name by accident.

Everywhere she looked, her surroundings literally hummed with life. With lush, green trees bearing flat, waxy leaves, far taller and fuller than anything she'd seen in Mytica. The flowers—mostly shades of purple, which had been the emperor's favorite color—were each as big as a serving platter.

The air was fresh and fragrant with the smell of the flowers and of the salty sea that surrounded the small island. Amara closed her eyes and tried to focus only on the feel of the humid air on her bare arms, on the intoxicating scents of the Jewel, on the cheers from crowds they passed.

When she opened her eyes again, the palace stretched up into the very clouds like a priceless shard of glittering emerald. It had been her father's design, built years before she was born. He'd never been happy with it, thought it not high enough, not sharp enough, not impressive enough.

But Amara loved it.

And now it belonged to her and her alone.

And, for a moment, she pushed aside her doubts, her fears, her guilt, and allowed herself to bask in her victory—truly the greatest victory by any woman in history.

The future for all the people who had cheered upon her arrival would be as bright as the ancient scepter she would raise at her public Ascension.

It would be a grand ceremony, much like her father's had been many years ago, long before her birth, that would live forever through the paintings and sculptures commissioned to document it.

And then all—whether they liked it or not—would have to worship and obey the first empress in mortal history.

Wearing purple robes, her hair arranged into a thick, neat bun at the back of her head, Neela waited for her in the grand, shining entryway to the Spear. The old woman reached her arms out toward her granddaughter. Guards lined the circumference of the palace's ground floor.

Amara's cane made a clicking sound on the green metallic floors as she closed the distance between them, then Amara allowed her grandmother to take her into a warm embrace.

"My beautiful *dhosha* has returned to me," Neela said.

Amara's throat tightened, and her eyes stung.

"I've missed you, *madhosha*," she whispered.

"And I you."

Amara couldn't take her eyes off her grandmother. The old woman looked anything but old today. She was vibrant. Her skin glowed, her eyes sparkled. Even her steel-gray hair seemed shinier and fuller.

"You look wonderful, *madhosha*," Amara told her. "Clearly, staving off a revolution does wonders for the skin."

Neela laughed lightly, touching her own smooth, tanned cheeks. "That's hardly to account for this. My apothecary created a special elixir for me, one that has certainly contributed to my renewed strength. During your stay in little Mytica, I knew I couldn't allow my age and ailments to slow me down."

The apothecary was a mysterious man who had worked secretly for the Cortas family for many years. Amara made note to meet him in person very soon. She knew he was also responsible for the magical potion that had brought her back to life as a mere baby, the same potion that had made Ashur's resurrection possible.

This was a man she needed to know. A man she needed to control.

"I have so much to tell you," Amara said.

"Perhaps not as much as you think. I have been kept fully apprised of all that has gone on in little Mytica, despite the rather short and cryptic messages I've received from you. Come, let's speak in private, away from curious ears, shall we?"

Mildly surprised, Amara followed her grandmother through the long, narrow hallways of the Spear to the east wing, out into the rock garden in Amara's private courtyard.

She gazed around at her favorite place in the palace—a place that her father had hated since he thought it ugly and uninspired. But Amara had acquired each of the tens of thousands of rocks—shiny, ugly, beautiful, all sizes and colors—over her lifetime and thought them each a treasure.

"I've missed this place," she said.

"I'm sure you did."

A servant brought them a tray of wine and a selection of exotic fruits unlike anything available in Mytica. Amara's mouth watered at the sight of them.

Neela poured them both a goblet of wine, and Amara took a deep drink.

Paelsian wine.

The same wine she'd used to poison her family.

She swallowed it down, although her stomach churned at the memory.

"Ashur is still alive," Neela said after she too drank from her goblet.

Amara froze mid-sip, then took a moment to compose herself. "He is. He acquired the resurrection potion from your apothecary."

"I am also told that after you captured him, he managed to escape."

Again, Amara exhaled slowly, evenly, before she replied. "He won't be a problem."

"Your Ascension isn't for nearly a week. If your brother shows his face here, if he claims the right to the title of emperor—"

"He won't."

"How can you be sure of that?"

"I just am. My brother is . . . preoccupied with other issues in Mytica."

"The young man he's come to care for far too deeply for his own good. The one who is currently the vessel for the fire Kindred."

Amara just stared at her now, stunned. "Who told you all this?"

Neela raised her brows, taking a plump red grape from the top of the platter, inspecting it carefully before popping it in her mouth and chewing slowly. "Do you deny any of it?"

Uneasiness spread through her. Her grandmother didn't trust her. If she did, she would have felt no need for a spy.

A very well-informed spy, it would seem.

"I don't deny it," Amara said, pushing back against her uncertainty. "I've done what I felt I must. I tried to find a way to control the Kindred. It was impossible. And now . . . well, I've left quite a mess behind." Amara's voice was shaking. "Kyan could destroy the world, *madhosha*. And it would be all my fault."

Neela shook her head, her expression serene. "I've learned in my lifetime to control only what is possible. When something is out of my hands, I let it be free. What is done is done. The problems in Mytica are Mytica's problems, not ours. Do you think there is a chance these elemental gods will succeed against the sorceress?"

Amara's grip tightened on her goblet. "I don't know."

"Is there anything you can do to be of assistance to her?"

"I could only make things worse, I think. It's best that I'm here now."

"Then it is done. And what will be will be." Neela poured herself more wine. "You should know that King Gaius Damora is dead."

"What?" Amara fell speechless for a moment. "He's . . . dead? How?"

"An arrow to the heart. He was halted in the middle of a speech about how he meant to defeat you and take back his precious tiny kingdom."

Amara allowed the shock of this incredible news to wash over her.

Gaius was dead.

Her enemy. Her husband. The man who'd married her for the chance to align with her father. The man she'd briefly believed might be an asset to her reign until he betrayed her at the first opportunity.

She knew she should be pleased by this news. Had she not feared Lucia's wrath, she would have had him executed herself.

Still, it seemed so strange that a man as powerful and as ruthless as Gaius Damora could be taken from the world by a mere arrow.

"Unbelievable," she whispered.

"I chose the assassin well, *dhosha*," Neela said.

Amara glanced up from her goblet, shocked by her grandmother's words. "It was your doing?"

Neela nodded, her gaze steady. "King Gaius presented a potential obstacle to your future. Now you are a widow, ready to marry anyone of your choosing."

Amara shook her head. Perhaps her grandmother expected gratitude, rather than shock, for taking this extreme step.

Could she have made such a choice?

Gaius was most definitely a problem, but one—like everything else she'd left behind—that she'd decided to deal with after her Ascension, when her power was absolute and unshakable.

"Of course, you were right to have made this choice," Amara finally said. "However, I do wish you'd consulted me first."

"The result would have been the same, only delayed. Some problems require immediate attention."

Amara limped a few paces away, her grip on her cane painfully tight. "I'm curious who it is in my compound that has been sending you so many detailed messages."

A small smile touched Neela's lips. "Someone who will be arriving soon with a very special gift I have acquired for you."

"Intriguing. Care to share more?"

"Not just yet. But I believe this gift will be incredibly useful to us both for many years to come. I will say no more since I want it to be a surprise."

Amara forced herself to relax. Despite the jarring news of Gaius's assassination, she knew she needed to give thanks for her grandmother's intelligence, strength, and foresight, rather than question it.

"The Jewel is beautiful and calm again," Amara said after a peaceful silence fell between them. She had strolled around her garden, touching her favorite rocks and remembering the very place she'd put the aquamarine orb when it had briefly been in her possession.

"It is," Neela agreed. "Most of the rebels were put to death immediately upon arrest, but we have their leader here in the palace awaiting execution. Since he was previously a servant here, I thought it would be fitting for him to meet his death publicly at your Ascension ceremony. Symbolic, really." She raised her chin. "A symbol that we shall survive despite any threats to our rightful power."

Amara picked up a sun-warmed piece of jagged obsidian, its shiny black edges reflecting the sunlight. "A servant, you say? Anyone I may have known?"

"Yes, indeed. Mikah Kasro."

Amara's grip on the stone tightened painfully.

Mikah was a favored guard who'd been at the palace since the two of them were children.

"Mikah Kasro is the leader of the revolution?" she repeated, certain she'd heard wrong.

Neela nodded. "The leader of the local faction, anyway. He was responsible for the prison break, which killed nearly two hundred guards, after your departure for Mytica." Her expression flashed with disgust. "Shortly after that, he made a direct attempt on my life here at the palace. But he failed."

"And I'm so very grateful he did fail."

"As am I."

"I want to speak with him." It was out before Amara even realized what she was asking.

Neela's brows raised. "Why would you want such a thing?"

Amara tried to think it through. To visit a prisoner, especially one whose goal was to overthrow her rule, seemed ludicrous, even to her. "I remember Mikah was so loyal, so kind, so honest—or at least I thought he was. I don't understand this."

He liked me and I liked him, she wanted to add. But she didn't.

It seemed that spending so much time in Mytica, with its deceptive and passive-aggressive people, had stolen her gift for the absolute bluntness Kraeshians prided themselves on.

Her grandmother now frowned deeply, regarding her with curiosity. "I suppose it can be arranged. If you insist."

Amara needed this. Needed to speak with Mikah and understand what he wanted, understand why he would choose to rise up and try to destroy the Cortas family—even now that her hateful father and all but one of his male heirs were dead.

Amara glanced at her grandmother. "Yes, I insist."

Amara had threatened the guard at the Paelsian compound, the one who had shifted his loyalties to Lord Kurtis, with turning his cell into a forgetting room.

Mikah Kasro had been locked in such a room in the Emerald Spear for several weeks.

Amara leaned on her cane as she entered the empty, windowless room, flanked by guards, to see that Mikah's hands and feet were shackled. He wore only ragged black trousers and had several weeks' growth of beard on his face.

There were deep cuts on his chest and arms, and his left eye was bruised and swollen shut. His shoulder-length long black hair was matted and greasy, and his cheeks were gaunt.

But his eyes . . .

Mikah's eyes burned like coals. He was only a couple of years older than Amara, yet his eyes were wise and steady and filled with bottomless strength, despite everything he had endured.

"She returns," Mikah said, his voice not much more than a low growl. "And she blesses me with her luminous presence."

He sounded so much like Felix that she had to wince.

"You will speak to the empress with respect," one of the guards snapped.

"It's fine," Amara said. "Mikah can speak to me however he likes today. I'm strong enough to take it. Hold nothing back, my old friend. I don't mind at all."

"*Old friend*," Mikah repeated, snorting softly. "How funny. I once thought that might be possible—that a mere servant and a princess could be friends. You were kind to me, so much kinder than your father. And much kinder than Dastan and Elan combined. When I heard you killed them, I celebrated."

Amara pressed her lips together.

"What? You think it's still a secret?" Mikah asked, raising a dark eyebrow at her.

"It's nothing but a poisonous lie," she said.

"You are a murderer, just like your father, and one day you will answer for your crimes."

Before Amara could say a word, the guard kicked Mikah in the chest. He landed flat on his back, coughing and wheezing.

"Speak with respect to the empress, or I will cut out your tongue," the guard snarled.

Amara looked at the guard. "Leave us."

"He was disrespectful to you."

"I agree. But that's not what I asked of you. Leave me to talk with Mikah in private. That is a command."

With obvious reluctance, the guards did as she said. When they left, closing the door behind them, Amara turned toward Mikah again. He'd sat up, cradling his injured ribs with his thin arms.

"You're right," she said. "I did kill my father and brothers. I killed them because they stood in the way of progress—the progress that both of us want."

"Oh, I doubt that very much," Mikah replied.

She was used to servants doing as she said without question, but Mikah had always been argumentative and challenging. Over the years, she'd come to expect it. And, at times, she enjoyed their banter.

"I thought you liked me," she said, then regretted it, since it came out sounding needy. "I will make a good empress, one who puts the needs of her subjects before her own, unlike my father."

"Your father was cruel, hateful, selfish, and vain. He conquered others to amuse himself."

"I'm not like that."

Mikah laughed, a dark and hollow sound in his chest. "Who are you trying to convince—me or yourself? It's a simple question, really. Will you follow in your father's footsteps and continue to conquer lands that don't belong to Kraeshia?"

She frowned. "Of course. One day soon, the world will belong to Kraeshia. We will be as one, and my rule will be absolute."

Mikah shook his head. "There is no need to rule the entire world. No need to possess every weapon, every treasure, every piece of magic one can get their hands on. Freedom is what counts. Freedom for everyone—be they rich or poor. The freedom to choose our own lives, our own paths, without an absolute ruler telling us what we can and cannot do. That is what I fight for."

Amara didn't understand. The world he proposed would be one of chaos.

"There is a difference between those who are weak and those who are strong," she began carefully. "The weak perish, the strong survive—and they rule and make the choices that help everything run smoothly. I know I will be a good leader. My people will love me."

"And if they don't?" he countered. "If they rise up and try to change what has been thrust upon them through no choice of their own, will you have them put to death?" Amara shifted uncomfortably on her feet. Mikah raised his eyebrows. "Think about this before your Ascension, because it's very important."

Amara tried to swallow the lump in her throat. She needed to block out what he said—to pretend that it didn't resonate with her.

"Let me ask you one thing, Mikah," she began. "Had you been successful in your siege of the palace—had you killed my grandmother and then been faced with me—what would you have done? Would you have let me live?"

His gaze remained steady, burning with the intelligence and intensity that made her unable to disregard everything he said as nonsense.

"No, I would have killed you," he said.

Amara stiffened at his blunt admission, surprised he hadn't taken the opportunity to lie. "Then you are no better than me."

"I never said I was. However, you're too dangerous right now, too intoxicated by your own power. But power is like a rug beneath your feet: It can be pulled away without warning."

She shook her head. "You're wrong."

"Be careful with your grandmother, princess. She has her hands upon that rug beneath you. She always has."

"What do you mean?"

"She's in control here," he said. "You think yourself so smart to have achieved so much in such a short time. Never doubt that everything that's happened, everything including your Ascension, is according to *her* plan, not yours."

Amara's heart pounded at his words.

"How dare you speak that way about my grandmother!" she hissed. "She is the only one who's ever believed in me."

"Your grandmother only believes in her own desire for power."

It had been a mistake to come here. What had she expected? Apologies from someone she once liked and trusted? For Mikah to prostrate himself before her and beg for forgiveness?

Mikah thought she wasn't worthy of ruling the empire. That she was as flawed and myopic as her father had been.

He was wrong.

"The next time I see you will be at my Ascension," Amara said evenly, "where you will be publicly executed for your crimes. All gathered will witness what happens to those who stand against the future of Kraeshia. Your blood will mark the beginning of a true revolution. *My* revolution."

CHAPTER 19

LUCIA

PAELSIA

She'd departed the palace with nothing but the dark gray gown on her back and a small purse of Auranian centimos. She'd left everything else behind, including the fire, earth, and air Kindred orbs that were locked away in a large iron box in her chambers.

She'd traveled far enough from the City of Gold that the original rush of panic and fear and confusion had dissipated, and now intelligent thought returned.

"So careless of me to leave them behind," she chastised herself under her breath, seated in the back of the horse-drawn carriage she'd hired to take her to her destination.

She should have kept the invaluable orbs on her at all times, like Cleo did. The princess had refused the offer to place the aquamarine crystal in the locked box with the others.

Lucia had told no one where they were, trusted no one with the secret.

She prayed this journey would not take her long before she could return.

When she'd realized Lyssa was missing, panic had controlled her thoughts and actions.

Since then, she focused on one thing to help ease her maddening fear about her daughter's kidnapping.

The fire god believed she had both the means and the magic to imprison him.

If he harmed Lyssa, if he so much as singed a single piece of her downy hair, he would surely expect that Lucia would go to the ends of the earth in order to end him rather than help him.

She believed that the fire Kindred would keep Lyssa safe. The baby was an assurance that he had something that Lucia valued above all else.

It had taken her nearly a week of travel to reach Shadowrock, a small village in western Paelsia. It was one of the few villages in this area close to the Forbidden Mountains, and it had once had a neighboring village five miles south.

As Lucia's carriage drove past the deserted, blackened remains of that village, she peered out the small window and winced at the sight. She clearly remembered the screams of terror and pain from those who'd made this their home, those who'd watched that home burn or burned with it.

Lucia knew she couldn't change the past. But if she didn't learn from it, and do better going forward, then those people had suffered and died in vain.

As Shadowrock loomed in the distance, she glanced down at the palm of her hand. The cut she'd made to draw enough blood in her attempt to summon Kyan would have taken a month to heal, but she had found enough earth magic within herself to help the process along. Only a scar remained, though at her best and most powerful, there would not have been a single trace of the injury.

Scars were good, she thought. They were an excellent reminder of a past not meant to be repeated.

Lucia acquired a room at the inn where she'd previously stayed. It had comfortable beds and decent food. She would rest here for the night before continuing into the mountains tomorrow.

And now, she supposed, it was time to deal with *him*.

Jonas Agallon had followed her from the City of Gold all the way to Shadowrock, by foot at times, by horseback at others. He'd been far enough in the distance that he probably thought she hadn't noticed.

But she had.

Lucia had chosen not to confront him and instead allowed him to think that he was as stealthy as a shadow in the night.

She left through the inn's back kitchen door so he wouldn't see her exit through the front. Then, she walked up a narrow side-street so she could approach Jonas from behind.

He stood on the stoop of a cobbler's shop across the street from the inn, leaning against a wooden beam with the cowl of his dark blue cloak over his head to help shield his identity.

But Lucia had come to know the former rebel leader well enough that she would recognize him no matter what disguise he wore.

She recognized the lines of his strong body that always appeared tense, like a wildcat about to pounce upon its prey. She recognized the way he walked without any hesitation, picking a direction and swiftly taking it even if it meant he got lost in the process.

Not that he would ever admit such a thing, of course.

She knew without even seeing his face that his mouth was set in a determined line and that his cinnamon-brown eyes looked serious. They were always so serious, even when he joked around with his friends.

Jonas Agallon had lost so much over the last year, but it hadn't changed who he was deep inside. He was strong and kind and brave. And she trusted him, even when he secretly trailed after her. She knew without a doubt he'd done this in a misguided attempt to protect her.

Now, observing him from distance of only six paces, she sensed the magic Jonas held within him—a pleasant, warm, and tingling sensation that she'd begun to associate with the rebel.

It had felt much stronger ever since leaving Amara's compound, and she had to admit that it troubled her that Jonas's magic had grown stronger while hers had continued to weaken just when she needed it the most.

She drew even closer to him, his gaze remaining fixed on the inn.

Close enough that she could hear him mutter to himself.

"Well, princess . . . just what is your plan in this little village now that you're here?"

"I suppose you could simply ask me," she said.

He jumped, then spun around to face her, his eyes wide with shock.

"You . . ." he began. "You're right here in front of me."

"I am," she said.

"You knew—?" he began.

"That you've been stalking me like a hungry ice wolf for days? Yes, I knew."

"Well, there you go." He scrubbed his hand through his brown hair, then he turned his painfully earnest gaze toward her. "Are you well?"

"What do you mean?"

"You were so distraught at the palace. Rightfully so, of course. And your hand . . ."

Lucia showed him the palm of her previously injured hand.

"I'm better now. Thinking more clearly. And I have a plan."

"You want to talk to Timotheus."

"Yes, that's the plan." It would be so much easier to continue on alone, without anyone to answer to or concern herself with. But if that had been her decision, she would have confronted Jonas earlier and told him to go back to Auranos.

"Tell me, are you hungry?" she asked.

He turned a frown on her. "What?"

"Hungry. We've been traveling for many hours today, and you've kept me in your sight all that time. I assume you're starving."

"I . . . suppose I am."

"Come." Lucia began walking toward the inn. "I'll buy you some dinner."

Jonas didn't argue. He followed her into the tavern connected to the inn. It was a small room that held a dozen wooden tables. Only three were filled with patrons. One table held a pair of Kraeshian soldiers.

"The occupation continues, even here," Jonas said under his breath.

"It doesn't bother me." Lucia watched him as he removed his cloak and placed it over the back of his chair. Something gold at his belt caught the last remaining traces of early evening sunlight coming through the large window. "Don't tell me you went back to that inn during our journey here and retrieved that horrible dagger of yours."

Jonas's hand shot to the sheathed weapon, covering it from view, his brows drawing tightly together. Then he took a seat, a smile stretching his cheeks. "You guessed it. I'm an idiot, what can I say?"

She shook her head. "That's not the word I'd use to describe you."

"Oh? And what word would you use?"

"Sentimental."

Jonas held her gaze for a moment. "Princess, I wanted to say that I am sorry for your loss. How I felt toward the king . . . it certainly doesn't lessen your grief."

"My father was a cruel, power-hungry man who hurt many innocent people. You have every right to have hated him." Lucia blinked, her eyes dry. She had cried more than enough tears in the last few days to realize that they were no help to her at all. "But I still loved him, and I still miss him."

He reached across the table and squeezed her hand. "I know. And know that I will help you in any way I can to find Lyssa."

"Thank you." Lucia frowned down at her hand in his. "I feel so much magic in you, Jonas. More than ever before."

He released her hand immediately. "Apologies."

"No, that's not what I . . ." Lucia trailed off as a server approached them, a girl with bright red hair and a wide, friendly smile.

Lucia recognized this girl immediately and stared up at her in shock.

"We have potato soup today," the red-haired girl said. "And some dried meats and fruits. The cook apologizes for the lack of variety on today's menu, but our shipment of supplies from Trader's Harbor has been delayed."

"Mia . . . ?" Lucia asked, her voice cautious.

The girl cocked her head. "Yes, that's my name. Have we met before?"

Oh, they absolutely had. After the battle with Kyan when his fiery, monstrous form had been destroyed near the mysterious crystal monolith, Lucia had found herself in the Sanctuary's grassy meadow with the Crystal City visible in the distance.

Once she'd reached the city itself, finding the massive, sparkling metropolis as quiet and empty as a ghost town, her path had crossed a lovely and helpful immortal who had taken her to see Timotheus.

"Don't you remember?" Lucia asked. "It wasn't so long ago."

"Apologies," Mia said. "Please don't think me rude, but I've recently forgotten much of my past. I've visited several healers who tell me that amnesia like this can happen from a hard bump on the head."

"Amnesia," Lucia repeated, her heart quickening. "Impossible."

"Not impossible." Mia shook her head. "I do hope to regain my memories soon, but until then the owner of this inn has promised to look after me."

Jonas leaned forward. "Promised who?" he asked.

Mia's gaze grew faraway, her brow furrowing. "I remember it like it was a dream, really. Unclear and distant. But there was a woman—a beautiful, dark-haired woman. She was so kind to me and promised that everything would be all right, but that I had to trust her."

Lucia listened, barely breathing. The girl wasn't lying; this is what she believed.

"Trust her with what?"

"I don't remember." Mia's frown deepened. "I know she had a sharp, flat piece of black rock." She looked down at her arm. "I think she cut me with it, but it didn't hurt very much. And after that, I found myself here. Oh, and the strangest thing . . . her hand . . . it wasn't a hand at all. I can't really explain it." She shrugged. "I must have hit my head very hard."

Lucia searched her face. "Is that all you remember?"

"I'm afraid so. So if I've met you before, please forgive me for not recognizing you. Hopefully I will again one day. Now, can

I get you both some of the potato soup? I assure you, it's delicious."

Lucia wanted to stand up, to shake Mia and have her tell her more, to try to use her magic to extract every last bit of truth from her lips.

None of this made any sense.

Mia was an immortal who lived in the Sanctuary with the handful of other immortals still in existence. Timotheus had recently chosen not to let any of them leave through their stone gateway into this world, not even in hawk form, for fear that Kyan would kill them.

How did this happen? And who was the dark-haired woman who'd cut Mia's arm?

"Yes, soup would be lovely," Lucia said instead. "Much gratitude."

Mia nodded and moved off toward the kitchen.

Lucia fell silent, lost in thought about what could have happened to Mia. Had it happened to anyone else?

"Trouble?" Jonas asked her.

"I think so, but I don't know what it means yet."

He watched her, his close scrutiny distracting her from her thoughts. "Your brother wants you to come home. He's worried about you."

"I'm sure he is." Lucia hated the thought that her decisions were causing Magnus even more pain. "But I'm not going back yet. I need to talk to Timotheus. I can't believe he's abandoned me now, at my greatest time of need. He wants the Kindred imprisoned as much as I do. Yet I haven't had a single dream in ages, and I have so many questions for him."

"He says his magic is fading," Jonas said. "That he can't use it all up to visit the dreams of mortals."

It took a moment for Lucia to register what he'd just said.

Her eyes went wide. "How do you know that?"

Jonas stiffened. "What?"

"What you just said—that Timotheus's magic is fading. When did you learn this?"

"He . . . visited my dream when we were at the compound."

"Your dream?" A mix of anger and annoyance flashed through her. "Why did he visit your dream and not mine?"

"Trust me, princess, I would have preferred he visited yours. He is a very difficult man. Everything he says is like a new riddle to decipher. He . . . wanted me to continue to watch over you, to keep you safe. And Lyssa too. He knew about her and that you survived her birth. He said he . . . trusts me."

Lucia couldn't let herself be distracted by Timotheus's choices. She'd always had a difficult time with the immortal; their relationship had been fraught with tension and distrust from the very beginning.

Finally, she nodded. "He's right to trust you."

"Why do you say that?"

"Because you're the most trustworthy person I've ever known," she said with complete sincerity. "Even my father and brother have lied to and manipulated me, but you never have. And I appreciate that more than you'll ever know."

Jonas just watched her now, silently, his expression pained.

Perhaps he didn't feel comfortable with her compliment. But that didn't make it any less heartfelt.

"You're coming with me," Lucia said after silence fell between them.

"I am?" Jonas raised a brow. "Where?"

She nodded out the window. "Into the Forbidden Mountains. We'll leave at dawn."

Jonas looked toward the jagged black mountains in the near distance. "What's in the mountains?"

"The gateway to the Sanctuary." At his look of shock, Lucia gave him the edge of a smile. "You followed me all this way. Are you really going to stop now?"

CHAPTER 20

MAGNUS

AURANOS

A week had passed since his father's murder.

The city had not gone into deep mourning for their lost king. In fact, they were currently in the midst of a celebration. Auranians always seemed to be celebrating something.

The last festival had been called the Day of Flames, and citizens wore red, orange, and yellow to represent the goddess Cleiona's fire magic. This festival was in celebration of her air magic, and it allegedly lasted for half a month.

Half of an entire month dedicated to a festival called the "Breath of Cleiona."

Ridiculous, Magnus thought.

Cleo had explained to him that citizens of Auranos far and wide would come to the palace city during this time of celebration to read their poetry and to sing songs in praise of the goddess. The breath they used to speak and sing was their tribute to Cleiona's air magic.

But really, she'd explained, it was simply an excuse for drinking great amounts of wine and boisterous social interaction that lasted until the wee hours of morning.

While such celebrations carried on in the city beyond the palace walls, Magnus stood in the royal cemetery, looking down at the patch of dirt that marked the king's temporary grave. The king's remains would eventually be returned to Limeros and buried next to Magnus's mother. Until then, Magnus had had him placed into the earth by nightfall of the day of his death, true to Limerian tradition.

How odd that he now felt some strange sense of solace from leaning on the same traditions he'd all but ignored his entire life.

A small black granite marker lay upon the bare soil, chiseled with the Limerian crest of entwined snakes.

He'd dreamed about his father just last night.

"Don't waste time mourning me," the king had said to him. *"You need to focus only on what's important now."*

"Oh?" Magnus had replied. *"And what's that?"*

"Power and strength. When news of my death spreads, there will be many who would fight to control Mytica. You can't let them. Mytica is yours now. You are my heir, you are my legacy. And you must promise to crush anyone who stands against you."

Power and strength. Two attributes Magnus had always struggled with, much to his father's disappointment.

But he would do as the dream version of his father suggested.

He would fight. And he would crush anyone who opposed him and wanted to take what was his.

Beginning with the Kindred.

He sensed Cleo's presence before he felt her lightly touch his arm.

"It's so strange to me," he said before she uttered a single word.

"What is?"

"I hated my father with every fiber of my being, yet I still feel this incredible . . . loss."

"I understand."

He laughed darkly, finally glancing at Cleo out of the corner of his eye. She wore a gown of pale blue today, the bodice trimmed in small silk flowers. Her hair fell over her shoulders in long, messy golden waves.

A vision of beauty, as always.

"I wouldn't expect you to understand," he told her. "I know how you felt about him. You hated him even more than I did."

Cleo shook her head. "You didn't hate him. You loved him."

He stared at her, not understanding. "You're wrong."

"I'm not wrong." She cast a glance down at the grave. "You loved him because he was your father. Because of his moments of kindness and guidance, even in the worst of times, even when barely perceptible. You loved him because at the end you began to see a glimmer of the strong relationship that could have become a reality between you."

Cleo reached out and took his hands in hers.

"You loved him," she said, "because you'd begun to have hope."

Magnus turned his face away so Cleo couldn't see the bottom-less pain in his eyes. "If so, that was very stupid of me."

She placed her hands on either side of his face and guided his gaze back to hers. "To love a father like Gaius Damora meant that you were brave, not stupid."

"I hope you're right." He leaned over to kiss her forehead. Cleo's skin was cold against his lips. He placed his hand on her cheek. "You're struggling today."

Cleo smiled up at him. "I'm fine."

"Lies."

Her smile turned into a scowl. "I'm *fine*," she said more firmly.

Magnus eyed her for a moment in complete silence. "Your hair, while stunning as always, looks like it hasn't been properly attended to. Is your current handmaiden lacking in such skills?"

"Nerissa is the best when it comes to making sense of my hair," Cleo said, twisting a long lock of it between her fingers. "I miss her very much. I hope she returns soon."

"Hmm."

Before she had the chance to stop him, he swept her silky hair back over her shoulder. She gasped and clamped her hand down on her exposed skin.

But he'd already seen the painful truth.

The blue lines that had been working their way up her arm were now visible on the left side of her throat.

"When did this happen?" he demanded. "When did you have another incident?"

That was what they'd started to call the drowning spells that seized her unexpectedly at any hour.

"Recently." Cleo glared at him, as if angry that he'd discovered her secret.

He swore under his breath. "I'd counted on Lucia to help you, but she's nowhere to be found."

"She's searching for her daughter. That is her priority right now, and I don't blame her. She's seeking a solution to all this, just not here, trapped within these walls. You saw what Kyan did to the nursemaid!"

The memory of the charred corpse returned to him, the smell of burning flesh. The thought that his newborn niece was in the clutches of the fire Kindred made Magnus's blood boil.

Strength and power. The only things that mattered. He would find Lyssa and his sister. He had to.

"I need to find answers myself," he muttered.

"I've been reading," Cleo said.

"Books won't help."

"I don't know about that. The right book, the right legend . . . there are so many in the library, and it seems as if the accounts of what happened a thousand years ago vary from scribe to scribe. We might find the answers in one of these books if we keep looking."

Magnus shook his head, uncertain. "Have you learned anything tangible from these books you've been reading?"

"Well . . ." She twisted her hands. "One of the books reminded me about Lucia's ring—the ring that belonged to the original sorceress. It controls Lucia's magic, keeps it from overwhelming her. I was going to ask her if I could try it on to see what would happen now that I have this magic inside me, but she left before I could suggest it."

Magnus stared at her. "I can't believe I didn't think of it before now."

"If she returns in time, perhaps—"

"No, not her ring. Mine." He pulled the bloodstone off his finger, took Cleo's right hand in his, and slid the ring onto her slender index finger. Then he looked into her eyes. "Well? Do you feel anything?"

"I . . . I'm not sure." Cleo held her hand out in front of her, shaking her head. Then her skin went deathly pale, and she began to tremble. "No . . . it hurts. It hurts! Magnus . . ."

Death magic. Lucia had been repelled by the same magic that was now hurting Cleo.

In a flash, he wrenched the ring off Cleo's finger and watched in horror as she had another incident, choking and gasping for breath as if she were drowning in a deep, black ocean and he couldn't do a damn thing to save her. He gathered her in his arms, rubbing her back and praying for it to be over soon.

A moment later it passed, and she collapsed into his arms.

The magic in this ring had affected Kyan the night Magnus had crawled from his grave. And now he'd proven that it hurt Cleo.

It was the last thing he'd ever want to do.

"I hate this," she said, her words coming out in gasps. "I wanted this magic. I wanted it so badly that I would have given anything for it. And now I have it and I hate it!"

"I hate it too." He kissed the top of her head, so sick of feeling powerless and weak when it came to finding a solution that would save her from this fate.

He knew only one thing for absolute certain: He would *not* lose her.

Magnus accompanied Cleo back to their chambers, and when he was certain she'd recovered and she'd fallen peacefully asleep, he went in search of Prince Ashur.

He found the Kraeshian with Taran Ranus in the palace courtyard.

Taran had his shirt off, and Ashur inspected the white lines that covered his entire arm and half of his chest.

More lines than Cleo had.

"What are you proposing?" Magnus asked when he reached them. "That we chop off your arm in hopes of delaying the progress? Seems too late for that, but I'm willing to give it a try."

Taran cast a dark look at Magnus, with equally dark circles beneath his eyes. "You think this is amusing?"

"Not even slightly."

"I want this poison out of me, by any means possible." Taran pulled his shirt on again. "Ashur knows things, knows magic. I thought he might be able to help."

Magnus looked at Ashur. "And?"

The prince's gray-blue eyes were stormy with uncertainty and doubt. "I'm trying to find a solution. But so far I've failed."

Magnus already knew that Taran's air magic manifested itself in frightening moments of suffocation. And after each incident, the white lines continued their progression.

It didn't take an expert in ancient magic to tell him that this was a sign that the elemental god was trying to break free and take control of Taran's body.

Taran snorted, a sound without any humor. "It's amusing, really."

Ashur looked up at him. "What?"

"My mother . . . she was an Oldling. She knew all about the Kindred, or at least the tales that had been passed down from generation to generation. She worshipped them. My mother was as powerful a witch as I'd ever known or heard of. It's possible she could have helped me now."

"Where is she?" Ashur asked.

Taran shared a look with Magnus before returning his gaze to Ashur. "She's dead."

Magnus knew this was only part of the truth. Taran had killed his own mother when she'd attempted to sacrifice him in a blood magic ritual.

Magnus also knew without a doubt that Taran's mother would have been no use to them, only a help to the Kindred, but he chose not to say this aloud.

"If I had half the resources I used to have," Ashur began, pacing back and forth in short, frustrated lines in the shadow of a tall oak tree, "I could find a way to help you. Help Olivia and Cleo . . . and Nicolo. But my hands are tied. If I show my face in Kraeshia again, I have no doubt that Amara will have me executed on sight."

Magnus winced at the name.

He'd refrained from sharing his plan to assassinate Amara with Ashur. He wasn't sure if the prince would care one way or the other, but he thought it best to say nothing for now. He would deal with the fallout if and when Felix and Nerissa were successful.

"Not willing to sacrifice everything to save your boyfriend?" Magnus asked drily. "I guess it isn't true love after all. If it was, you probably would have known he was in the city burning up nurse-maids and stealing babies."

Magnus turned, only to be met with Ashur's fist slamming into his face. After the blinding pain passed, he grabbed hold of the prince and shoved him against the thick trunk of the tree.

Ashur scowled at him. "You hit me before. Consider us even now."

Taran stood by, watching the two tensely.

With a grunt, Magnus released him, wiping his hand under his now bloody nose. "Cut a little too close to the quick, did I?"

"How I feel about Nicolo is no one's business but my own," Ashur growled. His shoulder-length black hair had come loose from its leather tie, and it fell into his face. "And you have no idea what I would be willing to do to help him. You may think you have me figured out, Magnus. But you're wrong. I'm not doing any of this with the thought that Nicolo would want to spend another day in my company."

"Then why?"

"Because I feel personally responsible that his life has been torn away from him. Had I not been complicit in Amara's original plans, he might be free of this tangled mess."

"Doubtful," Magnus replied. "He's Cleo's best friend. He would have been a part of this even if you'd never stepped foot in Mytica. Don't think yourself that important."

He knew it came out cruel and near hateful, but he couldn't help himself.

"Nicolo was in love with Cleo once," Ashur said. "Perhaps he still is. His romantic preferences are not the same as mine. There may never be a future for us. But that doesn't matter to me. I'm not doing any of this for my own gain. I'm doing it because I want Nicolo to live exactly the life he desires, whether I'm a part of it or not."

Magnus studied him for a long moment, his nose throbbing. "All right, so prove it."

"How?"

"I can't continue to wait for Lucia to return. That witch—or exiled Watcher you spoke of before . . ."

"Valia," Ashur said the name under his breath like a curse.

"You know of someone like that?" Taran said, stunned. "Someone who might be able to help us?"

Magnus nodded. "Let's go find her."

Magnus, Ashur, and Taran rode to the village of Viridy immediately, reaching it just before nightfall. Lit by lanterns and the light of the moon, its cobblestone streets sparkled, leading their way toward the Silver Toad.

The tavern was packed from wall to wall with patrons celebrating the festival. A band played noisily in the corner while a woman, a goblet clenched in her fist, announced that she was about to sing a song she'd written for the goddess, titled "Her Goldenness."

Magnus quickly wished for cotton to stuff in his ears when she began screeching drunkenly at the top of her lungs.

"Reminds me of my childhood," Taran said with a grimace. "It's one of the many reasons I left to join the revolution in Kraeshia."

Magnus spotted Bruno and beckoned the old man over to their table.

"Everyone!" Bruno waved his arms. "Look who we have here tonight! Prince Magnus and Prince Ashur and their . . . friend. I don't know who he is. Let's raise a glass to toast to their good health, shall we?"

"If we didn't need him, I'd kill him," Magnus said under his breath as everyone in the tavern clinked their drinks together in a drunken, if friendly, toast.

"He's certainly enthusiastic," Ashur replied.

"My father would cut the tongues from those half as enthusi-astic as he is if it annoyed him enough," he said.

"I have no doubt about that."

"So much for remaining as incognito as possible." Magnus scanned the area, worried that there might be Kraeshian guards in attendance, but saw no one in their green uniforms.

"I'm Taran, by the way," Taran said to Bruno.

Bruno clasped Taran's outstretched hand and shook it. "A plea-sure, young man. An absolute pleasure. Welcome to the Silver Toad."

The band started up again, drowning out their conversation, and the patrons' attention shifted back to the next volunteer, a man who'd composed a poem in honor of the goddess's beauty.

"What would you all like to drink?" Bruno asked. "The first round is in honor of your father, Prince Magnus." He spit to the side. "I didn't have an ounce of respect for him, but it is a horrible thing that happened to him all the same."

"Your heartfelt condolences are appreciated," Magnus said drily.

"We're not here to drink," Ashur said. "We're here about Valia."

Bruno frowned. "On such a night as this?"

"Yes. We need your assistance in the summoning ritual, unless you think she will not respond tonight. Perhaps she's celebrating somewhere else, somewhere unreachable."

"Oh, not a worry—I've never known Valia to celebrate anything." Bruno took off his apron and flung it onto a nearby table. "Very well, let's go out back. I am honored to assist in such an exciting prospect."

After disappearing into another part of the tavern for a few moments, Bruno returned with a lantern to light their way and a rolled piece of parchment tucked under his arm. Magnus and the others followed him outside into the cool evening air.

"What is that?" Magnus asked, nodding at the parchment.

"The instructions, your highness." Bruno shrugged. "My mind has a difficult time remembering such things at my age, so I make sure to write everything down."

Magnus shared a bemused look with Ashur.

"I do hope this isn't a waste of our time," Ashur said under his breath.

"Indeed." Magnus cast a glance over his shoulder at Taran to see that the white lines, now showing on his exposed hand and throat, glowed softly in the darkness. This sight sent a shiver of overwhelming dread through him. "I don't think we have much time left to waste," he added.

Magnus had left Cleo asleep at the palace without saying a word about where he was going. If he returned with good news, that was one thing. If this ended in nothing but disappointment, she didn't have to know.

But if she had joined them, he knew he'd be far too distracted to focus on the task at hand.

They followed Bruno to a wooded area just outside of the village borders.

Bruno put the lantern down on a piece of moss, then unrolled the parchment, peering at it through his round spectacles. "Ah, yes. I remember. Blood sacrifice." He glanced up at the three. "Do you happen to have a dagger on you?"

"Of course." Taran pulled his dagger from the sheath at his belt, presenting it to Bruno hilt-first.

"Excellent, yes, very sharp. This will do nicely." Then Bruno's gaze moved to the glowing marks at Taran's throat. "Huh. That is very curious indeed. Have you been dabbling in *elementia*, young man? Or did a witch cast a curse upon you?"

"Something like that," Taran said, then indicated the parchment. "May I read this?"

Bruno held it out to him. "Of course."

Taran glanced at Ashur and Magnus. "My mother kept notes on spells and her experiences with magic. I've read this sort of thing before."

"Does it look like it will work?" Ashur asked.

Taran scanned the page. "Hard to tell."

"For the blood sacrifice . . ." Bruno said, glancing around the area. "Perhaps we can find something slow to catch. A turtle, perhaps."

"Give me that." Magnus took the blade from Bruno and pressed it against the palm of his left hand, pressing down until he felt a sting. "No turtles need to die. We can use my blood."

Bruno nodded. "That should be fine."

Magnus held his hand out and watched his blood drip to the ground.

"Good," Taran said, nodding. "According to this, you need to smear it into a circle."

"How large of a circle?"

"It doesn't say."

Begrudgingly, Magnus did as instructed, creating a circle only two feet in diameter. "Now what?"

"Speak her name," Taran said. "Ask her to join us . . ." He winced as he looked up from the parchment. "And ask politely."

Magnus hissed out a breath. "Very well. Valia, we wish for you to join us here and now." He gritted his teeth. "If you please."

"Good," Bruno said, smiling. "Now we wait."

"My confidence wanes more and more every moment we're out here," Ashur said, shaking his head as Magnus bound the wound on his hand. "But I will remain hopeful awhile longer."

"My expectations are extremely low," Magnus said. "Even if we manage to contact this Valia, we have no idea if she can help us."

"I suppose," a calm, cool, feminine voice said, "you could start by asking me nicely. I do value proper manners, especially in young men."

Magnus turned around slowly to see a beautiful woman now standing behind them in the shadows of the trees. She wore a long black silk cloak, a color that matched her long hair. Her skin was pale in the moonlight, her cheeks high, her chin pointed. Her lips were stained a dark red.

"You're Valia," Magnus said.

"I am," she replied.

"Prove it."

"Prince Magnus!" Bruno said with a gasp. "We must speak respectfully to Valia."

"Or what?" he asked, keeping his gaze steadily on the witch's. "Will she turn me into a toad?"

"I don't think you'd make a very good toad," Valia said as she moved closer, eyeing them one at a time.

Ashur bowed his head. "We are honored by your presence, my lady."

"See?" Valia raised a brow toward Magnus. "This one knows how to behave in the presence of great power."

"Is that what you have? Great power?" Magnus's patience for a common witch—and he had no reason yet to believe she was anything but that—was quickly dissipating.

"It depends on the day, really," she said. "And the reason I've been summoned."

"Or perhaps you simply lurk in the shadows waiting for Bruno to bring you willing victims." He sneered at her. "Are you about to ask us for coin in order to perform your magic? If so, you can spare your breath. Save it for a poetry reading or singing a song during the festival."

"I have more than enough coin to not have any need of more." Valia approached Taran now, her thin dark brows drawing together as she studied him. Taran remained as still as a statue as she reached toward him and traced her finger along one of his glowing white lines.

"Very interesting," she said.

"Do you know what this is?" he asked.

"Perhaps."

"And can you help me?"

"Perhaps."

Magnus laughed out loud, drawing a sharp look from the witch. "You know, do you? And what exactly do you think it is?"

"This young man is currently possessed by the air Kindred." Valia took Taran's right hand in hers, turning it over so she could see the spiral air magic mark on his palm. "And yet he still has control of his body and mind. How interesting."

Magnus found he did not have an immediate reply for this.

She was far more knowledgeable than he'd expected.

He squinted in the darkness. Something seemed odd about the woman. At first glance, she appeared to be beautiful and young, but her features were *too* perfect, her skin *too* unblemished and flawless.

If she was an exiled Watcher and not just a common witch, that might explain it.

But her left hand—it wasn't the hand of a mortal, it was the taloned foot of a hawk.

"Your hand . . ." he said, his breath drawing sharply in as he realized what he was looking at.

"My hand?" Valia held out her hands in front of her. "Do you see something odd about them?"

Magnus shook his head, now seeing only two graceful hands with short, perfectly manicured fingernails.

"Nothing," he said, frowning deeply. "My apologies."

Valia drew closer to him, taking Magnus's hand in hers and unraveling the handkerchief he'd wrapped around his bloody wound.

"Let me help with that." She pressed her palm against his. A glowing light appeared, and sudden pain sliced through his skin. He wanted to pull away, but he forced himself to remain still. When she removed her hand, his wound had healed.

"All right," he said, trying very hard to keep his tone steady and controlled. She had enough earth magic within her to be able to heal just like Lucia could. "You're for real."

Valia didn't reply. She took his hand in hers again. "Where did you get this?" she asked, touching the golden bloodstone ring on his finger.

Magnus took his hand away. "It was a gift from my father."

"Quite a valuable gift," she said, raising her gaze to meet his. "Many would kill for a ring like this. Many *have* killed for it."

"You know what this is," he whispered.

"I do."

"What?"

"Dangerous," she replied. "As dangerous as the one who created it with his death magic and necromancy a thousand years ago."

He found he couldn't speak for a moment. Silence stretched between them until he found his voice again.

"Just how old are you, Valia?" Magnus asked. Bruno had said he hadn't seen her for three decades, yet she appeared only a handful of years older than Ashur.

She smiled, her green eyes sparkling with amusement. "That is a not a question a gentleman should ask of a lady."

"I'm no gentleman."

"Take care of that ring, Prince Magnus. Wouldn't want someone to steal it away from you, would we?" Valia turned to Taran again, her gaze moving over the white lines on his throat and hand. "So, you want my help. And you think I would willingly become involved with this?"

"If you can help in any way," Taran said, "I would hope that you would. And it's not only me, it's also Princess Cleiona. She's in trouble . . . we both are."

"And you need to help the other two," Ashur said to Valia. "A young man named Nicolo and an immortal named Olivia. However, they are not as fortunate as Taran and Cleiona to still have some semblance of control."

"He was right," Valia said under her breath. "We're close now. Too close."

"Who was right?" Magnus asked.

"A friend of mine who likes to give advice and ask for difficult and time-consuming favors." She swept her gaze over the four of them. "Bruno, it was lovely to see you again."

Bruno bowed deeply. "And you as well. A vision of beauty, as always."

Valia nodded. "Take me to the other one . . . this Princess Cleiona. I want to see her."

"And then . . . ?" Magnus asked, his voice tight.

She met his gaze directly. "Then I will determine if there is anything I can do to help you, or if it's far too late for that."

CHAPTER 21

CLEO

AURANOS

Cleo woke up in the large canopied featherbed and sleepily reached for her husband.

But there was no one there.

She pushed up on her elbow to see that the silk sheets on the other side of the bed did not show any wrinkles.

Magnus hadn't returned last night.

When she'd searched for him yesterday evening, she'd learned that he wasn't the only one missing from the palace without explanation—so were Prince Ashur and Taran.

She wasn't sure if she should be concerned or annoyed.

As she was thinking about it, her handmaiden arrived, a young Auranian girl named Anya who was attentive and polite. Her smile held even when she noticed the web of strange blue lines that now covered the entirety of Cleo's right hand and arm.

Anya asked no questions but made polite conversation as she helped Cleo dress in a simple yet beautiful pale rose-colored gown with golden laces at the bodice.

It was one of the dresses Cleo had had modified by the palace tailor to include a pocket for her aquamarine orb.

"Have you seen Prince Magnus this morning?" Cleo asked.

"No, your grace," Anya replied as she gently dragged a brush through Cleo's long, tangled hair.

"And not last night either?"

"I'm afraid not. Likely, he's enjoying the festival like everyone else is."

"I highly doubt that," she muttered. "He's up to something."

"Perhaps he's out acquiring you a gift."

"Perhaps," Cleo allowed, although she was certain this wasn't the case. If Magnus was with Taran and Ashur, she doubted that they would be doing anything frivolous. It would have been nice to have been kept informed of any plans.

He's trying to protect you, she thought.

"I'm not a simpleminded child who needs to be kept away from steep cliffs," she muttered.

Anya cleared her throat nervously, her smile remaining fixed upon her pretty face. "Of course you aren't, princess."

How Cleo longed for the company of Nerissa again. She needed her friend's guidance and straightforward way of looking at the world, especially when it seemed to be completely falling apart.

Nerissa had told her only that she was going on an important journey with Felix and that she would return as soon as she could. When Cleo had pressed for more information, Nerissa simply shook her head.

"Please trust that I am doing only what I need to do," she'd said.

Cleo trusted Nerissa because Nerissa had more than earned that trust in the past.

Yet it still seemed as if everyone had left her all alone with her thoughts, her worries, and her fears.

"I heard the most beautiful song last night at the Beast," Anya said as she pinned Cleo's hair back from the left side of her face. Cleo had requested that it remain down on the right to hide the lines.

The Beast was a popular tavern in the city, frequented by nobles and servants alike.

"Did you?" she asked absently. "What was it about?"

"It was about the goddess Cleiona's final fight against Valoria," Anya said. "And that it was not one of vengeance and anger, but painful necessity. That, in their truest hearts, they loved each other like sisters."

"What a tragic song," Cleo said. "And how fantastical. I've read nothing about them that would lead me to believe their battle was anything but two enemies who had finally declared war upon each other."

"Perhaps. But it was very pretty."

"Very pretty, just like you, my dear. Such a pretty vessel—I can see why you would fight so hard to keep it."

Cleo's breath caught as she stared at her reflection, Anya busily tending to her hair.

Who said that?

"You must give in to the waves," the voice continued. Cleo couldn't discern if it was a male or female voice; it could easily have been either. *"Let them take you under. Don't resist. Resisting is what makes it hurt the most."*

The water Kindred.

Cleo's fingertips flew to her throat, to the lines that had crept up higher yesterday.

"Leave me," she said suddenly to Anya, far more harshly than she'd meant to.

Anya didn't argue, didn't say that she wasn't finished with

Cleo's hair yet, she simply bowed her head and left the room without a word.

"I need you to leave me too," Cleo said, staring fiercely into her reflected eyes. "Immediately."

"*That won't happen,*" the voice replied. "*I chose you, I'm keeping you. It's as simple as that.*"

"There is nothing simple about this."

"*The fact that I'm even able to communicate with you now means that I am close to taking full control. I've never taken mortal form before. I think it will be wonderful to finally live on that plane of existence. To see all this world has to offer, to taste it, smell it, touch it. It is something that has been denied me for far too long. Won't you help me?*"

"Help you?" Cleo shook her head, her heart pounding hard in her chest. "Help you to kill me?"

"*A mortal life is fleeting. Seventy, eighty years, if one is lucky. I will be eternal.*" As Cleo watched her reflection, her eyes began to glow with an otherworldly blue light. "*You must go to Kyan. He will help you to make this transition as painless as possible. My brother does not possess a great deal of patience, and his anger can be quick and unpredictable, so you would be doing yourself a great favor, along with so many others who might come to harm, to do as I say.*"

Cleo learned forward, studying her now strange and foreign gaze. It was like looking at someone else entirely.

"Never," she snarled. "I will fight against you until my very last breath!"

She picked up the silver-handled brush that Anya had left behind and threw it at the mirror, shattering the glass on contact.

The water Kindred didn't say another word.

Cleo burst out of her chambers, knowing that if she stayed a moment longer in there all by herself she would go mad.

She slammed into something solid and warm. And very tall.

"Cleo . . ." Magnus took hold of her shoulders gently. "What's wrong? Another drowning spell?"

"No," she managed, breathless. It would worry him so much if she told him what had happened. She wasn't ready for that, not yet. "I . . . I just wanted to leave. I wanted to find you. Where have you been? Were you with Ashur and Taran?"

He nodded, his expression grim. "I want you to come with me."

Panic gripped her heart. Had something horrible happened to Taran? Had he been taken over completely by the air Kindred?

"What is it?"

"There's someone I want you to meet."

He took her hand in his and led her out of the room and through the hallways of the palace to the throne room.

"Who?"

"Someone I hope very much might have the power to help you."

Afternoon light streamed into the throne room through the stained glass windows and bounced off the gold veining on the marble columns, making them glitter.

Ashur waited there with Taran.

The "someone" Magnus had mentioned stood between them. A beautiful woman who used berry stain on her lips and cheeks, even though she had no need for such enhancements. Cleo wondered why she would bother.

"Princess Cleiona Aurora Bellos," Magnus said in formal introduction, "this is . . . Valia."

"Just Valia?" Cleo asked.

"Yes," Valia said simply, her green-eyed gaze focused intently upon Cleo as if assessing her value. "So this is the girl with the name of a goddess, is it?"

Cleo didn't answer the question. "I have been told you might be able to help us," she said instead.

Valia raised a brow. "May I ask a question out of sheer curiosity, your grace?"

"Go ahead."

"You have not taken your husband's surname as your own. Why is that?" At Cleo's surprised look, Valia tempered her question with a smile. "It strikes me as interesting."

It wasn't the first time that Cleo had been asked this question in her travels across Mytica. Usually a noble posed the question, peering at her over their goblet or dinner plate.

"I am the last in the Bellos family line," Cleo said simply. "I felt it was respectful to those who have come before me that I not let it fade away to nothing."

"How curious." Valia glanced at Magnus. "And you allowed this?"

Magnus's attention remained on Cleo, his hand pressed to the small of her back. "Cleo makes her own choices. She always has."

An excellent reply, Cleo thought.

"It is a good name, Bellos," Valia said. "I knew your father quite well."

Cleo regarded her with shock. "You did?"

Valia nodded, then turned to walk toward the marble dais. "I met with him right here, in this very spot, on several occasions."

Cleo grappled for a response to this unexpected information. "For what reason?"

"He'd had a dream that his palace was under attack. He didn't believe in magic, not like your mother did, but after Queen Elena's death he had come to consider many options that would strengthen his reign and was willing to open his mind to more possibilities that could help him." She took the stairs to the top of the dais and rested her hand on the back of the golden throne, gazing down at it as if King Corvin was seated there as they spoke. "He convinced me to help him. I used my magic to put a ward on the gates of this palace, to help keep everyone within it safe. I think he did this mostly to protect you and your sister, your grace."

Cleo remembered the magical ward placed on the gates. It was magic that Lucia had broken through with her own *elementia*, causing an explosion near the end of the bloody battle that had cost hundreds of lives.

"Impossible," Magnus said, shaking his head. "My father found the witch that had cast that spell. When she proved to be of no help to him, he . . ." He hesitated. "He *dismissed* her."

"Actually, King Gaius killed her," Valia corrected. "Or, at least, he killed the woman he *thought* was responsible. And then he sent her severed head to King Corvin in a box. But your father was wrong. His victim was certainly a witch, but not the correct one."

Cleo listened to all this, her thoughts spinning. "If this is all true, why didn't you help my father when he needed you the most? If you are so powerful that you could cast a spell of protection like that, why didn't you help him when the palace was attacked, when he was dying in my arms?"

Valia didn't speak for a moment. Cleo searched for any trace of regret or doubt in her eyes, but found nothing but hardness.

"Because that was his destiny," Valia finally said, then cast her gaze down toward Cleo's marked left hand. "And perhaps your destiny is already set as well."

Cleo wanted to resist. She wanted to stomp her foot and demand that this witch be cast from this palace forever, but she took a moment to calm herself.

Every time she thought of the water Kindred's voice in her head—thankfully silent now—a deathly chill spread over her skin.

She would not let herself be frightened of something that had not happened yet.

She still had control. And she would fight until the very end.

"Very well," Cleo said, her chin held high. "The past is over and cannot be changed. What can you do for us now, at this very moment?"

"That is an excellent question, your grace. Let me see your marks up close."

Valia descended from the dais and reached for Cleo's hand. Cleo allowed this, only because she didn't want to push back too much against someone who might have the power to help her.

Valia inspected the lines spreading out from the water symbol on her left palm, then swept the hair off the left side of her neck to see where they ended.

"Does it cover your entire arm?" she asked.

Cleo nodded stiffly.

"Taran's marks have progressed much farther."

Taran remained silent, standing straight-backed and square-shouldered like a trained soldier.

Ashur watched Cleo and Valia, intent on every word the witch spoke.

"What is your verdict?" Ashur asked. "Can you help them?"

Valia reached under the folds of her black shirts and withdrew a shiny black dagger that looked as if it had been chiseled from the same material as the earth Kindred orb. Obsidian.

"Just what do you mean to do with *that*?" Magnus asked.

"I need to draw blood," Valia said.

"You will not cut Cleo with that weapon," he snarled.

"But I must," Valia replied. "The princess's blood will give me more insight into how much I can help her."

"We need Lucia," Cleo said to Magnus.

"I agree," he said, his expression strained. "But Lucia is not here, and we have no way of knowing if or when she will return."

"Lucia," Valia repeated. "Princess Lucia Damora, the prophesied sorceress. Yes, she would be quite helpful, wouldn't she? I would enjoy meeting her in person. The stories I've heard, especially of her travels the last couple of months, are very interesting."

Cleo didn't like this woman. Didn't like how she looked, how she stood, how she spoke. She didn't like that Valia had known her father and had turned her back on him when she could have helped during that fateful battle, yet she seemingly felt no sense of responsibility or remorse over his death.

Valia's demeanor held an arrogance, a snide confidence that Cleo found repelling.

But Magnus was right. Lucia wasn't here. So she would have to swallow her pride and hope very much that this witch could help them.

"I'll go first," Taran said, moving forward to stand between Cleo and the witch. He pulled the sleeve of his shirt up and offered his right arm to her. "Cut me if you need to."

"Where is the moonstone orb?" Valia asked. "I think that would help greatly."

Magnus and Cleo shared a concerned look. This witch knew a great deal about the Kindred, far more than many others would.

"I don't have it," Taran said. "I gave it to Princess Lucia when she asked for it. Only she'd know where it is right now."

"I see." Valia glanced at Cleo. "And the aquamarine?"

"The very same," Cleo lied. "Lucia has all four of them."

Her crystal orb was where it always was: in the pocket of her gown, enclosed in a velvet pouch so Cleo wouldn't have to physically touch it.

"Very well. We will try to make do without." Valia nodded and, with Cleo, Magnus, and Ashur looking on, traced the tip of her blade against Taran's marked skin. It wasn't a straight cut; she twisted and turned the blade, as if drawing specific symbols upon his flesh.

Taran didn't flinch as his blood welled to the surface.

Valia swiped her hand against his arm and looked down at the blood on her palm.

"You have made some choices in your life, choices that have caused you great pain," she said. "What you did to your mother haunts you to this very day."

"What is this?" Taran growled. "I'm not looking to have my fortune told."

"Your blood is the essence of who you are. It contains your past, present, and future. This is not a simple fortune-telling, young man." Valia returned her gaze to Taran's slick blood on her hand. "I can see your jealousy toward your brother: the well-behaved one, the one who followed all the rules. When you heard of his murder, your need for vengeance did not stem only from the love of a brother but from your guilt at turning your back on him to seek your destiny far away. True?"

Taran's face had gone pale, making the circles under his eyes look even darker. "True."

Magnus cleared his throat. "Let's move this along, shall we? No need to dwell in the past."

"Do you hear the voice inside you?" Valia asked Taran, ignoring the prince. "The one that tells you to let go of your control?"

A shiver went up Cleo's spine.

"Yes," Taran said, nodding with a jerk of his head. "I can hear it even now. It wants me to go to Kyan. It says it will lead me there if I let it. But I don't want to. I'd rather die than let this demon inside me take over my body and my life. I want to—"

He started to tremble then, and his hands flew to his throat as he gasped for breath.

"He's suffocating," Ashur said. "Stop this, Valia. Whatever you're doing to him, stop it right now!"

"I'm not doing anything to him," Valia said, shaking her head. "I see now that I can't do anything. It's too late for him—too late for either of them."

"Get out," Magnus growled. "You've done enough. Just leave, and don't come back."

"I believe I can still help in other ways," Valia replied calmly.

"We don't want your help! Go now!"

Cleo grabbed hold of Taran's face. He was starting to turn a frightening shade of blue. Glowing white lines now spread over his jaw and up his cheeks.

"Look at me," she said frantically. "Please look at me! It's all right. Just try to breathe."

Taran held her gaze, his brown eyes filled with pain and fear just before they rolled back and he slipped from her grasp. Ashur was there to catch him before he hit the marble floor. He put two fingers to Taran's pulse at his throat and then held his hand under Taran's nose.

"He's unconscious, but he's still breathing," Ashur said.

"That witch did this," Magnus said darkly.

Cleo looked around to see that Valia had disappeared from the throne room. It was a relief to see she was gone. And it was an even greater relief that Taran was still alive.

Then she focused her attention on Magnus.

"You should have told me where you were going last night," she said. "All of this could have been avoided."

His lips thinned. "I was trying to protect you."

"You think you can protect me from this?" She wrenched her hair from the left side of her throat. "You can't. Like Valia just said, it's too late."

"It's not too late. I refuse to believe that."

She didn't want to fight with him, didn't want to say anything she'd regret later. "Ashur, please take care of Taran. I . . . I need to leave this place, clear my head. I'll take Enzo with me for protection."

"Where are you going?" Magnus asked as she moved toward the exit.

She wasn't sure.

Somewhere that wasn't here. Somewhere that would make her think of happier times, times long ago and mostly forgotten.

Somewhere she could try to regain her strength and focus.

"To the festival," she said.

CHAPTER 22

MAGNUS

AURANOS

Of course, Magnus immediately followed her.

He watched Cleo and Enzo from beneath the heavy black hood of his cloak, which helped to shield his identity from prying eyes, through the labyrinth of streets filled with citizens in the midst of their celebration. In the bright sun of midafternoon, the gaudy, colorful festival banners and temporary paintings sloshed onto the sides of buildings were impossible to ignore.

The original Cleiona must have enjoyed her hedonistic lifestyle every bit as much as her current citizens, Magnus thought. Valoria was said to be of much calmer demeanor. She valued silence rather than revelry, calmness and thoughtfulness over drunken debauchery.

This gave Limerians, as a whole, a sense of superiority over their southern neighbors.

But Magnus knew not all were as devoted as the law decreed. He'd found a Limerian tavern that secretly served wine to those who asked for it, and surely it was not the only one. Also, a large part of the gold his father had obtained, at least until the expensive war against Auranos had stripped him of any access to his fortune, had come from fines levied against those who did not observe the two days per week of silence.

Frankly, Magnus couldn't remember the last time he'd observed them himself.

He watched Cleo and Enzo pass storefront after storefront: bakers and jewelers, tailors and cobblers. Cleo had not disguised herself in any way, other than by wearing a pair of white silk gloves to cover her water Kindred marks. She greeted all who approached her with a warm smile, allowing them to bow or curtsy before she took their hands in hers and said something kind enough to make them glow with happiness.

The Auranian people loved their golden princess.

She deserves their love, Magnus thought, his throat tight.

After some time had passed and Cleo had spoken to dozens upon dozens of people, Magnus watched her indicate a specific building to Enzo. Enzo shook his head, but Cleo persisted. Finally, he nodded, and the pair disappeared inside.

Magnus looked up at the sign.

The Beast.

He hadn't recognized it in the stark light of day, but he knew the tavern quite well. He decided it best to remain outside, where he wouldn't be recognized and he could watch from afar.

A steady stream of patrons entered sober and left drunk and singing at the top of their lungs, but Cleo and Enzo still didn't emerge. Magnus's impatience grew as the afternoon wore on.

And then concern set in.

What could be taking so long?

He crossed the street to the tavern and pushed through the entrance. Inside the Beast, it could be any hour of the day or night.

There were no windows to let in the light, so the walls were dotted with lanterns, and a chandelier heavily laden with candles hung from the ceiling.

The room was packed, every table filled to capacity. Magnus could barely hear himself think over the din of loud conversation blended with a fiddler's music.

The placed smelled of cigarillo smoke, alcohol-laden breath, and hundreds of bodies that hadn't bathed today.

He wondered with dismay if the tavern had always been like this and he'd simply been too drunk to notice during previous visits.

Cleo was nowhere to be seen, so Magnus drew his cowl closer to his face and pushed forward through a mass of sweaty bodies dancing to the fiddler's tune upon a sawdust-covered floor. He grimaced as a scantily clad couple, kissing passionately, stumbled across his path, spilling wine from their goblets onto his leather boots.

Cleo would wish to spend more than a heartbeat in such a place?

A bearded man tripped over his own feet and landed hard in front of Magnus. Then, laughing, he immediately sprang up and continued on his way.

Auranian heathens, he thought.

The fiddler ended his song to cheers of appreciation from the drunken crowd. He stood up and spoke loudly to be heard over the din: "We have someone who wishes to make a toast to you all! Silence please, allow him to speak!"

The room quieted, and Magnus saw a flash of a red guard's uniform out of the corner of his eye. He turned slowly as Enzo, a large tankard of ale in his grip, climbed upon a long wooden table.

"I'm not sure I want to do this," Enzo said tentatively. "I think I've had far too much to drink today."

The crowd laughed as if he'd made the most hilarious joke they'd ever heard.

"It's fine!" the fiddler called up to him. "We all have! Speak from your heart in honor of the goddess and her magically sweet breath. Make your toast!"

Enzo didn't say anything for a moment, and the crowd began to murmur among themselves as the silence became more awkward.

Then he raised his tankard high in the air. "To Nerissa Florens, the girl I love."

The crowd cheered and drank, yet Enzo was not quite finished.

"The girl I love," he said again, "who never loved me! The girl who took my heart, chopped it up into tiny pieces, and threw them into the Silver Sea as she set sail with another man! A man with only one eye, might I add, when I have two perfectly fine eyes! Goddess, how I hate him. Do you know what she told me? 'It's my duty,' she said. Her duty!"

Magnus stared up at the guard. He'd known Enzo to be very loyal, very quiet, and very subdued—until now.

Just how much ale had he drunk since they'd arrived?

Enzo continued. "If any of you know Felix Gaebras, and I'm sure many of you do, he's not to be trusted."

Surely, he had to be finished now, Magnus thought.

Enzo stomped his foot, sending several tin plates flying from the surface of the table. "Nerissa does not value commitment, she says! This she told me many times, but what am I to believe? That her attentions were only temporary? That her kisses were meaningless?" His voice broke. "Does she not know my heart is shattered by her absence?"

Magnus's gaze moved over the crowd as Cleo, her blond hair trailing behind her, hurried toward Enzo.

"Please come down from there, Enzo," Cleo implored.

Seeing her loosened some of the tightness in Magnus's chest.

"The golden princess wishes to make a toast as well!" the fiddler announced.

Cleo waved her hands. "No, no, I don't. I'm just trying to retrieve my friend before he says something he will deeply regret."

"If you ask me," Enzo said loudly, ignoring the princess entirely, "I think there was something curious going on between Nerissa and the empress. Yes, you heard me correctly. Something much more than an attendant and a ruler." He took a deep drink from his tankard before raising it again. "You know what they say about Kraeshians."

"What?" someone called out. "What do they say about Kraeshians?"

"That the only cold bed for a Kraeshian is their deathbed." Enzo's shoulders then slumped, as if he'd just run out of his last bit of energy. "My gratitude to you all for joining me in this toast."

The crowd fell completely silent for a moment before they cheered again, and the fiddler started his next song.

Magnus approached Cleo as she helped Enzo down from the tabletop.

"That was . . . fascinating," he said, no longer interested in keeping his presence unknown.

Cleo spun to face him. "You followed us!"

"I did. If I hadn't I wouldn't have heard such intriguing gossip about your favorite attendant."

"Enzo's drunk," Cleo explained. "He doesn't know what he's saying."

Magnus eyed the guard. "I see that the princess has managed to corrupt you to her Auranian ways in a shamefully short amount of time."

Enzo leaned heavily against a nearby wall. "Your highness, I don't think—"

"Clearly there was a profound lack of thinking here. Your one job is to keep Cleo safe, not to publicly and drunkenly pine away for your lost love."

Enzo opened his mouth to speak, perhaps to protest, but Magnus raised his hand.

"You're dismissed for the rest of the day. Go . . . drink as much as you see fit. Find another girl to help take your mind off Nerissa. I'm sure there are plenty under this very roof who would be willing to help. Do whatever you wish, as long as it's out of my sight."

Enzo's gaze flicked to Cleo with uncertainty for a moment before he bowed deeply, nearly losing his balance. "Yes, your highness."

Magnus watched him disappear into the crowd before Cleo turned a glare on Magnus.

"That was rude," she said.

"Your point?"

"Enzo has earned respect."

"Not today he hasn't." Magnus crossed his arms over his chest. "Now, what to do about you?"

Her pale eyebrows lifted. "I would strongly suggest you don't try to order me around."

"If I did, I certainly wouldn't expect you to listen," he growled.

"Good."

Magnus reached for her left hand, and she didn't pull away. He ran his thumb over the silk glove. "Hiding it doesn't change what is happening."

Cleo looked down at the floor. "It helps me forget for a few moments so that I can try to feel normal again."

Magnus was about to respond, when he felt a hand on his shoulder. He turned to face a woman with a large bosom looking at them with a wide, toothy smile.

"Yes?" he said.

Her smile widened further. "You two make such a lovely couple."

"Much gratitude," Cleo said to her tightly.

"Seeing you here," the woman said, "together, celebrating with us all. It warms the heart."

"Indeed," Magnus said drily. "Please, don't let us keep you any longer from your . . . fun." He took Cleo by her upper arm and moved her a safe distance away. "We're leaving."

"I'm not ready to go yet. I like it here." She glanced around at the dingy tavern.

"I find that hard to believe."

"I've never been here before."

"I have." He took in the surroundings, as memories—mostly unclear—flooded back to him. "It was right before I found you in the temple that night."

She frowned, her gaze growing faraway. "When I offered you a tentative alliance, but you were too drunk to listen to me, and then you spent the night in Amara's bed."

He grimaced. "Actually, it was *my* bed. And I had greatly hoped not to be reminded of that unfortunate mistake ever again."

Cleo's annoyed expression eased. "Apologies. It's behind us, just as many troubles are."

"Good," he said. He searched her face. "Do you really want to stay here?"

"No." She shook her head. "Let's go back to the palace."

The fiddler ended his song and announced that there was someone who wished to make another toast.

"I certainly hope it's not Enzo again," Magnus muttered.

Out of the corner of his eye, he saw someone climb up onto the very same table that Enzo had used as a makeshift stage, a silver goblet in his hand.

"My toast is to Prince Magnus, the rightful heir to his father's throne!" the painfully familiar voice called out. "A true friend and—believe me when I say this—a true survivor."

"Magnus . . ." Cleo's grip on his arm became painfully tight.

Heart pounding, Magnus turned on his boot heels to face Lord Kurtis, whose cold gaze was fixed on him.

Kurtis raised his goblet. "Cheers to Prince Magnus!"

The crowd cheered and clinked their glasses again, drinking deeply, before the fiddler filled the noisy air with music.

The former kingsliege descended from the table and headed toward the exit.

"Magnus—" Cleo began.

"Stay here," he bit out.

Without another word, Magnus took off after Lord Kurtis.

He burst outside of the Beast, looking to the left and right, trying to spot Kurtis fleeing through the swell of the crowd outside. Finally, his gaze narrowed on the familiar pale, weasel-like face grinning back in his direction.

Magnus shoved past several men standing in his way.

The cold splash of a drink spilling on his boots distracted him long enough for Kurtis to disappear.

He swore in frustration.

"Up ahead," Cleo shouted. "Around the corner, he took a left."

Magnus cringed. "I told you to stay put."

Her face was flushed as she reached his side. "Yes. And I ignored you. Move, would you? He's getting away!"

Instead of arguing, he did as she suggested, leaving the main crowded area and heading down a street that had already been lit with fewer torches to compensate for the dwindling light as dusk began to fall over the City of Gold.

Magnus had dreamed of this moment. Fantasized about it. Along with picturing hungry beetles and death by spoon, his endless time in the maddeningly small coffin had included imagining his hands around Lord Kurtis Cirillo's throat, choking the worthless life out of him.

The dark form of Kurtis slipped behind another corner. Magnus had gained on him; Kurtis's steps were swift, but not fast enough.

The alleyway came to a dead end at a stone wall. Kurtis came to a staggering stop. He turned slowly to face Magnus.

"Nowhere left to run?" Magnus said. "How unfortunate for you."

"I wasn't running."

"You should have been."

Cleo caught up to Magnus and stood at his side, her arms crossed, her long blond locks tucked behind her ears. Her face was set in a most magnificent mask of icy judgment, her blue-green eyes narrowed.

A blue wisp curled along her left temple. Magnus might have mistaken it for a pleasant decoration applied by a talented face-painter at the festival had he not known otherwise.

The water Kindred marks had extended even further.

"You must tell me your secret," Kurtis said.

"What secret?" he growled.

"How you managed to survive to stand before me tonight." Kurtis's gaze swept the length of him with appreciation. "I heard your bones break—far too many bones for you to be up and walking about so easily. And I helped shovel the dirt upon your grave. There was no way you should have survived that."

"I will kill you myself," Cleo snarled at him.

"How? With your excellent archery skills?" Kurtis gave her a cold smile before returning his attention to Magnus. "Did your sweet young sister heal you with her now legendary *elementia*?"

"No," Magnus said simply.

Kurtis furrowed his brow. "Then how?"

"It's a mystery, isn't it?" Magnus glanced down at the stump at the end of Kurtis's right arm. "Much like where your right hand now is."

Kurtis's cheek twitched, and hate flashed in his eyes. "You'll regret that."

"I regret many things, Kurtis, but chopping off your hand is not one of them." Magnus did regret leaving the palace earlier without a sword. Foolish of him. But he didn't need one to end this maggot's life.

He took a menacing step toward Kurtis.

"Don't you want to know why I'm here?" Kurtis said, his eyes glittering with malice. "Why I would put myself in harm's way like this?"

Magnus glanced at Cleo. "Do we care?"

She nodded. "I must admit, I am vaguely curious."

"As am I," he said. "Perhaps he's here because he heard that my father slit his father's throat."

"Could be," Cleo allowed. "Perhaps we should be lenient. After all, he is in mourning, just as you are."

Kurtis's upper lip curled back from his teeth in a feral grimace. "I know my father is dead."

"Excellent." Magnus clapped his hands together. "Then we can continue without interruption. It isn't my preference to kill you during a joyous festival like this, but I will make an exception today."

Kurtis's voice dropped to a whisper. "Kyan sent me here."

Magnus's stomach lurched. He struggled to take his next breath. "You're lying."

Kurtis pulled open the front of his shirt to show a painful-looking brand on his chest in the shape of a hand. "He marked me with his fire."

It was the same mark that Kyan had threatened to give Magnus. One that would have made him the fire Kindred's mortal slave.

Kurtis ran his hand over the mark, cringing. "It's an honor, of course, to be marked by a god. But it feels like the fangs of a demon sinking deeper into me every moment. The pain is a constant reminder of where my loyalties now lie."

"Why?" Cleo asked, her voice tight. "Why did Kyan want you to come here?"

"Because he wants me to take you to him, princess," Kurtis replied.

"Then he will be disappointed," Magnus bit out. "Because Cleo is not going anywhere with you."

Kurtis smiled thinly. "I must say, I will regret not learning how you escaped your grave. But one cannot know everything, I suppose."

"You think I'm letting you leave? This ends here and now."

"Yes, it does." This voice came from behind them, and Magnus turned sharply to see Taran Ranus standing in the opening of the alleyway.

Magnus looked at him, confused. "How did you find us?"

Taran opened his mouth to answer, but at the same moment Cleo let out a sharp shriek.

Magnus whipped his head in her direction to see that Kurtis had grabbed her from behind and clamped a cloth over her mouth.

A chill exploded in the air. An icy mist burst from where the princess stood and raced up the walls, coating them with frost in an instant.

Then Cleo's eyes rolled back into her head.

Magnus lurched forward toward her.

Taran waved his hand, and Magnus froze in place, unable to move.

"What are you doing, you fool?" Magnus demanded. "Help Cleo!"

Cleo had gone limp in Kurtis's grip. The cloth must have had some sort of sleeping potion on it, Magnus realized with dismay.

"I *will* help her," Taran said calmly. "And then the four of us will be reunited, all-powerful. Unstoppable."

Magnus turned a look of horror on the rebel. "What are you—?"

"Kill him now," Kurtis barked.

Taran flicked his wrist again. Magnus found himself airborne for a split second before he hit the frost-covered wall hard enough to shatter bone. He fell to the ground in a heap.

"Pick her up," Kurtis said to Taran. "You're stronger than me, and it's a bit of a journey."

Taran did as he suggested, lifting Cleo's limp body easily into his arms. "Where are the others? I'm still gaining my senses. Everything is unclear. I can't yet sense them."

"The Temple of Cleiona," Kurtis replied.

Their voices grew more distant. Magnus couldn't move, could barely think. They believed they had left him for dead, and yet . . . he wasn't dead. The cold weight of the bloodstone on his middle finger was a constant reminder of the magic he wore, pressed against his skin.

But he feared that magic wouldn't be enough this time, especially when the world faded away around him—to utter blackness.

He was woken up by a gentle nudge.

"He's so dreamy, isn't he?" It was a girl's voice, slurred and drunken.

"Oh my goddess, *yes!*" another girl responded. "I mean, when I saw him on the balcony at the palace, he seemed so cold, so unapproachable. But up close like this? So cute, right?"

"*So* cute," her friend agreed. "The princess is so lucky."

"Should we fetch a medic to help him?"

"I think he's just drunk. You know what they say about Prince Magnus and wine."

"Good point." Another nudge. "Prince Magnus? Your highness?"

Magnus blinked, trying to clear his mind of the darkness, trying to focus on what little light there was in the conscious world. He was still in the alley where he'd cornered Kurtis. The sky above had darkened, the sun gone from the sky. It was early evening now. His eyes focused on two girls about Cleo's age looking down at him with great interest.

"Where . . . is she?" he managed. "Where is Cleo?"

In unison, they both cooed with happiness. "We were hoping you two would find happiness together," the first girl said. "I mean, you are so perfect for each other."

"I didn't like her at first," her friend responded. "But she's really grown on me."

The first girl nodded. "You're so dark and broody, your highness. And she's, like, a ray of sunshine. So perfect."

"*So* perfect," her friend agreed.

"I need to go." Magnus tried to push himself up to his feet, and the girls knelt to help him. He let them, since he still felt incredibly unsteady, then he staggered off in the direction of the palace.

"Farewell, my prince!" the girls called out behind him.

Magnus's mind was racing when he got back to the palace.

Ashur, his arms laden down with books from the library, was the first person who crossed his path.

"Magnus . . ." Ashur began, his eyes wide with concern.

"He has her," he managed.

"Who?"

"Kyan." Magnus gripped Ashur by his shoulders. "The Kindred—the air Kindred—it's taken control of Taran's body completely. He and Kurtis Cirillo took Cleo."

Ashur dropped the books, and they scattered across the floor with a thud. "Taran was resting in his chambers. I left him only a short time ago."

"Trust me, he's not there anymore."

Magnus wished very much he hadn't sent Valia away. He needed all the help he could get, but there was no time to find her again. "I need to get to the Temple of Cleiona," he said.

"Is that where the princess has been taken?" Ashur asked.

Magnus nodded. "They have a substantial lead, so I need to go immediately."

Ashur nodded. "I'm going with you."

CHAPTER 23

CLEO

AURANOS

The first thing Cleo saw when she opened her eyes was a white marble pillar.

She foggily registered it as familiar, similar to the pillars in the palace throne room. But this was larger and even more ornate, its surface carved with the images of roses.

She'd seen something exactly like it at the Temple of Cleiona.

Cleo took a sharp breath in.

This is the temple, she thought.

She stared around at the massive hall. It was three times the size of the palace throne room with a high arching ceiling. The last time she'd been here, when she had joined Lucia, Alexius, and Magnus to retrieve the newly awakened earth Kindred, it had been abandoned and in ruins after the elemental earthquake during her wedding. The floor split with wide cracks that descended into darkness. The high roof shattered and broke away, sending chunks of stone crashing to the ground.

But it wasn't crumbling anymore. Miraculously, it had been restored to its former glory.

"Did you sleep well, little queen?"

Cleo's stomach flipped at the sound of the familiar voice. She pushed up from the cold stone floor so quickly that a wave of dizziness crashed over her.

Nic.

Nic was there, standing in front of her, smiling his crooked grin, his carrot-red hair as messy as always.

Cleo's first instinct was to rush into his arms.

Her second was to clench her fists and attack.

This wasn't Nic. Not *her* Nic. Not anymore.

Frost began to snake from beneath Cleo's thin leather slippers, coating the floor of the temple.

"Excellent." Kyan glanced down at this, arching a red eyebrow. "I like to see that. It means we're very close now, the magic within you so near the surface."

"You bastard," she spat.

He casually moved to his left and took a seat on one of the long wooden benches that lined the temple, the same benches that had seated the hundreds of guests at Cleo's wedding.

"Wrong," he said. "I have neither a mother nor a father, so that label cannot possibly apply to me. Unless you simply meant it as an insult thrown at one you despise." He cocked his head, his expression thoughtful. "How sad that mortals would choose this particular word as a curse. It's not as if actual bastards have any say in their parents' decisions, is it?"

She clenched her fists at her sides, not wanting to give him the satisfaction of a reply.

"I forgive you, by the way," Kyan said.

"Forgive me?" She gaped at him. "For what?"

"For trying to put a knife through this chest only moments after I first acquired it." He pressed a hand to his heart. "I know you were confused. It was a difficult night for us all."

The dizziness hadn't left her yet, and it took all her strength just to remain standing.

Olivia then entered the temple, walking down the aisle until she stood at Kyan's side. Her face was as beautiful as any Watcher Cleo could have imagined, her dark flawless skin a beautiful contrast against her saffron gown. Beautiful, yes, but Cleo knew she never would have guessed Olivia's secret had Jonas not told her directly.

But now she wasn't a Watcher. She was the earth Kindred.

"Greetings, Cleiona," she said.

Cleo moistened her dry lips with the tip of her tongue, desperately trying to find her voice. "I assume you're the one responsible for the restoration here."

Olivia smiled, then waved her hand. A hundred paces away from Cleo, next to a window etched with a beautiful spiral design, a fallen column she hadn't noticed until now rose up and mended itself before her very eyes.

"It's my honor to bring the beauty back to this magnificent building," Olivia said.

Cleo grimaced at the blatant display of magic. It was a reminder that she had to be very careful about how she addressed the earth goddess. "Very impressive."

"Thank you," Olivia said with a smile. "You need to know that we are not your enemies. We want to help you through your transition so that it won't have to be as traumatic as Taran's was."

Taran. Cleo remembered that he'd been in the alleyway, appearing as if out of nowhere.

As if summoned by his name, Taran approached them from Cleo's right. The web of fine white lines that had appeared on his face during his most recent suffocation spell had disappeared completely, as had all his other lines. His skin was unblemished, apart from the air magic spiral on his palm.

"Taran . . ." Cleo whispered, her mouth dry.

"Yes, I've decided to keep that name," he said to her, "as a tribute to this strong, capable vessel, to show how much I appreciate it."

Cleo went very still. "So Taran is gone?"

He nodded. "Once the ritual is completed properly, all remaining traces of him will be only a memory."

"And that will be very soon," Olivia said firmly.

Cleo's heart clenched. So that meant Taran *wasn't* gone. Olivia *wasn't* gone. Not yet, not completely. There was still hope.

Out of the corner of her eye, Cleo saw Kurtis Cirillo emerge from the shadows of the cavernous temple behind her, his arms crossed over his chest.

She spun to face him. "Where's Magnus?" she demanded.

Kurtis smirked at her. "Let's just say that he won't be coming to your rescue any time soon, princess."

Panic swelled within her, thick enough to choke her. She wanted to launch herself at him, to claw out his hateful eyes. But she forced herself to take a breath.

"Kurtis . . ." Kyan began.

"Yes?"

"Wait outside."

"But I want to be here," he replied tightly. "I want to watch the princess lose herself to the water Kindred. You said I could!"

"*Wait outside*," Kyan said again. Not a suggestion, a command.

Kurtis's face blanched, his body stiffened, and he nodded with a jerk of his head. "Yes, of course."

Her gaze narrowed, Cleo watched the weasel leave the temple.

"Apologies for Kurtis's rudeness, little queen," Kyan said evenly. "His presence isn't necessary, and I know he causes you great anxiety."

"That's one way to put it," she muttered, now watching Kyan very closely.

"How do you feel?" Kyan asked, studying her. "There's no pain, I hope."

"You're very lucky that Kyan is in such a fine mood tonight," the voice of the water Kindred said inside Cleo's mind. *"You'd be wise not to make him angry."*

Surprisingly good advice, really.

Advice Cleo chose to take. For now.

"No, there's no pain," Cleo confirmed.

Kyan nodded. "Good."

She scanned the temple for any sign of Lyssa, knowing that Kyan had kidnapped her. "Do you think Lucia will come to you? That she'll help you?"

"I have no doubt of it," Kyan replied.

Such cool confidence. Was he right? Or was he delusional?

She couldn't forget that this monster with the face of her best friend had burned villages to the ground and killed thousands, including her beloved nursemaid.

Cleo brushed her hand against the side of her skirt to feel for the aquamarine orb that had been in her pocket, relieved to feel it was still there, and knowing it was a miracle that no one had discovered it while she'd been unconscious.

She needed to use this opportunity to gather information she might be able to use. As much of it as she could.

Cleo swallowed back her fear. "So what happens now?"

"For now, it's enough that we're together, the four of us," Kyan said. He tucked her hair behind her left ear and traced his finger along the blue wisp on her temple. She forced herself not to shove him away from her.

"As close to true freedom as we've been as a family," Olivia added. "Access to my magic already feels stronger."

"It's incredible, this mortal form. I can feel everything." Taran looked down at his hands, grinning. "I like it."

"I hope you more than like it," Olivia said. "This will be your vessel for all eternity."

"Your vessel is perfect," Taran replied with a nod. "As is mine."

Cleo noticed as a muscle in Kyan's cheek twitched.

"Are you unhappy with *your* vessel?" Cleo asked tightly. "You should know that I love that vessel very much."

"I know," Kyan said, his voice tight. "And it's fine, really. However, it has not been without . . . difficulties. All souls of fire are challenging beings, hard to control. But after my little sorceress properly completes the ritual, all will be well."

Cleo tried very hard not to physically react to his words, but they had shaken her. Did he mean that Nic was fighting him for control?

"I never would have guessed Nic had a soul of fire," she said instead, as calmly as possible.

"Oh, no? There were many clues of this." Kyan placed his fingers at his temples. "Memories of his bravery, his recklessness. His tendency to fall in love in the flash of an eye or nurture an unrequited and impossible love over many years. I have his memories here . . . of you, little queen. Much younger, much smaller, yet willing to take incredible risks. Leaping off high cliffs into the sea— your soul of water calling out to you even then."

That Kyan was able to access Nic's private memories shocked her. "I have always loved water," she forced herself to admit.

"Running as fast as many boys could, and willing to trip the ones who were faster than you so you could win the race—including Nic. You're the reason he broke his nose when he was twelve years old!" A smile stretched his freckled cheeks. "He was mad that it was always crooked afterward, but he never blamed you. Oh, yes, he loved you very much."

She pressed her lips together, memories of someone she'd lost coming to her as pure and painful as if they'd been yesterday. Good memories of innocent times, stolen now by a monster.

It was jarring to be reminded of such fond memories through Nic's own visage, as if they might endear her to the fire Kindred who'd stolen her best friend's life.

"*Kyan likes you,*" the water Kindred told her. "*That is deeply helpful.*"

Yes, Cleo thought. *It just might be.*

Kyan's gaze grew faraway. "I can see you riding your horse fast and free—no saddle, at least not until your father reprimanded you. 'That's no way for a young princess to behave,' he told you. 'Try to be more like your sister.' Do you remember that?"

"Stop it," she hissed, unable to listen to this anymore. "These are not your memories to tell like they're nothing but amusing stories."

"I'm just trying to help," he said.

"You're not." A sob rose in her throat, but she desperately swallowed it back down.

Cleo took a deep breath, fighting to control her emotions before they overwhelmed her.

Kyan's brows drew together. "This grieves you, and I do apologize for that. But there is no other way this ends, little queen. Allow my sibling to take control of you. It will happen soon, even if you continue to resist. It will be much easier and less painful if you comply. Your memories will also live on through her."

Cleo clasped her hands together and turned away from him to study the roses carved into the marble pillar. She counted them, getting to twenty before she felt her heart begin to slow to a more manageable rate.

Taran and Olivia watched her every move, every gesture. Not with kindness or understanding in their eyes, but with curiosity.

Much like she would watch a newly trained puppy, amused by its antics.

Cleo reached out and touched one of the marble flowers, the cold, hard surface helping to ground her. "There has to be another way. You're asking me to forfeit my life, my body, my future, so the water Kindred can just . . . take over? I can't. I just can't."

"This is much bigger and more important than one mortal life," Taran said.

Olivia frowned at her. "You are only making this more difficult for yourself. It's illogical and rather frustrating, really."

"Is there nothing of Olivia left inside you?" Cleo asked, desperate to know how this worked.

"Memories," Olivia said, her expression now thoughtful. "Just like Kyan has retained Nicolo's memories of Auranos, I remember the beauty of the Sanctuary. I remember taking flight in hawk form and flying through the porthole to the mortal world. I remember Timotheus—someone Olivia respected far more than many of the others who thought him far too secretive and manipulative. The others all believed in Melenia, but Olivia thought her to be a liar and a thief."

"Melenia did a few things right," Kyan said with a smile. "She acquired my first vessel—one that was, admittedly, superior to this one in many ways."

Again, Cleo noticed a muscle in his cheek twitch.

"Does Lucia know where to find . . . us?" Cleo said, forcing the last word out.

"She will," he said.

"How?"

Kyan cocked his head, studying her. "I can summon her."

"How can you summon her?" she asked again.

"Be careful," the water Kindred said, although its tone held amusement now. *"Too many questions and he will lose his patience with you."*

But Kyan's calm exterior didn't shift at all. "The magic Lucia has—the magic every common witch or immortal has—it is *our* magic. A part of each of us is within her and within everyone touched by *elementia*. I have not been strong enough before to use this ability, but now that the four of us are together, I feel . . . very good. And very strong. When I know it is time, I will summon her, and she will take her rightful place by my side."

Olivia muttered something under her breath.

Kyan's eyes flashed from brown to blue in an instant. "What was that?"

"Oh, nothing," she said. "Nothing at all."

Kyan turned back to Cleo. He gave her a small smile, but any trace of warmth had disappeared from his eyes. Cleo could see that his patience was beginning to wane. "My siblings don't share the confidence I have in my little sorceress. Lucia and I have fallen upon difficult times in the recent past, but I know she will fulfill her destiny."

Interesting. And chilling. Did Taran and Olivia not know that Kyan had kidnapped Lyssa as an assurance of the sorceress's help?

If Lucia did anything to help Kyan, surely it would only be to protect her daughter.

Cleo believed this almost completely. But the memory of Lucia coming to the Limerian palace as Kyan's more than willing assistant still colored her confidence in Magnus's sister.

She desperately wanted to ask where Lyssa was, if the baby was all right and being cared for properly, but she held her tongue.

Kyan would not harm the child. She was far too valuable alive.

At least, he wouldn't harm her until Lucia resisted his demands.

Cleo needed to keep talking, to draw the truth from Kyan's lips so she could learn if there was something she could do to stop this.

"Kyan," she said as calmly as possible.

"Yes, little queen?" he replied.

"At Amara's compound, you told me that I could help you because I am descended from a goddess. Was that true?"

"It certainly was." He narrowed his eyes, peering at her as if inspecting her closely. "Your namesake . . . Cleiona herself is your ancestor."

She gasped. "But the goddess didn't have children."

"Is that what you think?" He smiled. "That is only more proof that written history does not hold all secrets to the past."

"Cleiona was destroyed in her final battle with Valoria," she countered.

"The word *destroyed* can mean so many things," he said. "Perhaps only her magic was destroyed. Perhaps she was then free to live the life of a mortal at the side of the man she'd fallen in love with. Isn't that possible?"

Kyan could be lying. In fact, Cleo was quite sure of it.

Breathe, she told herself. *Don't let him try to distract you.*

"Is that why the water Kindred chose me?" she whispered. "Because I have . . . some sort of magic already inside me?"

Magic that I can use to fight this, she thought.

He shook his head. "No. You have no magic naturally within

you, but don't feel badly about that. Most mortals don't, even those descended from immortals."

Disappointment seeped through her.

That same muscle twitched in Kyan's cheek again. "Taran, Olivia, I want to speak with Cleo alone. Do you mind giving us some privacy for a few moments?"

"What do you have to say to her that you can't say in our presence?" Taran asked.

"I'll ask again," Kyan replied tightly. "Allow us a moment of privacy. Perhaps I can convince Cleo to stop fighting against the water Kindred and make this easier for all of us."

Olivia sighed with annoyance. "Very well. Taran, come, we will take a walk around the temple."

"Very well." With a nod, Taran joined Olivia as they left the temple.

Kyan stood silently in front of Cleo.

"Well?" Cleo said. "Speak your mind, although I assure you it will take more than words for me to give up this fight."

"That's what I've always loved most about you, Cleo," he said quietly. "You never stop fighting."

Her breath caught. And she looked up into Kyan's eyes.

Kyan never called her Cleo. Just "little queen."

"Nic . . . ?" she ventured, her throat tight.

"Yes," he said, his expression strained. "It's me. It's really me."

She covered her mouth with the back of her hand as shock swept through her. Then she searched his face, fearful of letting herself feel any joy. "How is this possible? Are you back?"

"No," he said. "He'll regain control soon—that's why we need to be quick."

"What happened?" she asked. "How is this possible?"

"In the woods, not far from Amara's compound"—Nic touched

his arm—"Magnus was there, and he grabbed me—or, rather, he grabbed Kyan—and I don't know why, but it was like a slap to the face, waking me up. Ashur was there too. I—I thought he might have done some kind of magic, some spell that caused me to regain a tiny bit of presence ... I don't know. It might have been my imagination that he was even there."

"Ashur is still with us," Cleo said. "He won't leave, not for any reason. He's determined to help save you, Nic."

Hope filled his brown eyes. "I've been such an annoyance to him from the moment we first met."

"Funny ..." A small smile pulled at her lips. "I think he believes the opposite."

"Ever since then, I have moments of control, like this, when the fire god isn't conscious. Kyan blames the interrupted ritual, but I know it's more than that. It doesn't happen to Olivia that I'm aware of."

Cleo reached toward him, touching his freckled cheek. He clasped his hand on top of hers and squeezed it. Hot tears spilled down her cheeks.

"Can we stop them?" she asked, her throat raw.

Nic took a breath before he replied. "Kyan wants the orbs. All four of them. And then he needs Princess Lucia to do the ritual again. He truly believes that she will do it without argument and it will go perfectly, giving the four of them ultimate power. They don't have it yet. Their magic has its limits."

"When does he want the ritual to happen?" she asked.

"I don't know exactly. Soon. Very soon. He met with Lucia at the palace, presented his plan to her. Left it in her hands to decide, but he has no doubt that she will join them." His voice dropped to a whisper. "Cleo, I think Lucia's still evil."

Cleo shook her head. "No, I don't believe that. Kyan has her baby. He stole Lyssa from her cradle. Don't you remember that? Where is she right now?"

"Lyssa? I—I don't know." Nic's eyes full of shock at this news, he shook his head. "I'm not always conscious. I see very little, but what little I do see and hear, I remember. Like . . . I very clearly remember when Kyan marked Kurtis—made him into his slave. I remember the way he screamed."

"I don't care about Kurtis."

His expression grew pained. "I'm trying to think, but I don't remember ever seeing Lyssa here. I remember Kyan went to visit Lucia at the palace, but . . . I don't remember him taking the baby. She could be anywhere."

Cleo tried to think it through, tried to piece together this puzzle. "What happens if Kyan doesn't possess the crystals?"

"Then he will burn the world," the water Kindred told her. *"And everyone in it."*

A shiver went down Cleo's spine.

"Nothing good," Nic said, then he swore under his breath. "I can't hold on to this control for much longer. But you have to. You can't let what happened to Taran happen to you. You can't let the water Kindred take you over."

Cleo pulled off one of her silk gloves and touched the blue lines on her hand. "I don't know how much longer I can resist. Every time I feel like I'm drowning, I'm certain I will die."

"Stay strong," Nic urged. "Because you need to gather the orbs together and destroy all four of them."

She gasped. "What?"

"Ridiculous. He doesn't know what he's saying," the water Kindred sneered, yet there was something now in its voice, something pained. *"Ignore him. Listen only to Kyan. He will help you."*

"Kyan helps no one but himself," Cleo muttered, and then

louder: "Nic, what do you mean *destroy* them? The orbs are the Kindred's prisons."

He shook his head. "Not prisons . . . not exactly. The orbs are *anchors*, princess. Anchors keeping them on this level of existence. If you destroy all four, then there will be no remaining ties to this world for them."

"You know this? You know this for certain?"

Nic nodded. "Yes."

"Foolish boy," the water Kindred snarled. *"He speaks his last words, full of falsehood and desperation. So mortal, so pathetic."*

The more fiercely the water Kindred protested, the more Cleo was certain that Nic was right.

"I . . . I can't hold on," Nic managed, then he cried out in pain. "You need to go . . . go now and do as I say. Don't let them catch you!"

A wall of fire blazed up around him, forming a circle of flames and blocking him from Cleo's view.

She wanted to help Nic, wanted him to escape with her, but knew that couldn't happen. Not now.

Cleo turned and ran out of the temple, as far and as fast as she could.

CHAPTER 24

NIC

AURANOS

All he could see were flames, as tall as he was, surrounding him on every side.

Then Nic felt as if he'd been punched in the gut, rendering him immobile as Kyan took control again. That had been the longest he'd taken control of both his body and of Kyan's fire magic.

He'd called for flames to shield Cleo's escape. And flames had appeared.

It had hurt like hell, but he took pride in his accomplishments tonight.

He didn't know how he'd been able to push through. Perhaps it had been the sight of Cleo, with frightening blue lines curling around the left side of her face, glaring at Kyan with so much courage and strength that it broke Nic's heart.

He knew he had to do something to help her.

Kyan and Taran and Olivia would not have allowed her to leave. They would have put her in chains had she tried to escape.

With Cleo here, even without the water Kindred being in

control of her body, Nic had felt Kyan's power double in strength.

Kyan waved his hand, and the fire disappeared. It left a black, scorched circle on the pristine marble. Nic sensed that Kyan found it distasteful and imperfect—a physical marking of his failure to control the mortal inside him. He scanned the temple for Cleo, but she was gone.

"You think you're clever," Kyan said under his breath. "So very clever, don't you?"

Actually, yes. Nic did think he was clever.

And, if he'd had any significant control over his body now, he would have made the rudest of gestures toward the fire Kindred.

"Not much longer now and you will be nothing but a memory," Kyan said darkly. "One I will toss away and forget as if you never existed in the first place."

That was rude, Nic thought. And it only made him want to fight harder to survive.

Kyan moved toward the exit, searching for Kurtis and finding him lurking outside in the shadows.

"Come here," he growled.

Nic had swiftly gone from empathizing with Kurtis's pain when he had received his branding to hating his pathetic guts again. Kurtis was a coward, willing to do anything if it meant he would not personally suffer. Surely, he'd offer up his own grandmother's soul if it meant avoiding even a moment of discomfort.

It helped a little that Kyan, too, deeply disliked the former kingsliege.

"Did you see her escape?" Kyan demanded.

"Who?" Kurtis asked.

Fury rose up inside Kyan, and his fists and forearms lit with flames. Kurtis's eyes filled with fear at the sight.

"The princess," Kyan hissed.

Kurtis began to tremble. "I'm so sorry, master. I didn't see her."

"Go after her. Find her and bring her back here immediately. She couldn't have gotten far."

Kurtis scanned the forest. "What direction did she take?"

"Just find her," Kyan boomed. "Fail, and you will burn."

Kurtis ran down the temple stairs and dashed into the forest.

"If I go after the little queen," Kyan muttered, "I might mistakenly scorch her beyond repair. Wouldn't want that, would we, Nicolo?"

How Nic desperately despised this monster.

"You see? You've only made it worse for her," Kyan continued. "There is no escape for the little queen. The water Kindred will rise whether she allows it or not. We cannot be stopped. We are eternal. We are life itself. And we will do anything to survive."

Blow it out your arse, you burned-up piece of cow dung, Nic thought.

"This evening has proven one thing to me, Nicolo." Kyan leaned against a marble pillar, running a hand absently through his stolen red hair. "The time has come to fully embrace the power that is already ours. The pieces are in place, the means to perform the ritual perfectly is at my fingertips. The little queen will rejoin me, Olivia, and Taran, and all will be well. For all eternity."

He gazed up at the temple with distaste.

"But not here." Kyan went silent, thoughtful. "I believe I know the perfect place."

CHAPTER 25

MAGNUS

AURANOS

The temple lay before Magnus, utterly and completely restored to its former grandeur. Apart from the massive statue of the goddess Cleiona that still lay shattered at the top of the thirty chiseled stairs leading to the entrance, the temple was pristine.

Juts of fire rose up from the ground and lined the marble walls, giving light to an area that would have been otherwise in darkness.

At the forest line, with the temple in clear sight before them, Magnus and Ashur tethered the horses they'd taken from the palace stables. They'd ridden so fast there had been no chance for conversation.

Magnus was about to say something to Ashur, some comment about it being earth magic that had to be the reason for the temple's restored appearance, when Ashur hushed him.

"Look," Ashur said, nodding toward the temple grounds.

Magnus peered around the trunk of a tree to see Kurtis emerge from the palace. He lingered at the top of the marble steps leading into the temple's sanctuary for several moments, glancing behind him with annoyance before he stomped down the steps to the ground, where a long, winding stone pathway led through a series of overgrown flower gardens with several grand statues of the goddess.

"I'm going to kill him," Magnus growled.

"Best not to show ourselves quite yet," Ashur replied. "Just observe."

"Cleo's in there."

"Likely, yes. And so are three elemental gods who could kill us with a single thought."

Magnus squeezed his eyes shut, summoning patience he did not possess. But he knew Ashur was right. They had to watch, observe, and then, when they got their chance, they would make their move.

Kurtis lit a cigarillo, then disappeared around the left side of the temple.

A moment later, two other figures emerged.

Olivia and Taran.

They walked side by side, leisurely, as if there was no rush, no worry, no urgency.

Magnus knew they weren't who they appeared to be. Not Olivia, Jonas's friend, the one Magnus had believed to be a witch until his shocking discovery that she was much more than that. And Taran, a young man who had initially wanted Magnus dead for the murder of his twin brother, at least until they'd come to an understanding about past mistakes and regrets.

Olivia and Taran were gone. Stolen.

And Magnus swore he would do whatever he could to help restore them to their former selves, vanquishing the demons who'd stolen their bodies.

Ashur gripped his arm, startling him from his thoughts. "It's Cleo."

Magnus's gaze shot back to the temple, where he was shocked to see Cleo's golden hair, glowing from firelight along her path, as she ran down the stairs of the temple and into the forest a hundred paces away from him.

He immediately started to move, to go after her. Ashur's grip on him tightened.

"Don't try to stop me," Magnus growled.

Ashur's expression was grim. "Are you sure it's the princess anymore? It may be the water Kindred."

Magnus's blood turned to ice at the thought. "I'm going after her."

"Magnus—"

"Go," he snapped. "Summon Valia again. If she can help us in any way, I will beg for her forgiveness for how rude I was to her earlier. Meet me at the Silver Toad tomorrow morning. If I'm not there . . . well, you'll know that the princess is gone, and likely so am I."

He didn't wait for any confirmation from the Kraeshian prince. He turned and ran in the direction Cleo had taken, into the woods on the east side of the temple. He ran as fast as he could in the near darkness, trying not to stumble and fall over the roots of trees along the forest floor.

For a moment, Magnus feared he had lost her, but then he saw movement ahead.

If she is the water Kindred, she may be trying to lure me to my death, he thought.

That was not a hopeful thought. Or remotely helpful.

His mind would do well to stay silent for now.

The forest opened to a small clearing at the edge of a twenty-foot-wide river. Magnus staggered to a halt at the tree line and

watched Cleo also come a stop, scanning right and left as if looking for a bridge in the meager moonlight.

Magnus stepped out from the shadows.

"I'm not sure it's the best time for a swim," he said.

Cleo's shoulders tensed.

Magnus was ready for anything as she slowly turned around
to face him.

In the moonlight, her eyes shone, but their color was lost
in darkness—grays and blacks with no trace of aquamarine. The
frightening, vine-like lines on her throat, moving up over her jaw
to her left temple, were almost black against her pale skin.

"You found me," she said in a half whisper.

"Of course I did." His throat thickened, making it hard to
swallow. "Is it you?"

She stared at him. "Who else would I be?"

Magnus let out a sharp, nervous laugh at that. "Taran lost his
battle against the air Kindred. And then they . . . they took you.
What am I to think?"

A small smile touched her lips. "It's still me."

The knot in his stomach loosened a bit. "Good. You're not getting away from me so easily. I swear, Cleo, I will fight for you until
my very last—"

And then something hit him hard from behind.

Something sharp and painful.

Cleo's eyes went wide. "No!" she cried out. "Magnus, no!"

He forced himself to look down.

The bloody tip of a sword now protruded from his chest.

He blinked, then fell to his knees as the weapon was yanked
from his body.

Vaguely he registered that the ground was cold and wet. It had started to rain hard, yet only a few moments ago there had been no clouds in the sky.

"I don't know how you did it before," Kurtis's reedy voice met Magnus's ears as the kingsliege moved out from behind him. "I thought surely your little sister's magic helped you out of your grave, but that doesn't explain the alleyway. But no matter . . ." His teeth glittered in the moonlight as he grinned. "You're dead, Magnus. Finally."

Magnus's foggy vision found Cleo still standing at the water's edge, her skin as pale as the moon itself. Her hair was slick from the torrents of rain beating down.

The ground all around her was now coated with an icy layer.

"I will kill you," Cleo snarled.

"I know you have no conscious control over this." Kurtis gestured toward the ice. "So stop being a nuisance and let me return you to your new family."

Magnus tried to speak, but he couldn't form words.

"What is that?" Kurtis held a hand to his ear. "I'm always intrigued by the last words of my enemies. Louder, if you please?"

"You thought . . ." Magnus managed, "it would be . . . that . . . easy?"

Kurtis rolled his eyes. "Just die already, would you?"

It took a moment before Magnus felt the wound begin to knit itself together.

The look of utter shock on the young lord's face as Magnus rose to his feet was almost worth the agony Magnus had just experienced.

"Magnus . . ." Cleo gasped, tears spilling to her cheeks. "I thought yet again that I'd lost you. Just like I lost—" Her voice broke.

She didn't have to finish her thought.

Just like she'd lost Theon.

"I know," he said grimly.

Kurtis hadn't tried to escape. He stood there, stunned by the sight before him. "This is dark magic."

"Oh, yes." Magnus moved toward him, his fists clenched at his sides. "This is the darkest, blackest, foulest magic there is. If there is an opposite to *elementia*, I am in full possession of it."

He grabbed Kurtis by his throat and slammed him hard against the nearest tree trunk.

"Mercy," Kurtis sputtered. "Have mercy! I am branded by Kyan's fire! I have no choice but to do what he says!"

"Did you even know Kyan when you had me buried six feet beneath the ground?"

Kurtis grimaced. "I beg for your forgiveness for every transgression I have ever committed against you. Please have mercy on me!"

"You are a pathetic, sniveling coward," Magnus spat.

His absolute hatred for this piece of worthless shit who had threatened Cleo and tried to murder Magnus on three separate occasions spilled over.

He had never wanted to kill anyone as much as this.

"Listen to me," Kurtis sputtered. "I think you will find me incredibly helpful if you let me go—" Then he gasped, a dry, wrenching sound from deep in his throat. "What are you . . . doing . . . to me?"

As Magnus tightened his grip on his neck, Kurtis's face began to turn gray and sallow in the moonlight. Thick black veins raced up his throat and covered his entire face in a gruesome web. His dark hair turned stark white from root to tip.

The life faded from his eyes.

When Magnus finally let go of him, the desiccated corpse of Kurtis Cirillo collapsed to the ground, his brittle bones snapping like dry twigs.

Magnus stared down at him, astounded by what he'd just done.

"Magnus . . ." Cleo was beside him now, her voice not more than a whisper. "How is this possible?"

"The bloodstone," he replied softly, sliding his right hand over the ring on his left middle finger.

She looked up at him, her eyes wide. "Did you know it could do that?"

"I had no idea." He waited to feel horror for what he'd done, but it didn't come. "All I know is I wanted him dead. And now he's dead. And I feel . . . relieved."

Cleo reached out a trembling hand toward him.

"Be careful," he managed. "I don't want to hurt you."

She let out a small, nervous laugh. "I assume that you don't want me dead as you did Kurtis."

"Of course not."

"Good," she managed. "Because I desperately need you to kiss me right now."

And so he did kiss her, breathing her in and gathering her so tightly in his arms that her feet lifted off the ground.

"I love you," he whispered against her lips. "So damn much it hurts."

Cleo pressed her hands to either side of his face, looking into his eyes. "I love you too."

She was his goddess. His love. His life. And he would do anything to save her.

On his finger was a piece of dark magic that had now saved his life three times. The one who created it a thousand years ago had surely been a god of death. This had been his ring then.

But now it was Magnus's. And he would not hesitate to use its horrible, terrifying, incredible death magic on anyone who might get in his way.

CHAPTER 26

AMARA

KRAESHIA

A week had passed since she'd returned to the Jewel of the Empire, and the world had not yet ended.

Amara took that as an excellent sign to forget Mytica and enjoy every single moment of her day of Ascension. The day she would officially—and in all ways—become the absolute ruler of the Kraeshian Empire.

She hoped very much that the ceremony would help to burn away any remaining traces of pain, uncertainty, or weakness unbefitting an empress.

But even a strong, capable, and powerful ruler needed a pretty gown for a formal ceremony.

"Ouch," she said when she felt the prick of a needle wielded by clumsy hands. "Be careful!"

"My deepest apologies," the dressmaker said, jumping back, his gaze filled with horror.

Amara stared at him through the reflection in the tall mirror in her chambers.

What an incredible overreaction. It wasn't as if she was going to kill him for being clumsy. She almost laughed out loud.

"It's fine. Just be careful."

"Yes, my empress."

Lorenzo Tavera was from Auranos, where he ran a famous dress shop in the city of Hawk's Brow. Amara's grandmother had learned that he'd been a favored dressmaker of nobles and royals alike. He'd even made Princess Cleo's wedding gown, which by all accounts had been breathtakingly beautiful before being soiled by the blood of rebels.

The golden gown Lorenzo had created for Amara fit tightly to her curves, the skirt flouncing outward from the knee in what looked like golden feathers. The bodice had intricate embroidery made of tiny crystal beads and larger emeralds and amethysts.

The color of the gown made Amara think of the golden princess herself, and she wondered how Cleo fared in her current situation. Was she suffering, or had she already been lost to the water Kindred?

My fault, she thought.

No. She couldn't dwell on such things. She couldn't dwell on how she'd helped a demon gain power and how she'd left everyone, including her brother, far behind her.

She couldn't think about how Kyan was a god with an extreme distaste for the imperfect mortals that swarmed over this world, mortals he believed were led only by greed and lust and vanity, weaknesses he wanted to erase.

Everyone everywhere would perish.

"*Dhosha*, is everything all right?" Neela asked as she entered the room.

"Yes, of course. Everything is fine." Amara forced the words out, feeling as very *un*-fine as she possibly could, despite the glory of the day and the beauty of this gown.

"Your beautiful face . . ." Her grandmother met her gaze in the mirror's reflection. "You looked so pained and worried for a moment there."

She shook her head. "Not at all."

"Good." Neela came close enough to touch the fine stitching of the gown. "Lorenzo, you have created a true masterpiece."

"Much gratitude, my queen," the dressmaker said. "It is only by your grace that I have been given the incredible honor to dress the empress."

"It's everything I dreamed it would be," Neela said, sighing with appreciation. "What about the wings?"

"Yes, yes. Of course. They are the most magnificent part of my creation." Lorenzo reached into a silk bag and pulled out a large but delicate golden piece. It fit over Amara's shoulders and gave the illusion of golden wings.

Amara gritted her teeth, finding the addition to be a rather heavy and unnecessary burden. But she chose not to complain, since they added an ethereal, otherworldly touch.

"Perfect," Neela breathed, clapping her hands. "Today you will have everything I have ever wanted for you. I am honored to have been able to make all this possible."

In the week since Amara had visited Mikah Kasro in his forgetting room, where he would stay until he was brought out for his execution during the ceremony, she'd tried not to think about their conversation. A part of it had stayed in her mind, though, like a piece of stubborn food between her back teeth, nearly impossible to dislodge.

"Your grandmother only believes in her own desire for power," he'd told her.

"I'm so glad you approve," Amara said softly. "Did you come

here just to get a glimpse of the gown, *madhosha*?"

Lorenzo pricked her again with his needle, and she slapped his hand away. "Enough," she scolded him. "Enough fixing of things that are already perfect."

Lorenzo backed away from her immediately, bowing deeply. "Yes, of course." Again, there was that fear in his eyes. It was the same kind of fear she remembered seeing in the eyes of those who looked upon her father.

Such power over others should please her.

Instead, it gave her a cold, empty feeling in the pit of her stomach.

"I will be a good leader," she'd told Mikah. *"My people will love me."*

"And if they don't?" he'd countered. *"If they rise up and try to change what has been thrust upon them through no choice of their own, will you have them put to death?"*

"Dhosha," her grandmother said sharply, as if she'd tried to get her attention more than once while Amara was lost in her thoughts.

"Yes?"

She looked around, pulling herself from her thoughts. Lorenzo was no longer in the room. She hadn't even noticed him leave.

"You asked me if I was here only to see the gown," Neela said. "I am not. I'm happy to say that your gift has finally arrived from across the sea."

Amara shook her head. "You really didn't need to get me a gift, *madhosha*. You've already done so much for me."

Neela smiled. "But this gift is special. Come with me now to receive it."

Amara changed back into her casual gown and shawl. The rest of the day would be one of relaxation, meditation, and rest. Then she would be coiffed from head to toe, paint applied precisely to her eyes and lips, her black hair plaited and threaded with jewels, and the finished gown would be the last touch before the ascension ceremony itself.

Leaning on her cane, Amara followed Neela through the hallways of the Emerald Spear. They passed several servants, all with eyes lowered to the ground. To look the Kraeshian royal family directly in the eyes was not permitted, since Amara's father had felt it was confrontational.

Priests and augurs also filled the halls, clad in long purple robes. They had journeyed to the Emerald Spear from across the empire to be a part of the Ascension.

The long corridors were lined with intricately embroidered rugs that had taken a commissioned artisan half a lifetime to complete. Amara realized she'd never paid much attention to the beauty of her surroundings, to the exquisite vases and sculptures and paintings that peppered the palace halls, many obtained from the kingdoms her father had conquered.

Stolen, not obtained, she reminded herself.

These were the possessions of former kings and queens slain by the emperor as he moved across this world like a plague.

What am I thinking? She shook her head to clear it of such dark thoughts.

Her father was gone. Her older brothers gone.

She'd heard not a word about Ashur.

Amara knew she would be different from those who had ruled before her.

They climbed the private spiraling staircase to the sixth floor and walked down another long hallway. At the end of the hallway was a familiar face, one that made Amara's worries disappear and her smile return.

"Costas!" As she drew closer to her trusted guard, he bowed

before her. "How lovely to have you here to help me celebrate this important day."

"Empress," Costas said. "I am here by request of Queen Neela."

Queen Neela. She'd noticed that many addressed her grandmother in this way now.

But of course they would. She was the closest relative and the most trusted advisor of the empress.

Her grandmother deserved such a title.

Amara turned toward Neela, smiling. "Did you secretly summon Costas here as my gift? If so, much gratitude."

Neela shook her head. "No. However, Costas did acquire your gift, and he brought it here at great risk to himself." She gestured toward the door next to the tall guard. "Your true gift is within this room."

How intriguing. What rare treasure had Costas brought for her at her grandmother's request on the day of her Ascension?

Amara went to the door, pressing her hand flat against its cool, smooth surface. Despite any misgivings or doubt, she swore she would enjoy every moment of today. To taste it. To savor it.

Whatever this mysterious gift was, she had earned it.

Amara opened the door and entered the small room. A woman dressed all in white turned to face her, then dropped her gaze to the floor. She bowed deeply and moved away from the small piece of furniture she stood before.

It looked very much like a cradle.

Her breath shallow, Amara moved forward, slowly, and looked inside.

A baby with sky-blue eyes and a dark tuft of hair stared up at her.

Amara gasped, clamping a hand over her mouth.

Neela came to her side. "Do you like my gift?"

"*Madhosha*, what have you done?" Amara asked, breathless.

"Do you know whose child this is?" Neela asked.

Amara could barely think, let alone speak. "It's Lucia Damora's daughter."

"You made no mention of her existence. I had to learn it from Costas. This child is the daughter of a prophesied sorceress and an immortal. A child of such extraordinary parents will contain incredible magic—magic we can use for so, so many things."

Amara's grip on her cane tightened. "*Madhosha . . .*"

Neela reached down into the cradle and stroked the baby's tiny, velvet-smooth cheek. "What shall we name her?"

"She already has a name. It's Lyssa." Amara turned to Costas. "You did this. You took her from her cradle—from the arms of a mother who will level the world to find her."

Costas's expression remained steady. "She won't."

"She will! The moment Lucia learns that you took her—"

"I thought of that," he interrupted her. "Of course I did. Queen Neela gave explicit instructions to make it appear as if the fire Kindred had stolen her. The only one who witnessed me enter the palace is dead. Burned as proof."

"More reason for the sorceress to focus her attention on this fire Kindred you could not find a way to control," Neela said. "We will raise this child as your daughter, just as King Gaius raised Lucia herself. My apothecary tells me he can use her blood to create powerful elixirs to strengthen your reign. Elixirs to keep you young and beautiful for many, many years."

"Elixirs," Amara repeated, again looking down upon the face of this stolen child, "to keep me young and beautiful."

"Yes." Neela then kissed Amara on both of her cheeks. "I am so happy to have been able to give you this gift, one you will appreciate more with every passing year."

Every passing year that Queen Neela advised her on how to rule her people, how to control them, and how to punish those who would oppose them.

I don't want the gift of a stolen child, Amara thought with a sudden, clawing desperation in her chest. *I don't want any of this.*

What have I done?

Still, uncertain how her grandmother would react if she blurted out the truth of how she felt, Amara instead forced a smile to her lips. "My gratitude to you, *madhosha*, for always looking out for me. For making today possible."

Neela squeezed her hands. "They will all bow before you. Every man who has ever made a Kraeshian woman suffer. And you will be the greatest and most fearsome ruler this world has ever seen."

Amara continued to smile her false smile as she left the nursery and headed back to her chambers.

She walked as quickly as she could, fighting against the tears pricking the backs of her eyes.

It had been her grandmother's idea to poison her family.

It had been her grandmother's idea for her to kill Ashur if he proved to be a problem.

It had been her grandmother's idea to kidnap the child of a sorceress.

Amara had trusted her grandmother all her life, had been willing to do whatever she said, knowing that Neela only wanted to help her gain power.

Power that Neela could wield for herself.

Her thoughts jumbled and unclear, her vision blurry, Amara didn't see the person hiding around the corner that led to her wing of the massive royal residence.

At least, not until they grabbed her.

Her cane fell away from her grip before she could use it to fight back against the large hand that grasped her throat and pinned her up against the wall.

The tip of a sharp blade pressed to her cheek.

"Well, that was easier than I would have predicted," Felix Gaebras growled. "Not enough security in the big green pointy palace to keep escaped criminals like me at bay. What a crying shame."

The sight of him was such a shock that Amara didn't react, didn't struggle, as he dragged her into her vacant chambers. He shoved her, and she stumbled backward and fell to the floor.

The door clicked shut, the lock sliding into place.

Amara glanced to the door. Felix had not sneaked into the Emerald Spear alone.

"Nerissa," Amara whispered.

Her former attendant's eyes narrowed coldly on her. "With Mytica so far behind you, I would have thought you'd have forgotten my name by now."

"Of course not." Amara tried to swallow, tried to breathe. Tried not to seem afraid. "Are you going to stop Felix from killing me?"

"No. Actually, I'm here to help him."

Amara stared at both of them for several long moments. And then she started to laugh, drawing glares from both Nerissa and Felix. The day had been so surreal—from the golden wings, to the fear in the dressmaker's eyes, to the gift of a stolen baby with magical blood.

"Stop laughing," Felix shouted.

"What is this?" Nerissa asked. "Are you mad?"

"By now?" she managed. "Very likely. But you, Nerissa, an accomplice to the murder of an unarmed woman? I never would have taken you as that coldhearted."

Amara was struck by the certainty that the punishment she deserved had arrived far sooner than she'd expected.

"I wish I could say the same in return," Nerissa said softly.

Amara sobered, narrowing her gaze on her former attendant. One who had looked at her not so long ago with kindness and patience. One who had shared stories from her painful past. "You told me that you and your mother survived so much under my father's reign. You know what it's like to be oppressed by men, to need to use them to get what you want. I would think you'd understand, if only a little, why I've done what I've done."

"What I told you about my mother being a courtesan was a lie." Nerissa raised a thin eyebrow. "She did what was necessary to survive, yes. But on most days, my mother was an assassin."

Felix gasped. "You never told me that. We have so much in common!"

Nerissa glanced at him. "Your mother wasn't an assassin."

"No, but I am. Oh, Nerissa, you get more interesting to me every day. We could be partners after this. Vigilantes who slay horrible, evil creatures across the world! Although, if we could avoid sea travel, that would be wonderful. I'm still ill from our trip here."

Nerissa scrunched her nose. "That—all of it—is unlikely, Felix."

He frowned and brushed his fingers over his eye patch. "Is it the missing eye? Can't do much about that, I'm afraid. Oh, wait. That's the empress's fault too. Another reason she needs to die." He looked down at his knife, and his single eye narrowed. "I'm going to enjoy this *so* much."

Nerissa sighed wearily. "Are you trying to talk yourself into yet another dungeon?"

"Definitely not." Felix spun his dagger around on his hand with the skill of someone who played with sharp weapons daily. "Before I finally and happily do this, empress, I am obligated to let you know that this is on Prince Magnus's orders. He's not happy that you had his father killed."

Amara finally pushed herself up to her feet, balancing her weight on her good leg. Despite her problems, her will to survive remained as strong as ever. "It wasn't me. My grandmother enlisted that assassin. I only learned of it when I arrived here last week."

Felix shrugged. "You say all of that like it matters. It doesn't. The result is going to be the same. You being dead, that is."

Amara shot a look at Nerissa. "And you're going to just stand there and watch him kill me?"

"Yes. I am." Nerissa crossed her arms and tapped her foot as if Amara's death couldn't come soon enough.

"Before that night . . . with Kyan, when I betrayed all of you . . . I thought you believed in me," Amara said, horrified by how weak she sounded. But it was still the truth. She had no more lies left within her.

"I did. Against my better judgment, I really did." Nerissa exhaled and shook her head. "But you've shown no remorse, no regret. Every decision you've made has been for your own gain, and countless people have suffered because of it."

Felix spun his dagger again. "And you say I talk a lot. Can we end this and get out of here?"

End this.

End *her.*

Felix had countless reasons to want Amara dead. She actually didn't blame him at all.

She'd hurt him very badly.

No. She'd tried to *destroy* him. But he'd survived.

"I admire that," Amara said.

"What?" Felix growled.

"You. I see now that you would have made a much better ally than an enemy."

He frowned at her. "I was hoping for more satisfying begging for your life at this point. This is extremely disappointing."

"It's over," Amara said.

"Exactly my point." Felix gave her a cold smile and stepped forward.

She raised a hand and lifted her chin. "But you can't kill me. Not right now. Later, perhaps. But not now. There's far too much for you to do first, and you're going to need a great deal of my help to do it."

"Nah. I think I'm just going to kill you," Felix insisted and raised his dagger.

Nerissa grabbed his wrist in midair, her eyes trained on Amara. "What are you talking about?"

Amara racked her brain, trying to figure out exactly where to begin.

"All right," she said. "Listen to me very carefully . . ."

CHAPTER 27

JONAS

PAELSIA

They left the inn at dawn.

Mia, the serving girl with amnesia—the one Lucia insisted was an immortal—was already awake, serving breakfast, and she provided them with some stale bread and honey for their journey.

On their way into the Forbidden Mountains, Lucia barely spoke. She moved swiftly along the rough-hewn path, clearly determined to make headway.

Jonas peered up at the jagged black peaks rising all around them and drew his cloak closer around his shoulders. There was a chill here, the temperature far colder than in the small village they'd departed earlier.

It was a chill he felt more profoundly than just on the surface.

It sank deep, all the way to his bones.

"Do you know what I was told as a child about these mountains?" he said, feeling the need to make conversation.

"What?" Lucia asked, her eyes still trained on the path ahead.

He'd all but forgotten them until now—all the stories told by adults to children about the Forbidden Mountains. Jonas never had patience for tales of fantasy or magic. He much preferred to be out hunting, even when he could barely lift a bow.

"I was told that they're ancient witches, cursed for using their dark magic against the first king of Mytica, just after the world was created."

"I've heard other legends about them, but yours doesn't surprise me at all," Lucia said under her breath. "Witches are always blamed for everything when most of them don't have enough magic to light a single candle."

"Why is that, do you suppose?" he wondered aloud.

"What?"

"Witches . . . they definitely exist. I know that now. But their magic is harmless, unlike the stories."

"I wouldn't say that. Even the weakest *elementia* can be strengthened by blood, which is apparently how my grandmother managed to help Kyan with his ritual. So if a witch strengthens her magic to a dangerous level, and if her intentions are dark, she is most definitely not harmless."

Jonas didn't know how many witches there were—only that if one was descended from an exiled Watcher they had a chance to have magic within them. "I suppose you're right. And we should be thankful that only you have as much magic as you do."

Lucia didn't reply.

"Princess?" he asked, frowning. "You still have your magic, don't you?"

She flinched. "It's weakened again. I don't know how much time it will take to return fully to me—or if that's even a possibility." Lucia looked at him over her shoulder. Her eyes were wide and glassy. Jonas felt his heart drop.

"You aren't just a common witch," he said, shaking his head. "You are a sorceress. *The* sorceress."

"I know. But it's Lyssa . . . somehow she's stolen my magic ever since I was pregnant with her. But I swear to the goddess, even if I don't have a shred of *elementia* within me, I will save her, no matter what I have to do."

"And I will help you," Jonas said firmly, even though the thought that her magic was no longer reliable enough to aid them in battle against Kyan chilled him. "I promise I will."

"Thank you." Lucia held his gaze for a moment before she nodded and turned away from him. "Now keep walking. We're almost there."

Jonas did as she said, one foot in front of the other.

He forced himself to keep walking even though every step was a test of his courage. These mountains had always been a part of his life—a chilling sight in the far east, no matter where in Paelsia one went.

They entered the foothills, and any remaining, struggling vegetation they'd passed in the previous dusty miles disappeared completely. The skies were gray, as if a storm stirred, and in the distance, above the mountains, even darker clouds blocked out the sun.

As they moved deeper into the black mountains, Jonas realized it felt even colder than Limeros here. It was a frigid kind of cold; an iciness that sank into his bones and settled there. The kind of cold he knew couldn't be chased away by a warm blanket and a campfire.

He rubbed his chest over the spiral Watcher's mark. The cold seemed to push deeper into him precisely in that spot, like the tip of a blade searching for his heart.

"This place," he began. "It feels like death."

Lucia nodded. "I know. There's an absence of magic here . . . an absence of life itself. From what little I understand, that's what has bled into Paelsia over generations, causing your land to wither and die."

Jonas looked around at their barren surroundings. He shuddered. "Like the rotten part of a peach that starts to spread through the whole basket."

"Exactly. Luckily, in the midst of all this death, is . . . that."

They'd breached a gray, rocky hill, and on the other side, where Lucia now gestured, lay a sight that made Jonas's breath catch.

A thick shard of purple crystal as tall as three men jutted up from a small patch of greenery in the distance. Beyond that small circle of life and beauty lay only black, scorched ground.

"This is where I fought Kyan," Lucia said grimly as she climbed the steep hill leading to the monolith. "He wasn't in mortal form then. He looked like he did in the dream that you witnessed."

A gigantic monster made of fire.

"You were so brave in that dream," he said, remembering the cloaked girl who stood in front of the fire god and swore she would stop him.

"I can't honestly say I was that brave in real life. But this"—she slid her hand over the amethyst ring she always wore—"protected me like it would have protected Eva when she wore it. And Kyan— he exploded. I thought surely it had killed him, but it only destroyed the body he'd been using as a vessel. I blacked out, and when I came to, I was in the Sanctuary."

Jonas couldn't fathom how frightening that must have been, to be faced with a true monster with no one to turn to, no one to help. He had misjudged this girl for far too long. She'd been through so much, it was a miracle she'd made it out alive and sane.

He looked up at the monolith as they drew closer to it. "So this is a gateway to another world, like the stone wheels."

"Yes," she said. "This is where that magic originated from—the ability to walk between worlds. I just hope, now that we're finally here, that it works with my magic being so unreliable."

"I have faith in you," Jonas said. "And your magic."

Lucia turned to him with red-rimmed eyes, as if expecting him to follow up that statement with something harsher, something more judgmental.

Instead, he gave her a small smile. He'd meant what he'd said.

Despite any dark intent Timotheus ascribed to Lucia, Jonas's faith in her had only grown since the immortal had given him the golden dagger.

Jonas thought back to the vision Timotheus had told him about: Lucia with the dagger in her heart and Jonas standing over her.

No, Jonas thought. *It's impossible.*

Either he'd been wrong or he'd been lying. Timotheus said himself that he glimpsed many possible futures. That had been only one of them.

Jonas needed answers from the immortal. And he would demand to be told the truth about everything.

Lucia had scrambled farther ahead, and Jonas took several long strides to catch up with her.

"All right," she said, turning to face him. "Now we will learn whether this journey has just been an incredible waste of time."

The closer he stood to the monolith, the better Jonas began to feel. The chill had completely dissipated, and a tingling warmth flowed through his body.

"Do you feel that?" he asked, meeting Lucia's gaze.

"Yes," she replied.

"Look," he said, pointing to her hand. "Your ring . . . it's glowing."

Lucia raised her hand, her eyes wide as she nodded. "I'm going to hope that's a good sign."

Then the monolith began to glow as well, emitting a violet haze all around them.

"I think it recognizes me," she whispered.

Jonas followed Lucia's lead and placed his palm against the cool crystal. "Let's just hope it doesn't explode."

Lucia laughed nervously. "Please, don't even think that."

The brightness of the monolith quickly became so intense that Jonas had to squeeze his eyes shut to protect them from the light.

When he opened them only moments later, they were not in the same place as before. Not at all.

He turned in a circle to take in the new surroundings. They were now in a grassy field—one that reminded him of the backdrop of his last dream with Timotheus.

"Did it work?" he asked, then raised a brow at the sorceress standing next to him. "Or are we dead?"

"You sound so calm, considering we just traveled to another world," she said. Lucia looked him up and down, studying him from every angle. "I wasn't sure if you would be able to come here with me. The magic you have inside you must be stronger than I thought. I'm sure what happened . . . it wouldn't have worked for just anyone."

Jonas would have replied, but he was too busy staring at the shining city in the distance.

"It *did* work," he said, stunned. "This is the Sanctuary."

"It is."

"I'm going to need a moment," he said. Jonas bent down, resting his hands on his knees as he tried to catch his breath. His mind was racing—one moment they'd been in the Forbidden Mountains in front of a big shiny rock.

Now they were . . . here. In the Sanctuary.

He always said he believed only in what he could see with his own eyes. And he could see this. All of it in one sweeping glance.

This was real.

"No time to rest." Lucia began walking away from him, in the direction of the city. "We need to find Timotheus."

At first glance, everything seemed normal enough—blue sky, green grass, colorful flowers—and in the distance, a city made of tall golden buildings loomed.

But it also wasn't normal at all, Jonas thought as they walked past two massive stone wheels that lay in the stretch of green land between the meadow and the crystal city itself.

"What are they?" he asked.

"Those are the gateways immortals use to enter our world," Lucia explained. "In their hawk form."

Jonas realized then that he hadn't seen any hawks lately. At least, not the kind that were as large and golden as the ones he knew to be spying immortals.

Perhaps he just hadn't been paying close enough attention.

After the stone gateways, Jonas spotted other differences between the Sanctuary and the mortal world. The colors here were more vivid and jewel-like. The grass was a bright emerald green, and the red flowers that dotted the field resembled sparkling rubies.

The sky was bright blue—the true color of a perfectly cloudless summer day.

But there was no sun here, only an undetermined source of light.

"Where's the sun?" he asked.

Lucia looked up at the sky, shielding her eyes from the brightness. "They don't seem to have one. But it's always day here."

Jonas shook his head. "How is that possible?"

"Let's focus on getting to the city, shall we? Then you can ask Timotheus any question you want. Hopefully you'll have better luck getting answers than I ever have."

The city had tall protective walls, much like the City of Gold, but its gates were open and unguarded.

Lucia hesitated only a moment before she walked through them and into the city itself.

Jonas couldn't keep up with all the sights before him. The City of Gold and Hawk's Brow were the two wealthiest cities in Auranos. Gold was inlaid into the stonework of the sparkling roads, and both cities were immaculately clean. Both cities, however, paled in comparison to the beauty and wonder of this one. It seemed to be entirely created out of crystal and silver and transparent, delicate glass. Shining, colorful mosaics coated the maze of roads that led them deeper into this waking dream.

The buildings were taller than anything Jonas had ever seen before, even taller than either the Auranian or Limerian palaces, with spires that reached high into the sky. Here, the individual structures were narrow, with angular, jagged edges that reminded him of the monolith itself. They stretched up twice as tall as a sentry's tower, but he'd never seen a tower made from anything but stone and brick.

"Incredible," Jonas muttered. "But where is everyone?"

Lucia didn't seem to be as awed by the sights as he was; she was far too busy walking deeper into the city. "There are not many immortals here, considering the size of this city," she said. "Perhaps two hundred or so. It makes this place seem completely empty."

"Yes, it certainly does," he agreed.

"Strange, though," she said with a frown. "I would have thought we'd have seen someone by now."

He heard the uneasiness in her tone, and it worried him.

Jonas followed Lucia to a clearing that looked to be two hundred paces in diameter. In the center of this space stood a tower three times as tall as any other in the city, one that stretched high into the sky like a shining beacon of light.

"This tower has been home to the elders," Lucia told him. "It's like their palace. When I was here, all the other immortals gathered in this square to hear an announcement from Timotheus."

Jonas scanned the vacant area, frowning.

"Something seems wrong, princess," he said. "Do you feel it?"

He couldn't exactly put his finger on it. It was like the same chill in the air he'd felt in the Forbidden Mountains, just before they'd reach the crystal monolith. For all its exquisite, otherworldly beauty, this city felt like . . .

Death, he thought.

Lucia nodded. "I feel it too. Where is everyone? This isn't right."

"Wouldn't they be concerned that two people just strolled through the city gates unexpectedly?" he asked.

"They didn't notice me the last time, not right away. But then I met Mia, the girl in the tavern."

"The one who couldn't remember anything."

Lucia nodded gravely.

Then, out of the corner of his eye, Jonas saw something flicker on the wall of one of the towers nearby. Light and dark, light and dark, like the rapid blinking of an eye.

It was changing color from a shining silver to . . .

The image of an old man.

Lucia gasped. "Timotheus?"

Jonas stared up at what indeed looked like a very old Timotheus, with white hair and a wrinkled face.

"Yes, it's me," the image said. "Your eyes do not deceive you."

Jonas realized then that this wasn't just an image—it *was* Timotheus, somehow appearing on the side of this tower to look down upon them standing in the middle of the massive, empty square.

"What happened?" Lucia asked, her eyes wide. "Why do you look like this?"

"Because I'm dying," Timotheus replied, his voice was small and distant.

"What do you mean *you're dying*?" Jonas demanded. "You're immortal. You can't die!"

"Immortals most certainly can die," he replied. "It just takes us a lot longer than mortals."

"Timotheus . . ." Lucia stepped forward, her shoulders tense. "It's urgent that I speak with you."

Timotheus shook his head. "You shouldn't be here. I saw in a vision that you would both come, but I hoped very much you would change your minds. Alas, you didn't. But now you need to leave immediately."

Lucia's hands fisted at her sides. "I can't leave! Kyan's taken my daughter and my magic . . . it's weak right now. I don't know if I can imprison him and the others." Her voice was shaking. "I need to save my daughter, and I don't know how. I came here to ask for your help."

"I can be no help to you," he replied grimly. "Not anymore."

"But you have to be," Jonas said, stepping forward. "We need answers. We came all this way. I don't even know how it's possible I'm here."

"You don't?" Timotheus chuckled. "Young man, you have so much magic within you right now I'm surprised it's not bursting through your very skin."

He could sense that? Jonas didn't feel any different than ever before. "How do you know that?"

"I know that because I've placed a great deal of that magic within you myself."

Jonas gaped up at him. "You *what*?"

"Some mortals over the centuries have proven themselves to be excellent carriers of magic. You are one of them."

Lucia looked back and forth between the two of them. "What do you mean, he's a carrier of magic?"

"Just like a rich mortal uses a bank to store his gold—and the same bank to borrow from," Timotheus explained. "This is Jonas's purpose and part of his destiny. I thought he would prove very useful, and he has."

"Wait," Jonas said. "What are you saying? You put most of this magic inside me? How did you do that?"

Timotheus gazed down at him patiently. "You wouldn't understand even if I told you. And there's no time to explain."

"Make time," he growled. "I already know the magic inside me is from Phaedra, when she died after saving my life, and Olivia, from the magic she used to heal me . . ."

"Yes. And that is how I knew you were a vessel. I gave you more magic in the last dream of yours I entered—as much as I could. You already know that whatever is shared in your unconscious mind can become reality."

The golden blade. So Timotheus transferred magic into Jonas just as he'd given him the blade, which had traveled from one world to another.

He stared up at the massive form of Timotheus on the side of the tower in awe. The immortal looked like a man, walked and talked like a man.

But he was no man. He was a god.

All the immortals were gods.

For someone who had never believed in anyone or anything . . . this was a stunning realization.

"Why did you place this magic inside me?" Jonas began, more tentatively now. "Was it because you knew you'd become weak like this?"

"Partially," Timotheus allowed.

"And now what? You take it back, recharge yourself, and you're good as new?"

Timotheus gazed down at them for a moment, his lips pursed in thought. "No."

"No?" Lucia said, stunned. "What do you mean *no*? I need you, Timotheus. There's no one else who can help me. Kyan has kidnapped my daughter, and I am afraid I can't save her!"

"I've seen your future, Lucia Damora," Timotheus said then, evenly. "I've seen you standing next to the fire Kindred with the crystal orbs before you, your lips moving as you complete the ritual that will empower him and the other three like they've never been empowered before. And you do so of your own free will, just as you stood on the side of the cliff that night—that fateful night—ready to help him destroy the world. You are aligned with Kyan, and any excuses having to do with Lyssa are only that—excuses."

Lucia's face was red, her eyes full of fury. "How dare you say that to me? I am not aligned with Kyan. I hate him!"

Timotheus shrugged his shoulders. "We don't change. We are who we are throughout our lives. We can try other paths, other roads, but it never works. I am no different. I was created to be a guardian to this place"—he waved his wrinkled hand toward the land beyond the city gates—"and to the mortal world. I tried . . . I did. And I'm still trying at this very moment, but I am failing, as all the others of my kind have failed. It is over, Lucia. The fight is over, and we have lost. We were never meant to win."

Jonas had listened silently to what the immortal said and to Lucia's reaction, and now he joined her in her outrage. "Is that it? You're giving up, just like that?"

"You don't know how long and how hard I've fought to reach this point," Timotheus said wearily. "I thought there was a chance, and I did what I could to help. But in the end, none of this matters. What will be will be, and we must accept it."

Jonas's fury began to boil over. He moved closer to the tower as if he could reach into the image and pull Timotheus out. "That's so typical of you, speaking in riddles, even now. Lucia needs your damn help to fix this bloody mess, and you're up there on your . . . *whatever* magic that is that you're on right now, looking down your nose at us. Detached from it all, safe and sound in your tall tower while we're out here fighting, bleeding, and dying."

"Fighting, bleeding, dying . . ." Timotheus shook his head. "It is the way of mortals. Past, present, and future. What little future is left, anyway. Everything ends. Nothing is truly immortal."

"Timotheus . . ." Lucia's tone had calmed. She clasped her hands before her as she gazed up at the image of him on the side of the tower. "Where are the others to help you?"

"The others are gone," he replied flatly.

"I . . . I saw Mia. I saw her in a Paelsian village not far from the monolith." She shook her head. "She couldn't remember any-thing—not being an immortal, not the Sanctuary, not meeting me before."

"You did that to her," Jonas said, filling in the blanks for him-self. "You hurt her . . . you stole her memories. And the others as well."

"Jumping to conclusions, like always," Timotheus replied.

"Hasty in your decisions, rash and bold and, so very often, wrong."

"Then what actually happened?" Lucia asked.

Jonas didn't want to listen to any more lies. It had been a waste of time to come here. He was about to say so when Timotheus finally replied.

"I called in a favor from an old friend," he said. "One with the means and the magic to erase memories. There were so few of us left, and no one but me knew the truth of what this place has become. They only thought it to be a beautiful prison, one they could leave in hawk form to gaze upon the lives of mortals. Over the centuries, some chose to stay in your world as exiles, their magic fading over the remainder of their limited lives. Exiles, as a whole, I've found, are happy with their decision to leave. To live a mortal life that is imperfect and short and beautifully flawed."

"So you gave them that chance," Lucia said, her voice barely more than a whisper. "All the others that were left. You exiled them and had their memories erased so they could live a mortal life without ties to the Sanctuary."

Timotheus nodded.

Jonas wanted to hate him. He wanted to pull the golden dagger that Timotheus had somehow given to him that night through his dream and throw it at the tower right here and right now.

But he didn't.

He studied the old and weary face of this man, this man who had lived for countless centuries, with one question rising in his mind that he desperately needed answered.

"Why not you too?" Jonas asked. "If what you say is true, why wouldn't you choose to live a beautifully flawed life as a mortal?"

"Because," Timotheus said sadly, "I had to hold on for just a little while longer. I had to hope that in these last moments, someone somewhere might surprise me."

"Surprise you how?" Lucia asked.

"By proving me wrong."

"Come down here," she urged him. "Help me imprison the Kindred. Everything will return to normal then—here and in the mortal world. You can recover from what has happened to you, and . . . and then you can be whatever you want to be, wherever you want to be it."

"I had hoped that might be possible, but it's far too late for that now." He looked down, shaking his head. "The end is here. Finally, after all these years. And now, if you have any hope of survival you must—"

He flinched then, as if a wave of pain had hit him. When he looked up at them, his eyes were glowing with a strange white light that was nearly blinding.

"What?" Jonas asked as Lucia clutched his arm. "What must we do?"

"You must run," Timotheus said. And then he yelled it. "RUN!"

The glow from his eyes brightened so much that the entire image of Timotheus turned stark white, and then he disappeared completely.

A piercing beam of light exploded from the narrow spire, along with a painful screeching sound. Jonas staggered backward, away from the tower, and clamped his hands over his ears, meeting Lucia's wide-eyed gaze.

When the sound ceased, Lucia turned back toward the tower. "He's dead. Timotheus is dead!"

Jonas stared at her with shock. "Dead? But how can you know that for sure?"

She frantically looked around as if searching for something specific. "His magic is gone. It was the only thing keeping this world from complete destruction. That's why he stayed here.

That's why he never physically left this place."

And then Jonas heard a cracking sound in the distance that reminded him of thunder during a powerful Paelsian rainstorm. But much louder. Much bigger. When he looked toward the tall silver tower again, the new reflection on its surface turned his blood to ice.

Beyond the city walls, the world was falling apart. Literally falling apart. Massive chunks of earth crumbled off the side of a cliff. The eternally blue and cloudless sky shattered like glass and dropped away to reveal darkest night. Green hills and fields fell into a bottomless black abyss.

Jonas was frozen in place by the horror of it all—a nightmare come to life.

"Jonas," Lucia shouted. "Jonas!"

He finally looked at her as the first crystal tower fell, shattering into the gaping chasm.

"I refuse to die here," she said as she grabbed his wrist. "There's too much left to do. Come on!"

He didn't argue. He ran by her side as they moved toward the tower itself. Lucia searched frantically for a door until one slid open seemingly out of nowhere.

"Where are we going?" he demanded.

"There's another monolith in here. It's how Timotheus sent me back to the mortal world last time."

They ran down a long corridor with a heavy metal door at the end of it. Lucia pressed her hand flat against it.

Nothing happened.

"Come on!" she yelled at it as she tried again, this time pressing both hands against cold metal.

It finally slid open.

"We can use the monolith to escape this?" Jonas asked.

"To be honest, I don't know for sure if it will work. So if you believe in any god or goddess that's ever existed, it's time to start praying."

He almost laughed at that. "How about I just believe in you?"

Lucia's gaze locked with his for a moment before she pulled him into the next room with her. Inside was a glowing violet monolith—a smaller version of the one in the mountains.

"He knew," Lucia said, and Jonas could barely hear her over the sound of the Sanctuary's destruction. "Timotheus made sure we had a way out before he died."

The ground shook, and with every step they took, pieces of it began to fall away.

"Close your eyes," Lucia yelled, grabbing Jonas's hand in hers as she reached for the crystal's surface.

Upon contact, it became blindingly bright. The noise that came from it was deafening, like rolling thunder.

Jonas felt Lucia squeeze his hand harder.

This world was ending, and it was taking them with it . . .

But then the monolith was gone. The room was gone.

And they were standing in the middle of another field, next to an ancient, crumbling stone wheel jutting out of the ground.

Jonas turned around in a circle, barely believing what he'd just experienced. "We made it. We made it! You, Lucia Damora, are absolutely brilliant!"

"It worked," she said wearily. "I can't believe it actually—"

Jonas grabbed her face between his hands and pressed his mouth against hers, kissing her hard and deep. When he finally broke away, he staggered back from her, stunned.

She's going to kill me for that, he thought.

Lucia looked at him, her eyes wide and her fingers pressed to her lips. "Why would you say that?"

"Say what?" he managed.

"That I'm going to kill you."

He stared at her, confused. "I didn't say it. I . . . I *thought* it."

"You thought it?" She studied him closely.

"Can you hear this?"

Lucia's lips hadn't moved, but he still distinctively heard her voice. Every word.

Jonas's heart pounded. *"I can hear your thoughts. How is that possible?"*

"You have Timotheus's magic inside you. It has to be the reason you were also able to enter my dream."

"Did he know this would happen?" Jonas thought, both disturbed and intrigued by the possibilities.

Then Lucia spoke aloud. "I can't deal with this right now. I have to focus on Lyssa and on—"

She cried out and fell to the ground in a heap. Jonas was at her side in an instant, kneeling on the tall green grass.

"What's wrong?" he asked, stroking her dark hair back from her face.

"It's Kyan . . ." she said in a pained whisper. "I felt him just now, in my head."

"What? How?"

"I didn't know it was possible. I . . . I tried to summon him at the palace after Lyssa was taken, but I failed. Now I think he's . . . summoning *me*."

Jonas swore under his breath, then helped her to her feet. "Whatever he's doing right now? Ignore him. He has no power over you."

"He has Lyssa." Her voice broke.

Jonas scanned the area, spotting the outline of a familiar city in the distance. "I think we're in Auranos. That . . . that's Hawk's

Brow over there. That means we're only a few hours away from the palace."

Lucia's face had gone pale, her eyes haunted. "That's where he is."

"What?"

"The City of Gold," she whispered. "He's in the City of Gold right now. He wants me to come to him. He's stronger . . . so much stronger than before." She drew in a shaky breath. "Oh, Jonas . . . I am so sorry."

He frowned. "Sorry for what?"

She touched his face, placing her palms against his cheeks, and drew him closer. He didn't resist. For a moment, a heartbeat, he was certain she would kiss him again.

Lucia looked deeply into his eyes. "I need to take it all this time. Timotheus had to know I would need this. That I'd do this. He knew everything."

"What—?"

Then he began to feel a painful draining sensation, like he'd felt the night of the rainstorm, the night he'd given her his magic to survive Lyssa's birth. But this was worse—deeper somehow, like she was stealing not just magic but life itself from him, as if she'd stabbed him in his gut and his blood left him, not in a slow drip but in a sudden and massive gush.

Before he could process what this meant, coldness fell upon him like a heavy blanket. He tried to move, tried to pull away, but it was impossible. He fell into a bottomless darkness from which he didn't know if he'd ever return.

But he did.

Jonas woke slowly, unsure how much time had passed. It was still light, and he lay next to the stone wheel.

Lucia was gone.

He weakly pushed himself up to his unsteady feet, then pulled open the front of his shirt. Only the lightest trace remained of the spiral mark on his chest.

Lucia had stolen his magic, and, he knew without a doubt, she had nearly taken his life in the process.

Jonas felt at his belt for the golden dagger, the one given to him to allegedly destroy magic and kill an evil sorceress if there was no other option.

Lucia had gone to Kyan's side the moment he'd summoned her. Whether she did it to save her daughter's life didn't matter. There'd been other solutions, other options.

Jonas would have helped her if only she'd asked.

But she hadn't changed after all.

Timotheus had believed it was Lucia's destiny to help the Kindred destroy the world.

And Jonas knew it was his destiny to stop her.

CHAPTER 28

MAGNUS

AURANOS

Magnus and Cleo followed the river to the next village. Once there, they stole a pair of horses and rode to Viridy, where, Magnus hoped, Ashur and Valia would meet them.

The weight of the ring on Magnus's hand felt heavier than before. He'd known it was powerful enough to save the life of its wearer, but not that it could also take a life . . .

This ring had also affected Kyan, allowing Magnus the chance to escape him.

This ring had caused Cleo pain when it had been momentarily on her finger.

What else could it do? Magnus wondered grimly.

As they drew closer to their destination, Magnus realized that Cleo was watching him, her grip tight on the reins of her horse.

"Are you all right?' she asked. "After . . . after what happened with Kurtis?"

"Am *I* all right?" His brows went up at the question. "You are possessed by a malevolent water goddess who wishes to help her siblings destroy the world, but you are worried about me?"

She shrugged. "I guess I am."

"I am fine," he assured her.

"Good."

Cleo had told him on the ride that the water Kindred could speak to her, urging her from inside her mind to let the waves in her drowning spells take her under. To give up control of her body.

It infuriated Magnus that he didn't know how to save her from this demon that wanted to steal life away.

Cleo also shared that Nic had been conscious enough to allow her to escape from the temple. That he'd told her to destroy the orbs. That they were the Kindred's physical anchors to this world. That without them, they would be vanquished.

He hadn't believed her at first, convinced it had been a trick Kyan had played to manipulate her. But she'd been certain it was Nic.

Certain enough that Magnus had stopped their journey long enough to take the aquamarine orb from her and attempt to shatter it with a rock. He'd tried until his hands bled and his muscles ached, but it didn't work. The orb remained intact, without even a crack.

He had damaged the earth Kindred in the past, throwing it against a stone wall at the Limerian palace in a fit of rage. This had triggered an earthquake.

But that, Cleo reminded him, was when the earth Kindred had been within the obsidian orb. An orb that had healed its damage after the Kindred had escaped from it.

It was more than obsidian, he realized. More than aquamarine.

The orbs were pieces of magic unto themselves.

And, despite his initial desire to find these priceless, omnipotent treasures, he now hated every single one of them because their very existence threatened the life of the woman he loved more than anything or anyone else in this world.

He knew Cleo wasn't helpless. Far from it. He'd witnessed her defend herself both verbally and physically in the past. But this threat wasn't as simple as escaping an assassin's blade or thrusting arrows into the throats of enemies at close range in a desperate quest for survival.

They needed a sorceress.

But they would have to settle for a powerful witch.

They entered Viridy just as the morning sunlight began to move across the large village. Their horses' hooves clip-clopped along the sparkling cobblestone roads lined with stone buildings and villas. It was much like the maze of the City of Gold; one could get lost along a road if they weren't careful. Magnus forced himself to concentrate, to remember the way to their destination. Finally, thankfully, they arrived at the large inn and tavern in the center of the village, the one with a black wooden sign in front emblazoned with a gilded name: *The Silver Toad*.

Leaving the horses with a waiting stableman, Magnus directed Cleo in through the entrance to the tavern, currently vacant but for one person seated at a table in the corner near a blazing fire-place. At the sight of them, Ashur rose to his feet.

"You made it," he said to Cleo as he took her hands in his, his expression filled with relief.

"Yes," she replied.

"And you saw Kyan . . ." he ventured.

She nodded. "I did. And Nic—he's still here, and I managed to speak with him for a few moments. He helped me escape. He's fighting as hard as he can."

Ashur sat down heavily in his chair. "He's not lost to us."

"No. There's still hope."

"I'm very glad to hear that," he whispered.

"Where is Valia?" Magnus asked, scanning the dark tavern. "Did you get her a room at the inn?"

"She's not here," Ashur replied.

Magnus's gaze shot to the Kraeshian. "What?"

Then he noticed the bloody bandages wrapped around both of Ashur's hands.

"I tried to summon her," Ashur said. "Multiple times. I followed the instructions perfectly, but she never arrived."

Magnus hung his head, pressing his hands to his temples.

"Where is Bruno?" he asked. "Is he here?"

Ashur nodded. "He's here."

"Who's Bruno?" Cleo asked.

"Bruno!" Magnus yelled at the top of his lungs.

The man in question appeared from the kitchen area, wiping his hands on his dusty apron. Deep lines fanned out from the corners of his eyes as he smiled broadly at the sight before him.

"Prince Magnus, such a great delight to see you again!" He looked at Cleo, and his eyes widened. "Oh, and you've brought your beautiful wife with you this time. Princess Cleiona, it is a true honor."

He bowed deeply before her.

"And it's lovely to meet you too," Cleo said kindly when he rose from his bow, absently tucking a piece of her hair behind her ear.

Magnus was dismayed to see that the blue lines had extended further along her left temple.

He tore his gaze from Cleo to look at Bruno. "Where is Valia?"

"Prince Ashur asked me the very same question last night," he replied. "And I have the same reply for you: I'm afraid I don't know."

"Ashur tried to summon her, but it didn't work," Magnus said.

"Sometimes it doesn't. Valia chooses when and where to appear." At the furious expression that fell over Magnus's face, the old man took a step backward. "Apologies, your highness, but I don't control her."

"We didn't even know if she could help," Ashur said. "We were only hoping."

"Hoping," Magnus muttered. "There's that useless word again."

"It's not useless," Cleo said. "Hope is powerful."

Magnus shook his head. "No, a sorceress is powerful, and that's what we need. Valia was useless too, a waste of time. I need to find Lucia."

"Where?" Ashur said, his tone sharp. "She's been gone a week with no message. She is on her own quest, Magnus, one that doesn't align with ours."

"You're wrong!" Magnus threw the words at Ashur like weapons, hoping to inflict injury. "My sister won't abandon us. Not now. Not when I need her the most."

But he had to admit, in his heart, he didn't believe this anymore.

Lucia was gone, and he didn't know when and if she'd ever return.

And Cleo . . .

He turned to her. Her earnest, hopeful expression crushed his heart.

He roared out in anger, grabbed hold of a heavy wooden table, and flipped it over.

Bruno staggered back, horrified.

Magnus's current increased strength—strength he'd had since crawling out of his own grave—was courtesy of the bloodstone.

Powerful death magic existed within the ring on his finger. But death magic couldn't help Cleo.

"Magnus," Cleo said sharply, pulling him from his thoughts. "I need to speak with you in private. Now."

He knew she was angry with him for scaring Bruno, for acting disrespectful and ungrateful toward Ashur. For wanting to crush anything that stood in the way of finding the answers he needed to save the girl standing before him.

To hell with rest of the world; Cleo was all he cared about.

Sullenly, he followed her to a room in the inn that Bruno swiftly provided for them.

"What do you have to say to me privately?" he said when she closed the door. "Do you wish to scold me for my behavior out there? To make me see reason and embrace hope like you do? To make me believe that we still have a chance to make this right again?"

"No," she replied simply.

He frowned. "No?"

Cleo shook her head. "There's nothing right about this."

Magnus inhaled deeply. "I acted like a bully to Bruno."

"Yes, you did."

"I think I scared him."

She nodded. "You can be very scary."

"Yes. And I can also be scared. And I am, right now." Magnus took her hands in his, his gaze locking with hers. "I want to help you."

Tears welled in her eyes. "I know."

"What do we do, Cleo?" He hated the weakness that had crept into his voice. "How am I supposed to save you from this?"

She frowned. "It's talking to me right now—the water Kindred. It wants me to leave you, to return to Kyan. It says that I've made him incredibly angry for leaving when he'd been trying to help me."

Magnus took her by her shoulders and stared deep into her

blue-green eyes. "Listen to me, demon. You need to get out of my wife now. Do so of your own volition and find another body to steal—I don't really give a damn who it is. But leave Cleo alone, or I swear I will destroy you!"

Cleo's frown deepened. "It finds you amusing."

Magnus had never hated anything so much in his entire life, nor had he ever felt so powerless. "I don't know what to do."

She took his hand in hers. "Wait . . . Nic . . . he told me that when you found Kyan in the forest, after you escaped from the grave, you touched him. And that—whatever you did—is what jarred him awake and allowed him to start fighting Kyan for control." Cleo held up his hand. "It's because of this ring. It has to be."

"Yes," he whispered, thinking hard. "I know."

"*Elementia* is life magic," she said. "And whatever this is, wherever it came from, it's the opposite."

He nodded. "So what? I'll ask Kyan to try this ring on and see what happens?"

"No," she said immediately. "He'd kill you before you get within three paces of him."

Magnus met her gaze. "It might be worth the risk."

"You will *not* do that," she said firmly. "We will find another way."

"You think it's that easy?"

"I know it's not." She bit her bottom lip, then moved to the window that looked out at the Viridy street outside the inn, already busy with citizens emerging from their homes for the start of a new day. "Tell me, Magnus, do you ever wish you could go back to before all of this? When life was normal?"

"No," he replied.

She turned a look of surprise on him. "Just no?"

"Just no."

"Why?"

"Because far too much has changed for me to wish for exactly how it was before." Magnus allowed himself a moment to think of life before war, before the Kindred, and before Cleo. He hadn't been happy, even then. He'd been lost, searching for meaning in his life, half-aspiring to be like his father, half-wishing his father were dead. "Besides, I don't really think the two of us would have gotten along very well before." He raised a brow at her. "You were an insufferable, vacuous party girl, from what I've heard."

"True." She laughed. "And you were a cold, brooding jackass with feelings for your sister."

Magnus cringed. "Times change."

"Indeed they do."

"I remember you, you know," he said softly. "When we were only children. From the visit when I got this . . ." Magnus brushed his fingers over his scar. "You were a shining light even at . . . what? Four or five years old?" He pictured the small golden-haired princess that had captured his attention and interest, even as a young boy. "I had a fantasy for a time that I would come to live with you and your family instead of my own."

Cleo's eyes widened. "Really?"

He nodded, the long-repressed memory coming back to him vividly. "In fact, once I ran away from home and got into a great deal of trouble with that goal in mind. My father . . ." He sighed. "My father was not kind. Not even on his kindest day."

"Your father loved you. In his own way." Cleo smiled at him. "And I know for a fact your mother loved you very much."

He raised a brow. "What makes you say that?"

"She told me once that she would kill me if I ever hurt you."

He stared at her, then shook his head. "That sounds like my mother."

A shadow crossed her expression, and her smile fell away. "I went on to hurt you quite a lot."

"And I you, far too many times to count." Magnus took her hands in his, pulling her closer to him. "We will figure this out, Cleo. I swear that to you."

He leaned in to kiss her, needing to feel her lips against his, but was interrupted by a loud bang on the other side of the tavern.

"So much for our private discussion," he said with annoyance.

He crossed the room and opened the door, shocked at who stood on the other side.

It was Enzo, his face bloody, half the hair on his head burned off.

The guard fell to his knees, gasping for breath, a rolled-up piece of parchment dropping from his grip.

Cleo was at his side in an instant, helping him to his feet. Magnus reached down to grab the parchment.

"Enzo!" Cleo gasped. "What happened to you?"

"Kyan knows where you are," Enzo managed. "He can sense you because the water Kindred is inside you. You're all connected."

Heart pounding, Magnus crossed the room to look out the window, searching for any sign of their enemy. "Where is he now?"

"He's not here," Enzo said. "He sent me with this message. For you, princess."

Magnus quickly unrolled the parchment, holding it out for Cleo to read along with him.

> I've tried to be patient and kind with you, but that didn't work. Come to me immediately. If you don't, everyone in your beloved golden city will burn. There's no other way for this to end. Deny me, and I promise endless suffering for everyone and everything you love.

At Cleo's pained gasp, Magnus threw the parchment away from him.

"He's bluffing," Magnus growled.

"He's not," Enzo said, his voice strained. "I saw what he could do. His fire . . . it's not like normal fire. It's deeper, more painful than anything I've ever felt before. I never thought that could be possible."

"You're not helping," Magnus snapped.

"Magnus, I know you want to save me," Cleo said, her eyes filled with tears. "But there's no way. I'm so close now to losing control of this. If Taran couldn't resist, I won't be able to. And I believe what Kyan says. He will burn the city."

"No, you're not going to him. We're going to find another answer."

"But he'll destroy the city."

"I don't care about the damn city!"

"I do," she said fiercely.

"Damn it!" Magnus's anguished gaze met Cleo's. "Stay here. I need to get Ashur. We need to try summoning Valia again." He glared at Enzo. "Stay with her."

He left the room and rushed down the stairs, searching for Ashur. He found the prince talking with Bruno near the kitchen.

"What?" Ashur exclaimed when he saw Magnus's pained expression.

"Whatever it takes," Magnus managed to say. "We need that witch's help. Kyan's in the City of Gold, holding it hostage until Cleo comes to his side."

"No," Ashur said, his voice pained. "We need time."

"There's no time." He looked down at Ashur's bandaged hands. "We'll use my blood. Or we'll find a dozen turtles to sacrifice to that woman. But we must be quick about it."

"The princess should be with us," Ashur said, nodding grimly.

"I agree. And Enzo's here—he delivered the message. He has plenty of blood in him to help. Come with me."

With Ashur in tow, Magnus took the stairs to the second floor two at a time and burst into the room where he'd left Cleo.

All that was in the room was a hastily scrawled note on a torn piece of parchment left on the cot.

I'm sorry, but I have to do this. I love you.

Magnus crumpled the note in his fist and threw it onto the floor. Ashur picked it up and scanned his eyes over it.

"She went to the city, didn't she?" he said.

Magnus was already out of the room, headed toward the exit to the inn.

He had to get to her before it was too late.

CHAPTER 29

AMARA

KRAESHIA

"Let me see if I understand this," Felix said when Amara was finished explaining everything to him and Nerissa. "Your granny kidnapped Lyssa from right under Princess Lucia's nose to use her blood in magic potions, and Mikah, the leader of the revolution, is going to be executed at your Ascension ceremony. And you're not all right with either of those things."

How could he sound so calm when Amara had just shared so much she felt exhausted from the confession? "That's right."

Felix glanced at Nerissa. "I'm going to go ahead and kill her now."

"Felix," Nerissa snapped. "Try to think, would you?"

"I *am* thinking. She's a proven liar and manipulator, one who uses others for her own gain and their great misfortune." His upper lip curled back from his straight white teeth as he studied Amara. Amara's mind flashed to a time not so long ago when Felix had desired her. Judging by the look in his eye, none of those feelings remained. "And the moment the game is up and she has nowhere to limp off to, she suddenly wants to be a hero? How convenient."

"I'm no hero," Amara said, refusing to show him any more fear.

She was through with fear and doubt. She had only certainty within her now—certainty that the baby would be returned to Lucia and that Mikah would not die today.

It surprised her how fiercely she clung to the need for Mikah's life to continue. He was a rebel, one who would kill her in an instant if he got the opportunity, just like Felix.

But what he'd said in the forgetting room—about her grandmother, about Amara's deluded idea of achieving a peaceful and benevolent world by force and absolute rule.

He'd been completely right.

A *man* had been right in telling Amara she was wrong.

It was a deeply annoying realization, but that didn't make it any less true.

"I know what I've done," Amara said. "I'm not seeking redemption for it—I know that's impossible. But you're here, and you're capable of helping me with these tasks."

"Tasks? You make it sound so simple." Nerissa shook her head as she moved through Amara's expansive chambers, brushing her hand along the back of a green velvet chaise. "You're suggesting we mount an immediate rescue of two heavily guarded prisoners, but we're only two people. It was difficult enough getting to this wing of the palace."

"Not that difficult," Felix growled.

"You will have my full cooperation." Yet even Amara had to agree that what she proposed would not be simple. "Still, this is my Ascension day . . . so, yes, it will be tricky. Security is doubled throughout the Spear."

"Oh, yes, excellent plan," Felix said. "You sending us off for slaughter so we're out of the way of your shiny ceremony."

He would not listen to her, no matter what she said. She knew that. But she couldn't let it stop her.

"Nerissa," Amara began. "You have to believe me that I want to help."

"I do believe you," Nerissa replied. "And I agree that ensuring the safety of Lyssa needs to be a priority. She must be returned to her mother immediately."

"Good. So where do you suggest we start?" Amara eased herself down upon the chaise to take the pressure off her leg. The sun streamed in through the windows along the opposite side of the room. Through the windows she could see the crystal-blue waters of the Silver Sea.

"Let's say I go along with this," Felix said, pacing the gilded ceramic floor of Amara's chambers like a caged beast. "I go and scour the city, checking Mikah's old hideouts for rebels that are still breathing, and I enlist them to join us in his rescue. After that, we wrestle the baby away from the clutches of evil granny. And what then? What happens to you?"

"Then . . ." Amara carefully considered this. "I will still rule as empress."

Felix groaned. "Isn't that convenient."

Amara's heartbeat quickened. "I can! I've seen the error of my ways, that my grandmother has been far too instrumental in the darkest of my decisions. I don't place the blame fully on her, of course. I chose to do what I did . . . just as my father would have selectively listened to his advisors." She winced at the thought that she'd turned out to be exactly like the man she'd hated all her life. "But I *can* change, I *can* be better. And now that I've discovered that my grandmother has been manipulating me for her own gain, she will no longer be such a strong influence on me."

Felix raised his one visible eyebrow. "You honestly believe every piece of that soggy horse dung coming out of your mouth, don't you?"

He spoke with such disrespect that she got the overwhelming urge to scream so that her guards would arrive and have him arrested.

Then Amara reminded herself, yet again, how much Felix had endured because of her. Most men wouldn't still be standing, let alone breathing.

He was strong. And she needed that strength today of all days.

"It's not horse dung," she said firmly. "It's the truth."

Felix looked at Nerissa, shaking his head. "I can't listen to this for much longer."

Amara realized Nerissa's attention hadn't shifted from her for a moment. Her former attendant studied her carefully, her dark eyes narrowed, her slim arms crossed over her chest.

"There's no time for debate," Nerissa finally said. "Felix and I will go search for local rebels, and I pray that we find enough who are willing to help."

Felix finally sheathed his blade, but his expression hadn't softened even a fraction. "If we find them, I know they'll help. Mikah was a great leader." He frowned. "*Is* a great leader. Nothing has changed there."

"I'll go with you," Amara said, wanting to assist in any way she could.

"No," Nerissa replied. "You will stay here and get ready for your Ascension. Act as if everything is normal."

Frustration coursed through Amara, and she awkwardly pushed herself up from the soft chaise and back up to her feet. "But everything is not normal—far from it!"

"All the more reason for you to pretend that it is. We do not want to raise the suspicions of your grandmother more than they already are. If that happens, she won't let anyone within sight of either Mikah or Lyssa. And Mikah will die, executed in a dark room with no one to help him."

Amara wanted to argue more, but she saw the wisdom in Nerissa's words. Finally, she nodded. "Very well. Please return as soon as you possibly can."

"We will." Nerissa moved toward the door without further hesitation.

Felix backed away from Amara slowly, as if he expected her to plunge a dagger into his back the moment he turned away.

"If you're lying yet again," he said before he left the room, "you will regret it very, very much. You hear me?"

And then they were gone, and Amara was alone, wondering if she'd made the correct decision. Then again, any other decision would have resulted in her bleeding on the floor right now, gasping for her last breath.

This had been the right thing to do.

Still, it felt as unnatural and awkward as trying to walk on a broken leg.

Amara tried her best to go about the rest of her day as originally planned. She meditated, bathed, and then took a midday meal of fruit and light pastries, which she barely touched.

She had a final fitting for a new leg brace that would allow her to walk from now on unassisted by a cane. It was better, but she still couldn't hide her limp.

Then she waited as long as she could before allowing an attendant to paint her face, lining her eyes heavily in black coal, brushing her lips with a dye that would make them appear as red as rubies.

Another attendant styled her long black hair, creating an intricate maze of braids.

Finally, they helped Amara into her Ascension gown with Lorenzo supervising, pride for his magnificent piece of artistry shining in his eyes.

"You are as beautiful as a goddess today, your majesty," he said as the heavy wings were placed onto her shoulders.

Amara looked into the mirror at her heavily made-up eyes, the color of her irises the exact same pale gray-blue as Ashur's were.

She'd wanted what Lorenzo said for so long. To be a goddess. To have ultimate power at any cost—any cost at all.

And a part of her still wanted that. Still wanted that shiny, exquisite bauble that now lay just out of her reach.

I can have both, she silently told her golden reflection. *I can have power* and *make the right decisions. Today is the first day of my new life.*

After she left Lorenzo, she shrugged off any cloying guard who wanted to escort her to the ceremony hall.

"I know the way," she told them. "And I wish only for silence and solitude to help collect my thoughts."

They didn't question her. The guards bowed, let her pass, and didn't follow.

Of course they obey me, she thought. They knew they would be harshly punished if they didn't.

Fear was a powerful weapon, forged over time and by example.

Generations of fear for the punishments issued by the Cortas family line had created total and complete obedience.

Could people be ruled without fear to keep them in check? Was it even possible?

She didn't know for certain, and that question troubled her deeply.

Amara took the long way to the hall where, by now, every Kraeshian who had received a personal invitation to the event of the century would be lining the large, ornate room where her father and mother had been married. Where her three brothers—but not their "lesser" sister—had been officially presented to important friends of the emperor after their births.

Where her mother had been displayed after her death, fully painted and coiffed and wearing her wedding gown, for all to see.

A thousand would fill the hall as Amara received the scepter—a symbol of power for a Kraeshian ruler since the very beginning—that bore the chiseled golden head of a phoenix. A symbol of eternal life and eternal power.

Within the scepter there was a sharp blade.

And with this blade, the ascending ruler would make a blood sacrifice to bring good fortune to her reign.

Today it would be Mikah's blood, unless Felix and Nerissa were successful in their quest.

Amara took her time walking to the ceremony hall. She wove through the palace and passed the large windows that looked out onto her courtyard. She paused. She knew exactly what would calm her. Amara made her way out into her rock garden.

To her surprise, waiting for her on a table was a bottle of wine with two goblets, just as there had been when she'd arrived.

There was a message there, which read:

> *Dhosha,*
>
> *I anticipate that you will visit your favorite place before joining me and the others. Please take a moment to appreciate how much you've accomplished, and how very much I appreciate you.*
>
> *Your Madhosha*

Yes. A sip of sweet wine might be exactly what she needed to calm her nerves to face what was to come. Her grandmother knew her very well indeed. She poured some of the golden liquid into one of the goblets and then raised it to her lips.

"Empress!"

She jumped at the sound of the voice.

Costas approached her, his expression grim.

"Did the queen send you to fetch me?" she said as sharply as she could. "Or did you decide to interrupt my privacy all on your own?"

"Queen Neela sent me to find you. The ceremony is ready to begin."

"I'm sure it is. And I'm equally sure that it can't start without me."

He took a step closer. He looked pained. "I know you're angry with me for all that's transpired."

"Angry?" she said, cocking her head. "What reason would I have for being angry with you, Costas? For shamelessly spying on me for my grandmother for months now? For kidnapping a child from a sorceress who could kill us all with a flick of her wrist?"

"Yes. That, all of that. But I need you to know . . ." The guard glanced over his shoulder as if assuring himself that they were alone. "I didn't do this with disrespect intended toward you, empress. I know I had earned your trust, and I valued that."

"And yet you destroyed that trust in an instant," Amara said. "Which was a grave mistake, I can assure you."

His eyes searched hers. "I need to explain why I did it."

"Lower your eyes to the ground," she said curtly. "You are no longer allowed to look at me as anything but a servant."

He did as commanded. "Queen Neela threatened my family, said she would have them killed if I didn't do as she said. She said that, by doing as she instructed, I would be helping you, not hurting you. I felt had no choice."

Amara wasn't sure why this explanation felt like a shock to her. Of course it made total sense. "The royal guard are not permitted to have a family for this reason, so that they can't be used against you."

"I know. I thought I could hide the existence of my wife and son, but I couldn't. I broke the rules—that much I know and accept. But it tells you that I was without a choice. I had to do what Queen Neela commanded."

"You should have come to me with this earlier—much earlier."

"I know. I can only beg for your forgiveness and assure you that I would die to protect you, empress. My life is yours."

It explained everything. It didn't excuse what he did, but she understood now why he'd done it. It wasn't because he'd shifted his loyalties to her grandmother.

He'd acted out of fear.

"We'll have to move your family somewhere more secure," Amara said. "Somewhere my grandmother won't be able to find them."

Costas let out a breath, and Amara saw his shoulders relax a bit. "Much gratitude, empress."

Amara picked up the wine bottle and poured the other glass. "Have a drink with me. Quickly, before we need to go to the ceremony."

Costas looked down with surprise at the goblet she handed to him. "Me, your grace?"

She nodded. "Make a toast, will you? Something that will give me the strength to continue on with this challenging day."

"Of course." He raised the goblet, his brow furrowed in thought.

"To the reign of Amara Cortas, the first empress in history. May that reign be one of light and hope and happiness for all who fall within her view."

He drank deeply from his goblet.

Amara paused to consider his words.

Could she really do this? Could she be the first empress in the world—someone who would rule with a message of hope instead of fear?

She had to try.

If she was successful, she could truly be the legendary phoenix brought to life.

Amara raised the goblet to her lips just as Costas collapsed to his knees.

His face had turned red and purple, with blotches of sickly white. Blood spilled over his bottom lip.

"Costas!" she cried, dropping her goblet. "What's happening to you?"

He couldn't speak. He clutched at his throat and toppled over on his side, his eyes wide and glassy.

Amara staggered back from the body, from the bottle of wine that had fallen to the mossy ground of the courtyard, its golden contents leaking out.

In the space of a few heartbeats, a horrible clarity dawned on her.

The wine had been poisoned.

Poison like the kind Neela had supplied Amara to put in the wine she'd given her father and brothers. And now Costas was dead.

But Amara knew he wasn't the intended victim.

She left Costas there, sidestepping his body so she wouldn't get blood on the golden skirt of her gown. She summoned every piece of control she had over herself to keep any tears from spilling. She wouldn't want to mess up the coal around her eyes, the stain on her lips. Her perfect hair and perfect wings and perfect day.

She thought her father might be proud of how she managed to pull herself together and head to the tall emerald-colored doors of the ceremony hall, where a flank of guards waited to escort her inside.

She let them.

Amara entered the hall, and a thousand people she'd kept waiting rose from the gleaming wooden benches to their feet. She moved down the aisle toward the front, where there were ten steps leading to a raised stage.

On that stage were three people. The Grand Augur, wearing magnificent purple velvet robes. Her grandmother, wearing a gown of silver finery nearly as beautiful as Amara's. And Mikah, on his knees, his hands bound behind his back.

She forced herself not to hesitate. To take each step as proudly as she'd be expected to by all witnesses. Finally, she stood next to the woman who had just tried to murder her and take her power.

After Amara, Neela was the next in line for the title of empress.

"Beautiful," Neela cooed. If Amara had expected to see surprise at her arrival from her grandmother, there was no hint of it at all. "Even more beautiful than I expected. We should keep Lorenzo in Kraeshia forever, don't you think?"

Amara pushed a smile onto her lips. "Oh, yes. Most definitely."

How could she untangle herself from this deceptive, lying creature of darkness and make everything right again?

Not now, she thought. *Later. I'll think about this later.*

Now, all she could do was hope that Nerissa and Felix had done what they'd promised.

She barely heard a word the Grand Augur spoke during the

ascension ceremony she'd dreamed about all her life. Something about history and family honor and the duties of a ruler.

All she knew was that it was over far too quickly.

Now Neela held the golden scepter, facing Amara on the stage.

"You are worthy to wield this, *dhosha*," Neela said, her smile fixed upon a face far younger-looking than should have been possible. Amara wondered if her mysterious apothecary was responsible for poisons as well as youth-inducing elixirs.

Amara watched her grandmother carefully, looking for any sign of guilt, but she found none. Had Neela expected Amara to show up at all? It could only have been a best guess that Amara would go back to her courtyard and find the wine.

How many other traps had been set for her by someone she'd loved and trusted?

"Now," the Grand Augur said, opening his arms wide as he addressed the silent, obedient audience. "The last piece of this Ascension must now lock into place: a blood sacrifice. A rebel who attempted to overthrow the royal family, who colluded in the murder of the former emperor and princes. Today his blood shall spill to wash away the past and welcome the future of Empress Amara Cortas."

Amara moved toward Mikah, mindlessly separating the scepter she held into its two parts—sheath and blade.

Mikah didn't flinch, didn't try to escape.

"Do what you must," he told her with a sneer. "Prove to me you're as evil as your father was."

Despite this show of bravery, he inhaled sharply as she pressed the edge of the blade to his throat.

One simple thrust of her wrist and she would officially be empress, and no one could oppose or control her.

It was so tempting. Then, she could send her grandmother far away, where she would never be heard from again.

Amara could have all the power she ever desired and do with that power everything she ever dreamed.

But before she could decide what path she would now take, the hall erupted in chaos. A group of masked, armed figures swarmed inside, battling against the guards in a blur of arms and legs and weapons. The clash of blades quickly became deafening.

Heart pounding, Amara turned back toward Mikah just in time for him to kick her hard in her broken leg. The pain shot up her spine. She dropped her weapon as she fell to the floor. Then he was gone, out of her sight. She searched for her grandmother but couldn't spot her either.

Amara turned around to find a sword pointed at her face, and the dark and hateful glare of a rebel's eyes.

The man took a step forward, moving the blade to her throat, but just as he did he was shoved aside. The sword clattered to the ground as the rebel fell. Felix stood before her, offering his hand. "I should have let him kill you. But I'd rather keep that honor for myself one day."

"Not today?" she asked tensely.

He frowned at her. "Unfortunately, no."

Nerissa came to Felix's side as the battle between rebels and guards continued behind them. Guests fled for the exit in a frenzied, frightened stampede.

"We did our part," Nerissa told her as she elbowed her way through the crowd. "This will be an excellent distraction for us to get to Lyssa."

Amara nodded. With no time to speak or make suggestions or do anything except try to avoid being struck down by a rebel's blade, she led Nerissa and Felix out of the ceremony hall to the nursery her grandmother had taken her to earlier that day.

Each step on her newly injured leg hurt. She hoped very much the brace would continue to hold as she hobbled along as fast as she could down hallway after hallway, passing swarms of guards headed in the opposite direction.

Of course Amara was recognizable in the Spear even without her golden gown. She knew she couldn't hide from these guards as she hurried down the hallways toward her destination, so she didn't try.

"We will control the situation, empress," one guard told her. "You do not have to fear."

A lovely promise, she thought. *But not possible at this point.*

She feared. She feared very much the outcome of this day.

After awkwardly ascending the stairway to the floor of the nursery, Amara led her personal pair of rebels down the last hall-way to the unguarded door at the end.

"Lyssa is in there." She gestured toward the door, while scanning the area. "The guards on duty must have been called away to join the fight, but the door will be locked."

"That's not a problem," Felix said. He kicked the door hard, and it flew open.

Amara entered the room first, expecting to deal with nothing more than a frightened nursemaid.

But, of course, things couldn't be that simple.

Neela was already in the room, alone, holding the baby in her arms.

"So nice of you to join us," Neela said, barely glancing up after the door broke open.

Amara felt her heart sink in her chest. She tried to speak, but no words came.

Nerissa stepped forward.

"Put her down right now," she demanded.

Neela smiled at her. "I don't know you, do I?"

"No. But I know you. And you're going to put that baby back in her cradle and leave this room right now."

"No, actually, I don't think I will."

Felix stepped closer. "You know, I really don't make it a habit to mess with old ladies if I can help it. But some old ladies need messing with." He flashed his blade at her. "Step away from the baby and no one has to get hurt."

Neela swept her gaze over him. "I recognize you, don't I? Felix Gaebras, one of Gaius Damora's bodyguards. The one that my granddaughter took to her bed at her first opportunity. And the one who was arrested for poisoning the emperor and my grandsons. How surprising it is to see you again."

Felix's eye narrowed on her. "And you're the evil granny who's responsible for everyone's pain and misery around here. Every kingdom's got one, it seems."

Neela's smile held. "I advise you to stay exactly where you are, Felix. We wouldn't want this darling child to get hurt, would we?"

Lyssa cooed and stretched her little arms over her head. Amara eyed her uneasily.

"We need to give the baby back to Lucia Damora, *madhosha*," she said aloud. "Felix and Nerissa will take her from here."

Neela made no move to put the baby down. "*Dhosha*, are you being forced to comply with these rebels' demands? Be honest with me. There'll be consequences for lying, as I'm sure you know."

Amara's mouth went dry. "Why did you poison the wine, *madhosha*?"

Neela raised a brow. "What did you say?"

"The wine you left for me in my courtyard rock garden. You left me poisoned wine, because you hoped I'd drink a glass before the ceremony."

"What? I admit I left you some wine, but it wasn't poisoned! If it was, someone else is certainly to blame. You are my jewel, *dhosha*. My treasure beyond any other from the moment you were born."

Amara searched her face, now uncertain. Could this be the truth? That someone else had found the wine and poisoned it? "I know you called my mother that. *Your jewel.* And I know she died for me . . . because of the potion. Perhaps you blame me for that."

"No, I don't blame you." Neela's eyes narrowed. "Your mother died because your father was evil and cruel and heartless. And now he's dead, and I can dance upon his grave—and the graves of all men like him in this world. Now, I ask you again, are these rebels forcing your hand?"

Amara looked down at the peaceful face of Lyssa, nestled in Neela's arms. Surely, her grandmother had held her like this, had cared for her when she was only a baby—a baby whose mother had been taken before her time.

And then the clouds parted outside. A ray of sun shone through a window at the far end of the room. Amara noticed something glinting in Neela's grip, partially hidden beneath the blanket and pressed against the baby's stomach.

A knife.

Amara took a shallow breath in. "Yes," she forced the word out. "They are. They rescued Mikah and told me that if I didn't bring them here, they would kill me."

"I knew it!" Felix growled. "I will kill you before you leave this room, you deceitful bitch."

"No, you won't," Neela said, revealing the blade for them to see as well.

"Please don't!" Nerissa held out her hands and shook her head. "Don't hurt the child!"

"If I do, it will only be because you gave me no other choice.

It will be your fault entirely." Neela shook her head. "And such a waste to spill even a drop of this baby's precious blood. So here is how this will work. The two of you will leave here immediately and rejoin your friends downstairs, who, no doubt, have been captured by now, as they were the last time they attempted a siege upon the Spear. Then you will all be executed—the more blood spilled at my granddaughter's Ascension, the better and more memorable it will be."

Amara hadn't moved, had barely breathed, as she'd listened to her grandmother calmly explain all this.

"And you . . ." Neela addressed Amara now. "I must say, your actions today worry me."

Amara shook her head. "They shouldn't. I am still with you in all ways, *madhosha*. If it weren't for you, I wouldn't have everything I have today." She needed to play along, needed to convince her grandmother she was trustworthy.

And a horrible part of her, a scared and dark part she wasn't proud of, wanted to erase her deal with Felix and Nerissa, to have everything go back to the way it was before, when the world was hers to do with as she pleased now that she had enough power to wield.

"I have been your greatest advisor," Neela said. "I know you've struggled with some decisions you've had to make, such as with Ashur. But you did choose to kill him, just as you killed your father and two other brothers. *You* did that, not me."

"I know," Amara whispered.

Neela took a step forward. With Lyssa cradled in one arm, she reached her other hand out and stroked Amara's check.

"You need me, *dhosha*. I've given you everything you've ever desired, and yet now you look at me with such doubt that it breaks my heart. But it can still be all right."

"Don't listen to her," Nerissa hissed. "She fills your head with lies."

Amara tried to ignore her, tried to focus only on her grandmother's face.

"It can?" she whispered.

"Yes. However, sadly, today it seems that you lost your mind, *dhosha*."

Amara shook her head. "I haven't lost my mind."

"But you have," Neela insisted. "I have seen this madness coming upon you ever since you lost your beloved father and brothers. I've documented it, but I had hoped it wouldn't escalate to this."

"What are you talking about?" Amara's heart began to beat fast and hard. "I'm not mad!"

"I've found a place for you, somewhere safe, where you can recover your mind. It will be peaceful, so very peaceful, and I promise to visit you regularly. There are others like you there, others afflicted by this confusion that has caused you to hurt so many people I know you love, including me. I hope that the actions I've taken will help you heal, my beloved *dhosha*. And during your absence, for as long as it takes, I will rule in your place."

Amara stared at her grandmother as the rest of her world began crashing down all around her.

"You planned this all along," she said, the words like jagged rocks in her throat.

Those of a lower class, if they lost their minds, were allowed to leave this life gently, with the hope that they would be cured for their next life. But those of the royal class were given the opportunity to heal during this life.

Locked away in a forgetting room—but one in a madhouse, where its prisoners were told it was for their own good, not because of a specific crime they'd committed.

But Amara knew the experience was the same in all other ways. Forgotten for years—decades.

Sometimes until their natural death.

Neela sent a glare toward Felix and Nerissa, who were still watching silently. "Put down your weapons and walk away, or I fear my granddaughter will hurt this child, and I can't do a thing about it." She moved the tip of the blade upward to Lyssa's small, vulnerable throat.

Nerissa and Felix finally did as instructed, their expressions dark and pained. They moved backward until they were on the other side of the open door.

"I've won," Neela said. "Admit it and all of this will go smoothly, *dhosha*. I promise it doesn't have to hurt."

Amara tasted the bitter tang of the red dye as she licked her lips, trying to find the strength to reply, to say what she knew she had to say. Her grandmother controlled her life—she always had. Amara just hadn't realized it until now.

"You've won," Amara whispered. "Now please, *please* put the baby back in her cradle."

"Very well." Neela smiled and gently placed Lyssa down. "Now I want you to thank me for the beautiful gift I've given you."

Amara smoothed the sides of her golden skirts. "Thank you for the beautiful gift you've given me."

"A gift that is valuable and precious."

"Yes. Yes, it is."

"Not *it*, my darling. *She*. And we still need to pick a new name for her."

"Oh." Amara frowned. "I didn't mean *that* gift."

Neela cocked her head. "Then what gift did you mean?"

"This gift." Amara drew her wedding dagger out from beneath the folds of her skirt and pulled her grandmother into an embrace. "Thank you, *madhosha*. Thank you so much."

Then she sank the tip of the blade into her grandmother's chest. The old woman gasped, stiffened, but Amara held on.

"You poisoned the wine," Amara whispered in her ear. "I know you did. But even if you didn't, this still had to happen."

She yanked the blade out. The front of her golden gown was now stained with her grandmother's blood.

Neela stood there for a moment, her hand pressed to her chest, her eyes wide with disbelief.

"I did everything for you," she managed.

"I suppose I'm just an ungrateful grandchild," Amara replied as Neela fell to her knees. "Always thinking of herself and no one else."

"This isn't over," Neela gasped, but her words grew weak as her blood flowed over the floor. "The potion . . . the resurrection potion. I've taken it. I will live again."

"That potion requires one who loves you more than any other to sacrifice their life in exchange for yours." Amara raised her chin. "That might have been me before today. But no longer."

Neela dropped to her side, and the life faded from her gray eyes.

Amara then turned to Felix and Amara, standing in the doorframe, staring at her as if she'd just performed the most incredible feat of magic they'd ever witnessed.

"I really hate to admit it, but I think I'm impressed," Felix said, shaking his head.

Nerissa had no such reaction as she moved quickly to the cradle and picked up Lyssa.

"Take her and go," Amara said, surprised that she sounded so calm. The dagger she held continued to drip her grandmother's blood to the floor. "I have some things to clean up here."

Nerissa shook her head, then opened her mouth to say something in reply.

Amara held up her hand to stop her. "Please, don't say another word. Just go. Take Lyssa back to Lucia and tell her . . . tell her I'm sorry. And if you see my brother, tell him I know he hates me and always will, but that I . . . I hope one day to make amends even though I have no idea how I'll do that. Now just go, before we waste any more time."

Nerissa's eyes had turned glassy. She swallowed hard and nodded.

"Farewell," she said, and then she and Felix disappeared with the baby.

And Amara, alone in the room with the body of her grandmother, waited to see who would arrive first.

A rebel to kill her.

Or a guard to arrest her.

She knew she'd more than earned either outcome.

CHAPTER 30

CLEO

AURANOS

Cleo knew Magnus would follow, just as he had when she'd gone to the festival. And if he found her before she reached the palace, she knew he would try to stop her.

And the city would burn.

She couldn't let that happen.

Cleo held tightly onto Enzo as he raced his horse across the green hills and valleys of the Auranian countryside until her beautiful city finally came into view.

She gasped at the sight before her.

The City of Gold had greatly changed since yesterday.

Frightening, thick green vines now covered the golden walls, reminding her of the blue lines on her skin. The vines looked as if they had been there for years, growing from a deserted and untended garden. But they hadn't been there before, not at all. The walls had always been clear of any debris.

This was new.

"Earth magic," she managed to say aloud.

Enzo nodded grimly. "Olivia has been changing the city to please herself."

"The Kindred have taken over completely in such a short time."

"I'm afraid so," he said. "They control everything within the walls. Citizens who aren't now imprisoned in pits Olivia created or cages of fire are hiding in their homes and businesses, afraid to come outside."

Kyan wanted everyone to know of their existence, Cleo thought. And to fear their power.

The main gates themselves were coated in flames. Cleo could feel the painful, intense heat even thirty paces away, as if she'd stepped close to the face of the sun itself. Enzo's horse wouldn't take another step toward it, bucking in protest until they finally had to dismount it.

There were no sentries stationed above the fiery gate or to the sides of it.

"How do we get inside?" she asked.

Just as she spoke the words, the gates opened all on their own, allowing entry into the city.

As the flames parted, Cleo saw someone waiting for them. Lucia's long, raven-black hair blew away from her face.

"Don't worry," she called out to them. "I won't let the fire burn you."

"Lucia . . ." Cleo said, stunned.

"Welcome," Lucia said, spreading her arms. She wore a plain black cloak that bore no embroidery or adornments at all. "It's nice of you to finally show up. I've been waiting here for a while."

She sounded so calm and collected, as if this weren't a nightmare come to life.

"You're helping him," Cleo said, the words painful in her throat.

"He has Lyssa," Lucia replied simply. "He won't show her to me, won't confirm that she's fine. But he has her. And therefore, he has me as well. It's as simple as that."

Cleo wrung her hands as she walked through the entrance and into the city. Enzo stayed at her side. True to Lucia's promise, they didn't feel the heat of the flames anymore, even though the opened gates still burned.

Cleo hadn't seen Lyssa at the temple. Perhaps she should have demanded that Kyan show her the baby to ensure her safety. Instead, she'd been too focused on her own well-being.

She could have prevented all this.

"You . . ." Lucia addressed Enzo. "You've done what Kyan asked of you. Now leave us to speak in private."

"I won't go," Enzo said gruffly. "I will protect the princess from anyone who means her harm."

"That certainly must be a long list by now. I'll say it again: Go away." Lucia flicked her hand, and Enzo staggered back toward the flames.

"Stop it," Cleo snapped. "Don't hurt him!"

Lucia raised a brow. "If he does what I say, he won't come to further harm."

"Princess . . ." Enzo said, his voice pained.

Cleo's heart pounded. "Go, do as she says. I'll be fine."

They both knew it was a lie. But Enzo nodded, turned, and walked directly toward the palace along the main pathway to the entrance.

"Come with me," Lucia said. "We'll take the long way."

"Why?" Cleo asked. "Doesn't Kyan want to know I'm here?"

"Just follow me." Lucia turned away from Cleo and strode in the opposite direction from Enzo.

Cleo forced herself to move. She had to be brave.

Finally, the water Kindred said from within her. *This long and tiresome journey is almost at an end.*

Not if I have any say in the matter, Cleo thought fiercely.

She followed Lucia along the city's main concourse. Tiled with sparkling stones, the concourse was usually filled with citizens going about their daily business. With carriages and wagons bringing both guests and wares to the many businesses and the palace itself. Its emptiness was so eerie, Cleo felt a shiver run up her spine.

"Please! Please help us!"

Cleo froze at the mournful sound of cries coming from a deep pit in the ground ten paces away, at the edge of a grassy garden.

Legs stiff, she moved to the side of it and looked down at thirty faces looking up. Her heart wrenched.

"Princess!" The trapped Auranians reached up toward her. "Please help us!"

"Save us!"

Cleo staggered back from the side, her breath now coming in gulps as she tried not to allow her fear and desperation to overwhelm her. "Lucia," Cleo barely managed to speak. "You have to help them."

"I can't."

A sob rose in Cleo's throat, but she refused to let it out.

Lucia might be helping Kyan in order to save her daughter, but at what cost? Thousands of people called this city their home. Countless others would be visiting for the day.

Kyan would kill them all.

"You can!" Cleo insisted.

"Trust me, they're safer in there than anywhere else." Lucia's expression was grim. "Kyan arrived in this city in a foul mood. He burned fifty citizens in a single burst of his fire before Olivia created pits like this."

Cleo stifled a gasp. Kyan's foul mood was surely because she'd run away from the temple. And now fifty citizens were dead.

She tried to find her voice in the face of this realization. "Olivia is trying to help?"

"I wouldn't say that." Lucia exhaled shakily. "I think she's simply trying to keep Kyan from becoming distracted from the task at hand."

"Which is?"

"Kyan wants me to perform the ritual again," Lucia told her.

"The ritual?" Cleo repeated. "No. Lucia, no! You have to listen to me. You can't do this."

"I have no choice."

"You do have a choice. I can help you defeat him."

Lucia laughed. "You don't know Kyan like I do, Cleo. He can be charming when he wants to be. Curious about mortals and their amusing behavior. But he's not a man who can be reasoned with. He is fire, and it's in his very nature to burn. The others are the same."

"You've seen them."

Lucia nodded. "They're all at the palace waiting for you. I thought I might be able to reason with Olivia, that she might have some kind of maternal instinct and want to protect Lyssa. She is the earth Kindred—that magic is what makes healing and growth possible. But she's not like that. She's just like Kyan. She wants to use her magic for evil. And she will destroy everything on a whim. Mortals aren't important to them, not individually. We're . . . like insects—annoying pests that are easily swatted away."

Cleo waited for the water Kindred to add something, but it stayed silent.

Perhaps that meant it agreed with everything Lucia said.

Cleo wasn't surprised by any of this. Last night, Kyan had pretended to be kind as he'd offered to help her through this—as both Olivia and the water Kindred had called it—"transition."

But Kyan gave her no choice in the outcome.

He would win. She would lose.

"Is Lyssa here?" Cleo asked. "Have you see her?"

Lucia's expression grew pained, her sky-blue eyes filled with anguish. "She's here, I'm sure of it. But I haven't seen her yet."

"If you haven't seen her, how can you be so sure she's here?"

Lucia turned a glare on her, one so sharp that Cleo nearly flinched away from it. "Where else would she be? Kyan has her—he's using her to keep me in line. And it's working very well."

Cleo's stomach sank. Lucia sounded so despondent, so hopeless. Yet she'd also never sounded more dangerous.

Part of Cleo had begun to doubt that Kyan had taken Lyssa. She would have seen some sign of the baby last night at the temple.

Surely, Nic would have known about her.

But if Kyan didn't have her, who would?

It didn't make any sense.

"When did you come back?" Cleo asked more tentatively now.

"Kyan summoned me earlier today."

She frowned. "What do you mean he summoned you?"

Lucia paused as they passed the city gardens. A portion of the hedges were shaped into a maze that children could run through, searching for a way out the other side. Cleo knew it reminded Lucia of the ice maze back at the Limerian palace.

She saw a very familiar emotion cross the sorceress's blue eyes.

Wistfulness. It was the same ache Cleo felt for a simpler, happier time.

"I was with Jonas and . . . I felt it here." Lucia pressed her hands to her temples. "My magic—it's fully connected to theirs. In an instant, I knew where he was, and I knew he wanted me to come to him. I didn't hesitate."

"Where is Jonas now?" Cleo asked.

"I don't know."

There was something in the way she said it . . .

"Did you hurt him?" Cleo demanded.

Lucia turned a bleak look on her. "He's strong. He'll survive."

For a moment, Cleo couldn't speak. "You could fix this, all of this. You are a sorceress. You could imprison them."

"I would be risking my baby's life if I even tried."

Cleo grabbed her arm, finally getting angry. "Lucia, don't you get it? Your baby's life is already in danger. But the whole world will be in danger if you do what Kyan says! You know this already, yet you're still siding with a monster. Perhaps you've just been looking for an excuse all this time to join his side. Is that it?"

Outrage flashed in Lucia's gaze. "How can you say that?"

"You are your father's daughter. You only want power, and if that power is given to you by an evil god, you'll gladly take it."

"Wrong," Lucia growled. "You've always been wrong about me, so quick to judge from your perfect golden tower and your perfect golden life."

Cold anger flowed through Cleo then, and ice formed at her feet, expanding out to coat an abandoned carriage on the side of the road.

Lucia looked at it with a frown. "You can control the water magic within you."

Cleo fisted her hands at her sides. "If I could, you would be a block of ice right now."

But then a wave of water hit Cleo from out of nowhere—an invisible wave that covered her mouth and nose. She couldn't breathe. It took her under, drowning her.

No, it couldn't happen again. She wouldn't survive it this time.

"*Yes,*" the water Kindred whispered. "*Let me take over now. Don't resist. Everything will be much better the moment you stop struggling.*"

It was too hard to keep fighting when the inevitable loomed in front of her.

The Kindred would win.

Cleo would lose.

And she had to admit the truth of it: It would be so easy to just stop struggling . . .

The sensation of Lucia grabbing hold of her hand and pushing something onto her finger drew her out of the invisible waters.

She gasped for air. "What? What are you doing to me?"

"Cleo, you're all right," Lucia told her firmly. "You're alive, you're all right. Just breathe."

She forced herself to take one breath and then another. Finally, the drowning sensation ebbed away.

Lucia gripped her upper arms. "You have to fight this."

"I thought you didn't want me to."

"I never said that. Hopefully, this will give you just a bit more strength, like it did for me in the beginning. After all, it rightfully belongs to you. You've just let me borrow it, really."

Cleo frowned, not understanding. And then she looked down at her hand.

Lucia had given her back the amethyst ring.

"What—?" she began.

Lucia raised her hand to silence her. "Tell no one. The longer you keep fighting, the longer I'll be able to make him believe the ritual needs to wait. Now, follow me. If we take any longer, he'll send his personal servant back out to find us."

Cleo reeled from having her ring back—the ring that helped Lucia control her magic. "Who, Enzo?"

"I know you like him. I like him too. But he's been marked by fire—he has no choice but to obey Kyan. That's why I sent him away."

Cleo realized then that Lucia was fighting just as hard as she was, just in a different way. They weren't enemies, not anymore. Perhaps they never were.

They were allies. But they were both at an extreme disadvantage.

"Lucia," Cleo said, her voice hushed. "I know how to stop them."

"Do you now?" An edge of wry humor entered Lucia's voice. "Did you find this nugget of information in a book?"

"No. This nugget of information came from Nic himself last night."

Lucia's brow furrowed. "Impossible."

Cleo shook her head. "Kyan isn't as in control as he might present himself to be. He's vulnerable right now, and Nic's found a way to break through at times."

Lucia's gaze moved around them as they walked past a yard they'd once been seated at together. Cleo remembered very vividly the day they'd shared, part of which had been spent watching a group of attractive young men practice their swordplay.

The yard was empty today, more like a graveyard than a place that had contained so much life.

"What did he tell you?" Lucia asked, her voice low.

Cleo was still hesitant to tell her, but she knew they were each other's best chance. "The orbs—the crystal orbs. They're the Kindred's anchors to this plane of existence. If they're destroyed, the Kindred won't be able to walk this world any longer."

"Anchors," Lucia repeated under her breath, frowning deeply. "Anchors to this world."

"Yes."

"And they need to be destroyed."

"Yes, but that's the problem. Magnus tried to destroy the aquamarine orb, but it didn't work, no matter how hard he hit it with a rock."

Lucia shook her head. "Of course not. They're not crystal, not really. They're magic." She pulled her cloak tighter around her as if she'd just become chilled. "This makes sense, all of it. I've been trying to understand where the Kindred were all this time—this last thousand years. The Watchers and countless mortals have searched Mytica from north to south looking for this treasure."

Cleo's gaze scanned the concourse, cringing as she noticed another deep prisoner pit to the north. "But it wasn't until your magic came into being that they could be awakened."

"Yes, *awakened*," Lucia nodded. "Because that's exactly what happened. They were asleep, as in *not conscious*. They had no consciousness like they do now. They're joined—the Kindred and the crystals. To destroy the crystal is simply to destroy its physical form. The magic would still exist in the air. In the earth beneath our feet. In the water of the sea. And in the fire in the hearth. All would be as it should be. How it should have been from the very beginning."

Cleo's head swam with all this information. "I'm glad to see you seem to be understanding all of this far better than I could ever hope to."

Lucia smiled nervously. "I understand it—but far less than I'd like to."

"So that's what we have to do," Cleo said with a nod. "Figure out a way to destroy the crystal orbs."

Lucia didn't reply. Her gaze grew distant again as she paused just steps away from the palace entrance.

Cleo eyed it uneasily, not wanting to enter. Lucia appeared just as hesitant.

"I can try to figure it out," Lucia said. "But there's one large problem I can see."

"What?"

A shadow crossed her expression. "You. And Nic, and Olivia, and Taran. Your bodies—they're mortal and fragile, flesh and blood. You are the current vessels for the Kindred, and I have no way of knowing if you'll survive the impact this much magic would have upon you. I saw what happened to Kyan the last time he came face-to-face with counter-magic. It destroyed his shell. And that shell had been immortal."

Cleo blinked.

But of course, Lucia was right. There was no easy way for this to end.

To destroy the crystals, to send the Kindred into a form of being that had no conscious hold upon this world . . .

It would kill them all.

But it would save her city. And it would save her world.

"I can't speak for the others, but I can speak for myself," Cleo said firmly. "Do whatever you have to do, Lucia. I'm not afraid to die today."

Lucia nodded once. "I'll try."

The two continued through the palace. Similar to the vines outside, the walls of the corridors were coated in moss. Flowers grew from cracks in the marble.

Small fires burned, not in lanterns and torches set into the wall, like usual, but in shallow pits carved into the floor.

They passed a room, the door wide open, where a dozen guards clutched their throats, gasping for air.

"Taran," Lucia said. "He too enjoys using his magic wherever possible."

Cleo's stomach lurched. "The real Taran would be mortified."

"I have no doubt."

Finally, they reached the throne room.

Cleo couldn't believe it'd only been a day since she'd been here last.

It looked completely different. The high ceilings were covered in a canopy of vines and moss. The marble floor was now that of a forest floor; dirt and rocks and small plants poked through the surface. Several man-sized tornadoes spiraled and danced around the room, threatening to knock Cleo off-balance if she came too close to them.

Air magic, she thought. The air Kindred was playing with his magic to create yet more obstacles.

She looked ahead to see that the aisle that led to the dais was lined with blue fire, courtesy of the fire Kindred himself.

Kyan sat upon the vine-covered throne with Taran at his right and Olivia at his left.

Cleo's fury peaked when she saw that he'd found her father's golden crown and placed it upon his head, just as King Gaius had done when he'd taken over.

"And here she is," Kyan said without rising. "I was worried about you, little queen, running away like that with no warning. Rather rude, really. And all I'd wanted to do was help you."

"I guess I am rude. My deepest apologies for offending you."

"Ah, you say that, but I know you don't mean it. What do you think, Taran? You know, this little queen was quite enamored with your vessel's twin brother. I think she would have married him, despite his low social ranking as a mere palace guard."

"I'm surprised," Taran replied. "My memories of Theon show that he much preferred tall brunettes, not short blondes."

"But she *is* a princess. That excuses a myriad of shortcomings." Kyan grinned. "*Shortcomings*, because she's short. I am very funny, but so was Nic—right, little queen? He always made you laugh."

Again, a sheet of ice formed beneath her feet, triggered by her rising fury.

"How sweet," Olivia said. "She's trying to access the water magic inside of her."

"Oh, yes," Kyan said, clapping his hands and laughing. "Let's see you try. Go on, little queen, we're watching."

And she did. Cleo tried so hard to harness the magic within her. To freeze the room solid like she'd frozen the guard. To make the three monsters on the dais choke and sputter on a magical lungful of water, like she'd done to Amara the night of the first ritual.

Cleo thought that perhaps, with this ring on her finger, she might have a chance to control this, to end it.

But she couldn't. This magic wasn't hers to yield—not in any way she could control.

The sound within her of the water Kindred's laugh only made her angrier and more frightened than she already was.

"Now," Kyan said after he sobered. "Little sorceress, shall we begin?"

Lucia stepped forward. "I don't have the aquamarine orb."

"She keeps it in a velvet pouch in her pocket," Taran said.

Kyan glared at him. "And you only mention that now?"

He shrugged. "My memories are improving. Yesterday was a bit of a blur, to be honest. This vessel fought hard to retain control."

"But he lost," Olivia said. "Just as the princess will."

Cleo clasped her hands in front of her, keeping the ring covered from view. "Will I? Are you sure about that?"

Olivia smiled thinly. "Yes. I'm sure."

"Give us the orb," Kyan said. "It must now join the others."

He gestured to a long table to their left. It was adorned with a

Morgan Rhodes

blue velvet cloth—the backdrop for three crystal orbs.

Cleo turned a glare toward Lucia.

Lucia shrugged. "He asked. I delivered."

Cleo shook her head. "I will give you the orb, Kyan, but I demand to see Lyssa first."

"Ah, yes. Lyssa," Kyan said evenly. "The sweet little missing baby that I kidnapped from her sweet little nursery, leaving the sweet little nursemaid in ashes. That was . . . so unkind of me, wasn't it?"

Cleo watched him carefully. Every gesture, every look.

"Incredibly so," Olivia agreed.

"But an excellent way to ensure the sorceress's commitment to the cause," Taran said. "You were very smart to think of it, Kyan."

"Indeed, I was."

There was something off about their delivery of this, as if they were mocking her.

"You don't have her," Cleo guessed. "Do you?"

Kyan's smile fell. "Of course I do."

"Then prove it."

His eyes narrowed. "Or what?"

"Or . . . I won't cooperate. I won't give you the orb, and you won't be able to do the ritual properly this time."

Kyan sighed and pressed back into the throne, running a hand through his carrot-orange hair. "Taran?"

Taran waved his hand, and a strong gust of wind hit Cleo, wrapping itself around her like a large, hungry snake.

She watched with horror, unable to do anything to stop it, as the velvet pouch exited her pocket, sailed through the air, and landed in Kyan's waiting hand.

He undid the drawstrings and looked inside. "Excellent. Over to you, little sorceress."

He tossed it to Lucia, who pulled the orb out and placed it next

348

to the others, exchanging a brief, pained glance with Cleo.

Four orbs, all ready to be used in the ritual that would solidify the Kindred's existence here in this world and strengthen their power to the point where they could destroy the world with a thought.

Or four orbs ready to be destroyed, which would, very likely, kill Cleo, Nic, Taran, and Olivia.

For all Cleo had envied Lucia for her magic, she didn't envy her current choice.

"I think it was a good idea to come here," Kyan said, gazing around at the overgrown throne room that smelled of fresh life and acrid fire. "It has a sense of history, of eternity. Perhaps it's all the marble."

"I like it too," Taran agreed. "We should reside here indefinitely."

Olivia trailed her fingertips along the edge of the throne. "Oh, I don't know. I think I prefer Limeros. All of that delicious ice and snow. Princess Cleo, you would do well there once my sibling takes over. Ice and snow is only water, isn't it? Perhaps you could form a palace of ice."

"Only if I could crush you underneath it," Cleo replied.

Lucia snorted, but covered the sound with a cough.

"Oh, I don't know," another voice came from the throne room's entryway. "The princess doesn't favor the Limerian climate. She does look incredibly beautiful in her fur-lined cloaks, but she's an Auranian girl through and through."

Cleo spun around to face him.

Magnus leaned against the mossy doorframe as if he'd been there all the time, without a care in the world.

He pushed away and took several steps inside the room.

"I've come to negotiate a truce," Magnus said. "One in which we are left in peace and the Kindred are sent directly to the darklands."

CHAPTER 31

LUCIA

AURANOS

Clearly, her brother had lost his mind.

Lucia didn't need this further complication added to an already impossible situation. But Magnus was here anyway.

While Kyan had taunted Cleo, Lucia had been studying the crystal orbs, trying to figure out how best to break them. Anything she thought of—blunt force, dropping them onto a clear area of marble on the now overgrown floor—seemed too expected, too easy. Cleo had already said that Magnus had tried to break the aquamarine orb and failed.

This would need something special. Something powerful. But what?

And even if she could figure it out in time, the more she considered it, the more she feared she'd been right about the effect on the Kindred's mortal vessels.

She'd watched Kyan's monstrous, fiery form shatter like glass.

He still hadn't recovered from that. Cleo was right—the fire Kindred was currently vulnerable until Lucia performed the ritual.

But if she destroyed him, she'd destroy four people whose lives she valued.

And she might never find Lyssa again.

She could try to imprison them—but it would be slow, painful, and with an uncertain outcome. And she could only try to focus on one Kindred at a time.

The others would stop her.

Lucia turned toward Magnus as he approached. "What are you doing here?" she snarled at him.

He nodded at her. "Lovely to see you too. Beautiful day, isn't it?"

"You shouldn't be here."

Magnus hadn't arrived alone. Prince Ashur entered the throne room right behind him. He gazed around at its new decor.

"Very nice," Ashur said, nodding. "It reminds me of home."

"Lovely Kraeshia," Magnus replied. "I mean to visit the Jewel someday."

"You should," Ashur agreed. "Despite the current corrupt government led by my blackhearted sister, it's the most beautiful place in this world."

"I would argue that Limeros is, but I'd like to see for myself." Magnus then turned toward Cleo. Despite his calm demeanor, there was a storm brewing in his brown eyes. "I got your note. I hope you don't mind that I came after you anyway."

Cleo's expression was tense. "I mind."

"I figured you would." He looked up at Kyan and the others. "And here you are, seated upon a throne that far better men than you have possessed. And, quite frankly, I include my father in that statement."

Kyan smiled down at him. "I do enjoy your sense of humor."

"You are one of the few who do."

"Kyan," Lucia said, stepping forward. She had to do something, say something, to keep this from getting worse than it already was. "Spare my brother. Let him leave here without harm. He doesn't know what he's doing."

"Oh, I disagree." Kyan's smile only grew wider. A line of blue fire ignited in front of him, zipped down the stairs, and formed a shallow circle around Magnus and Ashur. "I think he knows exactly what he's doing, don't you, little prince?"

Magnus eyed the blue flames uneasily. "I'd really prefer that you never call me that again."

"But it suits you," Kyan replied. "Little prince, one who marches in to save his little queen, like the hero you aren't and will never be. Your princess is lost to you, little prince. She belongs to us now."

The flames rose to knee level.

"Stop," Lucia hissed. "If you hurt my brother, I swear I won't help you."

"But what about Lyssa?" Kyan asked evenly.

"Lucia, it's a bluff," Cleo told her. "He doesn't have her, I'm sure of it now. She wasn't at the temple last night, and Nic hadn't seen her. He didn't know anything about the kidnapping."

Lucia's breath left her as she considered this possibility.

If Kyan didn't have her daughter, who did?

A thought occurred to her then, one that hadn't even entered her mind until this very moment. Amara. It could have been Amara, using the chaos surrounding the king's assassination, to kidnap her daughter.

Oh goddess, she couldn't think about this now. Surely, she would go mad.

No, she had to stay focused or everything, absolutely everything, would be lost—including Lyssa.

Kyan stood up from the throne and descended the stairs. He stood in front of Magnus, studying him carefully. "How did you get past the gates?" he asked.

"There are other entrances into this city," Magnus replied. "What, you think there's only one way in, one way out? That's not how a city like this works. There are books about this in the library. Perhaps you'd like to borrow a few and read up on the subject."

Kyan narrowed his eyes. "Did you come here to sacrifice yourself to save the girl you love?"

"No," Magnus said. "In fact, I'm very much counting on us both walking out of here alive and well. I believe she's promised me another wedding very soon, and I intend to hold her to it."

Kyan glanced at Cleo. "But you know the hard truth that your husband does not. There will be no happy ending for you—either of you."

Lucia fully expected Cleo to break down, to start to cry and beg for her life and Magnus's, but instead she watched the princess's expression harden.

"Wrong," Cleo said. "There will be no happy ending for *you*, Kyan. Today is the last day you will have the privilege of walking this world. A world that you could have embraced rather than tortured. One you could have helped rather than hurt. And here we are."

"Yes, here we are," Kyan repeated, nodding. Then he shot a look at Lucia. "Start the ritual *now*."

"We need to wait for the water Kindred to fully take control," Lucia lied.

Although she honestly didn't know for sure whether it was a lie or not. She'd never done this ritual before, never wanted to do it. She only knew the steps because Kyan had described them to her.

The ritual needed her blood and the blood of an immortal—
Olivia's blood, which is what her grandmother had used during
the last ritual at Amara's compound—combined. The orbs would
react to it, even without the wisp of Kindred magic within.

More proof that the orbs were more than prisons.

Magic. Pure magic.

"How long must we wait?" Kyan hissed.

"I don't know," Lucia replied.

"Perhaps this will help speed things along." He gestured toward
Taran, who came down the stairs, grabbed hold of Cleo's hand, and
wrenched the amethyst ring off her finger.

Cleo gasped.

Lucia turned to Kyan, clenching her fists at her sides to stop
herself from lunging at him.

"Don't push me, little sorceress," Kyan hissed. His eyes were
glowing—a striking blue color that matched the flames. "Or you
will be very sorry you did."

The fire surrounding Magnus rose higher, to his waist now,
and the fire Kindred turned a cold smile toward her brother.

"Do you feel that?" he asked. "My fire burns brighter and hot-
ter than any other."

"Do you feel this?" Magnus asked, then his hand shot out and
he grabbed Kyan by his throat. "That's the bloodstone my father
gave me to save my life. It's full of death magic, and it has a rather
interesting effect on people I hate. I think you felt it once before.
Let me show you what it can do."

Kyan scratched at his hands but didn't succeed in breaking free.
The skin at his throat where Magnus clutched him had started to
turn a sickly gray color.

Lucia watched this unfold in shock. She'd known Magnus's

ring contained death magic, but she didn't think that it might affect Kyan.

"Apologies, Nic," Magnus growled. "But this has to happen."

Kyan began to shake, and his eyes rolled back into his head. Olivia had descended the stairs to stand next to Taran, but neither of them made a single move to stop Magnus.

Lucia didn't understand why. They could stop him so easily.

She shot a worried glance over to Cleo, and the girl didn't appear at all surprised by what Magnus was doing.

Had her brother tried to kill someone with this death magic before today?

The next moment, the ring of fire extinguished around both Magnus and Ashur.

"Don't kill him," Ashur snarled, just as Kyan fell to his knees.

Magnus pulled his hand away, glaring at the Kraeshian prince over his shoulder. "You broke my concentration."

"You promised me that you wouldn't kill him."

"Some promises were meant to be broken," Magnus snapped. "Nic would understand."

Kyan hissed out a breath as he collapsed to the floor.

Magnus nudged him with the toe of his boot. "He doesn't look nearly as bad as Kurtis did. Much less dead."

Lucia shook her head. "Oh, Magnus, do you even know what you've done?"

"Yes. I stopped the bad guy." Then Magnus eyed the other two Kindred who were observing silently from a dozen paces away. "Don't come a step closer, or you'll get the same."

Lucia held her breath as she watched the red wisp of fire magic rise from Nic's unconscious body.

Then that wisp of magic swirled around Magnus for a moment

before it morphed into a ball of fire and shot into his chest. He jumped as if he'd been struck by lightning, then doubled over, bracing his hands on his knees, gasping for breath.

In a single motion, Magnus then pulled the golden ring off his finger and threw it to the mossy floor.

Then slowly, very slowly, he straightened up, squared his shoulders, and swept his gaze around the throne room.

Lucia's heart stopped at the sight of the fire magic mark now on the palm of Magnus's ringless left hand.

"Yes . . ." Kyan now spoke with Magnus's familiar deep voice. "I like this vessel very much."

"No!" Cleo cried out. "No, you can't do this!"

"I didn't do anything." Kyan walked over toward her, then hunched down so he could level his eyes with hers. "The little prince did this because he thought he was smart. That he was the hero. He thought he would save his beautiful bride and all her friends. He should have stayed in the shadows, where he belonged."

"Get out of him right now," Cleo snarled.

When Kyan smirked it was Magnus's smirk. Lucia's heart sank at the sight. "No. In fact, I think I'll keep this vessel for all eternity."

Out of the corner of her eye, Lucia saw Ashur move to Nic's side, where the prince pressed his fingers against the young man's throat.

"Is he dead?" she asked.

"No. Not yet, anyway." Ashur scowled at her. "This is your fault. I blame you for all of this."

"You're right," she replied. "It is my fault."

Confusion crossed Ashur's expression. Perhaps he'd expected her to argue with him.

"Kyan," Lucia said, and her brother turned to face her. She swallowed hard. "I will begin the ritual now."

"Good," he said with a nod. "And here I thought you might give me more of a problem than you already have."

"Why would I? You have everything that I care about at your mercy. My daughter, my brother, my . . ." She frowned. "Well, that's about it, really."

He raised a dark brow. "No more tricks?"

"I'm finished fighting," she said, and it felt as honest as anything else she'd said that day. "Now I just want this to be over."

"This is your destiny," Olivia said, nodding. "You should take pride in this, Lucia."

"You will be well rewarded," Taran added.

Lucia cast a glance at Cleo, who watched the fire Kindred's every step, every movement.

She's searching for some small sign that Magnus is still here with us, Lucia thought. *She still has hope.*

However, Lucia wasn't as optimistic.

Lucia moved behind the table that bore the four crystal orbs—aquamarine, obsidian, amber, and moonstone.

Olivia stepped forward and presented Lucia with her bare forearm.

With a small blade Lucia kept in the pocket of her cloak, she sliced a shallow cut into Olivia's perfect dark skin. Blood welled to the surface and then dripped onto each of the four orbs.

Even without any words spoken, or any specific magic focused toward them, the orbs began to glow with a soft inner light.

Olivia nodded, then backed away.

All eyes were on the glowing orbs. Lucia considered her next step as she held the blade against her own skin.

Follow through with the ritual as Kyan had described it to her?

Magnus . . . he stole Magnus. Her brother, her best friend. She'd failed him again . . .

No. She forced herself not to despair, not to dwell on what had already happened.

How could she do this? To hand Kyan so much power, to ensure his hold upon her brother's body . . .

But she couldn't figure out how to break the orbs. She could try, but if she failed, the ramifications would be catastrophic.

Before she could decide whether to bleed or not to bleed, an arm came around her from behind, yanking her back against a firm chest.

The tip of a blade pressed against her throat.

"I'm not dead, in case you were curious," Jonas whispered.

"Jonas," she managed.

Kyan, Taran, and Olivia stepped forward, but Lucia held up her hand to stop them from doing anything rash.

No one had seen the rebel's approach through the overgrown, vine-covered throne room. They'd all been watching the orbs, watching the blade at Lucia's arm.

Lucia would have been impressed by the rebel's surprising stealth if this hadn't been the worst possible time he could have arrived.

"Let go of me," she urged.

"I believed in you, and you betrayed me," Jonas growled. "I would have given you all of my magic if you'd asked me for it. Hell, I would have offered it to you if you'd given me half a chance. Now I'm in a difficult spot, princess."

Lucia didn't move, barely breathed. "Is that so?"

She'd wanted a way to delay the inevitable, and it seemed as if she now had a very good one.

"Now, now," Kyan said. "I'd appreciate very much if you'd step away from my sorceress before I have to make you."

Jonas hesitated for a second. "Magnus?"

"Not exactly," Kyan said, smiling his stolen smile. "I think I remember you . . . yes, a beautiful day in a Paelsian market. A lovely girl got in the way of my fire and your body."

Jonas stiffened. "Kyan."

Kyan nodded. "There you go. I'm sure more memories will come to me from this vessel. You've met before, many times."

"I will kill you," Jonas said.

"I doubt that very much."

"Stop it," Lucia thought, hoping very much this strange telepathy still worked between them. *"Stop baiting him, or you're going to die. Do you want that?"*

Jonas froze. *"I can still hear you. I wondered if I could after all the magic you took from me."*

"Little sorceress," Kyan said evenly. "Shall I take care of this for you?"

"No," she said aloud. "I can handle this."

The fire Kindred's eyes narrowed. "Then handle it."

Jonas's grip on her tightened. *"Timotheus gave this dagger to me, told me it can destroy magic. Didn't think I'd need to use it on you. Yet here we are."*

Lucia had gone very still.

A dagger that could destroy magic.

Right here, in this very room.

And currently pressed murderously close to her throat by someone who had every right to want her dead.

CHAPTER 32

NIC

AURANOS

When Magnus arrived, a part of Nic held on to the hope that this prince, this former enemy, had a secret way of defeating Kyan and his siblings.

He did. Nic just hadn't realized how much it would hurt.

He remembered Magnus's hand clutching his throat as Kyan screamed internally at the cold wash of pain that crashed down upon them both.

And then everything went black again for a while.

The next thing he knew, he was opening his eyes and staring up at the face of Prince Ashur Cortas.

Relief filled the prince's gray-blue eyes.

"What happened?" Nic managed to say.

"You're alive, that's what happened," Ashur whispered.

"This isn't a dream."

"No. Not even close. But don't move, not yet."

Nic heard raised voices from close by. Lucia, Magnus . . . Jonas. They were arguing.

Wait.

How was he speaking words right now? How was he having an actual conversation with Prince Ashur if this wasn't an incredibly vivid dream?

Then he realized what had happened.

Partially, anyway.

Kyan had chosen a new vessel—that of Prince Magnus Damora himself.

Through narrowed eyes, leaning against Ashur for support, Nic watched the others. They paid him no attention at all, so engrossed were they in their argument.

Jonas had a golden knife pressed to Lucia's throat.

And then, before Nic's eyes, that knife was invisibly lifted from Jonas's grip. It floated in midair, where Lucia snatched it.

"Thank you for bringing this to me," Lucia said, gazing at the sharp blade. "It will be very useful, I hope."

"Do you want to kill him, little sorceress?" Magnus—no, *Kyan*—asked. "Or should I?"

"Do you have a preference, Jonas?" Lucia asked, slipping the golden dagger beneath the folds of her black robe. "I mean, you did wander in here and threaten the life of a sorceress while observed by three elemental gods. Clearly, you knew your death would be the result."

"Do whatever you have to do," he snarled.

"That is my current plan," she said. Then she glanced at Kyan. "I'll kill him myself later."

"Very well." Kyan gestured toward Olivia. The earth Kindred waved her hand, and thick green vines curled around Jonas's legs and torso, locking him into place.

"What do we do?" Nic whispered. "How can we help?"

"I don't know," Ashur replied, his tone frustratingly calm. "I fear there's nothing we can do. We may very well die here. And it's unfortunate, really. I had plans for us, you see."

"Plans? For us?"

"Yes."

Suddenly, something nearby caught Nic's eye. A small flash of gold.

It was the ring Magnus had worn on his hand, the hand that had clutched his throat.

Kyan had discarded it the moment he'd taken over. Now it lay ten paces away from the Kindred, who were currently and thankfully ignoring Nic and Ashur's hushed conversation.

"What is that ring?" Nic asked. "The ring Magnus wore."

"It's the bloodstone ring," Ashur whispered. "It's magic . . . death magic. It's what drove Kyan out of you."

Death magic.

Nic watched Kyan move around, stretching his long, muscular limbs, running his fingers through Magnus's thick, dark hair.

Clearly, Kyan was happy with this change. Confident. Hopeful. Ready to claim victory over this scattering of mere mortals.

"I need to know something," Nic said, keeping his voice low.

"What?" Ashur asked.

"On the ship, when we were bound for Limeros, you told me that you had a question for me, one you'd ask when everything was over. Do you remember?"

Ashur was silent for a moment. "I remember."

"What was the question?"

Ashur exhaled slowly. "I'm not sure if it's appropriate anymore."

"Ask it anyway."

"I . . . I wanted to ask if you would allow me the chance to steal you from the shores of Mytica, to show you more of the world."

Nic frowned. "Really?"

Ashur's expression shadowed. "Silly, isn't it?"

"Yes, very silly." Nic sat up, turning so he could look directly into the prince's eyes. "My answer would have been yes, by the way."

Ashur's brows drew together. "*Would* have been?"

Nic grabbed Ashur's face and brushed his lips against his. "Apologies, but I have to do this."

Then he reached forward and took hold of the ring.

Ashur's eyes widened. "Nicolo, no . . ."

On shaky legs, Nic rose to his feet and closed the distance between him and Kyan as swiftly as he could.

Kyan turned to him with surprise.

"Well, look who's nicely recovered," the fire Kindred sneered. "Are you going to cause more problems for me?"

"I certainly hope so," Nic said. Then he grabbed Kyan's hand and thrust the ring back onto his left middle finger.

He held on tight as Kyan burst into flames.

CHAPTER 33

MAGNUS

AURANOS

M agnus didn't enjoy admitting fault. Ever.

But he'd made a horrible mistake.

It was his last thought before the fire Kindred stole his body. And then there was nothing but darkness—a darkness even more intense, more empty, and more bottomless than what he'd experienced in the grave.

That Kyan had won had been the worst feeling ever. Worse than having his bones broken on Kurtis's command. Worse than learning of his mother's murder. Worse than watching his sister slip away from him, little by little, the tighter he tried to hold on to her. Worse than his father dying just as they'd begun to mend their broken relationship.

But then it was as if someone had reached into the darkness and grasped hold of him, pulling him back up to the surface.

The bloodstone was back on his finger.

Cold death magic mingled with fire and life, combusting, creating something new.

It hurt—it hurt like being raked over burning coals. But he could think again. And he could move. It felt like he was coming up for air.

His arms were on fire, but as soon as he realized that, the flames extinguished.

Nic stared at him. His hand was red and blistered from the fire, but Magnus's skin was unblemished.

"Get back," Magnus growled.

Nic did as he said, returning to Ashur's side. Ashur bound Nic's burned hand quickly in a torn piece of his shirt.

"Get the ring off your finger. Do it now, or I will destroy you."

It took Magnus a moment to realize it was Kyan who snarled this. Kyan's voice inside Magnus's head.

Magnus grimaced as he swept his gaze through the throne room. Everyone watched him with different expressions on their faces.

Lucia, with dread. Jonas, bound by vines—who must've foolishly shown up just minutes ago—with disdain.

The look on Cleo's face nearly undid him: pain mixed with fury. Her golden hair was a tangled mess, wild and free. The blue lines on her face and arms were still as disturbing as ever.

But she'd never been more beautiful to him.

"I hate you," Cleo hissed at him as he held her gaze.

He drew closer to her. She stiffened but didn't stagger back from him.

"I'm sorry to hear that, Cleiona," he said softly. "Since I feel very differently toward you."

Her blue-green eyes widened a fraction at the use of her full name, and she drew in a sharp breath.

It had become their signal—when he used her full name.

She now knew the truth that no one else did. Magnus was in control of his body. But he didn't know how long it would last.

Taran and Olivia studied Magnus carefully.

"Are you well?" Olivia asked.

"I'm very well," Magnus said smoothly, knowing it would be best if they didn't realize what had happened. "Everything is under control."

A bigger lie has never been spoken in history, he thought.

"*I will kill your niece*," Kyan hissed from inside him. "*I will burn her until she's nothing but ashes.*"

Magnus leveled his gaze at Olivia. "Fetch the child."

She cocked her head. "Child?"

"Lyssa. Bring her here immediately."

Olivia exchanged a look with Taran. "That's not possible."

"What?" Lucia exclaimed. "What are you talking about? Why isn't it possible?"

"Princess!" Nic shouted at Lucia. "Cleo's right. Kyan didn't kidnap Lyssa. They never discussed her, I never saw her. I don't know where your daughter is, but she's not with them."

Taran flicked his hand, and Nic went flying backward, hitting a column hard enough that Magnus heard the far too familiar sound of breaking bones.

But when Ashur moved to his side, Magnus saw that Nic still moved.

That boy was definitely resilient. Magnus had to admire him for that.

The bloodstone hadn't stopped hurting him for one moment. It was like his hand was on fire, the searing pain sinking deep into his bones.

But he didn't dare take it off his finger.

Lucia had a blade in her hand, a golden dagger Magnus hadn't seen before. She raised it up. "Do you know what this is?" she asked.

Magnus shook his head.

Olivia and Taran came to his sides, but both their gazes were fixed on Lucia.

"Sorceress," Olivia said gently. "I think you need to use a different blade. That one could be problematic."

Lucia raised her chin, her gaze now filled with raw maliciousness. "I'm hoping it will be, actually. I'm hoping it's incredibly problematic for you."

"Stop your stupid sister from whatever she's thinking of doing," Kyan growled. *"Or I will burn everything you've ever cared for!"*

"Quiet," Magnus muttered. "Lucia is speaking."

"What did you say?" Taran asked.

"Nothing, nothing. Just enjoying the show." Magnus gestured toward his sister. "Lucia, will you be getting on with the ritual? Time grows short."

Her bleak gaze met his, but there was no recognition there. She still didn't see him past the threat of Kyan.

"I wanted to find another way," she said as she drew the edge of the golden blade across her palm, then dripped her blood onto each of the crystal orbs. "But there's no choice. I don't know if this will work or if it will kill you—" Her voice broke off. "Magnus, I'm sorry. If I'd never been born, none of this would be happening."

"Don't say that," Magnus said firmly. "You have been a gift from the moment you came into my life. Never forget that."

Their eyes met and held. And . . . yes. There it was.

Tears spilled down her cheeks.

She knew it was him.

"Stop her," Kyan yelled from within Magnus. *"I demand that you stop her! I was meant to be free—free with my siblings. I was meant to rule this world! To reform it however I saw fit! You can't stop that! I am fire. I am magic. And you will burn!"*

The orbs had begun to glow brighter, like tiny suns.

"Do it, sister," Magnus said, steeling himself, since he knew very well how badly this could end for him. "Whatever you feel you need to do to end this, do it right now."

"What is happening?" Taran said, moving forward. "This isn't right. This isn't the ritual."

"No," Lucia said, shaking her head. "It definitely isn't."

Lucia raised the blade above her head and brought it down hard over the obsidian orb.

Olivia screamed.

Taran was closing the distance between him and Lucia as swiftly as a hurricane, but not before she shattered the moonstone with the dagger's tip. He froze in place, as if he'd hit an invisible barrier, his knees buckling from under him.

Magnus grabbed hold of Cleo's hand, pulling her against his side.

"Do it!" Cleo yelled.

Lucia destroyed the aquamarine orb, and Cleo's grip on Magnus's hand became painfully tight as she cried out.

"What are you waiting for?" Magnus roared. "End this!"

The amber orb shattered on contact.

Magnus felt something hit him. Something solid and sharp and painful. It felt like his flesh was being torn from his bones.

He tried to see through the pain—toward Lucia at the table. She looked down at the broken pieces of the Kindred orbs. They were still glowing, brighter and brighter until their light began to obliterate her from his view.

Move, Lucia, he thought frantically. *Get away from them.*

But she stood frozen in place, as if unable to move away from the magic that was going to explode and surely destroy them all in the process.

A moment before his vision went stark white, he saw a shadow—Jonas, free from his vines, leaping toward Lucia and knocking her out of the way just as a thick column of light shot up from the shattered orbs.

Light, too, shot out of Magnus's eyes, his mouth, his hands. He couldn't see, couldn't think. But he could feel.

Cleo's hand still gripped his.

"Don't you dare let go of me," he roared at her past the deafening whooshing sound sweeping through the throne room. A windstorm enveloped them, threatening to carry them away. A violent earthquake shook the ground beneath their feet.

"The others!" Cleo screamed.

Yes, the others. Magnus searched the chaos surrounding him until he saw Olivia. She held on to Taran like he held on to Cleo.

He reached toward her, and she grabbed hold of his hand. Cleo did the same with Taran. Taran's nose was bleeding, and his face was bruised and bloody. Olivia's gaze was wild, fearful, but still fierce and ready to fight.

Chunks of marble fell from the destroyed ceiling, narrowly missing them as the wind swirled around and the floor nearby split wide open.

"I'm sorry!" Olivia yelled, but it was barely audible above the sound of the elemental storm surging around them.

"None of this is your fault!" Cleo replied.

Magnus would like to argue that this was, in part, Olivia's fault, but there was no time.

"Bloody weak," Taran growled. "I should have fought harder."

"Yes, you should have," Magnus said. "But you're still here."

"Just in time for us all to die."

A monstrous burst of fire erupted in front of Magnus. He jumped back as the fire grew. He could feel its heat searing his skin.

"No," Magnus growled. "I didn't survive this long to give up now."

"Your sister is helping them," Taran hurled back at him, his words nearly stolen completely by a series of swirling tornadoes that circled them. Magnus eyed them uneasily, knowing each one could tear them apart if they got too close.

They should have been torn apart by now—by all of this. But they weren't. Not yet.

"My sister, in case you are incapable of understanding this," Magnus said without a single doubt in the world, "is helping *us*."

Lucia would save the world. Why had Magnus doubted her for even a moment?

He was such a fool.

He lost his grip on Olivia's hand, and she flew backward from him. "No!" he yelled.

Cleo squeezed his hand hard, and he looked at her, nearly blind from the beam of destructive light that had torn the throne room apart.

Taran was nowhere to be seen.

"Forever," she said, tears streaking her face. "Whatever happens—you and me are together forever. All right?"

"You and me," he agreed. "Until eternity. I love you, Cleo."

"I love you, Magnus."

He'd never heard more beautiful words in his entire life.

Cleo buried her face in his chest, and he wrapped his arms tightly around her, refusing to ever let go of her, no matter what happened.

The light grew brighter and brighter.

The wind howled. The fire burned. The earth itself shook and shattered beneath their feet.

And then . . .

Then it was all over.

CHAPTER 34

JONAS

AURANOS

It felt as if the Forbidden Mountains themselves had crashed down on top of him.

The throne room was in ruin. Light from the sky shone down onto Jonas, brightening the remains of what had once been the golden palace. He tried to turn his head to see who was there, who was hurt or dead, but the pain made him scream.

"Hold still, you fool," Lucia said. "You have a broken neck."

"Broken neck—?" he managed. "Nic . . . Nic is hurt. Worse than me. Help him first."

"I already did," Lucia told him. "Ashur insisted. He'll be fine. Now stay still and be quiet so I can heal you." She placed her hands on his neck, and a burning sensation made him yelp as it sank deep into his throat, his spine, so intense he thought he might pass out from it.

And then the pain was gone.

Lucia looked down at him.

"You healed me," he said weakly.

"Of course I did. I mean, it's your *elementia* I'm currently using."

He blinked. "I was dead."

"I hear you've been dead a lot."

"I think this is my third time. Or second and a half, anyway."

"It's the least I could do after . . ." Lucia drew in a shaky breath. "I'm sorry for what I did. At the time, I felt I had no choice."

Jonas touched her face, brushing the dark hair off her forehead. "Of course I forgive you."

She stared down at him with surprise. "That easily?"

He grinned. "Sure. Not everything has to be a struggle. Not today, anyway."

"I still don't know where my daughter is," Lucia said, her voice breaking.

Jonas took her hands in his. "We'll find her. Wherever she is, however long it takes, we will find her together."

She nodded. "Thank you."

"You just saved every one of our arses with that stolen magic . . . and that dagger . . ." Jonas strained to see the altar where the orbs had been, but there was nothing left, only a black scorch mark.

Lucia shook her head. "The dagger vanished, along with every last piece of the crystal orbs."

"Good riddance." Jonas pulled her gently against him, and she let out a shuddery sigh of relief.

"I'm glad Kyan's gone," she whispered. "But part of me really liked him in the beginning."

"I'm sure part of him was worth liking. A very small flicker of likability." Jonas finally and reluctantly released her. He rubbed his neck, which felt as good as new, then gazed around at the shattered remains of the throne room.

A hand appeared before his face then. A hand attached to the arm of Magnus Damora.

Jonas grabbed it, and Magnus helped him to his feet.

He'd seen light explode from Magnus, Cleo, Taran, and Olivia, just as it had exploded from the Kindred orbs. Anything with the power to punch a hole in a marble roof could easily have torn apart a mortal body. But it hadn't.

"You're alive," Jonas managed.

"I am."

Jonas blinked. "Good. I mean, yes. Glad you're not dead and all that."

"Likewise." Magnus hesitated. "I saw you protect my sister. You have my eternal gratitude for that."

It was all a blur now. The vines that had held him immobile had fallen away as soon as Lucia had crushed the orbs. He remembered her standing over them, the golden dagger in her hand.

Frozen in place.

Had she remained there, he doubted she would have survived that blast.

Jonas looked at Magnus. "It seems your sister needs protecting sometimes."

"She'd disagree with that," Magnus replied.

"I'm right here," Lucia said, pushing herself up to her feet to give her brother a tight hug. "I can hear you."

Cleo came to Magnus's side, accompanied by Taran and Olivia.

The sight of the three of them, free from the monsters that had used their bodies, made Jonas's throat tighten. "You're all right. All of you."

Olivia nodded. "I don't remember much at all, to tell you the truth." She gazed around the room at the moss and vines. "But it seems like I was quite busy."

"I tried so hard not to let the air Kindred take me over," Taran said. "That loss of control, it was worse than death for me. But I'm back. And my life . . . it's going to be different now."

"How?" Jonas asked.

Taran frowned. "Not sure yet. I'm still working on that."

Lucia embraced Cleo, gripping her tightly. "If you hadn't told me about the orbs . . ."

Cleo hugged Lucia back. "We have Nic to thank for that."

Jonas glanced to the other side of the throne room, where Nic and Ashur were speaking together in hushed tones.

"We survived," he said with shock. "We all survived."

Lucia's eyes were glossy. "I hurt you, Jonas. I lied to you. I manipulated you. And . . . I almost killed you. And you're still willing to forgive me? I can't understand it."

Jonas grinned. "I guess you're lucky I'm fond of complicated women."

Magnus cleared his throat loudly. "Anyway, we will immediately start a kingdom-wide search for my niece, including a reward no one will be able to resist."

"Thank you, Magnus," Lucia whispered.

She hadn't let go of Jonas's hand.

This girl will probably be the death of me, he thought with wry amusement.

But not today.

CHAPTER 35

AMARA

KRAESHIA

ONE MONTH LATER

Amara endured the uncomfortable, rocky ride in the back of the enclosed wagon that would take her to a locked room where she would spend the better part of her life, away from anyone she might try to hurt.

Her grandmother had made sure to document everything she'd done. With the very same Grand Augur who had almost completed Amara's ascension ceremony as her witness, she'd signed away Amara's life. Neela's accounts of her granddaughter's descent into madness would take everything away from her.

She was now known as a girl who'd murdered her loving family in the relentless pursuit of power.

The most amusing part of it all was that Amara couldn't argue with any of her grandmother's claims, since every single one of them was true.

But she was still alive. The rebels who'd attacked the ceremony hall had successfully rescued their leader, but their numbers were far too few to take control of the Emerald Spear or the city surrounding it.

For now, the Grand Augur would rule. Which, quite frankly, annoyed her because the man didn't have a single original thought in his idiotic head.

At the moment, however, she couldn't concern herself with power.

She was more concerned with escape.

Unfortunately, with her ankles and wrists chained, and the back of the wagon locked up tight after her last attempt to break free from her captors, that didn't seem remotely possible.

Very well. She would go to the madhouse. She would play along and behave herself and . . . well, very likely seduce a guard who would eventually help her escape. For now, however, she had to be patient.

But patience had never been an easy task for Amara Cortas.

After the incessant jerking motion of the wagon became so unbearable she wanted to scream, the vehicle came to an abrupt halt. She heard indiscernible shouting, a clashing of metal, and finally a frightening silence.

Amara couldn't see a thing, could only imagine a thousand possibilities of what had just happened, none of which ended well for her.

She waited, tensely, a line of perspiration trickling down her spine as the sound of footsteps moved around to the back of the wagon. The latch clicked, and then the door swung wide open.

Sunlight streamed into the darkness of Amara's temporary prison. She blocked the blinding brightness with her hand until she could register who stood right in front of her.

"Nerissa . . ." she whispered.

The girl's dark hair had grown a little since the last time Amara had seen her. It was now long enough to tuck behind her ears. She wore black trousers and a dark green tunic. And she carried a sword.

"Well?" Nerissa said as she sheathed the weapon at her waist. "Are you going to look at me like an absolute fool, or are you going to get out of there before your guards wake up from the knocks they just took to their heads?"

Amara stared at the girl in disbelief. "Are you here to kill me?"

Nerissa raised a brow. "If I were, you'd already be dead."

Perhaps this was only a dream. It had to be a dream. Or a hallucination of some kind from the heat and claustrophobia. "You should have returned to Mytica weeks ago, with Felix and Lyssa."

"I did return. You don't honestly think I would leave Felix Gaebras all alone with a baby, do you? He wouldn't have had the first clue what to do with her, even without his seasickness to contend with."

This was happening, Amara realized. It wasn't just a dream. "You went home . . . and now you're back?"

"Mytica was never my home, just a brief stop on my journey— one I certainly enjoyed for a time." She jumped up into the back of the wagon and, with the key in her grip, unlocked Amara's chains. "In case you're still confused about all this, I'm rescuing you."

Amara shook her head. "I don't deserve rescue."

I deserve escape, she thought. *And continued survival. But certainly not rescue by outside forces.*

Nerissa leaned her shoulder against the side of the wagon as Amara rubbed her sore wrists and tried to stand up. Her leg had mostly healed, but she still had a limp. Perhaps she always would.

"We all deserve to be rescued," Nerissa said simply. "Some of us take longer to realize it than others."

Amara stepped down into the daylight, again shielding her eyes from the sun. They hadn't made it very far—they were almost at the docks, the Silver Sea just a stone's throw away. She looked around at the unconscious guards, realizing that Nerissa wasn't alone.

She was with three other rebels, including Mikah.

Her breath caught at the sight of him.

Mikah gestured at Amara with the tip of his dagger. "I know you told Nerissa and Felix about me, and if you didn't, I'd be dead. But know this: If you show your face in the Jewel after today, it's over. You're not welcome here anymore."

Amara pressed her lips together and nodded, resisting the urge to speak. She could only make this worse by trying to explain herself.

Mikah didn't wait. He and the other two rebels walked away without looking back.

"I don't think organizing my rescue won you any friends," Amara said.

Nerissa shrugged. "I'm fine with that. Come, let's walk along the shore. I have a ship waiting for us at the docks so we can leave this place far behind us."

Amara followed her, her limp even more pronounced once they walked along the sandy beach. "Why did you do this for me?"

"Because everyone deserves a second chance." Nerissa cast a look at the white beach and blue ocean that spread out before them. "Besides, the dust has settled in Mytica. Kyan and his siblings were defeated, their magic returned to . . ." She shook her head, frowning. "Lucia explained it to me, but I still don't really understand it. The magic is everywhere now. It's spread out . . . in everyone and everything, where it always belonged, and where it can do no more harm."

Amara felt a knot in her stomach loosen.

Kyan was gone. The world was safe again.

"I'm glad," she said, her voice barely audible.

"I was happy to help out there for a while, to do what I could." A smile touched Nerissa's lips. "You're not the only one who's been given a second chance in this life. I'd been using mine the best I could."

"How curious. I'd like to hear more about that one day."

"One day," Nerissa agreed.

A thought occurred to Amara. "Did you see my brother?"

"Briefly. I told him what you did and that you'd helped us save Lyssa."

"And what did he say?"

"Not much." Nerissa grimaced. "You were right: He will need time to find forgiveness in his heart for you."

The very heart that I stabbed, Amara thought. "I don't think an eternity will be enough time," she said.

"Perhaps. But we all make our choices and then must deal with the consequences, whatever they are."

Yes, so very true.

So many choices and so many consequences.

"Tell me," Nerissa said after they walked in silence for a while. "Did you ever dream of anything in your life beyond being empress?"

Amara considered this. "To be honest, no. The only real option for me was marriage, but I'd put it off as long as I could. I suppose, before I became empress, I was waiting for the right powerful man that I knew I'd be able to control and manipulate."

Nerissa considered this. "And now?"

"Now I have no idea what I'm supposed to do with the rest of my life." The sea air was warm and smelled like salt. She breathed in the unexpected freedom that she knew she didn't truly deserve. "Why would you leave Cleo to come back here? I know she depended on you and considered you a true friend."

"The princess doesn't need me anymore," Nerissa replied simply.

Amara couldn't help but laugh at this. "And I do?"

Nerissa took Amara's hand in hers, squeezing it. "Yes, actually I think you do."

Amara looked down at Nerissa's hand. She didn't try to pull away.

"So," Nerissa said when the docks came into view up ahead, "where do you want to go now?"

Amara smiled at the sheer number of possibilities that now lay ahead of her—opportunities she never thought possible. But perhaps somewhere along the line, in some small way, she might find a way to redeem herself.

"Everywhere," she said.

CHAPTER 36

CLEO

LIMEROS

"Ouch!"

"Apologies, your highness." Lorenzo Tavera finally finished lacing up the back of Cleo's gown so tightly that she could barely breathe.

"I don't remember it being this uncomfortable during our previous fitting," she said with a grimace.

"Discomfort is temporary," he told her. "The beauty of silk and lace is forever."

"If you say so."

He took a step back from her, clasping his hands together with joy. "Absolutely stunning! My greatest creation to date!"

She took a moment to admire the gown in the mirror before her. The skirt consisted of layer upon layer of delicate, violet-colored silk and satin, like the petals of a rose. Golden threads woven through the material created a near-magical sheen whenever the gown caught the light. Several seamstresses—and Lorenzo himself—had spent weeks embroidering graceful birds in flight over the bodice.

They were hawks, which Cleo appreciated. Hawks were the symbol of Auranos, the symbol of Watchers and of immortality. They were every bit as meaningful to Cleo as the phoenix was to Kraeshians.

Life—Auranians had learned in the days following the Kindred's deadly siege upon the city—was about love, about friends and family, and about not putting one's own desires above the well-being of another person, no matter who they are.

Cleo gently stopped one of her two attendants from tugging at her hair in an impossible attempt to make it perfect. Her scalp felt as if it had been set aflame. Half of her golden locks had been coiffed into an intricate series of braids, the other half left free and flowing down her shoulders and back. Lorenzo had requested that all her hair be up so the crowd waiting outside in the palace square could appreciate the beauty of the gown that he'd made by hand, but she much preferred to wear her hair just like this.

"I think we're done," Cleo said as she looked at her reflection. She had mostly recovered from the ordeal of being possessed by the water Kindred. The only remaining sign was one faded blue tendril along her temple. One of her attendants, a girl from Terrea, told her it looked like a painted adornment worn by her ancestors during the half moon celebrations.

By the way she'd said it with such enthusiasm, Cleo took this to be a great compliment.

Lorenzo smiled as Cleo moved toward the door. "It's even more beautiful than your wedding gown, if I do say so myself."

"By a fraction, yes, I must agree. You are a genius." That gown had been incredible, but she'd never had a moment to truly appreciate it.

Today would be much different.

"I *am* a genius," Lorenzo agreed merrily. "This coronation gown is one that will be remembered throughout history."

"Without a doubt," she agreed, repressing a smile.

Nic waited for her on the other side of the door impatiently. "You took forever to get ready. Is that how queens are? Wait, now that I think of it, you always took forever to get ready, even as a mere princess."

"You didn't have to wait for me, you know," Cleo said.

"But how could I miss a single moment of today?" He walked beside her down the hall. Jonas was waiting at the other end as well, also ready to accompany her to the balcony, where she would be making her first speech as the queen of Mytica.

"Are you sure you haven't changed your mind?" Jonas asked, his arms crossed over his chest.

"Save your breath," Nic said to him. "I've tried to convince her otherwise during the entire trip here, but she refuses. If you ask me, this is the worst idea ever."

"Then it's very smart that I didn't ask you, isn't it?" She smiled at him patiently. "When is it that you're planning to leave on your journey to explore the world with Ashur?"

"Not for another week." He raised his eyebrows. "Don't try to get rid of me yet, Cleo."

"Wouldn't dream of it." Cleo cast a look at Jonas. "So you are yet another protestor?"

"It just seems . . ." Jonas spread his hands. "Problematic. At best. Then again, I'm not in favor of any ruler at all, let alone two who've chosen to equally share the throne."

Nic let out a grunt of frustration. "Co-reigning with . . . *him*. Do you have any idea how much trouble you're in for? Have you even looked at the history texts? It's never been done successfully before. Too much arguing, fighting . . . war, even! Death and mayhem and blood and pain are a given! And that's best-case scenario!"

"And that," Cleo said patiently, "is why we're going to take it a day at a time. And also why we have enlisted a very trustworthy council that won't be afraid to intervene, if necessary."

So far this council included Jonas as the Paelsian representative, Nic representing Auranos, and Lucia representing Limeros. The council would grow in time, but Cleo thought they were off to an excellent start.

On their walk, they passed Olivia and Felix, who'd both come to live at the Limerian palace.

Felix stayed at Magnus's request as a personal bodyguard for him and Cleo—and for any other "problems" they might need him to deal with on their behalf. Felix had enthusiastically agreed. Of course, Cleo truly wished such problems would be few and far between going forward.

As for Olivia, Lucia had broken the news to her of what had happened in the Sanctuary. That Timotheus was dead, the Sanctuary destroyed. That all others of her kind no longer possessed the memories of their formerly immortal selves.

After the initial shock and deep mourning over such an acute loss, Olivia consoled herself with the idea that she would be the one to keep the memory and history of the Watchers alive.

Taran had already departed Mytican shores, telling Cleo and Magnus that he wanted to rejoin the fight in Kraeshia. The revolution there had only just begun, and he knew he could help to overthrow an already shaky temporary government.

And then there was Enzo.

Looking handsome in his red guard's uniform, he nodded at Cleo as she passed him along the hallway. The fire mark on his chest had vanished immediately after the Kindred were banished from this plane of existence. He had joined them on their journey to Limeros for their coronation, but insisted on returning to Auranos immediately after to help in the reconstruction of the Auranian palace.

Cleo had a feeling it had a great deal to do with his desire to return to a pretty kitchen maid there at the palace who thought Enzo was the most wonderful man she'd ever met.

"Are they trying to talk you out of this?" Magnus greeted Cleo as the trio turned the next corner. "What an incredible shock."

She started. "You surprised me."

"You still need to get used to the twists and turns of this palace," he said. "Remember, you agreed to live here half of the year."

"That's one of the reasons this dress is lined in fur."

Magnus's appreciative gaze slid down the front of her and back up, meeting her own and holding. "Purple."

"It's violet, actually."

He raised a brow. "That's a Kraeshian color."

"It's a common color that is, yes, used by Kraeshians."

"It reminds me of Amara."

Ah, yes. *Amara.* Cleo had received a personal message from the former empress from an undisclosed location congratulating Cleo and Magnus on their victory against Kyan. Amara also conveyed that she hoped one day to see them again.

Nerissa claimed that Amara had value and deserved a second chance. She'd even chosen to accompany Amara to parts unknown.

Cleo had decided not to harbor any ill feelings toward Amara, but she didn't have any interest in ever seeing her again.

But it was impossible to know what the future held.

She looked up at Magnus. "This shade of violet, Lorenzo tells me, is the perfect blend of Auranian blue and Limerian red."

A smile touched his lips. "As clever as you are beautiful."

Nic groaned. "Perhaps I'll leave now—why wait a week?"

"If you insist," Magnus said. "I certainly won't try to stop you." His gaze moved to Jonas. "My sister is looking for you."

"Is she?" Jonas asked.

Magnus's lips twisted with disapproval. "She is."

Jonas grinned mischievously. "Well, then, I'll have to see what she wants, won't I?" He leaned toward Cleo and kissed her cheek. "By the way, that shade of violet is my favorite. And you look gorgeous, as usual."

Cleo couldn't help but notice that Magnus's eyebrows furrowed immediately whenever Jonas complimented her.

Perhaps they always would.

"And you . . ." Magnus eyed Nic.

"What about me?" Nic shot back.

A smile turned up the corner of his mouth. "I might surprise you yet."

"Oh, you do surprise me," Nic replied. "Constantly. Be good to her or you'll have me to answer to, *your majesty.*"

"Noted," Magnus replied.

Then Nic and Jonas left them to take the remaining walk to the balcony in privacy.

"I still hate both of them," Magnus told her. "Just so you know."

"No, you don't," Cleo replied with amusement.

Magnus shook his head. "What exactly is it that my sister sees in that rebel?"

She repressed a grin. "If I have to tell you, it would be a waste of my breath."

Whenever Lucia wasn't spending time with her daughter, she seemed to be with Jonas. The only one who seemed to have a problem with this was Magnus.

He'll get over it, Cleo thought. *Probably.*

The day after the Kindred had been defeated, they'd received a message from Nerissa explaining what had happened in Kraeshia.

It said that Amara's grandmother had commanded the assassin to take the life of King Gaius. And that she'd arranged to have Lyssa kidnapped, making it seem as if it had been the fire Kindred.

A week later, Nerissa and Felix returned from their journey and delivered Lyssa into her young mother's grateful arms.

"I do like your hair like this, very much." Magnus twisted a long, loose golden strand around his finger as he pressed Cleo up against the wall of the corridor. They were inches away from the balcony where they would be addressing the cheering Limerian crowds and making their first speech as king and queen.

"I know," she said with a smile.

He traced his fingers along the tendril that framed her temple. She gently touched his scar.

"Can we do this?" she asked, a sliver of doubt creeping in. "For real? Or are we going to fight every day about everything? We have vastly different outlooks on a million different subjects."

"Absolutely true," he said. "And I anticipate countless heated arguments that will stretch deep, *deep* into the night." A grin pulled at his lips. "Is it wrong that I look greatly forward to each and every one of them?"

Then he kissed her deeply, stealing both her breath and her thoughts.

They *would* make this work.

Mytica—Limeros, Paelsia, and Auranos—mattered to both of them. Their people mattered to them. And the future stretched before them, both frightening and enticing in far too many ways to count.

Magnus took her hand in his, rubbing his thumb over the thin gold band she now wore, a near match for his own. When she'd questioned him about the rings, he'd insisted that it wasn't the bloodstone melted down and made into two rings.

She didn't believe him, since she hadn't seen his thick gold ring since that fateful night.

If she was right, Magnus had created the most powerful pair of wedding bands in history.

"Apologies for interrupting," a voice cut between them, making Cleo gasp against Magnus's lips.

"Valia," Magnus said with surprise. "You're here."

"I am." The witch wore her long black hair loose. It cascaded down the back of her burgundy gown.

Several guards who stood along the walls nearby didn't make a single move toward her.

"You didn't answer Prince Ashur's summons when we needed you," he said darkly.

She smiled. "Perhaps I did. Perhaps I'm answering that summons now. But what difference does it make? You survived, both of you. And you're ready to begin the rest of your lives together."

True enough, Cleo thought. *But a little extra help would have been lovely.*

"Why are you here?" she asked.

"I've come to give you a gift. A symbol of luck and prosperity for the future of Mytica under the new rule of its young king and queen." Valia held out a small plant, its roots encased in a burlap pouch.

"What is it?" Magnus asked, eyeing it.

"A grapevine seedling," she said. "One that will yield perfect grapes year after year, just like those produced by the greatest vineyards of Paelsia."

"Much gratitude," Cleo said, taking the plant from the woman. "Alas, it will not last long if we don't get it into Paelsian soil soon."

"This one will do well wherever you plant it, even here in Limeros," Valia said with confidence. "I promise you that."

"Earth magic," Cleo guessed.

Valia nodded. "Yes. It certainly helps. And ever since the Kindred were defeated, I feel that my magic has increased. I am grateful for that."

It wasn't the first time Cleo had heard this claim. Lucia said her magic had also strengthened, that the drain that Lyssa had on it was no longer an issue for her.

"Will you be present for our speech?" Magnus asked.

Valia nodded again. "I plan to join those in the palace square now."

"Excellent," he said. "Much gratitude for your gift, Valia."

Cleo froze as the witch pressed her hand against Cleo's belly.

"What are you doing?" she asked, taking a step back.

"Your son will be very strong and very handsome," Valia said. "And in time he will discover a great treasure, one that will benefit the world."

"Our son . . . ?" Cleo began, sharing a shocked look with Magnus.

Valia bowed her head. "All the best to you, Queen Cleiona. King Magnus."

As the witch walked away, Cleo was certain she saw the brief flash of a gold dagger—one that looked very much like the dagger Lucia had used to destroy the Kindred orbs—in the sheath on her leather belt.

How strange, she thought.

But the thought quickly left her mind. She was focused on something else entirely that Valia had said.

Their son.

Her gown *had* been so much tighter this morning. And she hadn't been able to keep any breakfast down, but she'd decided that was due to her nerves about starting her and Magnus's coronation tour.

"A son?" Magnus asked, breathless. "Did she just say something about our son?"

Cleo tried to find her voice. "Yes, she did."

He searched her face, his eyes wide. "Is there something that you haven't told me yet?"

She laughed nervously. "Perhaps we can discuss this in further depth *after* our speech?"

A slow smile appeared on Magnus's face. "Yes," he said. "Immediately after."

Cleo nodded, trying very hard to keep her happy tears at bay.

Her hand in his, they approached the doors leading to the balcony.

"Seeing Valia again," Cleo mused, "her face seems so recognizable to me, like I've seen it somewhere before."

"Seen it where?" Magnus asked.

Then it came to her. "That book—the one about your goddess I'd recently started to read. It had some of the most incredible illustrations I've ever seen. So detailed."

"So who does the witch remind you of?" he asked.

"Valoria herself," Cleo said, unable to contain her grin. "Do you think it's possible that we were just given both a gift and a prophecy by your goddess of earth and water?"

"Can you imagine if that were really true? That Valia was ac-tually Valoria herself?" He laughed at this. How Cleo loved the rare sound of Magnus Damora's laugh.

"You're right," she agreed. "It's ridiculous, but they are both very beautiful."

"Not nearly as beautiful as you are, my lovely queen." Magnus leaned down and brushed his lips softly against hers. "Now . . . are you ready?"

Cleo looked up into his face—the face of someone she'd come to love more than anyone or anything else in this world, in this life.

Her friend. Her husband. Her king.

"I'm ready," she said.

ACKNOWLEDGMENTS

The Falling Kingdoms series has been an incredible, challenging, wonderful experience, and I have been so, so happy to share these books with the world. But I certainly did not travel this road alone over the last six years.

Thank you to my editor, the endlessly patient and truly delightful Jessica Harriton. Thank you to the fabulous Liz Tingue and Laura Arnold, who began this winding and exciting journey through Mytica with me. Thank you to my publisher Ben Schrank for giving me the best experience of my writing career. Thank you to my awesome publicist, Casey McIntyre, and to everyone at Razorbill Books and Penguin Teen who helped make Falling Kingdoms happen. Thank you to Vikki VanSickle and everyone at Razorbill Canada. You are all The Best!!

A million thank-yous to my agent of thirteen years, Jim McCarthy. I don't know how I would have navigated the writing world without his savvy, guidance, and wicked sense of humor.

Thank you to my friends and family, whom I adore and value and cherish. I love you all more than you even realize.

And thank you, thank you, THANK YOU to the readers of Falling Kingdoms. You are all made of magic, every single one of you!